one of the ...ighest rated women's fiction authors
on Goodreads. Here's what some of her
reviewers have said over the years:

Lucy in the Sky, 2007

'I loved it – I couldn't put it down!' – **Marian Keyes**

'A fab debut and a great summer read' – *Elle*

Johnny Be Good, 2008

'Pacy, highly enjoyable insight into life in La-La Land!' – *Closer*

'All the warmth and fun that I've grown to expect from
the talented Ms Toon' – **Freya North**

Chasing Daisy, 2009

'A fast-paced and funny read… Superior chick-lit with great
jokes and a thoughtful heart' – ***Daily Express***

'Laugh-out-loud funny and touchingly honest. This summer's
poolside reading sorted!' – ***Company***

Pictures of Lily, 2010

'An absorbing and emotional narrative – brilliant!' – ***Heat***

'Another perfect summer page-turner from Paige Toon' – ***Mirror***

Baby Be Mine, 2011

'Fun, summery, chick-lit with bite, if you want escapism,
this is perfect' – ***Cosmopolitan***

'Heart-...rming...' ... ...ddictive),
will ... ...letcher

Also by Paige Toon

Lucy in the Sky

Johnny Be Good

Chasing Daisy

Pictures of Lily

Baby Be Mine

One Perfect Summer

One Perfect Christmas (eBook Short Story)

The Longest Holiday

Johnny's Girl (eBook Short Story)

Thirteen Weddings

The Sun in Her Eyes

Young Adult

The Accidental Life of Jessie Jefferson

I Knew You Were Trouble

All About the Hype

Paige Toon

the ONE we fell in LOVE with

SIMON &
SCHUSTER

London · New York · Sydney · Toronto · New Delhi

A CBS COMPANY

First published in Great Britain by Simon & Schuster UK Ltd, 2016
A CBS COMPANY

Copyright © Paige Toon 2016

1 3 5 7 9 10 8 6 4 2

Simon & Schuster UK Ltd
1st Floor
222 Gray's Inn Road
London WC1X 8HB

www.simonandschuster.co.uk

Simon & Schuster Australia, Sydney
Simon & Schuster India, New Delhi

A CIP catalogue record for this book
is available from the British Library

Paperback ISBN: 978-1-4711-3843-0
Trade Paperback ISBN: 978-1-4711-5514-7
eBook ISBN: 978-1-4711-3844-7

Typeset by M Rules
Printed and bound by CPI Group (UK) Ltd, Croydon, CR0 4YY

For my beautiful editor, Suzanne Baboneau
and for my lovely readers, old and new.

Thank you for making my childhood dream
of becoming an author even better than
I could have imagined.
(And I imagine for a living, so that's saying something.)

Prologue

Angus

She's here. I'm instantly tense. The people around here are mistaken. They *don't* all look alike. She's special. She's different. She's the most beautiful girl I've ever seen.

I watch her in a daze through the crowded, smoky air as she gets herself a beer from the makeshift bar. I want to go over to her, but I stay where I am, leaning against the doorframe. After what happened last night, she has to come to me. But I don't know if she will. I've been worried she wouldn't even turn up.

She swigs from her bottle, then looks around the packed living room, taking everything in. She's late and everyone else is well on their way to oblivion. Turning up at a party alone at this hour is brave. It wouldn't surprise me if she walked right back out again. That thought messes with my head, and it's already messed up enough. I can't believe I've let her get to me like this.

I watch, fixated, as she puts the bottle back to her lips

1

and then suddenly her eyes lock with mine. I force myself to stare back at her.

She smiles at me and the relief is instant. I jerk my head backwards, willing her to come over. Still smiling, she slowly makes her way through the packed space, squeezing through bodies until she's right in front of me.

'Hey,' I say, reaching down to touch my fingertips to hers.

'Hi.' She closes her hand into a fist.

Okay, so we're not cool. Her gorgeous eyes are wide as she stares up at me. My gaze drops to her lips. They're shiny, like she's just applied lip gloss. I want to lick it off her.

Bloody hell, I'm drunk.

'How was dinner?' I ask.

'It was fine!' She shouts. I can't hear her next words because the music is too loud.

'What did you say?' I shout back, cupping her head with my hand and pulling her closer.

'I said it's noisy!'

'Yeah,' I reply with a grin. 'Sorry, I'm a bit pissed.' I speak right into her ear.

'Lucky you.'

She is so sexy. Her hair is soft under my fingers. I run my thumb across her temple and she puts her hand on my chest. I think she's trying to keep me at bay, but it's not working. Her touch almost does me in.

I take her hands and pull her closer.

'Angus?' She sounds uncertain as I touch my forehead to hers. I know I'm making her uncomfortable in front of all these people, but I need to be with her. I want her so much. *Too* much.

Determination surges through me. 'Come with me,' I say firmly, putting our beers on a nearby table. I grab her hand and tug her out of the living room. My head is spinning as I push open the door to the cloakroom under the stairs. I pull her inside and hear her gasp as I slam the door shut behind her. Then my mouth is on hers. I hear her sharp intake of breath as my tongue pushes her lips apart. She hesitates only a little before kissing me back. I could kiss her forever.

'I want you,' I murmur into her mouth, pressing myself up against her so she can feel how much.

Her breath quickens as I slide my hand up inside her T-shirt.

'I want you,' I say again, and then she silences me with fast, hungry kisses and I know that I've got her. She's mine.

Someone turns the doorknob and I whip my hand out from under her T-shirt and slam my palm against the door, keeping it shut.

'Go upstairs,' I shout, locking the door. 'Whoops.' I laugh under my breath as I pull her body flush to mine. But she's tensed again. 'It's alright,' I tell her, my hand returning to the hem of her shirt. But this time she catches it, stopping me in my tracks.

'What... We... What are you doing?' she asks, even more breathless than before.

'What do you think I'm doing?' I ask in a low voice, kissing her neck. We're picking up from where we left off last night. She needs to know what she does to me.

'Angus, stop!' she says loudly.

Oh fuck. Ice freezes my stomach and I jerk away from her, reaching for the pull cord to flood the room with light. She flinches at the brightness, instinctively lifting her hands up to block it. She squints at me from under the shade of her fingers and I stare back at her with horror.

Same greeny-gold eyes…

Same light-blonde hair…

Not the same girl.

'Oh…' I say. 'I thought you were—'

Rose

Phoebe

Eliza

You could say we're freaks of nature.

We look exactly the same with our blonde hair and green eyes, and we all carry the same genetic material. One of us could literally commit murder and blame it on the others without our DNA giving us away.

Identical triplets are formed when a single fertilised egg splits into two, and one of the resulting two eggs splits again. The odds of this happening could be anything from 1 in 60,000 to 1 in 200 million, but one thing's for certain: identical triplets are very, very rare.

When our parents brought us home from the hospital, they were *terrified* about mixing us up. Apparently we wore our hospital armbands until they grew too tight, and even after Mum snipped the bands off, she painted each of our little fingernails a different colour. Sometimes she's still baffled about who's who in our baby photographs.

But even though we look the same, and even though we came from the same, single, fertilised egg, we were separated into three before our mother even knew she was pregnant.

And here's the crux of it: we were born three *completely different* individuals.

As time passed and our personalities began to shine through, Mum and Dad came to realise that we actually had very little in common.

Yes, we could all scream very loudly.

And yes, we were all extremely stubborn.

But that was about it.

Until we were seventeen, that is. Because when we were seventeen, Angus Templeton moved in next door. And unfortunately, all three of us fell head over heels in love with him.

Part One

Chapter 1

Phoebe

When people say they're living in the shadow of the mountain, it sounds kind of ominous. But there's nothing ominous about this. The mountain is so close, I feel like I'm *in* it. I can't even see the top unless I sit down on the sofa, and then my eye line reaches right up to the snowy peaks. What I wouldn't give to be up there...

'Why are you sighing?'

I jolt at the sound of Josie's voice, glancing over my shoulder to see my best friend gazing down at me. 'Nothing. I'm just happy to be back.' I smile warmly.

It's been almost ten years since we first came to Chamonix together at the age of eighteen.

'What time did you get up?' Josie asks, belatedly noticing that I'm fully dressed.

'An hour or so ago,' I reply, tightening my ponytail high up on my head.

'What's wrong with you?' she grumbles, not expecting an

answer as she flops onto the sofa beside me and yawns. Her medium-length dark hair is all tangled and her blue eyes look half asleep. She's still gorgeous, though.

'Coffee?' I ask, bounding to my feet and heading into the small kitchen.

'Yes, please,' she replies.

We only arrived yesterday, and last night we hit an old haunt and drank one beer too many. To Josie's irritation, I rarely suffer with hangovers, but then again, *I* managed to avoid being roped into the shots she did at midnight.

I switch on the radio and set about making the coffee, humming along to the music while she chills out.

'What do you want to do today?' she calls.

'Climb a mountain.' I poke my head around the door and flash her a hopeful grin.

'Noooooo. No, no, no, no, no.' Josie shakes her head adamantly and I continue with my task, chuckling to myself.

'Sorry,' she says, taking her cup from me when I reappear. 'I don't want to spoil your fun.'

I frown at her. 'Don't be silly.'

I'm getting married in two weeks, and all I wanted to do hen-wise was to come back here for a few days with my closest friend. I've thought a lot about Chamonix over the years, and as Josie and I experienced it together, it felt right that we should return, just the two of us.

My sisters were a little put out at not being invited, but now they've made other plans. Eliza and I are going to see a band in Manchester and Rose has organised a spa day. It'll be great to have some one-on-one time with each of them. We don't get to do that nearly enough these days.

'So, aside from climbing a mountain, what else could we do?' Josie perseveres.

'Paraglide off one?' I ask hopefully.

She pulls a face. 'You know I don't do extreme sports. I'm a boring mummy these days.'

Josie has a one-year-old son, Harry, back at home and this is the first time she's been away from him.

'How about we go on the Aiguille?' I suggest. 'You haven't seen the top at this time of year.'

She went home towards the end of the winter season in March all those years ago, but I managed to secure a contract working on the Aiguille du Midi cable car. I loved life here so much that I ended up staying on through the summer.

'Okay, sure,' she agrees, nodding. 'Guess I'd better get cracking then. I assume we'll have to queue for ages like all the other tourists?'

'Mmm, unfortunately. I don't know anyone who works there any more.'

The thought makes my heart squeeze.

A couple of hours later, we're nearly 4,000 metres above sea level on the highest and most famous of the Aiguilles de Chamonix.

I feel giddy with elation. Or maybe it's the altitude. Whatever it is, I'm ecstatic to be back.

'Wow,' Josie murmurs as we stand in quiet reverence on the panoramic viewing platform. 'I'd forgotten how beautiful it is up here.'

I gaze around at the jagged browny-grey peaks of the surrounding mountains. Mont Blanc is ahead of us and carpeted with snow, nonchalantly indifferent to the fact that it's summer. It looks deceptively close, but the way from here to its summit is one of the more technical climbing routes. I know because I've done it, as well as another route that is slightly less challenging, but not to be underestimated.

'I can't believe you climbed the White Lady twice.' Josie appears to be reading my mind.

'Neither can I,' I reply, as another of Mont Blanc's nick-names comes back to me: *White Killer*... It's hard to keep track of how many people have lost their lives trying to reach the top of Western Europe's highest summit, not to mention those who have perished coming back down again.

'*Getting to the top is only halfway*', my dad used to say. The thought of him here, now, brings with it a sharp sense of loss.

Dad died of a heart attack eight years ago, and I miss him so much, especially here in the mountains. He was the person who taught me how to climb.

Josie snorts with amusement, oblivious to the dark turn my thoughts have taken. 'You are such a jammy git. Did you really get paid to stay overnight up here? What a view to wake up to!'

I can't help but smile again. 'Well, there are no windows in the staff apartment,' I tell her. 'But yeah, it was pretty ridiculous walking outside in the morning.'

When Josie and I first came to Chamonix, we started off as chambermaids, but when she went home, I set my sights higher – a *lot* higher.

I'd made friends with a few locals, and one of them, Cécile, worked here on the Aiguille du Midi. The likelihood of a non-Chamoniard securing a contract on the cable cars was so low that it barely seemed worth applying – once you got a contract, you didn't let it go. But my French was fluent and Cécile promised to put in a good word for me, so I sent in my CV. When a couple of full-timers unexpectedly quit citing personal reasons, I got a lucky break.

It's hard to convey how much I loved it. I had to do everything from manning the cable cars to picking up litter, but the icing on the cake came once a month, when two of us would be guardians of the top, staying overnight in the staff apartment three floors down from where Josie and I are standing now. We were the last people to see the sun set at night and the first to see it rise the next morning. The experience was unforgettable.

My thoughts flit away from me again and suddenly I'm on the footbridge, the sky tinged orange and the mountains jagged silhouettes all around. For a few moments, I let my mind drift, before gathering myself together.

'Let's go to the ridge,' I prompt Josie, bumping her arm.

Soon afterwards we're in a shiny, dark, hollowed-out, frozen tunnel and, as I breathe in the cold air, I hear the familiar scritch-scratch of crampons on boots digging into densely packed snow. In the oddest way, I feel like I've come home.

There are three climbers ahead, preparing to set off down the ridge, and as they make their way through the gate, I move out of the ice cave and into the light. I watch as they set off down the narrow snow track, tethered together by rope.

'Freaking nutters,' Josie says under her breath, casting me a look. 'And you're a nutter as well.'

I smile a small smile. 'It feels like a long time since I did that.'

'You don't really go climbing much these days,' she observes.

'Hardly ever,' I reply quietly.

'Do you miss—'

'Yes,' I interrupt, then smile at her properly. 'I need to get my act together.'

She smiles back at me. 'Plenty of time for that. What do you reckon, lunch?'

'Good plan.'

Chapter 2

Rose

Once, on a sleepover, I was playing a late-night game of 'Truth or Dare' and Becky Betts asked me to choose between my sisters.

'You can only save one, and the other one will *die*,' she declared melodramatically.

I didn't hesitate to respond.

I still remember the look of shock on her face as she glanced at her sister Laura. Neither of them could believe my blasé lack of diplomacy.

But of course I'd save Phoebe. Everyone would, Eliza included.

It's not that Eliza and I hate each other. We just don't get on very well. We never have. She thinks I'm boring and uptight and I think she's immature and disrespectful.

'You're as thorny as your name,' she never tires of saying. Or another variant: 'Don't be so prickly, Rose.'

If we weren't sisters, it's unlikely we'd be friends.

Phoebe, on the other hand, is like a ray of sunshine on a cloudy day. Her laughter is infectious.

Damn, I miss her. She's only been gone two days.

'You're not taking that with you, are you?' I ask Mum now, realising that she's been holding the same china plate in her hands for at least two minutes.

'I haven't decided,' she replies defensively, putting it down with a slight clatter.

'You won't need a formal dinner service in a smaller house,' I point out pedantically.

'I might do,' she snaps.

'You can't take *all* of it with you,' I warn wearily as she stalks out of the room. She stops abruptly in the hall, her face turned towards the front door. It breaks into a smile.

'Have you been busking?' she asks over the sound of the door clunking shut.

'Yeah, in town,' I hear Eliza's reply, and then a knock as she places her guitar case against the adjoining wall.

'I thought you must've been at work. Come and have a cup of tea,' Mum urges genially.

I roll my eyes. 'Or better still, come and help!' I call out, smoothing my hands over my floral summer dress as our mother heads spiritedly in the direction of the kitchen.

'Do you want one, Rose?' she calls out to me as an after-thought. She's already put the kettle on.

'Sure,' I reply, as Eliza appears in the doorway.

She's wearing ripped denim jeans with a bright orange vest top and her hair has been fashioned into pigtails.

The hairstyle is just one example of how she hasn't grown up. Others include busking and waitressing instead of getting a proper job, going through boyfriends like they're going out of fashion, and still living at home. I could go on.

'Seriously, are you going to help at all with this packing?' I ask, as she slumps into a chair at the dining-room table. I'm kneeling on the carpet in front of Mum's display cabinet, wrapping yet another of her beloved ornaments in bubble wrap.

'Why should I? I don't want to move,' Eliza responds sarkily.

I was the one who recently persuaded Mum to sell up and downsize.

Phoebe thought it was 'probably a good idea', but Eliza was just furious to be losing her free hotel room.

'This is not about you,' I point out.

She leans forward and rests her elbows on the table, gazing down at me intently. I shift uneasily, already bristling at whatever it is that she's going to say.

'Do you really have nothing better to do with your holidays?' she asks.

I'm a nurse and I live and work in London, doing an often harrowing and stressful job. I would love to be lying on a beach right now beside my boyfriend Gerard in a hot country, but instead I'm here in Manchester for the next two weeks, helping *our* mother to move, and *our* sister with her last-minute wedding preparations. What's Eliza doing? A big fat diddly squat, that's what.

My father's words ring in my ears: *'Rose is a giver, not a taker. Just like her mother…'*

Mum used to be a nurse – that's how she and Dad met. Dad had a climbing accident and Mum nursed him back to health, but she gave up work when we were born. It was all hands on deck after that.

'I'm just saying,' Eliza says, shrugging and looking away, dispassionately. 'Some of us have better things to do with our time.'

I raise my voice. '*Some* of us need to get a proper job and stop scrounging off their elderly parent!'

'Stop it!' Mum barks from the doorway, making me flinch guiltily. The mugs on her tray vibrate noisily against each other as she continues. 'You two turn into spoilt brats when you're together! When are you going to start acting your age?'

She has a point. We *are* twenty-seven.

'Why don't you go and make a start on the attic?' Mum prompts me.

'Fine, I will,' I reply, grabbing my tea and flouncing out of the room in much the same manner as she did a couple of minutes ago.

When Phoebe and I were at university, our parents decided to turn our family home into a bed and breakfast. All of our childhood bits and pieces went up into the attic – even Eliza had a tidy up, but she never moved out – and then Dad died and Mum lost interest in putting up strangers.

I've been meaning to sort through my stuff for ages.

On my way past the hall mirror, I catch sight of my reflection and see that my high bun has come loose into a ponytail – the no-fuss, sporty style Phoebe favours. For a split second, it's like I'm looking right at her.

She and I adopted our own hairstyles from an early age because we were fed up with our teachers collectively calling us 'Miss Thomson' when they couldn't tell us apart. But Eliza was responsible for me first embracing the bun.

I used to nick her scissors occasionally because I could

never find mine, but one day she went mad because she had an art project due – some bizarre collage made out of cardboard – and I told her I'd given them back. She stormed into my bedroom, vying for blood, and was so cross to see them sitting in my top drawer that she yanked my hair and snipped off a chunk. She got into a *lot* of trouble for that.

In some ways, though, she did me a favour. I had to wear my hair up the next day and I got so many compliments that it became my signature look. Sometimes she'd wind me up by wearing hers in a bun, too, but she never could do neat and tidy so the teachers always knew something was off.

I hunt out the pole from the airing cupboard and hook it onto the ring to open the hatch door and bring down the ladder. A few minutes later, I'm up in the dingy, dusty space surrounded by boxes. I have no idea where to start, so I grab one and haul it towards me.

It's almost an hour before I come across the first diary. I recognise it immediately, despite the stickers plastering the front cover. My sisters and I were given identical purple notebooks by our Uncle Simon for our seventeenth birthdays, padlocked with tiny locks. I wrote in mine religiously, although I'd probably cringe at reading it now.

I prise back one corner of the cover and start in surprise at the scratchy handwriting I can just make out inside.

I knew Phoebe kept a diary – everyone knew Phoebe kept a diary – she was always entering writing competitions and telling people she wanted to be an author one day. But Eliza? I never would have pegged her as the diary-writing type. Songs, sure. But pouring her heart out to inanimate objects? Not her style. Even her songs are weird and quirky – there's no soul-baring in her lyrics, not the ones that I've heard, anyway.

Yet this is definitely her scrawl. When did she start writing this?

I scrutinise the lock. I lost my own key once, so I have a fair idea how to crack it. I reach up and remove one of the bobby pins that were unsuccessfully securing my bun and poke it in the keyhole, wiggling it around. A moment later, there's a click and I'm in.

I jolt at the sight of the first entry date: Friday 13th May, a whole decade ago. Friday 13th May – that was the day Angus moved in!

I slam the diary shut again. I *knew* it! I *knew* he had got to her, too! She always went around with this couldn't-care-less attitude, but she didn't fool me.

Guilt slithers like a snake in my gut as I open up the diary again. A chance to get inside Eliza's head? How could I resist? She'd kill me if she found out, of course, but it serves her right for not helping to pack up the house.

I press back the pages and begin to read…

Chapter 3

Eliza

I'm sitting on the wall, swinging my legs as far back as they'll go before they hit brick and bounce off again. This has always been one of my favourite places to sit at home: out the front, squeezed between a gap in the hedge, watching the world go by. We live on a tree-lined street in one of the nicer parts of Sale, a small town about twenty minutes' drive southwest of Manchester. My friends wonder why I haven't moved closer to the city, seeking a buzz instead of what they perceive as suburban boredom – 'suboreban' – but I like it here. I close my eyes and tilt my face to the sun, trying to catch a few rays before it goes behind the hovering clouds. It's been a shitty summer so far. I hope Phoebe's having more luck with the weather in France. I still can't believe she didn't invite me. I picture her now, laughing and carefree with the sun on her face and the snow-capped mountains behind her, just like in the photos she used to send me. It makes me smile, too.

My ears prick up as a car turns into the road and, sure enough, it's Angus.

A few strays from the kaleidoscope of butterflies that resides in my heart burst out through the bars of my ribcage and make their way into my stomach. The buggers are under much better control these days, but I'm annoyed at the few that won't behave themselves.

I watch as Angus parks his old Land Rover Defender on his mum's drive, remembering with affection the day he brought it home from his uncle's farm. It was painted bright orange within weeks.

'Are you still driving that shitmobile?' I call as he gets out of the car.

'It's a classic!' he exclaims, flashing me a cheeky grin as he slams the door shut behind him. His dark–blond hair is as dishevelled and windswept as ever. Phoebe said he plans to tidy it up for the wedding, I recall with a pang.

'Hello trouble,' he says, coming over.

'Speak for yourself.' I don't get down from the wall and he doesn't try to kiss me hello.

'I haven't seen you for ages. How are you doing?'

I glance over my shoulder in the direction of my childhood home, although I can't see it for the foliage in the way. 'Bit gutted,' I reply with a shrug.

'Yeah.' He regards me with concern. 'I heard your mum's selling up.'

'She's already accepted an offer.'

'That was quick,' he comments.

'Mmm. I'm sure she could have got more if Rose hadn't been rushing her.'

He gives a small, pitying smile that makes me regret bitching. Angus has never liked it.

'Have you heard from Phoebe?' I change the subject before he does.

'Nah.' He shakes his head. 'She's only been gone a couple of days.'

'Feels like longer.'

There's that smile again.

Phoebe is my older sister by twelve minutes, my beloved middle sister. In a funny way, she has always come between Rose and me. She'd like to say she bridges the gap, but actually, she widens it. Rose and I have always fought for her attention.

'Are you back for the weekend?' I ask Angus.

'No, for the whole week. I want to get the apartment sorted out before Phoebe returns.'

'Trying to soften the blow?'

'Something like that.' He smiles half-heartedly.

Phoebe wasn't keen on moving back to Manchester. She's only doing it because she promised Angus years ago that they would. He wants to live closer to his mum and property is cheaper up here, so they can afford to buy something of their own at last. Plus they're both able to work freelance – she's a translator and he's a journalist – but she's planning to take a break from her translation work to pen the novel that she's always wanted to write. When we were younger, she was always bounding into my bedroom, desperate to tell me about her latest story idea before it slipped from her mind. I could've listened to her chat away for hours. She was very engaging. She still is.

'What about you? Have you found anywhere to live yet?' Angus asks.

'Nope.' I steel myself for his reaction. 'I'm thinking about moving to London.'

'You're shitting me.' He gapes at me. 'You're moving to London the second Phoebe and I leave? Are you avoiding us?'

I force a roll of my eyes.

No, just you.

'Come in for a coffee?' he asks hopefully, jerking his head towards his house.

'Nah, your mum will want you to herself. Maybe catch you later, though,' I say out of politeness.

'Are you up to anything tonight?' He ignores his cue to leave.

'I've got a gig at a working men's club. Should be fun.'

He smirks at my caustic tone. 'Give me the address and I'll pop in.'

'You don't have to.'

'I know I don't.'

His mum appears then, and proceeds to sweep him up in a hug. I take the opportunity to escape while I can.

Chapter 4

Phoebe

'What's your greatest fear?'

Josie and I are well into our second bottle of wine and the evening has taken a turn for the philosophical.

I think for a long time before replying to her question, distracted by the movement of the waiting staff and the irritating non-appearance of our food.

'Come on.' She presses me for an answer, and I'm too fuzzy-headed to come up with an alternative to the truth.

'That I'm not the one.'

'What do you mean?' she asks with confusion.

'I don't know if I'm the one for Angus.'

'Of course you are!' she scoffs. 'You guys are perfect for each other! What on earth would make you think you're not?' Josie is comically flabbergasted, but my corresponding smile is half-hearted.

The truth is, sometimes I think that Angus and I are together for one reason and it's very simple: I saw him first.

I was riding my bicycle home from netball practice after school one afternoon when I spied the hottie getting a box out of the back of the Roger's Removals truck parked on the Templetons' driveway.

You know how sometimes you drive into danger when you should be driving away from it? It is a fact that *loads* of people crash into cars parked on the hard shoulder of a motorway because drivers inadvertently follow the line of their sight.

Well, I'm not saying Angus was dangerous, but he was extremely attractive and I was understandably drawn to him.

'Whoa!' I remember him gasping, jumping out of the way as I swerved towards him.

'Shit, sorry!' I screeched to a halt.

He took in my netball uniform with a bemused, lovely smile, and I, in turn, took in his lack of a Roger's Removals T-shirt.

'Are you Mr Templeton's grandson?' I asked with delight, also taking in his long legs, toned arms and honey-coloured skin while I was at it. Our elderly neighbour lost his wife a few months ago, and Mum mentioned something about his daughter and grandson coming to live with him.

'Er, yeah,' he responded, shifting the obviously heavy box in his arms. His longish hair was partly obscuring his vision and, as he rested the box on a wall, I noticed the faded band T-shirt he was wearing, coated with a faint layer of dust. Radiohead – one of Eliza's favourites. He was *exactly* her type. I couldn't wait to show him to her.

But then he flicked his hair out of his eyes and they were so beautiful, they sort of stumped me.

'I'm Angus,' he introduced himself, his lips tilting up at the corners.

'Phoebe,' I replied, feeling inexplicably nervous. Suddenly the *last* thing I wanted was for him and Eliza to meet. His eyes were multi-coloured and unusual – one was mostly green and the other predominantly hazel. 'Have you.come to visit your granddad before?' I was perplexed as to how I could have missed him.

He nodded. 'A few times.'

Mr Templeton had always kept to himself. I sometimes saw him from my bedroom window sitting out in the garden, but the most we spoke was when one of our netball balls escaped over the back fence onto his property, and then it would only be returned with a lecture about flowerbed damage. I certainly hadn't got into a conversation about his drop-dead-gorgeous grandson, but I wished I had.

At that point an attractive woman in her forties interrupted us. She called out hello and waved, while ducking in and out of the removal men still ferrying belongings into the house like ants.

'Hi!' I called back, assuming this was his mum and preparing to go into full charm offensive mode.

'Making friends already!' she exclaimed with delight.

'Mmm,' Angus murmured. 'Mum, this is Phoebe,' he introduced us. 'And this is my mum, Judy.'

'Phoebe!' She clapped her hands together with glee. 'You're one of the triplets!'

So she knew more about me than I knew about her.

'You live next door?' Angus asked, his unusual eyes widening slightly. Okay, so they had *both* clearly been informed of our existence, but it had taken Angus longer to cotton on.

'Yeah,' I replied.

'And your sisters are Rose and Elizabeth, is that right?' Judy checked.

'Yes,' I said with a smile. 'But don't call Eliza "Elizabeth" if you want her to answer. She changed her name when she was twelve because she thought it sounded cooler.' I said this with a light-hearted eyes-cast-to-the-heavens look and felt an immediate stab of remorse for poking fun at her.

'I've never met identical triplets,' Judy mused. 'I know twins – beautiful little girls called Fifi and Bo – but they're not identical.'

People were *always* telling us their twin stories, so I'd had enough practice at smiling and looking interested. I'd even heard of a couple of sets of triplets over the years, but never any *identical* triplets. We won.

'You'll be able to play Spot the Difference with us later,' I joked.

Strangers had been known to stop us on the street to do this, and one time we even featured in a Guess the Triplet quiz at school – Mum and Dad supplied the photographs. Rose was mortified, bless her. She never liked being under the spotlight.

Angus seemed in no hurry to re-join the removal men, and I soon discovered that he and his mum had moved from Brighton because Mr Templeton had recently had a bad fall. Apparently he hadn't been managing at all well on his own since Judy's mum passed away, but I sensed that there was more to the move than that. I also got the impression that Angus was less than thrilled to be there.

'It's all a bit tough on you, isn't it, love?' Judy said, rubbing his back conciliatorily.

Angus shrugged and looked uncomfortable, but he didn't bat her hand away like other boys I knew would've.

'He's got his A Levels coming up, and starting a new school at this time of year is not ideal,' she explained.

That seemed to be understating it.

'That sounds hard,' I sympathised. 'I've got mine coming up, too.'

We discovered that we were going to the same school so I offered to show him around. He accepted, pleased, but then my thoughts darted to Eliza and it occurred to me that there was a whole weekend between then and Monday. If I wanted to get in with Angus before my sisters, I had to be quick about it.

'In fact,' I said, thinking on the spot. 'If you're not too busy unpacking tomorrow, we could go and have lunch in town?'

Angus looked slightly taken aback, but quickly agreed. 'Sure,' he said with a nod. 'That would be great.'

'Cool.' We smiled at each other for a moment and I only broke eye contact when I noticed Judy beaming at us from out of the corner of my eye. 'Guess I'd better let you get on,' I said before my face had a chance to betray me. It was a bit embarrassing to be organising a date in front of his mum. 'But see you tomorrow. Around eleven?'

'Sounds good,' he confirmed.

I lost it as soon as I went inside, tearing up the stairs.

'I've just met Mr Templeton's grandson!' I yelled, shoving open first Eliza's bedroom door and then Rose's. 'Oh my God, he's gorgeous!' I cried from the landing, straddling the space between their two bedrooms. 'But don't even think about stepping on my toes because he's having lunch with me tomorrow and *I saw him first!*'

Eliza was lying on her bed, half asleep, and barely looked up at me. Rose just tutted under her breath and continued with her homework at her desk.

It was only later, when they met him, that they realised what they'd lost, but by then it was too late. I'd already staked my claim on him.

Angus and I spent the whole day together that Saturday, wandering around Manchester after lunch and ending up at a pub until late into the evening. I was initially attracted to his looks and I was pretty sure that he fancied me as much as I fancied him, but there was so much more to him than that. We clicked immediately and made each other laugh. As the day progressed, our jokey banter transformed into more heartfelt conversation, and he confided in me about his family. I learned that he never knew his dad and his mum had raised him singlehandedly – he doted on her. She lost her job recently and couldn't afford the rent on their apartment in Brighton, so moving in with his ailing granddad seemed like a good solution. But Angus was gutted to be leaving his home and his friends. He didn't have a girlfriend. I asked. He had been seeing someone, but they'd broken up a few months ago.

Towards the end of the evening, our looks became longer and the sense of intimacy between us increased. The kiss we shared on the footpath outside our homes was sweet, and from that moment on, we were an item. Neither Eliza nor Rose ever stood a chance.

*

'Don't you think Angus and Eliza are better suited than he and I are?' I ask Josie now.

'*What?!* No!' she spluttered. 'Of course they're not! Why on earth would you say that?'

'They have so much in common. They're both such homebodies – he's thrilled to be moving back to Manchester, but he's dragging me, kicking and screaming. I'd give anything to come and do another stint here instead,' I say wistfully, looking out of the window at the mountains shrouded in darkness.

I like my job as a translator, and there's big money in interpreting. It's a high-pressure thrill to listen to a conversation through headphones in one language and then repeat it simultaneously into a microphone in another, and I do have a knack for languages: I'm fluent in French, German and Spanish, now.

But when we move back to Manchester, I plan to make a start on my book. I've had an idea kicking around in my head for years, about a girl who falls for a modern-day magician. I've kept notepads practically all my life and I still jot down my thoughts occasionally, in the hope that they'll come in useful for future characters or settings.

But as I sit here now, I realise that even writing – however much I love it – pales in comparison to the rush that I used to feel when I lived here for those few months in the mountains.

Dad always used to tell us to find our passion and then work out a way to do it. I haven't climbed in so long. Have I lost sight of what I love?

I continue with what I was saying to Josie. 'Also, Angus and Eliza are both really into their music, and you know how he's always refused to try rock climbing. He won't even go skiing, for pity's sake.'

'Shut up,' Josie interrupts me. 'That's all completely inconsequential. Angus loves you and you love him. It would be boring if you were the same.'

'Maybe,' I reply, and then Josie gasps, 'Finally!' at the sight of our approaching food.

As I move my wine glass aside to make room for the waitress, my thoughts drift back to when we first came here nearly a decade ago...

Josie and I had hit the ground running from the moment we'd arrived. After circulating our CVs to everyone under the sun, we walked straight into jobs as chambermaids for a small hotel. We had a minuscule two-bedroom apartment in Cham Sud, nicknamed The Ghetto, in a dark-wood-clad six-storey apartment block. Our days kicked off early, when we'd trudge through the snow with our pick-axes for a six-thirty start. We'd open up the hotel kitchen and lay out breakfast, then make beds, clean bathrooms and try to avoid the temptation of crawling under the soft duvets to catch up on some sleep. By eleven thirty we'd be ready to head up the slopes with the eclectic group of Swedish snowboarders we'd fallen into step with. Sleep in the early evening was an irritating necessity, but by nine thirty we'd be hitting the bars, drinking free shots and usually end up dancing on the tables. Midnight would see us move on to a club, and at around four a.m. we'd head home for a quick kip before beginning it all again two hours later.

It was *sooooo* much fun.

I didn't want to leave at Christmas, even temporarily, but our apartment was being rented out for the week by its owners and Mum and Dad would have been gutted, so I didn't have much choice. But the whole experience back home was hard.

For a start, I felt unusually disconnected from my sisters. I'd felt incredibly close to each of them individually for my entire life and I loved and trusted them more than anyone, but for some reason, when we were back together again, we jarred. At the time, I wondered if we'd taken to our new-found independence to such an extent that we struggled to find ourselves back in each other's pockets.

Rose was certainly itching to get back to university in Portsmouth where she was doing a nursing degree. She rubbed me up the wrong way a few times, looking unimpressed when I talked about dancing on tables and doing free shots. She acted like I was a silly girl, whereas she'd matured and grown up. She was a bit full of herself.

But Eliza was especially distant and cold towards me. I assumed at the time that she blamed me for leaving her, and I felt bitter in turn about being made to feel guilty. After all, she was the one who chose to stay in Manchester to pursue her music career – nobody forced her.

The other thing that happened at Christmas was Angus and I broke up properly. Back in September, we had made a tearful but, *we* thought, mature decision to take a break from what had been a very intense relationship. We had been distraught knowing we were going our separate ways – him to university in London and me to Europe before settling for the winter in Chamonix – but we convinced each other that if it was meant to be between us, we would pick up again when I returned.

But, at Christmas, we decided to make the break permanent. We had barely been in touch during the three months we'd already spent apart, and Angus felt that he'd been putting his life on hold for me and wanted a clean break. I was more upset than I let on, and I couldn't wait to escape back to France.

I met Remy in January. He was French, but lived a couple of hours away in Turin with his Italian girlfriend and would come through the Mont Blanc tunnel on weekends to snowboard. He knew some of the guys in our group so he hung out with us occasionally, but we didn't speak much. Sometimes Josie and I would see him in his bright yellow ski jacket expertly navigating the slopes and we wouldn't be able to look away. When he was out of sight, we'd flash each other knowing grins. Remy was cool and talented and different to the other guys we knew with their piercings and crazy-coloured hair. I adored them as mates, but I didn't fancy any of them in the slightest.

Remy I was attracted to, I'll confess to that. But I stayed out of his way because he had a girlfriend and, anyway, it would have been too soon after Angus.

Josie did hook up with a guy when we returned to Chamonix after Christmas, and when he went home to Birmingham in February she moped for weeks. We'd initially planned to remain abroad until April, but she called it quits in March. He didn't appreciate her dedication, sadly – they broke up soon afterwards.

I was sorry to see her go, but for me, my love affair was still with the mountains and I realised I had no immediate reason to leave. It was around this time that I became friends with Cécile and she encouraged me to move into her apartment in Argentière, the next village along. I traded chambermaiding for a job behind a bar at *The Savoy*, a brilliant après-ski venue that hosted live bands on a regular basis. But what I really wanted was to work on the Aiguille du Midi like Cécile. I couldn't believe it when I landed the contract.

The skiing and snowboarding my friends and I had done in winter gradually turned into rock climbing, hiking and mountain biking in the spring and summer. But the thought that I'd have to go home and start university in London was always at the back of my mind.

I sigh and look out of the window again at the dark night beyond, while Josie tucks into her meal beside me. I'm no longer as hungry as I thought I was.

If things had turned out differently, I could still be living here. I can't believe it's taken me until now to return.

'Phoebe?'

I glance away from the window and straight into the glacier-blue eyes of the one person in the world who I should be avoiding.

'Hello, Remy,' I reply, feeling oddly at peace as I stare back at him.

Chapter 5

Rose

There's a strange sort of melancholy in my heart as I gently place Eliza's diary down on my stomach, trying not to dislodge any of the old concert tickets or scraps of paper that meant something to her years ago. It's late at night and I'm lying in bed, my eyes sore from the strain of keeping them open. Mum seemed keen for company after dinner, but I was desperate to get back to my clandestine reading.

I have an unusual urge to give Eliza a hug. She's still out at her gig and I'm tempted to wait up for her, but I'd only freak her out. She wouldn't understand the reason for the gesture and I wouldn't be able to explain my sudden affection for her.

I had no idea she'd fallen so hard.

'Fuck.' That's her opening word. And then: *'It's him. That guy from the park. He's our new next-door neighbour. And Phoebe has a date with him tomorrow. How the hell did that happen?!'*

I just don't understand why she never said anything. I mean, okay, Phoebe had lined up a date with Angus within minutes of meeting him and when Phoebe wants something, the rest of us tend to step aside and offer our best wishes. She has that effect on people and no one holds it against her because she's personable and popular, not bullish. Well, not usually, although she was pushing it the day she met Angus with all her 'I saw him first!' nonsense.

But that's the thing. Phoebe *didn't* see him first. Eliza did. A whole year before he moved in.

She was at the local park and he was on the skateboard ramp. She sat and watched him for ages, but couldn't pluck up the courage to say hello. She went back looking for him for months afterwards, but never saw him again. Well, not until he bloody well moved in next door and, within minutes, her cherished Phoebe had got her claws into him.

Poor Eliza. She didn't even try to fight for him.

Unlike me…

My face burns as a few choice memories flood my brain…

I didn't meet Angus until the Saturday morning after he'd arrived. I'd gone outside to bring in the recycling box and he happened to be doing the same. I'd just reached the footpath when I heard his front door slam.

'Hey!' he called, jogging lazily down his driveway towards me.

I hadn't brushed my hair and was still wearing my dressing gown – mortifying.

'Hello,' I called back weakly, trying to hide my blushing

face. But I caught his smile and couldn't resist looking at him as he approached.

'Let me guess. Rose?' His eyebrows pulled together adorably. He was so tall – towering over me at about six foot two or three.

'Yes,' I replied, both surprised and flattered that he'd guessed right. 'And you're Angus.'

'Yeah. No identical siblings to confuse *you*.'

His eyes were curious – stunning. It was both a struggle to look away and to make eye contact. His dark-blond hair fell just so across his forehead and I remember I had a strong desire to run my fingers through it.

'I heard my sister is taking you out later,' I said, wanting to kick Phoebe.

'Hopefully,' he replied. 'If she's still up for it.'

'I'm sure she is.' I *knew* she was. She hadn't stopped going on about it.

Maybe he sensed the downturn of my mood, because the next thing I knew, he was inviting me.

'Come along, too, if you like?'

I could tell he meant it and I was genuinely tempted.

'Oh, thanks!' But Phoebe would kill me! 'Um, maybe,' I added, not committing either way. Perhaps Phoebe wouldn't mind *too* much. 'Guess I should go and get dressed, in any case.' I bent down and picked up our recycling box.

'Maybe see you later then,' he said amiably.

'Maybe.'

I caught his eye again and my blush intensified.

Phoebe was still at the kitchen table eating breakfast with

Dad when I went back inside. I casually mentioned that I'd met Angus and he'd invited me along today.

'Oh no, you don't,' Phoebe said firmly, putting her spoon down in her bowl with a clatter.

'What's this?' Dad asked, glancing up at me.

'Rose is trying to get in on my date with Angus,' Phoebe said and her unusually cold tone made me squirm.

'Rose,' Dad said, eyeing me with disappointment. I felt ashamed. Phoebe and Dad were very close and she had evidently already told him about her crush on the boy next door.

'I didn't say yes,' I snapped at them both. 'God!'

I stormed out of the room and we never spoke about it again.

I was still awake when Phoebe came in that night and I went to the landing and watched her moon her way up the stairs. I knew from the moment she looked up at me that they'd kissed. I tried to be happy for her – I didn't usually begrudge my favourite sister – but my heart sank. She always got the best of everything.

But it was done, and after that I had to live with it, had to witness The Angus and Phoebe Show. He was clearly besotted with her, but I wasn't convinced of the level of her affection for him. I knew that she liked him a lot, but she always acted so confident and independent, certainly not clingy or needy. I had the impression that his feelings for her ran deeper.

Sometimes he'd call round and she'd be off rock climbing with Dad, without even telling him that she'd be out for the day. I felt sorry for him when that happened, and I'd invite him in for a cuppa to try to cheer him up. Eventually we became friends on our own terms, but I still had a soft spot for him. Being completely honest, had Phoebe stepped aside, I would have picked up the pieces.

Angus was sweet. He still is, bless him. I love him to bits, but luckily not like *that* any more. Now he's just Gus, my gorgeous big brother who looks out for me.

I had absolutely no idea that Eliza, while acting like she couldn't be arsed to come downstairs and say hello when Angus called around, was actually avoiding him because it hurt too much to see him. That seems like an entirely different level to what I felt.

The urge to hug her returns.

I'm being ridiculous. All of this happened years ago and Eliza must be over her feelings for him by now. She'd better be, because she'll be seeing Angus all the time once he moves here.

I feel a stab of jealousy. I've been a core part of Phoebe and Angus's London gang for years, and now Eliza will have them all to herself. It makes me remember that hellish year at school when Mum and Dad decided to separate us. We constantly squabbled so they put us into different classes and Eliza was the one who got Phoebe. I feel a pinch even now as I remember them tailing off to go to their classroom together.

I sigh heavily. At least I'll still have Josie to spend time with in London.

I was disappointed when Phoebe didn't invite me on her hen holiday, although I did understand. Chamonix was her and Josie's thing, not mine, and Phoebe could hardly ask me without inviting Eliza. But I've got to know Josie well over the last few years and she feels almost as much my friend as Phoebe's.

Luckily she and her husband, Craig, will still be in my life when Gus and Phoebe leave. And Gerard, too, of course.

I jolt. What's the time? He was supposed to call me tonight.

Oh well. We'll speak in the morning. I pick up Eliza's diary and continue to read.

Chapter 6

Eliza

It's a pretty decent round of applause, all things considered. I smile at the crowd of predominantly pot-bellied baldies and give them a little bow, before taking off my guitar strap and hopping down from the tiny platform that they like to call a stage.

'The usual?' Bob asks from behind the counter. I tend to stick around for one drink, but only because the manager is paying.

'Sure.' I give him a curt nod and prop my guitar up against the bar, tensing as I notice a certain someone approaching out of the corner of my eye.

'That was good,' Angus says.

'What are you doing here?' I ask with shock.

He shrugs, amused. 'I said I'd come.'

'How did you know where I was playing?'

'I got the details from your mum after you nicked off without telling me. Don't you do any of your own songs any more?'

Bob plonks my half pint of beer down on the bar top and raises his chin at Angus.

'Same, please,' Angus says amiably. 'Actually, make mine a pint.'

'I'm not sticking around for long,' I'm quick to point out, as Bob waddles off.

'I'll drink fast,' he replies, shoving his hair back off his forehead. It won't stay in that position for long.

'So, why only covers?' he asks of my set list.

'It's what they asked for,' I reply with a shrug.

He nods thoughtfully and drops the subject. 'Did you come by Metro?'

'Yes,' I reply.

'I'll give you a ride home,' he says.

I raise one eyebrow. 'In your shitmobile?'

He shrugs. 'It's a classic.'

This makes me snigger. The two of us have been known to go on and on like this.

'So, Liza...' he starts, resting one elbow on the bar top and staring at me with his freakishly beautiful eyes. My heart contracts. I wish he wouldn't call me that. I love it when he calls me that. 'What's this crap about you leaving Manchester?'

I groan and look away.

'Phoebe will be gutted,' he says seriously.

'Yeah, well, it's not all about Phoebe.'

'You're the main reason I got her to move back here,' he continues, unfazed by my comment. 'She misses you. She wants to spend more time with you.'

'She'll get over it,' I reply.

He leans in closer. 'You know you're her favourite, right?'

'Bullshit.' I can't help but smile because this comment is ridiculous and he knows it. If anything, Phoebe is closer to Rose these days, not that she'd ever pick favourites. He returns my smile.

'I thought you loved it here,' he says gently.

My lips tug down at the corners. 'I do.' I feel downhearted, but the emotion morphs smoothly into annoyance. 'Is this the only reason you came here, to pester me about doing what's best for Phoebe?'

Angus looks wounded. 'No, I came to see your gig. I haven't seen you play for ages.'

I humph and turn back to the bar.

'I'm only teasing.' He elbows me in my ribs. 'It's up to you where you want to live.'

'Good. Glad we're agreed on that.' I take a gulp of my drink.

Later, I stare out of the car window as Angus takes me back to Sale. I've lived in Greater Manchester for most of my life. I've never gone anywhere else or done anything of interest. I'm twenty-seven and I've got nothing to show for it. I *am* going to move to London, I think determinedly. Maybe I'll go tomorrow and start flat hunting. I know Phoebe will be hurt. She's been encouraging me for years to move to the Big Smoke to be near to her and Rose, but I couldn't. And I can't be near her now, either. Damn Angus for driving this wedge between us! *This wedge that she doesn't even know exists.*

'What is it?' Angus asks, sensing the change in atmosphere. I'm angry, and he has always had an uncanny way of noticing, even when he's not looking at me.

'Nothing,' I snap.

'Liza…'

'Don't call me that!'

That shuts him up. Stupid man.

We ride the last few minutes in stressed silence. He pulls up on his driveway, cutting off the engine and turning to face me.

'Thanks for the lift.' I unclick my seatbelt and reach for the door handle.

'Wait,' he says with frustration.

I glare at him. 'You know I've broken up with Dave, right?'

He swallows. 'No, I didn't.' He shakes his head.

'Well, it was a total nightmare.' I'm overstating it. Dave was my boyfriend for about four months, but I was the one who ended it – he just clung on a little too hard. 'I need a break from this place, alright? Get over it.'

'Stop,' he says, his no-nonsense tone making my mouth go dry.

A shiver runs down my spine as he gives me a hard stare.

'Gah!' I erupt, pulling myself together and getting out of the car.

He does the same, going around to the boot to retrieve my guitar case. I don't meet his eyes as he hands it over.

'I'm sorry about Dave,' he says.

'You thought he was a dickhead,' I point out, looking up at him. They met a couple of months ago at Easter.

'He *was* a dickhead.' He nods definitively. 'I hope you find someone nicer.'

'Oh, piss off, Angus,' I mutter.

'Hey!' He grabs my arm as I turn away. 'I mean it.'

'And I mean it, too. Piss off.' I shake my arm free before thinking to glance quickly at my house. Rose's bedroom light is off, I notice with relief.

'Liza,' he says gently, stepping towards me. I stare up at him, scared that if he hugs me, I'll crumble. He makes a move to do just that, but a split-second before his arms come around my back, I stiffen my resolve and push him away.

'Fine,' he says flatly. 'Have it your way.'

I stalk off to the sound of him locking his car and our feet crunching across the gravel towards our respective front doors.

But this is not having it my way. If I had it my way, we never would have met.

I don't know what it was about Angus that drew all three of us to him. There was clearly something in his chemical make-up that was like a drug to us. If only there had been three of him, like there were three of us. Rose has swooned over him from the word go and she probably still fancies the pants off him. But deep down, I know that the reason I've grown less patient of my eldest triplet over the years is because I can see myself in her.

Screw Angus, and screw chemistry.

I go inside and only just manage to stop myself from slamming the front door behind me.

Chapter 7

Phoebe

It's late at night and my head is spinning and not from the wine. I sobered up after dinner, but Josie thinks I'm off my face – or out of my mind. In truth, it's probably both. I'm sure she thinks I'm going to come to my senses in the morning, but she's wrong. I've been lying here for an hour thinking about Remy and I'm becoming more and more certain that I need to see him again tomorrow.

He doesn't seem to have changed much. He's older, sure, but life here clearly suits him. He's done everything he set out to do – he's living in his favourite place in the world, climbing mountains every day and earning a salary from it. He's stuck to his guns and I expected nothing less of him. I'm happy that he's happy.

So why do I feel like crying? Maybe I'm drunker than I realised. I should phone Angus – he'd sort me out.

But no. I just want to think for a while, about Remy, and the night that we began…

*

'Nervous?' Cécile asked.

'Excited,' I replied with a grin as Marcel blew my friend a kiss. We stood and watched as he and the rest of our colleagues disappeared through the clouds on the last cable car of the day.

It was my first overnighter and Cécile had arranged for us to be guardians together. Usually she stayed up here with her boyfriend Marcel, but he hadn't minded swapping with me. Perhaps I should've been nervous about being one of only two girls sleeping in a tiny apartment at the top of a mountain, but all I felt was exhilaration.

Before we could kick back and relax, we had to go through our check-list to ensure that everything was clean and in order for the next day. This meant inspecting fuel and water tank levels, machinery, toilets and stairs. Fire doors had to be closed, the cable car needed to be turned off and put on charge for the next day and one toilet was to be left open for any climbers who had missed the last cable car home.

But before we got on with our tasks, we took a moment to stand on the footbridge and breathe.

'It's so still and quiet,' I murmured.

Cécile and I tended to speak in French, even though her English was good, too.

'You should see it in a snowstorm,' she replied, leaning over the handrail. Her wavy dark hair was blowing slightly in the breeze. 'It's really eerie and cold.'

'At least you usually have Marcel to cuddle up to,' I pointed out with a smile.

Jagged grey and brown peaks protruded through the fluffy

white clouds and the vast sky curved over our heads in a pale-blue dome.

In the name of God, stop a moment, cease your work, look around you.

It was a Tolstoy quote, but it always made me think of Dad because he said it aloud every time we went climbing. The memory of some of our summits filtered through my brain and I wished he was with me now. He had promised to try to come over in the summer so we could do Mont Blanc together, but first he needed to persuade Mum. He was in his early sixties, which she thought was too old to do a big climb, but I couldn't imagine going up there without him.

My family had almost come to see me at Easter, but in the end, Somerset had won out. Our Aunt Suzie had a cottage there and apparently both Eliza and Rose had been keen to go. Mum had been so surprised that they'd wanted to spend the break together that she'd agreed. She would've done anything to keep the peace where those two were concerned, but they also had to take finances into account now that Dad was retired.

On the one hand, I felt hurt that my sisters hadn't jumped at the chance to come and see me. Eight months earlier, when I'd first left home to go travelling, I'd cried so much. I felt like a part of my soul had been torn from my body when I said goodbye to them. But something happened to me in the days and weeks that passed. I began to enjoy my independence. It was the first time in my life that I'd been able to do exactly what I wanted, without having to take Rose or Eliza's feelings into consideration, and I liked it more than I could have predicted. A part of me was glad that they hadn't come to Chamonix and cramped my style.

I had also been sensing a detachment on their part, especially since Christmas when I'd briefly returned home. Rose took forever to reply to my emails, and Eliza was cold and standoffish when I called. Half the time Mum and Dad made excuses for her and she didn't even come to the phone.

But I knew that our distance – both physical and emotional – was only temporary. I'd have time to make things right between us when I went home. I just needed to make the most of the here and now.

It was with that thought at the forefront of my mind that I took a deep breath of the crisp, clean air and felt a little more at peace.

When I started work on the Aiguille du Midi, I did a couple of days training. The staff were expected to be 'all-rounders', so we pitched in and took turns on a rotational basis. I could've been a 'liftie', i.e. manning the cable cars; ticket inspecting at the bottom, middle or top stations; or working as a substitute for either of these. There were also elevator lifties who brought clients up to the top terrace; and when it was open in the summer, various roles working on the Panoramic du Mont Blanc cable car to Helbronner in Italy.

Everyone had a preferred and least preferred task. After being a chambermaid, I wasn't keen on picking up other people's rubbish for hours on end, but some of my colleagues preferred the cleaning shifts to riding repetitively up and down the mountain in a cable car.

Personally, liftie days were my favourites. I hadn't yet got bored of reminding tourists to take off their backpacks or hearing them exclaim how fast the cable car in the opposite direction was going. It was an optical illusion: we were on the same cable so when the cars whizzed past each other they were going exactly the same speed. I still smiled when my passengers squealed as we flew over the pylons, and I thought I'd never tire of breaking through the clouds to gasps of delight.

I wasn't sure how I would have fared if I were caught in bad weather, though. In Cécile's first summer season, she had been manning a cable car when the operators in charge heard of a huge storm on its way. They thought they had time to bring up the last clients of the day from Chamonix to the middle station, but the storm had come quicker than expected and Cécile had to stop the car en route and wait for the bad weather to pass.

Storms never lasted long, but she said it was scary swinging there for half an hour and calming down the passengers while huge gusts of wind blew the car this way and that. These days she just laughed if it happened, but I didn't think I'd find it very funny.

I quickly changed my mind – being a guardian of the top was now my preferred job. I suspected it could well end up being my favourite job of all time.

Or maybe not, I thought to myself a short while later as I scrubbed away at a toilet bowl. My head shot up and my blood ran cold at the sound of Cécile crying out for help.

I scrambled to my feet and ran outside in the direction of her voice, jolting with shock at the sight of a young couple coming through the ice cave from the ridge. The man was supporting the girl and her face was creased in pain.

'She fell. I think she's sprained her ankle,' he said in French. I did a double take. 'Remy?'

He stared back at me, disoriented.

'You know each other?' Cécile asked me.

'Yes. I'm Phoebe,' I reminded him, feeling a stab of disappointment as his face only belatedly registered recognition.

'Hello,' he gasped, panting.

I quickly came to my senses, rushing to his aid.

We went to the nearby staff canteen where Remy lowered his companion into a chair.

'What's your name?' Cécile asked the girl.

'Amelie,' she replied as Remy crouched down to unlace her left boot.

'What happened?' I asked.

The pair had been on a day trip doing the Midi Plan crossing. They'd come up on the first cable car this morning.

'I was too slow,' Amelie lamented.

'It was my fault,' Remy chipped in miserably, gazing ruefully at her foot, which we could now see was blue and swollen.

'No,' she cut him off firmly, putting her hand on his arm. 'You told me we shouldn't take so long for lunch. But we'd gone all that way.' She winced. 'It was my first time doing the route,' she explained.

The Midi Plan crossing takes about six or seven hours if you're good, but Remy had realised they weren't going fast enough and he knew they needed to step up their pace to catch the last cable car home at five thirty. Amelie had been at the bottom of the ridge when, tired and exhausted, she had got one of her crampons stuck in her trousers and fallen, twisting her ankle. Remy had had to help her the rest of the way.

I was intrigued as I listened to her speak. She was definitely French, but Remy's girlfriend had been Italian. Had they broken up? But if that were the case, who was Amelie?

Although Cécile was trained in first aid, she wasn't allowed to administer any medicine without first calling the doctor. The doctor in turn asked to speak to Amelie before determining that she'd be fine to stay at the top overnight. An ice pack, water and some pain relief tablets would see her through.

'Is there anyone you need to contact?' I asked Remy. Amelie had called her mother a little while ago, but Remy hadn't rung anyone to let them know he was safe.

'No.' He took off his red woollen hat and dragged his hands across his scalp, skewing his short, dark-brown hair. He had stubble that was bordering on a beard and his face was tanned and lean.

I couldn't help myself. 'You don't need to call anyone in Turin?'

He shook his head. 'My girlfriend and I split up a few weeks ago.'

'Aah.' I glanced at Amelie and he followed the direction of my gaze.

'Amelie is my cousin,' he explained.

'Oh. I'm sorry to hear that. I mean…' I stuttered. 'I'm not sorry to hear that Amelie's your cousin.'

When Remy was snowboarding, his eyes were hidden behind dark glasses, but at that moment they were a striking blue and sparkling with amusement.

'So, you work on the Aiguille now?' he asked, taking a sip of the coffee I'd just made him.

'Yes.' I smiled weakly, trying to regain my composure. 'For a little over a month now.'

'What happened to your friend?'

'Josie? She went home.' I shrugged. 'I wanted to stay for a bit longer. I don't go to university until September, and now I have a contract here, I think I'm going to find it hard to let it go.'

He looked impressed. 'I know a few people who've tried to get a job on the Aiguille in the past with no luck. How did you manage it?'

'Friends in high places.' I flashed Cécile a grin. She was sitting with Amelie, but must have been eavesdropping because she returned my smile.

'Should we carry on with the check-list?' I asked her, slightly reluctantly. I figured the sooner our work got done, the sooner we could come back here and hang out.

'I suppose we should.' Cécile stood up and reached for her coat. 'Help yourselves to anything in the kitchen,' she told Remy and Amelie. 'We'll be back in a bit.'

The moment we were outside, she gave me a comically meaningful look. 'So he's split up with his girlfriend, has he?'

I smirked and she laughed, continuing to tease. 'And he and Amelie are just cousins, are they?'

'Oh, shut up.' I shoved her arm as she giggled.

It wasn't protocol, but after our work was done, Cécile agreed to let Remy and Amelie join us for dinner in the staff apartment.

As we all walked across the footbridge with Cécile leading the way and me bringing up the rear, my eyes, for once, were not drawn to the view.

Remy was carrying Amelie and he looked so… well, *manly*. He was lean but strong – probably not quite six foot tall, but much taller than my five foot six inches. Older, too – I hazarded a guess at early twenties. In contrast, Angus seemed like a lanky teenager.

I made the comparison fondly, but I still felt a pang of guilt. Angus and I were no longer a couple, but we had been trying to stay friends. I had been trying a little harder than he had, in truth. In the five months since our break-up at Christmas, I'd instigated every single one of our very occasional email exchanges.

When I thought of Angus and how close we'd been the previous summer, my memories had a surreal quality to them. I'd loved him enough to lose my virginity to him and I remembered feeling incredibly lucky to have found such a funny, kind, drop-dead-gorgeous boyfriend. Sometimes I wondered if I'd been mad not to fight harder for him when he asked to make our break permanent, but I'd told myself that if it were meant to be, we would find our way back to each other again someday.

The staff apartment was pretty cosy with four of us inside. Cécile settled our guests and sorted out drinks while I prepared dinner: homemade Bolognese and, luckily, a whole packet of spaghetti. We thought we could stretch the sauce to four.

'What can I do?' Remy asked, making me jump as he joined me. 'You want me to grate some cheese?'

'Er, sure.' I got the Parmesan out of the fridge and found him the grater.

'Thank you for this,' he said as he got on with the task.

'You're welcome. It's good to see you again.' And boy, did I mean it. He had stripped down to a T-shirt and I was finding it hard not to stare at his tanned, muscled arms. I'd met a few attractive rock climbers in my time – I used to think of them as surfers of the sky, so often fit and sexy with thrill-seeking natures and a true sense of adventure. Usually Dad was around to keep me in line, but not this time.

In the nearby living room, Amelie laughed at something Cécile said. Remy smiled in their direction and then at me. 'I'm sorry I couldn't place you earlier,' he said. 'I wasn't expecting to see you at the top of a mountain.'

'I suppose the last time you saw me I was on the top of a table, so it's a fair comment.'

'You did like dancing on those tables,' he commented with a grin.

'I'm still prone to the occasional tabletop dance,' I replied as I scooped out a strand of spaghetti with a fork to check if it was cooked. 'I mostly hang out in Argentière these days,' I explained, draining the pasta. 'I live with Cécile and have a part-time bar job at *The Savoy*.'

'I'm surprised I haven't seen you there,' he said, watching as I served up.

'You must've been in on my days off. It's been, what, two months since I saw you last?'

'Something like that. I haven't been to Chamonix as much as I would have liked.'

'Why is that? You seemed to be here every weekend earlier in the year.'

'Mmm. My girlfriend, Cristina, wanted me at home more. It's part of the reason why we broke up.'

'Aah.'

I wanted to ask him more, but our food would've gone cold so I grudgingly put my questions on hold.

Amelie was in high spirits during dinner, which was amazing considering the state of her ankle. She stayed on the sofa with her foot on a chair, nursing her plate on her lap. If it weren't for her injury, we could have been four friends chatting merrily away, but I soon became distracted thinking about our forthcoming sleeping arrangements.

In the summer months, we encouraged stranded climbers to walk back down the ridge to the Refuge du Cosmique, which is about a forty-five-minute trek on the glacier. But if they were injured or didn't want to, then we would let them sleep on the floor of the public toilets. It might sound mean, but some people stayed at the top on purpose to avoid paying the refuge charges, and frankly, the Aiguille was not a hotel.

That evening, though, I couldn't bear the thought of sending our two new friends to the other side of the footbridge to sleep in the loos, however warm they might've been.

I could've kissed Cécile when we were alone in the kitchen and she made a different suggestion.

'I suppose they could sleep on the sofas,' she whispered.

'Really? Well, no, Amelie can have my bed. I'll take the sofa.'

'I bet you will.' She gave me a mischievous look.

'Cut it out.' My cheeks flamed. 'Are you serious, though? Can we let them stay here?' I asked hopefully.

'I won't tell if you don't,' she replied with a comedy wink.

Amelie was extremely grateful and really didn't take much convincing to sleep in my room. She was so exhausted that she went to bed straight after dinner. Cécile stayed up only a little while longer before calling it a night.

'What about the sunset?' I frowned at her as she stretched her arms over her head. Surely she didn't want to miss it – she was always going on about the fact that we got the last of the sun up here.

'Take Remy. I've seen enough sunsets. I'm shattered.'

It wasn't that late, but while her yawn looked genuine, I couldn't believe she was really that tired. She was meddling.

As soon as she went, I felt a flurry of nerves at being alone with Remy. I smiled across at him from my position on the second sofa.

'Do you think Amelie is feeling okay?'

I regretted my chosen topic of conversation when his face fell. He shook his head with dismay, but didn't answer.

'It could have been a lot worse,' I pointed out, soon regretting that comment, too.

He shuddered visibly. 'I keep imagining having to tell her mother that she'd...' He shuddered again, a morose look in his eyes. 'I can't believe I messed up so badly.' He looked utterly miserable.

'Hey.' Impulsively I moved to sit beside him.

'I should have insisted we turn back sooner, but I didn't, and then I rushed her...'

'You were just trying to get down in time,' I said, squeezing his shoulder consolingly.

'Better late than never,' he replied darkly.

We both fell silent, deep in thought. I let my hand drop, but didn't move back to the other sofa.

'You two are close, aren't you?' I said.

He nodded. 'We grew up in the same village. Our mothers are sisters.'

'How old are you both?' I asked curiously.

'She's twenty; I'm twenty-three. And you?'

'Eighteen.'

He reached forward and picked up his glass, taking a sip of his water. We weren't allowed to drink alcohol.

'Do you climb?' he asked casually.

'Ever since I was small.' He turned to face me with interest. 'We had a climbing wall around the corner from where we lived. It isn't in use any more, sadly. My dad tried to teach my sisters and me when we were seven.'

'You're an identical triplet!' he said suddenly, his face lighting up as he remembered.

'How did you know that?' I asked with surprise. I'm sure I never told him myself.

'Swedish Pete mentioned it,' he explained, pursing his lips. That was the nickname we had for one of our wacky snowboarding friends.

'Aah.' I nodded at him. 'Well, my sisters and I are very different. I took to climbing straight away, but Rose and Eliza struggled to get to grips with it. Rose didn't want to go in the first place, but my dad insisted and then she hurt her hand and gave up.' Rose had sat on the pavement in a sulk for ages, I remembered affectionately, although Dad had been less than impressed with her lack of effort.

'Eliza did try, but she kept slipping and bashing her knees. She's not the most co-ordinated person in the world, bless her, but she kept going and then suddenly, near the top, she freaked out. She was paralysed and started to scream and had to be rescued. She's still afraid of heights to this day,' I mused sadly, glancing at Remy. Was I boring him? I didn't think so, from his expression.

'Anyway, climbing became the thing that I did with Dad. We went back to the wall time and time again.' He had taught me all of my climbing techniques and all of the various hand, finger and foot holds, everything from a knee bar to a pinch grip. 'Then he started taking me hiking with a bit of scrambling thrown in.' Scrambling was the link between mountain walking and rock climbing and it was excellent preparation for Alpine climbing, which involved routes with both rock and ice and snow. It took us away from paths and rock walls and was often a sanctuary for rare plants and animals, so I used to get a lesson in nature as well, remembering always to take care with my footsteps. 'Scrambling graduated to bouldering.' This meant climbing big boulders without safety ropes and only a crash mat and Dad to catch my falls. 'And when I was old and strong enough to belay Dad, we'd go full-blown mixed ice and rock climbing.' In this case, Dad used to lead and fix bolts as he went, while I belayed him from the bottom – feeding the rope out and supporting him should he fall, which was incredibly rare. He would then wait at the top for me to climb up behind him.

'Sometimes we'd spend whole weekends away in Wales or

Scotland, just the two of us, and our family holidays usually took place near well-known rock climbing routes, so we'd escape together when Mum would let us.' These times alone with my father were among my happiest memories. 'How about you? How did you learn?' I asked Remy, suddenly feeling bad for hijacking the conversation, although he didn't seem to mind.

'Big brother,' he replied. 'Well, half-brother – my father's son from an earlier marriage. I grew up in a little village, surrounded by national parks. The Gorge du Tarn was my climbing playground. My brother used to take me when he came to visit. Amelie followed on when she was sixteen. My aunt blamed me for her new hobby, of course,' he said with a wry smile. 'A safer one would have been preferable.'

'Stop thinking about it,' I said firmly as he shuddered again.

'Do you have any photos of your sisters?' he asked, changing the subject. It was an age-old question. People always wanted to see photos, and then they'd become obsessed with meeting all three of us at once.

'They look exactly like me,' I replied, but indulged him by digging into my pocket and bringing out my phone. He leaned in close while I showed him.

'Whoa,' he murmured, staring first at the pictures and then at me with fascination.

I laughed lightly, trying to ignore my butterflies as I placed my phone on the coffee table.

'What's it like, being a triplet?' he asked.

'I get to see what I look like from behind,' I replied flippantly.

'Do you play a lot of tricks on people?'

I shrugged. 'Not really.' I wished we'd been more inventive, considering the amount of times I'd been asked that question. 'Eliza used to joke that we should train as magicians. We'd be able to do a great double act.'

'Triple act, you mean.'

I smiled. 'Exactly.'

'You must miss them.'

I paused before admitting the truth. 'Not as much as I thought I would.'

'No?' He looked intrigued.

'It's just… It's weird. We've had eighteen years of it being the three of us. We've been through *everything* together and there's a bond between us that can never be broken. I love them more than life and I can imagine us all growing old together and ending up living next door to one another. But then there's the flipside of the coin.' I stared at him levelly. 'It's not easy being constantly compared and having to share everything under the sun. It's nice to just be me for once. To follow my own path.'

He nodded attentively.

'What's the time?' I asked in a sudden panic, checking my phone and realising that it was almost ten o'clock. 'We're going to miss the sunset!'

We grabbed our coats, but still had to brace ourselves against the cold as we walked out of the apartment and down the stairs. The shop and café were dark and deserted.

'I can't get over how bizarre it is up here without the tourists,' I said.

'I love it.' He flashed me a grin and then stopped suddenly in his tracks.

'Wow.' We both spoke at the same time.

The sky had turned a deep mauve, fading to a line of brilliant orange across the cottonwool cloud-line. The sun's yellow rays were still potent, piercing my eyes and leaving impressions when I blinked. We were surrounded by mountain peaks, bathed in the last of the evening's light.

'What do you do, Remy?' I asked after a moment.

'I'm a web designer for a small company in Turin. I've worked there pretty much since I left school.'

'You enjoy it?'

'Yeah.' He nodded. 'I'm lucky. I don't have to work weekends, so I can come here. Most of my salary goes on the Mont Blanc tunnel.'

'There are worse ways to spend your money.'

'My ex does not agree with you,' he said drily.

'She doesn't like the mountains?'

'She doesn't mind looking at them, but climbing, skiing, hiking… no. We don't have a lot in common, to be honest. I don't know how we lasted two years.'

'Did you live together?'

'Yes. We still do, unfortunately.' He turned to face me properly, leaning one elbow against the handrail. A warm glow was cast across his face, lighting his blue eyes. He was insanely attractive, even when he was talking about his ex. I tried to concentrate as he continued.

'It's a great apartment. Neither of us wants to give it up, but we can't afford the rent on our own.'

'If you like it here so much, why don't you move?'

'And lose my job?' he replied.

'Couldn't you freelance?'

'I don't know if my boss would go for that.' He paused and then looked up at Mont Blanc. 'Maybe I'll ask.'

'Have you been to the summit?' I asked after a moment. His sightline hadn't changed.

He nodded. 'A couple of times. You?'

'Not yet. I'm hoping to go this summer with my dad. The last time he summited Mont Blanc, he was in his twenties and I know he's keen to do it again. But he's getting older now and my mum worries every time he talks about doing another big climb. I feel a bit guilty for putting the pressure on.'

'Well, if he decides not to come, you can give me a call.'

He said it casually, but I told him I'd need his number.

'I'll give it to you when we go back inside,' he promised with a smile. 'What about you?' he asked. 'What do you want to do with your life?'

'I like writing. I'm going to university in September to study French and English.' I shrugged. 'I guess I'll take it from there, see what happens.'

He must've picked up on my lack of enthusiasm. 'You're not looking forward to university?'

'Not yet.' My lips turned down. 'But only because I can't imagine leaving here.'

He regarded me thoughtfully. 'You don't miss your boyfriend?'

'My boyfriend?' I was taken aback. 'I don't have one.'

His eyes widened. 'No?'

'I did, but we broke up at Christmas.'

'Aah.' He gave me a knowing look. 'Swedish Pete got his facts wrong.'

'Swedish Pete again?' I asked with a disbelieving giggle.

He grinned. 'I think he was a little besotted with you.'

I laughed and pulled a face.

We fell silent as we returned our attention to the view. I tried to relax and recapture the sense of tranquillity from earlier in the day, but my breathing was shallow and I felt strangely skittish.

The sun was dipping below the clouds.

'Going…' I said.

'Going…' he said.

'Gone,' we both finished at the same time, turning to face each other. I shivered.

'You're cold. We should go back inside,' he said, placing his hand on my arm. I stared up at him for a long few seconds before lowering my gaze to see his smile slowly fading. I met his eyes again and involuntarily stepped closer. A moment later, his lips were on mine.

We barely slept that night, talking and kissing as we lay in each other's arms on the sofa. Occasionally Angus would flit into my mind and that would make everything seem unreal, but I knew I had no reason to feel guilty. It was thrilling being with Remy.

In the morning we rose in time for the sunrise and went to the ice cave, our view framed by icicles clinging to the ceiling as the sparkling sun rose over the mountains and up into a clear, blue sky.

Cécile and I put Remy and Amelie on the first cable car down and stood and waved them off. But I didn't feel sad to see them go because I knew it wasn't the end. It was just the beginning. The beautiful beginning of a beautiful relationship that would last only a few short months.

Falling in love with Remy was easy. Letting him go at the end of the summer was the hardest thing. Neither of us believed in long-distant relationships, so when we parted it was devastatingly final.

But we almost didn't part at all. I kept delaying my return home, and as autumn approached, I seriously considered staying in Chamonix permanently. It was Dad who talked me out of it, when he finally made it over to visit me in August.

'You're only eighteen!' he exclaimed. 'You can't throw away your career prospects because of a man,' he said, amongst other arguments he'd used to convince me to take up my place at university.

I told him I wanted to be a mountain guide, like Remy. He'd done as I'd suggested and moved from Turin, scoring a job with a tour company who took climbers up the mountains. He was doing what he loved, day in, day out, and getting paid for it. Why shouldn't I aspire to do the same?

'There's no money in it,' Dad said. Climbing for him had been a hobby, something he had done at weekends to get away from it all. Prior to retirement, he'd worked as a civil engineer for a large building company. He hadn't been passionate about his job, but it had paid well and had allowed him to live the life he'd wanted outside of working hours.

In the end, I succumbed to pressure and returned to England with a broken heart.

My sadness didn't stop me from throwing myself into life at university in London, but I knew I wasn't done with France. And I also believed that Remy and I would cross paths again one day.

*

The One We Fell in Love With

It turns out I was right. Two weeks before I'm set to marry Angus, here we are again. It should be Angus who's filling my head tonight, with happy thoughts about our future. Instead a snowstorm is brewing that's entirely Remy-induced. It's scaring me.

Chapter 8

Rose

What was *that* all about?

I jump back under the covers as I hear the front door close.

I was still reading Eliza's diary and only switched off my light a little while ago, peeking out of the window when I heard Angus's car pull up. It wasn't spying, I was just curious to see what he was up to, but now I'm more confused than ever.

What the hell were he and Eliza arguing about? The way he tried to embrace her... The way she pushed him away... It seemed so intense – almost intimate. I've never seen them act like that around each other before.

I listen as Eliza's footsteps reach the top of the stairs. She walks along the landing and pauses outside our bedrooms. I grab her diary and shove it under the duvet, then freeze at the sound of gentle knocking on my door. I close my eyes and pretend to breathe deeply as the door opens. A moment later it shuts and I hear her go into her room.

My eyes fly open. That was not an encounter between

platonic friends. There's something going on between those two. They have history. What sort of history? What the *hell*? *Eliza!* What did you *do*?

My conscience pricks me as the memory of my own betrayal comes back to me. New Year's Eve, almost a decade ago...

I'd gone to Darryl White's party on my own because Eliza was ill. I knew Angus was going to be there and I wanted to see him. He'd seemed down for a couple of days and it had been a while since we'd caught up properly. But then he spotted me and smiled and he was so drunk and... and... Oh God.

Phoebe had returned to France the day before so I thought − *hoped* − that he knew what he was doing when he started to kiss me, but he was so out of it, he'd obviously forgotten she'd left. Not only did I return his kiss passionately, but I let him feel me up. My face burns at the memory. I nearly died when he turned on the cloakroom light and realised his mistake.

I groan and slide further under the bed covers, pulling my duvet over my face. It's ridiculous that this still bothers me.

Angus and I never talked about what happened, although I think he tried. He called for me the morning after, but I was horrified. Eliza had been ill the night before so I pretended I'd caught her tummy bug and managed to escape to university without facing him. Even though I heard from Phoebe − *very* belatedly in a letter − that she and Angus had broken up before we'd kissed, I still felt disgusted with myself. In his drunken state, he must've thought Phoebe had changed her mind and come back to him.

I couldn't bear to face him at Easter either, so I jumped at the chance when Aunt Suzie offered to have us to stay in Somerset. The next time I saw Angus was in the summer holidays, well over six months after our encounter. He was warm and friendly and seemed genuinely happy to see me. Eventually, my blushes came under control and I realised he was cool to let it go – we never had to speak of it again. Thankfully we've been buddies ever since.

Oh, but his kisses… I shiver and do what I really shouldn't, which is remember the good bits. I've never had anyone kiss me like that, before or since. He was divine.

Mum rouses me from a deep sleep at ten forty-five the next day.

'Rose! Are you ill?' she exclaims, whipping back the curtains. I groan and bury my face in the pillow, but she's pulling me out again a moment later and checking my vital signs.

'Mum!' I squawk, batting her away. 'I'm fine! I'm just tired.' Too damn right I'm tired. I struggled to get to sleep last night after all that. Needless to say, my urge to hug Eliza has flown right out the window and is probably migrating to Africa.

'Are you sure you're my Rose?' Mum asks, sitting beside me on the bed and peering at me with amused blue eyes. We inherited our green eyes from Dad, but the rest of us is all Mum: similar height, similar build, and we did have a similar hair colour, before hers turned grey. Now she dyes it dark blonde and wears it in a bob. 'Did you and Eliza swap beds in the night?' she asks.

'No, we did not,' I snap indignantly. Eliza almost always oversleeps. 'I just had a bad night.'

'Aah,' she says, patting my cheek. I flinch with annoyance.

Sometimes I think my mum still sees me as a little girl and not the twenty-seven-year-old woman that I've become. Maybe if she came to London more to visit, she'd know the real me – the one who has a sophisticated, older doctor for a boyfriend and a busy job – but she rarely gets out of Sale these days.

'You'd better get up,' she says, standing. 'The new owner's architect is coming over soon to measure up.'

'Okay.' I yawn and swing my legs out of the bed. 'Is Eliza up yet?'

'She's long gone,' Mum replies.

'Where to?' I ask with alarm.

'London, flat hunting. Didn't she tell you?'

'No, she did not!' What on earth?

Mum fills me in. Eliza wants to move to London. I can't believe she didn't say anything! We may not be close, but I'm still her sister and I could have given her advice about where to look – she doesn't know London well at all. Even more proof of how little she respects me.

'She was out of here at the crack of dawn, raring to go. She reminded me of you when you've got ants in your pants.'

I humph and she smiles at me as she goes out the door.

Wait a sec. Why does Eliza want to move to London when Angus and Phoebe are about to come back here? I thought she hated that I've had them to myself all these years.

I'll never work her out, so I give up trying. Eliza's an enigma, that's for sure.

Right, then, I'd better get ready. I went out with an architect once and he was rather dishy.

*

71

Sadly, this one is not, as I discover half an hour later. He's up in the loft, grumbling about not being able to see the wood for the trees. The new owners plan to do a loft extension, apparently.

'I'm still in the process of sorting everything out, I'm afraid,' I call up to him, rolling my eyes.

Not that I'm looking for a boyfriend. Gerard is a catch, but frankly he could do with a firecracker or two up his jacksie. We've been seeing each other for six and a half months and he's thirty-four, tall, dark, handsome, *and* he's a doctor. However, he does unfortunately happen to be married. He's not still *with* his wife, mind. I would never do that. But it would have been nice if the divorce papers had been signed before he'd asked me out. I don't think they've actually been issued.

The thing is, although I admittedly did have a soft spot for Angus when I was younger, I wasn't deluded. I knew early on that he and I weren't meant to be, and I certainly haven't sat around pining for him since. I've moved on, dated, searched for the one true love of my life. I'll find him eventually, if I haven't already. I'm not sure it's Gerard. He is reasonably attractive, clever and definitely fancies my pants off, but he's no Angus.

What I mean by that is he's not the same with me as Angus is with Phoebe. Those two together are adorable. The way they laugh at each other, listen to each other, look at each other... The way he casually drapes his arm around her shoulder, when they're hanging out at a barbecue, a beer in his spare hand. I can picture them both, right now, standing on my London balcony in the early evening sunshine, the week before last. Gerard is far less attentive to me.

There is no doubt in my mind: Angus is absolutely besotted with Phoebe. So what the *hell* has been going on between him and Eliza?

'Are you okay up there for a minute?' I call up the ladder, feeling twitchy. I wonder if Eliza's diary holds any clues.

'I'm almost done,' the architect calls back.

'Do you need help getting down?'

'Yes, if you could just wait,' he replies a touch huffily.

I sigh, eager to get back to my reading.

But it's one thing after another, and then Angus rocks up. Mum answers the door to him and he doesn't waste much time getting to the point.

'Is Eliza there, by any chance?' I overhear him asking.

'Oh, no. She's gone to London to look for a flat,' Mum replies.

'Has she?' He sounds taken aback.

'I know, that's what I thought!' Mum exclaims. 'She was out the door before I'd even made breakfast. Rose was still fast asleep.'

'Hello, Gus,' I interrupt, squeezing between Mum and the doorframe.

'Hey, Rosie!' While he might sound jovial, I can tell that the news about Eliza has thrown him.

I turn to Mum. 'Do you think you should check on the architect?'

'Does he need me?' she asks with a frown.

'I think so.' Actually, he's fine, but I want to speak to Angus alone. 'You're after Eliza?' I ask him when Mum has moseyed off.

'Yeah.' He shrugs. 'It wasn't important. You okay?'

'I'm fine. Busy packing up.' I watch carefully for any signs of guilt as I ask my next question. 'Have you spoken to Phoebe?'

'I tried calling her last night,' he replies. 'But it went straight to voicemail.' His right eyebrow twitches. Oh, *Angus*! I want to ask him about his apparent intimacy with the *wrong* sister, but he distracts me before I can think of a way to phrase the question.

'Are you missing Dr Gerard?' He raises one eyebrow in a cheeky gesture.

'Yeah, but he's really busy at work, so I wouldn't have seen much of him this week anyway.'

'It's a shame you two couldn't have got some time off together.'

'What, so he could come here and help me pack?' I tease.

Angus gives me a sympathetic look and nods past me. 'How's it all going?'

'Slowly,' I reply. 'What about you?'

'Same. I have no idea how I'll get the apartment sorted before Phoebe returns.'

'Maybe I could come over and give you a hand?' I offer.

'Haven't you got enough on your plate?'

Er, yes. What am I thinking? 'I could just hang up Phoebe's clothes or something,' I find myself saying. 'I bet you're rubbish at that.'

He grins. 'Have you seen inside my wardrobe?'

'No, but I know *you*, Angus Templeton, and you're a right messy git.'

He chuckles. 'Alright. I'd love to show you the place. What are you doing tonight? Maybe I could order us in a pizza?'

'Sounds perfect. I want to see what you're leaving me for.'

'Aw.' He flashes me a fond smile and pulls out his phone. 'I'll text you the address.'

As he types out a message, it occurs to me that I could use this evening as an opportunity to find out what's going on with him and Eliza. I wish that had been my reason for offering to help him unpack, but no, I'm just being a martyr as usual.

'Rose is a giver, not a taker.'

You got that straight, Dad, I think wryly. I really should sort out my priorities.

Chapter 9

Eliza

There's a lump in my throat as I walk out of yet another estate agent's. So far, I've seen eight places and none of them have been right, nor can I see myself getting on with any of the people that I'd have to share with. My potential flatmates seem to be either a bit snotty, or grotty students with no one in between.

I can't believe I have to leave my home. Bloody Angus. And bloody Rose for being such a frigging driplet! Mum is happy living there with me, and I'm happy living with her. We keep each other company.

My eyes sting with tears because deep down I know that the time is right for her to move into something smaller and more manageable. She's almost seventy, but she's an old almost-seventy. I think having the three of us in her forties aged her, and she's definitely suffered since Dad died. I'm not there enough – if I'm not busking, I'm waitressing – and she's rattling around in that big house all by herself. I know she's lonely and could do with more company, people her own age, but I'll miss her and I'll miss my home. I'll even miss my stupid waitressing job and my stupid boss, Mario, who looks at my tits every day. No, maybe I won't miss *him*.

I sniff and begin a futile search in my bag for a tissue, but I give up and dry my eyes with the hem of my T-shirt instead, glaring at a guy passing on the pavement when he gawps at my bellybutton ring.

I'm tired. I wouldn't be so emotional if I'd got a decent night's sleep, but last night's argument with Angus put a stop to that. It was typical of what happens when we're alone for any length of time. Our defences slip and we fall back into the past to a place where we can speak openly, laugh, argue, cajole. We can be the best of friends or the worst of enemies.

But nobody else is allowed to see this side of us. They wouldn't understand how we got to be so close. In front of others, we have to keep our distance. Living 200 miles apart makes this easier.

Sometimes, when I feel like torturing myself, I imagine what could have been, how things might've turned out if I'd gone downstairs to introduce myself the moment I'd seen Judy's car pull up on Mr Templeton's driveway. I was watching from the window and my jaw nearly hit the sill at the sight of Angus climbing out of the car. He was as heart-skippingly sexy as I'd remembered. The moving truck arrived and he got stuck straight in with helping to unload it while I watched him, fixated.

And then Phoebe appeared.

I felt sick to my stomach because I had an idea how the next few minutes were going to play out. I thought about bolting downstairs and going outside to introduce myself, but I couldn't make my feet move, so I stayed, frozen at the window with a sinking heart as Angus's mum came outside and Phoebe won her over, too. You should have seen their faces when Phoebe headed into our house. Judy looked beside herself with glee and Angus was smitten. Phoebe had him, hook, line and sinker.

When she rushed up the stairs to warn us off, I threw myself onto the bed and pretended to be asleep.

I don't know why I didn't tell her that Angus was my mystery skateboarder — I'd mentioned him at the time and she knew I'd gone back looking for him — but I doubt it would have made a difference.

Phoebe is determined. If she likes something, she usually gets it — she's lucky like that — and I can't even hate her for it because I love her to death.

But also, I'm honest enough with myself to know that I couldn't have charmed Angus and his mum like Phoebe did. I'm a slow-burner, not a bright spark. Phoebe would probably still have offered to show Angus around, and at the end of the day, they still would have kissed.

I didn't meet Angus until the Sunday when Phoebe introduced us and I couldn't help but be a bit standoffish. I remember Phoebe glowering at me, willing me to be nicer to her new boyfriend, but I didn't have it in me and, after that, I went out of my way to avoid him.

My attempts only lasted so long, though, and a few weeks after he moved in, he overheard me singing. I was sitting on my windowsill, playing my guitar, but this was no Disney movie and I was no princess because it was late at night and

I was as drunk as a skunk and intermittently smoking a fag. Suddenly a ball of paper came flying through the window...

'What the hell?' I exclaimed, poking my head out into the cool night air.

'Hi,' Angus whispered loudly with a grin, waving at me from what I assumed was his own bedroom window a few metres away – our house was a semi and his bedroom backed onto mine.

'You scared the shit out of me!' I hissed.

'Sorry,' he replied cheekily, nodding at my cigarette. 'Have you got a spare?'

'No, it's my last one.' I narrowed my eyes at him. 'I didn't know you smoked.' Phoebe hated smokers.

'I don't usually, but I've had one too many beers,' he replied. 'Give us a drag?'

I hesitated, but then thought why not, putting down my guitar and leaning out of the window while he leaned out of his. We must've both been very pissed because there was no way in hell we were going to reach each other.

'Bollocks,' he said.

'Shall I throw it to you?' I suggested.

'Sure, if you want to burn the house down.'

I sniggered. 'Guess I'd better not risk it.'

He grinned at me, still hanging out of his window. 'Where have you been tonight?' he asked.

'Pub in the city. What about you?'

'Just down the local with a few mates.'

'You've made some, then.' I took a drag of my cigarette and blew the smoke out in his direction.

'Shit, I really want a drag,' he said, distractedly ignoring my jibe. 'I know!' His eyes lit up and he ducked back inside. I could hear him making a racket in his room and then he reappeared with a long plank of wood.

'What the hell is that?' I exclaimed.

'Skirting board.' He stuck it out of the window in my direction without further explanation. It wobbled this way and that from the effort of keeping it straight.

'There's not much left,' I said, indicating my almost-butt.

'Quick,' he urged, so I popped it on the end of the plank. It immediately rolled off and fell into the flowerbed below.

We both swore at the same time.

'Sorry,' he mumbled.

I smirked at him. 'At least you won't have dog-breath in the morning. Phoebe will still kiss you.'

'Where is she?' he asked.

'In bed.' Her room was at the back of the house, overlooking the garden.

'Didn't you go out for dinner tonight with your uncle?' he asked.

Uncle Simon – the youngest of Dad's three brothers – and his long-term partner Katherine were over from Australia.

'Yeah, but I stayed out afterwards.'

He nodded and we fell silent, neither of us making any move to go back inside.

'What was that song you were singing?' he asked after a while.

I shrugged. 'Just something I wrote.'

'Wow.' He looked impressed. 'Are you in a band?'

'Ha. If you can call it that,' I replied sarcastically. Our

drummer, Matt, couldn't keep time, and Gavin, the bassist, couldn't play anywhere near as well as he thought he could.

'Well, if that was a single, I'd buy it,' Angus said.

'How drunk are you?'

'I'm pretty fucking wasted,' he declared with a chuckle, smiling at me. The look in his eyes made my heart flip.

'I should hit the sack,' I said.

'Already?' he asked with surprise. 'I reckon I'll throw up if I lie down now.'

'Me too,' I reluctantly admitted.

'Stay and chat to me. I've hardly spoken to you since I moved in.'

I knew he was just being friendly. But I also knew that I shouldn't allow myself to get too close to him. Honestly, though? This was the first time I'd had him to myself and I didn't want it to end.

So we sat and talked about our favourite music, movies, comic book heroes, friends, everything, for another hour – it might have even been two. When we got the munchies, he remembered a squished Twix in his rucksack, and this time we managed to get the plank to work. I've never stifled laughter so much in my life. We formed a bond that night that never went away, but it was a bad thing for both of us.

The next morning, I woke up and cursed at the pounding in my head, but when I saw the ball of paper on the floor, I smiled the biggest smile. I don't know why I didn't just put it in the bin, but instead I flattened it out and the sight of Angus's messy handwriting made my heart swell. It was just the start of a piece of English homework – nothing special – but I couldn't throw it away.

As the days turned into weeks, I longed to have him to myself again, but I forced myself to keep my window shut. Sometimes I caved, but on those nights, he wasn't about.

Then, in June, just before our eighteenth birthday, his best friend from Brighton came to stay.

I was down the back of the garden, hanging out in the tree house that Dad had built for us when we were kids. Rose and Phoebe hadn't used it for years, but it had sort of become my sanctuary, my favourite place to go to write.

It was still light, only just, when Angus and Kieran came down to the back of his garden with a couple of beers. Phoebe and Rose had gone to the movies with a few friends, but I hadn't wanted to see the romcom they'd chosen, so I'd stayed at home.

I listened to Angus and Kieran's conversation as it carried across the fence to my ears, and it wasn't long before they started talking about us.

'I can't believe you live next door to triplets,' Kieran said. 'Jeez, mate, no wonder you're not missing Brighton.'

'They're pretty beautiful, aren't they?' Angus replied, his tone laced with dry amusement.

'Hot as hell.'

'Oi. That's my girlfriend you're talking about,' Angus said.

'I'm referring to the other two.'

They both laughed.

'Seriously, though, are Phoebe's sisters single?' Kieran asked.

'Rose and Eliza? I'm pretty sure they're both seeing people.' We weren't.

'What are they like?' Kieran asked. 'You're really into Phoebe, right?'

'Yeah, she's amazing,' Angus replied warmly. 'I reckon she could do anything and she'd be good at it. Rose doesn't have Phoebe's sense of adventure, but she's really sweet and she goes out of her way for people. And Eliza…' His voice trailed off and I felt like I could hear my heart beating in my throat. 'Liza is very cool, very smart, and she's fiercely protective, especially of Phoebe. But underneath it all, I think that she's the one who needs protecting, although she'd bite your head off if you ever suggested it.'

'You sound like you're in love with all three of them,' Kieran mused. 'Ever thought about, you know, getting it on with all—'

'Piss off!' Angus interrupted.

They laughed, but that was the end of the interesting conversation.

I stayed where I was, not wanting them to know I'd over-heard, and eventually they got sick of the midges and went back into the house.

But my head continued to reel. No one had ever had us – *me* – so well pegged. It seemed like everything Angus said or did made me fall for him a little bit more. I knew I was in trouble, and the feeling was unbearable.

Sometimes I would catch him looking at me and I'd sense a slight confusion radiating from him. Perhaps he also won-dered what would have happened if he and I had got to know each other before he'd jumped headfirst into a relationship with Phoebe. Did he ever regret doing that?

I know he's loved her from the beginning. Even when he

was with me, he loved her. But I suspect there's a small part of Angus that has always loved me, too.

With all of these thoughts still spinning around my head, I come to a stop on the pavement outside another estate agent's. Gathering myself together, I push through the door. If Angus and Phoebe are moving to Manchester, I really have no choice but to leave.

Chapter 10

Phoebe

And so here we are again.

I can't see Remy's blue eyes behind his dark glasses, but I watch his attractive, suntanned face as he checks over my equipment. He looks quite a lot older than he did nine years ago — more weather-beaten, somehow, but in a good way. He's in his early thirties, now.

'All good?' I ask in French.

'Oui,' he replies with a smile.

Josie was still asleep when I left her this morning, and it's probably just as well because I know she'd try to talk me out of this. I wrote her a note, reassuring her that I haven't lost my head. Honestly, I've never felt clearer about what I need to do.

I fell hard for Remy when I was younger. Our relationship was a rollercoaster ride of epic proportions, but there were times when I hated feeling out of control. So today I'm testing myself. I need to know that I'm in control now, and then I can walk down the aisle and commit to a life in Manchester with Angus, knowing with absolute certainty that I'm on the right path.

I doubt Angus would understand my mindset so I've begged Josie to tell him I've gone shopping if he calls. I hate the thought of him freaking out when I'm sure there's nothing for him to worry about. I love him so much – I always have, and never more than I do right now. When I think about what we've gone through, how many years we've been together, I can't imagine ever throwing it away...

It was Dad's death that brought Angus and me back together. We lost him suddenly in the spring, six months after I returned from France. I was only nineteen and it came as such a shock. Dad was fit and healthy – the least likely person to have a heart attack, it seemed. And then Mum woke up one day to find him gone, just like that.

Angus came to the funeral. We had vowed to stay friends, but he and I hadn't spoken much in the months since I'd got back. Seeing his beautiful but bloodshot eyes did something to me. Maybe it was my grief, but everything I'd felt for him came rushing back. I desperately wanted him to hold me, to be close to him again, and when he took me in his arms, I felt safe. He held me tight while I cried into his shoulder, and I didn't want to ever let him go again. I think I fell back in love with him then, right there, on that spot – if I'd ever fallen out of love with him in the first place.

We were both at different universities in London, so after

the funeral, we saw each other regularly and soon it felt as though we'd never been apart. I'd told Angus about Remy, but we rarely spoke about him or the couple of girls from university that he'd had fleeting relationships with – we were both keen to move forward and that suited me fine. Angus finished his journalism course a year before I completed my degree, but instead of moving back to Manchester to be close to his mum, which was always his intention, he found an apartment in Kentish Town, an easy tube ride away from my campus, and we moved in together.

Mum said I was too young to be living with a boy – even Angus, whom she adored – but her heart wasn't fully in the argument. I think she was glad that I had someone to love, someone to help me come to terms with our loss. She missed Dad terribly, and I was still beside myself with grief.

Living with Angus fortified our relationship, and when Rose finished university and moved to London, too, my bond with her strengthened. She got a job at the Whittington Hospital in Highgate, where Mum used to work, and the three of us hung out regularly. Angus to her was like the big brother she'd never had, always checking out her boyfriends and making sure she felt safe.

But Eliza kept her distance, and even to this day I feel a block between us. When I think about the years we spent as teenagers, lying on my bed with our limbs intertwined, reading magazines or pouring our hearts out over the boys we fancied, my chest hurts. She's grown up, gone her own way, and I still miss her so much. I miss the little girl that she was, the little girl who once punched Heidi Maunder in the face because she picked on me.

But you see, the thing that I couldn't admit to Josie at dinner yesterday, or to anyone else in the world, is this: I know that Eliza keeps her distance because she's in love with Angus.

And I know that he has feelings for her, too.

I've seen it on their faces and in their demeanour when they're near to each other, and a few years ago, it struck me like a bolt out of the blue that something had happened between them when I was on my gap year. The feeling was intuitive, and I sensed that they'd both laid whatever had passed to rest, but it made everything clear. *That* was why Eliza had begun to detach herself from me. I'd always thought she was bitter about being left behind at the age of eighteen – and maybe she was, a little. But the truth was entirely more complex. I suspect she gave up Angus because she didn't want to hurt me and had never come to terms with the loss.

Angus has always been easy to read – he's open and honest and I believe he would tell me the truth if I asked him about it.

But Eliza has tried so hard to keep her emotions hidden that I sense it would crush her if I brought it up.

So I never did.

Who am I kidding? I'm too scared to.

Sometimes I feel guilty that I got to Angus first because Eliza would be so much happier with him by her side.

But the problem is I would have to fall *spectacularly* out of love with him, or spectacularly *in love* with someone else, for them to ever stand a chance.

Last night, I came to the following conclusion, and my

words are still ringing around my head now as I stare at Remy trudging through the snow ahead of me: if Eliza and Angus are meant to be together, the stars and the planets will have to align to make it happen.

Because I can't let him go easily. And while Eliza knows that I still love him, she won't touch him with a bargepole.

Chapter 11

Rose

I find Mum at the back of the garden, staring at the rose that has climbed its way up into the branches of the old apple tree over the years.

'Are you okay?' I ask her.

She nods abruptly and turns her face away from me.

'Are you crying? Mum!' I exclaim with dismay, going around to her front to make her look at me. 'What's wrong?'

'Oh, I don't know, Rosie,' she laments, shaking her head, but still not meeting my eyes. Instead she stares up at the rose – *my* rose. I was eight when we planted it; when I asked if we could call it mine. Now it is so deeply intertwined with the apple tree that it seems almost part of it. It's currently giving the apple its second flowering of the year: a brilliant orange instead of its pale pink blossoms of spring.

'I'm not sure about all of this,' Mum says.

'Come and sit down,' I urge, guiding her across the lawn to the chairs on the deck. The garden is in full bloom:

flaming reds, sizzling oranges and hot pinks blazing out from around the border. I pull out a chair for her and take one for myself.

'What aren't you sure about?' I ask gently, resting my feet on the cool wrought iron of the matching coffee table.

'This house. This garden.' She shakes her head again, despondently. 'They hold so many memories. I don't know if I'm ready to let them go.'

My chest feels tight with worry. We've come so far. This is the right thing to do. Isn't it?

'Do you think you'll ever be ready?' I ask carefully.

'That man rummaging around,' she spits suddenly, and I presume she's talking about the architect who's just left. 'Do you know they plan to knock through from the sitting room to the kitchen?' she asks indignantly. 'What's wrong with the sitting room? They'll take all the cosiness out of it! Your father and I loved reading the papers there in the sunshine—'

Her voice cracks.

'Oh, Mum.' I lean across and put my arms around her, feeling her collarbone beneath my fingers. She's lost so much weight in recent years. 'It's normal to get cold feet. I love this house, too, you know. It's going to be hard for all of us to say goodbye.'

It was actually this garden that helped me to bond with Mum for what felt like the first time, on my own, away from my sisters.

We'd moved from a tiny two-bedroom apartment in London, and being in such close quarters for the first seven years of our lives had been stressful, to say the least. Phoebe had been no trouble at all, but Eliza would turn the room into a pigsty and we'd all get the blame for it. We had to share *everything*: birthday parties, toys, clothes, even our knickers, and damn, it would piss me off when Eliza managed to nab the ones with the unicorns on them. We all loved those knickers.

It was easier when we moved here and got bedrooms of our own. At least then, we had our own space.

Mum had got stuck straight into the unkempt garden and I found myself helping her. Eliza and Phoebe had no interest in gardening, but I discovered I loved it, and I hated it when our time was interrupted by my sisters – usually Eliza – seeking some attention of their own.

Later I decided to follow in Mum's footsteps with nursing, too.

I wanted to make my parents proud, so in that way my career choice was pretty much predetermined.

Mum draws away from me and flashes me a sardonic smile.

'Don't suppose you fancy taking care of me instead of your patients?'

'What, quit my job and move back home?' I ask with alarm.

She laughs and shakes her head. Okay, so she's not being entirely serious, but I can tell she's not entirely joking, either.

'What would I do for money?' I ask, humouring her.

'We could take in a lodger – you could keep the rent.' She raises her eyebrows hopefully.

'What about my life?' I ask, feeling a little panicky now. *Has she given this some thought?* 'My friends? What about Gerard?'

'Is he still married?' she demands to know, all teasing gone from her tone.

I tut. '*Technically*, but they're not together like that,' I add quickly. 'You'll like him when you meet him. He says he'll come to the wedding.'

'That's good of him,' she mutters.

We both start at the sound of the Templetons' French doors being opened. I peer over the fence to see Judy stepping outside.

'Hello!' she calls amiably. 'We seem to be getting a summer at last.'

'Yes.' Mum's reply is half-hearted. I flash Judy a reassuring look as her smile slips.

'Is everything okay?' she asks.

'We're a bit down about the move,' I explain.

'Oh dear,' she sympathises. 'Do you want to come in for a cuppa?' She and Mum have become good friends over the years.

'I've got so much to do,' Mum bemoans.

'Go on,' I urge. 'You could do with a break.'

She hesitates and then agrees. 'Okay. Thank you, Judy, that'd be grand.'

'I'll see you at the front door,' Judy says, going back inside.

'I don't know why we didn't just put a gate in at the end of the garden,' Mum mutters. 'It would have got enough use.'

'That would have taken all the fun out of shimmying over the fence,' I say.

'Since when have you ever shimmied over the fence?' Mum demands to know.

'All three of us used to sneak over when Angus had hot friends staying.'

'Rose!' she admonishes. 'Only *now* am I hearing about this?'

I laugh. 'Too bad you can't ground me.'

When she's gone, I walk into the kitchen and look around at all of the items that still need bubble-wrapping. Mum's right: there is still so much to do. I should get on. Or...

A minute later I'm lying on my bed with Eliza's diary open to the page I left it.

Ten minutes later I'm sitting bolt upright on my bed with my scalp prickling uncomfortably. All of the blood in my body seems to have rushed into my face.

Oh my *God*! When Angus drunkenly kissed me at that party, he didn't think I was his cherished Phoebe – he thought I was Eliza! The two of them had been at it the night before!

Chapter 12

Eliza

Well, *that* was a total waste of time. I'm on the train on my way back to Manchester after what proved to be a completely futile search for a new home. I'll have to come back again next weekend. The thought depresses me.

I rest my head against the cool glass and stare at the scenery flashing past outside the window.

I've often wondered, if I could go back in time, would I do anything differently? I felt so lonely after my sisters flew the nest. Would I have had the strength to keep Angus at a distance?

I was the only one left of us to wave Angus goodbye when he set off for university and I hated admitting it, but it was his departure that hit me the hardest. I remember him hugging me goodbye and being surprised to find there were tears in my eyes when he withdrew. He brushed them away with his thumbs and told me he'd be back in three weeks for his mum's birthday – maybe we could catch up then?

After he left, I would lie on my bed with my hand on the wall, imagining him on the other side. It was stupid, but I couldn't help it. I didn't feel like singing or writing. I lost the will to do much of anything at all.

'Cheer up, Lizziebeth, it'll be okay,' Dad kept saying. He didn't like seeing me so listless, but he was pleased that I was still around. Mum had been volunteering at Priory Gardens so Dad and I hung out a bit. I remember us brainstorming money-making ideas. I was the one who suggested he and Mum turn the house into a B&B to keep them occupied in their retirement, and it was he who encouraged me to start busking to build up my confidence after the band broke up. I enjoyed having him to myself, even if he was primarily trying to take his mind off the loss of his Number One climbing partner.

I still remember the first time Angus called to speak to me – *me*. My stomach fluttered at the sound of his voice at the end of the line.

'Liza,' was all he said.

'Hello,' I replied with surprise. It had been two and a half weeks since he'd left for university. He was coming home for the weekend – I'd been counting down the days – but I hadn't expected him to call.

'What are you doing on Saturday?' he asked.

'Nothing.' I'd kept it clear on purpose. 'You're home for your mum's birthday, right?'

'Yeah, it's on Sunday, but I'm free on Saturday. You want to hang out?'

'Sure,' I replied, trying to sound cool, even as nerves bounced around my stomach. 'What shall we do?'

'Want to take a drive out to the Peak District for a picnic?'

'Sounds great.'

We ended the call, but I sat staring into space for a long time afterwards. I knew he was just being kind because I was there on my own, but I wondered if Phoebe would mind me spending the day with him. If she rang before Saturday, I decided I'd double check with her.

But she didn't ring, and four days later I waited for Angus to come round. He'd arrived home late the night before – I'd heard his Land Rover pull up on the driveway.

Mum and Dad had seemed a bit surprised to hear we were going out together, although they hadn't specifically said anything against it. When the doorbell went, I jumped.

'I'm off!' I shouted down the hall.

'Have fun!' Dad shouted back.

I opened the door to Angus's lovely smile. He was wearing light-grey cords and a long-sleeved dark-grey top layered under a black Bloc Party T-shirt. He'd been to see them on tour recently.

'Got the sarnies?' I asked, going outside and closing the door.

'Yep.'

'Better not be any fishy ones.'

'You don't like mackerel?' he asked with surprise, opening the gate and standing back to let me pass.

I gaped at him. 'You know I don't like mackerel! I don't like anything fishy! Not even tuna.'

'Tuna's not fishy. Not really. Especially when it's mixed in with sweetcorn.'

'Angus!'

'I'm messing with you.' He wrapped his arm around my shoulder and gave me a squeeze. 'I've done us cheese and pickle,' he said, letting me go again.

I'd seen him do that casual gesture with Phoebe so many times, but it was the first time he'd done it to me.

I didn't think he noticed me blushing as we climbed in the car.

It wasn't long before we were out of Manchester and winding our way through the hills of the Peak District. I looked past Angus to see a stream carving its way along the gulley down below. He followed my gaze.

'How about somewhere around here?' he asked.

It was October and there was a chill in the air, but that day it was only partly cloudy and when the sun came out there was real warmth to it.

We spread out our picnic rug by the stream. Angus left his car door open with The White Stripes blaring out of the stereo.

'Show us your bits, then,' he said.

I smirked as I got out some grapes, millionaire shortbread and two packets of salt and vinegar crisps. He grinned, passing me a sandwich.

'I bet your mum and granddad were happy to have you home again,' I said between mouthfuls.

'Yeah.' He scratched his head. 'Well, Mum was. I think Granddad prefers the peace and quiet, but Mum misses me.'

'Of course she does.'

He glanced at me with his multi-hued eyes. 'How are

your parents? Going from three to one must have been a blow.'

'Yeah. I feel like an only child.'

'That must be surreal,' he said.

'It sure is.'

'Do you like it? Having them to yourself?' he asked.

I thought about that for a minute. 'Yes,' I admitted. 'But I'd rather have my sisters here. The house is very quiet without Phoebe.' Her constant laughter and chatter had been silenced so suddenly. No one else could compete. No one else even tried. 'And when Rose went to university, Mum moped for a week.' I had known she'd be sad to lose Rose, but it had upset me more than I'd expected. I even missed her banging on my wall and shouting at me to turn my music down.

Angus smiled at me sympathetically as I swallowed and looked down at my sandwich.

'What about you?' I asked. 'Are you pining for Phoebe?'

He didn't answer immediately and my eyes shot up in time to see him shrug. 'Yeah, but she's been gone a while now.'

'How often do you talk to her?' I tried to sound casual, hiding the hurt I felt about my favourite sister barely calling me.

'She's texted me twice,' Angus replied. 'That's it.' He sounded flat.

'She hasn't called you?' I asked with surprise.

'Well, we *are* on a break,' he said pointedly.

'*What?*'

'Didn't she tell you?' he asked with a frown.

I shook my head.

'We thought that this year would be too hard, trying to

keep a relationship going,' he explained. 'We decided to take a break and see how things are next year when she's back.'

I was shocked. I'd thought Phoebe and Angus were in far too deep to ever consider climbing out, even temporarily. She'd lost her virginity to him – oh yes, she'd told us, not that it was necessary because it had been written all over her face. How could she have let him go if she'd loved him so much? Why hadn't she confided in Rose and me?

'You okay?' Angus asked.

'Yeah, I'm a bit taken aback, that's all. It's odd that Phoebe didn't say anything.'

'Have you always told each other everything?' he asked.

'More or less. At least, I thought so.' Maybe she was more secretive than I knew. 'Anyway, it doesn't matter.'

We fell silent.

'Do you ever wish you had siblings?' I asked eventually.

His lips turned down at the corners and he shrugged. 'Maybe I do, somewhere.'

I stared at him with confusion so he enlightened me.

'I don't know much about my real dad, other than that he's American and he was in the army stationed near here. Oh, and he didn't want anything to do with us when Mum told him she was pregnant. Who knows where he is now, if he's married, if he has kids.'

I felt traumatised on his behalf. 'Do you ever think about trying to track him down?' I asked.

'No,' he replied. 'My mum is the only parent I need – or want. Anyway, it'd be like a kick in the guts to her after all she's done, raising me on her own.'

'You said he was stationed near here,' I said. 'Did your mum live around this area when she was younger?'

'She grew up in our house,' he replied. 'She was only eighteen when she fell pregnant – my grandparents threw her out. I didn't even meet them until I was about six. I don't think Mum's forgiven them for that, but Granddad's mellowed in his old age. They're closer now than they ever used to be.'

'No wonder you didn't visit them often.'

'Hmm, no great surprise. I was gutted when Mum said we had to move here.'

We fell silent. I was mulling things over, but eventually I just came out and said it.

'I saw you once, in the park,' I told him. 'About a year before you left Brighton.'

'Did you?'

'You were on your skateboard.'

His eyes widened. 'Did you speak to me? No,' he answered his own question. 'I would have remembered.'

I smiled at him and noticed something. 'Your eyes are the same colour as the hills.'

'Are they?' He looked half mystified, half amused.

'Yeah, look,' I said with a smirk, nodding at the hills behind us. 'A mottled mess of tawny brown and grassy green.'

'A mottled mess?' He raised one eyebrow. Then he said, 'Look at me. Let me see yours.'

'They're exactly the same as Phoebe's,' I replied with a laugh.

'No, they're not,' he said seriously. 'I'm not quite sure what it is, but they're not the same.'

'They're exactly the same,' I insisted drily. 'That's the definition of identical.'

'You're not completely identical,' he maintained. 'I can tell the difference between you.'

'Go on then, tell me how we differ. And you can't just say it's the way we wear our hair.'

'Rose's face is slightly rounder, softer,' he said.

'No, it's not,' I scoffed.

'Phoebe's eyes are ever so slightly a lighter shade of green.'

'Bollocks. You've just spent a lot of time looking at them in the sunlight.'

He carried on with his analysis as though I hadn't spoken. 'And they both have a tiny sprinkle of freckles, here.' He touched my nose and I flinched, surprised. 'It's probably because they spend more time outdoors. They're so faint, you can barely see them, but you don't have any at all.' He met my eyes.

Butterflies swarmed into my stomach as I stared back at him.

A moment later, he looked away. 'But before that, you're right, it was the hair.'

I laughed uneasily. 'Bet you couldn't tell the difference between us if you were drunk.'

'Bet I could,' he replied flippantly.

Angus called me again the following week.

'I just tried ringing Phoebe,' he said.

'I thought you weren't in touch?' I replied with confusion.

'We said we'd stay friends, but anyway, she didn't answer.'

'Aw, are you lonely?'

'Nah, just felt like a chat. Are you alright to talk for a bit?'

'Sure, I'm not busy.' I settled myself on the chair in the

hall for what turned out to be the first of many phone conversations.

At first, we talked a bit about Phoebe, but as the weeks went on, she barely featured in our conversations. He told me all about his journalism course, his professors, his classmates and his drunken nights out in London, and I told him about life at home: my stop-gap job as a waitress at an Italian restaurant, my pervy boss Mario and the random amusing things that happened with my customers.

Every time the phone rang, my stomach swirled with jittery nerves. I knew I was in dangerous territory, but I couldn't stop it.

Phoebe, on the other hand, barely called home. I was hurt and upset and just a little pissed off about it. She rang towards the end of November, just before setting off for Chamonix in France. She'd been inter-railing around Europe up until that point, but she and her friend Josie were planning to remain in the mountains until the spring, with just a short break when they'd return home for Christmas. I asked her outright if she was missing Angus.

'Yeah, of course,' she replied flippantly. 'But I've been so busy, I haven't had time to think about him or home much.'

She was so casual about their relationship that it made me wonder if she had ever loved him at all. Even Angus seemed quite content without her.

In the middle of December, the university term ended. Rose stuck around in Portsmouth for a bit, in no rush to leave behind her shiny new friends, but Angus came straight home.

When he hugged me hello, I felt like my heart was going to expand through my ribcage.

'Hello, trouble,' he said, releasing me only enough to smile down at me. 'Miss me?'

'Might've done,' I replied.

Judy worked as a receptionist at a local lawyer's office, so Angus and I spent most of the next few days in each other's company. On Wednesday, he offered to drive me into the city to busk. He sat on a nearby bench, and every time I looked over he caught my eye and gave me an encouraging smile. At one point a couple of guys came and stood a bit too close and I saw him brace himself, ready to get involved if necessary. It was like he was my bouncer or something, but whatever it was, I felt protected.

'Have you had any luck getting a gig?' he asked me later, when we were hanging out in the tree house.

'No,' I replied edgily. 'I don't think I'm ready yet.'

'Don't be ridiculous, of course you are.'

I flashed him a sheepish look. 'Dad's been going on at me, too. But I'm busy with waitressing and busking, and it's not like we haven't been round to a few venues.'

It was Dad's idea to try to line something up, but with his thinning hair and my scratty pigtails, we probably looked like a right pair when we walked into places and asked to see the manager. I laughed at the knock-backs at first, but in truth, I was scared to death that I was screwing up my life. I had no career plans if the music thing didn't work out. It was the only thing I cared about.

Well, not the only thing.

'No one wants me,' I told Angus. 'They all say I'm too young, that I don't have enough experience.'

'Have you only been looking at bars in town?'

I nodded.

'What about trying some working men's clubs in the suburbs, just to get some experience?' he suggested. 'My granddad might know someone who'd be interested, that's all. I could ask?'

'Okay. Sure, why not?'

That evening, Angus came back over. His granddad's ex-colleague Ernie ran a club just ten miles away and was interested in meeting me. The next day, we went there together. Within a minute of our introduction, Ernie was asking if I was free on Monday night.

'He didn't even want to hear me sing!' I squeaked with delight on the way back home again. My first ever gig was four days away!

Angus chuckled. 'The look on his face when he saw you.' He shook his head with amusement. 'He thought all his Christmases had come at once.'

I beamed at him. 'Thank you!' I exclaimed, leaning across to impulsively peck him on his cheek.

His face flushed, but he kept his eyes on the road.

Once my initial excitement subsided, all I was left with was tense anticipation. I had no idea if anyone would even turn up. Angus helped me make fliers and we distributed them locally. We hung out in the tree house going over my set list and I was touched that he was helping me.

Dad noticed how much time we were spending together. On Saturday afternoon before the gig, he brought it up. 'You're seeing a lot of Angus, Lizziebeth.' He had taken to using my old nickname again and usually I loved it, but not that day.

'We're friends,' I replied defensively, wanting him to butt out.

'Do you think Phoebe would be okay with that?' He raised one browny-grey eyebrow at me, his green eyes challenging.

'Of course she would,' I replied snappily. 'Anyway, she knows. I don't think she could care less, to be honest.'

I had occasionally dropped it into conversation that Angus and I chatted to each other, but as conversation with her *was* so occasional, it was possible it hadn't properly sunk in.

'As long as you know what you're doing,' Dad said, making me squirm.

His anxieties were still playing on my mind the following day. Judy answered the door when I went to call on Angus.

'Oh! Hello, Eliza, I thought you were Phoebe there, for a moment!'

I forced a smile. 'No, she doesn't get back until Saturday.' She was coming home in time for Christmas, but would return to France before the New Year.

'What a shame she can't make your gig tomorrow night. I'm looking forward to it.'

'Are you coming?' I asked with surprise.

'Of course! Angus wouldn't forgive me if I didn't support you.'

It was a sweet, innocent comment, but it made my heart sing.

The problem was, nothing could stay innocent forever.

Angus was the first person I went to after I stepped down from the stage. He took me in his arms and hugged me hard. I was ecstatic. Despite the uninspiring surroundings, I had loved every minute of the set.

'What about me?' Dad interrupted. He and Mum had both come along to support me.

As I pulled away from Angus to hug him, I caught sight of Judy's face and the look of wary concern she was wearing. I was instantly on edge.

'Meet you in the tree house later?' I asked Angus before we left.

'Yeah, see you there,' he said in my ear, touching my arm.

I waited for forty-five minutes and it was flipping freezing. Just as I was about to give up and blow out the lantern candle, he appeared.

'Where have you been?' I exclaimed.

'Sorry,' he muttered. 'I got talking to Mum.'

'What's wrong?' I asked, noticing his mood. 'Has she said something about me?'

He looked alarmed at the question. 'Why would you think that?'

'I saw the look on her face, after we hugged.'

His eyes dropped to the floor.

'Does she know you're here?' I asked.

'No,' he replied uncomfortably.

'Tell me what's wrong,' I urged, leaning forward. I gave his forearm a small squeeze and he glanced down at my hand before looking up abruptly to meet my eyes.

'Do you think Phoebe would mind that we're friends?' he asked.

I let him go and sat back against the wall. 'She shouldn't. Why? What has your mum said?'

'She thinks that I'm being reckless.'

'Reckless, how?' I asked, my pulse jumping unpleasantly.

'She's worried I'm leading you on.'

'And what do you think?' I asked hotly, trying to cover up how mortified I felt.

'I think that I feel more for you than I should.'

The intensity in his expression made my heart skip a beat.

'Angus,' I warned, shaking my head. I knew I was playing with fire by getting close to him, but I thought I was the only one who'd get burnt. I didn't think Angus would be affected, and I certainly didn't expect to hurt Phoebe.

He hadn't taken his eyes from mine. 'This is where you admit that you have feelings for me, too,' he said in a low voice.

'No,' I replied adamantly, shoving open the rickety wooden door and climbing out into the dark, frosty night. He didn't try to stop me from leaving.

I was all over the place the next day. Luckily, it was snowing, so I could hibernate indoors.

But then another day passed without us seeing each other and I began to fret. It was clear that he was avoiding me as much as I was avoiding him, but did that mean he regretted what he'd said? I wished I could truthfully say that I hoped he did.

With Phoebe due home on Saturday, we were running out of time to smooth things over. But his mum had finished work for Christmas and I was too chicken to call on him for fear of bumping into her.

Then, on the Thursday afternoon, I was sitting on the windowsill when I saw Angus going outside to his car. Without thinking, I opened the window. He looked up at me.

'Where are you going?' I tried to force an easy smile.

'To the supermarket for Mum,' he replied flatly.

'Can I come for the ride?' I asked casually.

His brow furrowed, then he nodded hesitantly. I ran downstairs and grabbed my coat, calling out to Mum and Dad to see if they needed anything.

By the time I'd hurried them up for a list, the ice had thawed from his windscreen.

'Sorry about that.' I climbed in and pulled the door shut with a clunk. 'Mum and Dad asked me to grab a few things.'

'It's fine,' he said, putting his left hand on the back of my headrest and looking over his shoulder as he reversed. I snuck a glance at his face and my heart contracted.

'How have you been?' I asked when we were moving forward again. One of us had to bite the bullet.

'Fine,' he replied shortly.

'Have you been busy?'

'Liza, it's okay,' he said out of the blue. 'I get it.'

'Get what?' I asked carefully, tensing as he pulled up at the kerb and turned to face me.

'I know that you feel the same as I do.'

The blood rushed into my cheeks as he continued.

'But I also know that Phoebe will always come first for you. You'd never hurt her.'

'I wouldn't,' I agreed, fervently shaking my head at him.

'I know that this is a bit screwed up. I still care for her a lot, probably more than she cares for me, judging by how little she's been in touch.' He didn't even sound bitter; he was just stating a fact. 'But even if she and I call it quits for good, which feels like a distinct possibility at the moment, I know she wouldn't like you and me to be toge—'

'She'd hate it,' I interrupted.

We both fell silent. After a while, he spoke.

'Anyway, I'm sorry. I shouldn't have said anything, but I was confused and I can't shut up around you.' He smiled at me pensively. 'Do you reckon we can go back to being mates?'

'Of course we can,' I replied, relief intermingling with regret.

I somehow managed to convince myself that once Christmas was over and he'd returned to university, we'd be able to get back to the way we were. But then Phoebe came home and I was completely and utterly unprepared for the jealousy that I felt when I saw her with Angus.

Don't get me wrong: things weren't great between them. She seemed a little cool, and maybe he was more bitter than he'd let on about her not calling him much, because you could've cut the tension between them with a knife. Still, I backed right off.

Surprisingly, Rose proved to be a decent distraction. I found myself hanging out with her, asking her about her course and her friends. She loved telling me gruesome nursing stories and most of the time I enjoyed listening.

Phoebe headed back to France the day before New Year's Eve. That evening, I opened my window to have a sneaky cigarette. I'd only taken a couple of puffs when I heard Angus's window opening.

'Hey,' he said, leaning out.

'Alright,' I replied offhandedly. I knew I was going to find it hard even to look at him for a bit.

'You okay?'

'Fine.'

I felt him watching me, but I fixed my attention on the front garden below.

'What's wrong?' he asked eventually.

'Are you still going to Darryl's New Year's Eve party?'

He seemed surprised by my out-of-the-blue question.

'Um, yeah. Are you?'

'I think so. Do you know if your mate from the Leisure Centre, Jake, is?'

'Er, I don't know,' he replied uneasily. 'Why, do you want him to be going?'

I shrugged. 'Maybe.'

Angus and Jake had worked as lifeguards at the pool over the summer. Jake had come to my gig and I'd caught his eye a few times. He was a little older than us, good-looking, fit and, importantly, still lived locally. Why shouldn't I set my sights on him?

'I could ask him, if you like?' Angus said.

'Yeah, that would be good.' I felt a sudden, inexplicable swell of anger.

'Are you sure you're alright?' he asked again.

'Why wouldn't I be?'

He shrugged. 'I don't know. Are you missing Phoebe? Did you like having her home?'

'Did you?' I turned his second question around on him.

He shrugged again. 'It was okay. No, actually, it was pretty pants,' he admitted truthfully.

I frowned at him, meeting his eyes at last.

'You know we broke up properly, right?' he said.

'What, *permanently*?'

'She didn't mention it?'

'No, once more, she didn't.'

He nodded at my cigarette. 'Have you got any more of those?'

'Yeah.'

'Want to meet me in the tree house?'

I hesitated, but only for a moment. 'Okay.'

I snuck out of the house without telling Mum and Dad where I was going. It's not like I needed their permission to do things at my age – after all, I was eighteen – but they might've found it a bit odd. I hoped they wouldn't check up on me on their way to bed.

Angus was outside before me and I watched as he folded his long limbs over the fence, just missing the flowerbed as he dropped to the soggy grass. He had a bag in his right hand and he gave me a small smile before climbing up the ladder. I followed him up and pulled the door closed, then we both took off our boots. I lit a couple of candles and settled in one of the beanbags. He pulled out a small bottle of vodka, a big bottle of coke and a couple of disposable cups.

'Are you drowning your sorrows?' I asked as he cracked open the vodka.

'No,' he replied calmly. 'It's not like we didn't see it coming.'

'I can't believe Phoebe failed to mention it again.' I was upset, actually. I hadn't felt very close to her at Christmas. It had been partly my fault. I hadn't made much of an effort, but she hadn't even asked how my recent gig had gone. I kept getting the feeling that she hadn't wanted to be at home and that hurt.

Angus handed me a cup. I chucked him my packet of

cigarettes and surreptitiously watched him as he lit up. His face was so handsome highlighted by the flame, his cheek-bones even more pronounced. He took a drag and blew the smoke out through a crack in the door.

'So, what's this about Jake?' he asked. 'You've got the hots for him, now?'

'I've always thought he was good-looking.'

'You reckon?'

I was thrilled at the hostility in his voice. Was he jealous?

'Do you think he fancies me?' I asked, hoping to wind him up further.

'Of course he does.'

My eyes widened. 'Has he said anything to you?'

'Yeah, and you wouldn't like it if you heard it, so don't ask.'

'Tell me!' I exclaimed, prodding his stomach with my socked foot.

'No.'

'Go on.' I prodded him again and he grabbed the ball of my foot, holding it steady. My stomach fluttered as he stared at me with irritation.

'Let's just say he'd be happy with any one of you, or all three at once.' He shoved my foot away.

'Oh, is that all?' I said in a bored voice, adding a yawn for good measure. 'We've heard it before. *Loads* of times.'

'Yeah, well, I wanted to deck him when he said it to me.' He glared at me and took a swig of his drink.

'Aw, Angus.' I prodded him again, but this time when his hand closed around me, he didn't show any sign of letting go.

'I hate it when people lump you together like you're the same.' He held my foot against his chest and I could just about feel his heart beating beneath my sole. 'You couldn't be more different.'

I smiled a small smile at him, but I didn't know what to say. 'Give us a drag.' I leant forward and took the cigarette from him. He relaxed back into the beanbag and regarded me levelly as I inhaled.

'You don't really like Jake, do you?' he asked.

'Why do you care?'

He gave me a meaningful look, but didn't spell it out. My head spun. The vodka was already making me woozy and the cigarette wasn't helping.

'No,' I murmured.

He took a deep, shaky breath and sighed heavily, not taking his eyes from mine.

'How many guys have you been out with?' he asked.

'I don't know. Five.'

'Were you serious with them?'

'You mean sex?' I asked directly.

He nodded warily.

'I haven't been with anyone like that.'

His jaw hit the floor.

'Surprised?' I asked drily.

'A bit,' he replied, gobsmacked.

'You're not the only one. People generally think I'm the floozy triplet.'

I offered up his cigarette, but he shook his head, still looking a bit stunned. The smoke was adding to my dizziness so I sat forward, opened the door and threw the cigarette out.

'Remind me to hide the butt in the morning,' I said, starting in surprise as his hand slid up the back of my calf.

He froze, and then held both palms up. 'Sorry.'

'Did you forget who I was for a second?' I asked mockingly, removing my foot from his chest. I'd seen him do that to Phoebe.

'Fuck off,' he said with annoyance.

'Angus Templeton, you've got quite a temper on you tonight.'

'Eliza Thomson, you're a fine one to talk,' he replied in the same tone of voice.

'Do you think I'm an angry person?' I asked, taken aback.

'Well, you're not all hearts and flowers like Rose, that's for sure.'

'You think Rose is hearts and flowers? She's got some serious spikiness to her.'

'I'm not saying she's a push-over. But she's softer than you and Phoebe are.'

I narrowed my eyes at him. 'If Phoebe and I didn't exist, would you fancy Rose?'

'What a thing to ask!'

'Answer me.'

His eyebrows pulled together as he thought about the question. 'Well, no, probably not.'

That didn't sound very definitive.

He shrugged. 'I mean, she's beautiful, she's kind, she's funny. Technically I *should* fancy her, but I don't know.'

'I think I'm going to call it a night,' I said darkly, reaching for my boots and pulling them on.

'Hang on, what's wrong?' He sat up, sounding genuinely baffled. 'You did say if you and Phoebe didn't exist.'

I shook my head, suddenly feeling hopeless as I stared back

at him. 'I don't know, Angus. I shouldn't give a damn who you like, and you shouldn't give a damn who I like. What's wrong with us?'

We stared at each other for a long, heated moment. Butterflies crowded my stomach and went absolutely berserk.

'Shit,' he murmured.

'No,' I whispered, shaking my head a minuscule amount.

The next thing I knew our mouths were colliding.

Shivers rocketed up and down my spine as he tugged me onto his lap, my knees straddling his thighs. I kissed him back passionately, pushing my fingers through his hair as he pulled me hard against him. It felt so good, I couldn't bear for it to stop.

The more he kissed me, the more delirious I felt. The ache inside became more pressing, more intense. I needed more. He unzipped my hoodie and slid it down my arms, kissing my neck and biting gently as my head spun and I stared up at the candlelit ceiling.

'I want you,' he whispered, making me tremble.

I slid my hands inside his shirt and his kisses became more frenzied as they traced the waistline of his jeans, coming to a rest on his belt buckle.

He said my name at the same time as Dad shouted it.

'ELIZA! ARE YOU DOWN THERE?'

We both froze, but I came to my senses first.

'YES!' I shouted back, staring at Angus with wide-eyed alarm. If Dad found him here, he'd freak out.

'YOU'LL CATCH YOUR DEATH OUT HERE! IT'S MINUS TWO!'

'I'M COMING!' I shouted back, climbing off Angus and

pulling on my hoodie. 'I'm sorry,' I whispered. 'He'll be down here checking on me in a minute.'

'Hey,' he said as I pushed open the door. 'Wait.'

'What?'

He pulled me to him and kissed my lips. 'I'll see you tomorrow.'

Tomorrow came, and with it the guilt. It was overwhelming. I wanted to blame the alcohol, but we hadn't had that much to drink. I was so freaked out. If Dad hadn't interrupted us, how far would we have gone? Would we have had sex? Where would that have left me if we had? Absolutely broken.

It frightened me how much I'd lost my senses. In the cold light of day, I knew beyond any doubt that I could not have a serious relationship with the boy that my sister had lost her virginity to. The thought of the two of us giving ourselves to the same guy made me feel sick with shame. I would have been the floozy triplet that people joked about. The slag. The slut.

I got up the next day and went into town, telling my parents that I was going busking. Angus texted me to ask which street I was on so I assumed he'd called round looking for me, but I ignored him. I didn't want him to find me.

He tried ringing, but I didn't answer so he left a message saying that he'd see me at Darryl's later. Mum and Dad were planning to drive Rose and me to the party after a meal at a posh restaurant they'd booked weeks before. But there was no way I was going. They dropped Rose off and I went home to bed, claiming to be unwell. Early the next morning, I got up and went to visit an old school friend who'd moved to

Birmingham. Luckily she and her family were happy to put me up for a couple of days with next to no notice.

Angus didn't stop calling or texting. Finally he left a message that was bound to get my attention: 'I'm guessing that Rose told you what happened on New Year's Eve.'

Of course, I was desperate to know what he meant by that. So I called him back.

'Eliza!' he exclaimed. 'What the hell? Why haven't you returned any of my calls?'

'I'm returning them now,' I said. 'What happened with Rose?'

'Has she said anything?' he asked circumspectly.

'No.'

He fell silent. I heard him take a deep breath.

'Tell me,' I urged, feeling sick to the pit of my stomach because I had an idea of where he was headed.

'I thought she was you,' he said at last, confirming my suspicions.

'Oh God, *Angus*!' I felt faint.

'I'm sorry!' he blurted. 'I was drunk! I wanted it to be you. I wanted to see you there. And she didn't stop me!'

'Of course she didn't!' I raised my voice, but I wasn't angry. I was destroyed. I knew Rose had a crush on him. Her eyes had followed him around like a lovesick puppy from the moment he'd moved in, but I never thought she'd let it go anywhere.

'Liza, I'm so sorry,' he said urgently. 'I swear, I'll never—'

'Don't call me again,' I told him firmly, steeling myself. 'Can't you see how screwed-up this is? Let it go. Move on. I plan to.'

When we were invited to Somerset for Easter, I jumped at the chance. I wanted to avoid seeing Angus in person for as long as possible.

We saw each other that summer, but by then I was already going out with Jake. I hated the look of contempt in Angus's eyes when he found out that we were 'serious', but I told myself it was for the best. It was the closure we both needed. Angus ended up getting together with a girl from university after that – her name was Megan – but they didn't go out for long; only a couple of months. He had one other fling that I knew of, but it didn't amount to much either.

Sometimes I had second thoughts about him. Dad's death the year after almost broke me.

I was at my lowest ebb. I was nineteen and I'd had Dad to myself for only eighteen months. We'd grown very close. He had given up climbing the previous autumn under pressure from Mum, and he had no hobby to occupy his time or take him away from us. He had finally been showing a real interest in me and what I was about, and he'd help me set up gigs and drive me to and from the venues. He used to joke that he was my manager. We had such a giggle together. For the first time in my life, I'd felt like the apple of his eye.

I only just kept it together at the funeral. Mum asked me to sing Dad's favourite song and I was wrecked, because I knew he would have wanted it too, so I couldn't say no.

But it was the last thing I felt I could do. The idea of playing my guitar and singing a jaunty little song to a congregation of people, while my beloved dad was lying cold and lifeless in a box, was abhorrent. I did the best that I could, singing my song to the last person who would ever call me Lizziebeth, but towards the end, tears started to stream down my cheeks.

I couldn't sit back down. I had said my goodbye and didn't have it in me to endure any more.

I felt a jolt of electricity spark up my arm as I passed the third pew and the low whisper of my name as Angus's fingertips brushed against mine. I met his eyes and wanted nothing more than to hold him and to have him hold me.

But by the time he'd found me, I'd come to my senses.

'Liza,' he said, his voice choking at the sight of me sitting on the grass, leaning up against a gravestone. He knelt down, but I flinched when he tried to touch me. I'd gone all this time without crumbling and I was determined not to lose it now.

'I'm just trying to be a friend,' he said quietly, his eyes full of concern. 'I miss you. I miss my friend.'

'You and I could never have been together, Angus. You do know that, right?'

It was one of the very few times we ever spoke about what happened. Maybe if we'd both had it out properly at the beginning, we could have forgiven each other and eventually become mates, but instead it had always been awkward.

'It's Phoebe or no one for you. Do you understand? If you don't want her, you can't have any of us.'

His stare hardened and he stood up and backed away.

Later I saw him holding Phoebe in his arms as she cried. I felt a bittersweet happiness for them. I could almost see the cracks in their broken relationship gluing themselves back together. I was glad that he could comfort her. She deserved it. And they really did make a beautiful couple.

They still do.

But I would have preferred it if he'd chosen not to have any of us.

I arrive home from my futile flat search in London at eight o'clock, just as Rose is coming out of the front door. She recoils when she sees me.

'What's up?' I ask. 'Where are you off to?'

She glares at me. 'I'm going to see Angus's new apartment.'

'Are you?' I wrinkle up my nose. 'Why?'

'I'm helping him unpack Phoebe's things,' she replies, already on the defensive.

I can't help it. I let out a snort of laughter. 'Are you for real? Haven't you got enough sorting out to do? Or is Angus more important to you than Mum?'

'Fuck off, Eliza,' she hisses, and I don't even flinch because I know what I said was mean. She continues. 'Just because you're a devious little bitch who wants to get into his pants—'

'What are you talking about?' I interrupt, paling.

'I know about you! I know about you and Angus! You betrayed Phoebe years ago and you're probably *still* betraying her now!'

I shake my head. 'No. You're off your rocker. There is *nothing* going on between Angus and me. Nothing. If anyone wants him, it's you. You with your soppy, puppy dog eyes. You make me sick. Get a life.'

For a split-second, I think she's going to slap me. 'I'm telling Phoebe,' she warns, suddenly serious.

'Telling her what?' I snap.

'About what you and Angus got up to when you were eighteen. How you were *this close* to shagging him.'

I gawp at the thumb and forefinger she's holding in front of my face, a centimetre apart. How does she know that? Did Angus tell her? Is he *trying* to wreck his wedding? I'm stunned. But no, he wouldn't have done that. Hang on a second...

'You found my old diary,' I state as it dawns on me.

She looks away uneasily.

'You bitch! I can't believe you read it!' I hiss. 'Well, maybe *I* should tell Phoebe that you had it off with Angus at Darryl's New Year's Eve party! He thought you were me,' I say nastily. 'But *you* let him kiss you. *You* let him touch you.' I don't know this for sure, but I know Angus and I know how he was with me the night before.

I'm right, because Rose looks like she's going to throw up.

'Instead of accusing *me* of betraying Phoebe, why don't you take a good, long look at yourself, *Rosie*,' I spit. I laugh suddenly and look around. 'Wow, if Judy and Mum could hear us, they'd cancel the wedding themselves,' I say scathingly. 'Jesus, you know what? I *am* going to tell Phoebe that Angus would have had either of us, too. She deserves to understand what she's walking into before she marries the guy.'

'No, don't,' Rose splutters. 'You'd ruin everything for her. She'd be so cut up.'

I'm vaguely aware of the phone ringing inside the house, but I'm on a roll. 'I disagree. She needs to hear the truth.'

'IT'S PHOEBE!' Mum yells.

'*Perfect!*' I erupt. 'Perfect timing, Feebs.' I smile evilly at Rose. 'Maybe I'll tell her right now...'

Part Two

Chapter 13

Phoebe

Sometimes I can't believe I'm still here. I'm having a proper 'pinch me' moment, right now. I'm sitting on the balcony looking up at the mountains. The setting sun is casting a bright amber light across the snow-capped peaks. It is beyond beautiful.

Remy and I are heading into Chamonix tonight for dinner, but he was late coming back from today's climb.

Before he went inside, he asked me if I was happy. I think he worries sometimes when he catches me deep in thought, which admittedly, is quite often.

The truth is, the dream I had last night is still playing on my mind. In it, Dad and I were ascending a mountain and I was teasing him about the time he'd confided in me that he'd grown up amongst brothers so had always wanted sons, but instead he'd got daughters: three of them.

I was fifteen when he first said this. We were climbing in the Welsh hills and I had just reached the top of Cemetery

Gates. I remember him being so proud. He hugged me and told me that I was as good as any son.

In my dream he smiled and repeated these words, but then he vanished and I screamed, certain that he'd fallen. I woke up sobbing and Remy had to hold me until I calmed down.

I think Dad's on my mind because I know how much he would have loved the climb Remy and I did yesterday. It was the Rébuffat route on the South Face of the Aiguille du Midi. It was technical and it took us almost six hours, but Dad would have been proud.

Sometimes I feel so clunky, like I'm lumbering up the mountainside, but today everything just flowed.

I adore climbing with Remy. He's so beautiful and he has such grace – he's like a dancer, moving up the rock. I know that's what Dad once said about me, that I reminded him of Catherine Destivelle, my rock climbing heroine. Dad's hero was the legendary Joe Brown, the 'human spider' – Manchester born and bred.

The thing about Remy is that he's always challenging me and forcing me to step out of my comfort zone. The first time he ever did that was on our very first date when he took me paragliding. I was terrified, which was pretty unusual for me, so he really had to persuade me. What did he say? 'It's the purest, simplest form of aviation' or something like that. He said I'd feel like I was flying.

I remember indignantly telling him that I wasn't a fricking bird, and he laughed so hard. But he wasn't going to be deterred. He convinced me that doing something out of the ordinary would stimulate my mind. So many people go through life just coasting, but shifting my perspective would feel amazing.

He was right. We did a tandem flight together and when we ran down the hill, I was petrified, but then my feet were off the ground and we were floating over dark-green pine trees with the mountains all around. It was so incredible. My heart soared.

It's still soaring today.

So to answer Remy's earlier question, yes, I *am* happy. I just mustn't think too much.

Chapter 14

Rose

The knock on my bedroom door jolts me to attention. It's late afternoon and I've been lying on my bed, reading.

'Rose?' Mum calls as I quickly sit up. 'I'm making tea. Would you like one?'

'Sure! I'll come down.'

She doesn't usually seek me out when she's putting the kettle on. She must be lonely. Either that, or she has something to talk about.

In the end, both prove to be correct.

'I think it's time,' she says, her voice wavering when I appear in the kitchen.

I gather her in my arms and give her a hug, fighting back tears myself.

'I'll speak to the estate agent tomorrow,' I tell her.

'I've called them already,' she replies. 'They said they can use the same photos, so it might even go live in the morning.'

Unsurprisingly, last summer's sale fell through. It's not like

128

Mum hadn't been having her doubts, but it's been almost a year now so I'm relieved she's finally come back around to the idea.

'I've also found a little place that I think will suit me just fine,' she says brightly. 'It's a bungalow, not far from here. A rental, so I won't have to worry about being stuck in a chain.'

'That's great, Mum.' I pretend not to notice her watery eyes.

'I think I'll go quickly, this time,' she says. 'No delaying it. Will you return to London?' she asks.

'No.' I shake my head. 'I want to stay here.'

Her lips pinch together. 'Don't you think it's time you went back to work?'

'Not yet, Mum.'

'You mustn't let that man ruin your career, Rose,' she warns, and I can see that she'd quite like to shake me, but she manages to refrain.

'It's not just Gerard,' I say, although finding out that he knocked up his wife while telling me they were getting a divorce was admittedly quite a blow. 'I feel like I need a change from nursing.'

'What about taking a job at one of the hospitals here?' she suggests, not really listening to me.

'Maybe,' I reply, not wanting to make any promises.

In the end, quitting my job in London last October and moving home to Sale permanently to be with Mum was an easy decision. But living with her hasn't been as easy. Eliza moved out when I moved in – she and I were never going to last long in the same house. She claimed she was ready to live somewhere new anyway, but instead of moving to London, she shacked up with one of her waitress friends in the city.

Meanwhile, Mum and I soldiered on alone. We didn't get a lodger, and without my sisters the silence has been deafening. Mum has felt it more keenly than anyone. She needs to move on, meet new people and have a fresh start. I fear that this house is sending her to an early grave.

'What will you do?' Mum asks worriedly, bringing me back to the present. 'Where will you live?'

'I don't know yet, but I'll find something.'

As it turns out, I'm far too busy in the next six weeks to do much of anything other than deal with the house sale. We get a cash buyer quickly who wants to move in without delay and I'm overcome with déjà vu as I begin to pack. Mum can't do much – she's grown more frail over the last year – so I crack on with most of the work alone, although Judy, bless her, sometimes comes over to help. Mr Templeton passed away two years ago – Angus, who was pretty cut up at the time, fretted about his mum living on her own in that big house – but earlier this year, Judy made the decision to downsize, and luckily, she didn't move far.

As before, Eliza offers no help, but this time I'm thankful. It upsets Mum that we're still not speaking, and Phoebe would hate it, but she's not here to do anything about it.

I've been helping out Mrs Dryden, an elderly lady from down the street who had a hip operation a couple of months ago. Her Staffordshire Terrier, Bicky, needs walking, and usually we go to the local park. Today, though, I need to pick up a few groceries, so I head into Sale town centre, praying Bicky won't want to do her business on the pavement. The last time that happened, a good-looking guy was approaching and I had to pooper-scoop in front of him.

I've heard that the boarded-up shop around the corner from the Town Hall has reopened as an artisan bakery, so I decide to go and have a nose around. There's a stylish, modern, pale-green and grey sign jutting out from the red brickwork with the name *Jennifer's* painted on it. In the window, various fancy breads lie stacked in old-fashioned wooden boxes, and colourful cupcakes are piled high on the counter.

A couple of those would go down nicely for tea. We exchanged on the house today, but the feeling is bitter-sweet and Mum and I could do with a pick-me-up, if not a celebration.

'The dog has to stay outside,' the man behind the counter says the moment I push through the swing door.

'Oh, okay.'

I go back outside and tie Bicky to the lamppost.

'What can I get you?' he asks when I return. He's about six foot tall and heavy-set with thick eyebrows, greying hair and dark-brown eyes. He has a cockney accent, so it's a pretty safe guess that he's not from around here.

'Two cupcakes, please. One chocolate and one vanilla.'

He gets out a box while I scan the interior. The pale-green and grey colour scheme continues inside, with white accents on the skirting boards, windowsills and furniture. There's a small seated section at the back where a couple of people are sitting at a table, drinking coffee.

'Anything else?' the man asks.

'Um, maybe a loaf of bread,' I reply, turning back to him. The door opens and three women come in, two with prams.

'Which one?' he asks as they stand behind me, chatting noisily.

'I usually go for a boring wholegrain, but there's so much to choose from. What do you recommend?'

'Is it a special occasion? Or are you just planning to slice it up for sandwiches? Toby!' he yells before I can answer.

'Not for a special occasion, exactly,' I reply as the door behind him opens and a sullen-looking guy saunters out. He has a likeness to the man with the same dark hair and eyes, although he's a darn sight better looking.

'See to these customers,' the man barks, returning his attention to me.

'But it'd be nice to try something different,' I finish.

'Walnut and raisin bread? Goes well with cheese.'

'That sounds lovely, I'll give it a shot.' I look around again. 'This is a great place. When did you open?'

'Last week,' he says.

'Have you moved up from London?'

'Er, yes. Accent give me away, did it?'

I smile. 'Just a bit. I used to work in Highgate,' I tell him.

'The posh part,' he says with a knowing look.

'The area where I worked wasn't particularly posh,' I feel compelled to point out. 'It was closer to Archway. The Whittington Hospital. I'm a nurse.'

He looks away abruptly and I feel a bit silly for divulging all that information as he interrupts the discussion going on beside us. 'We're out of the rosemary and potato bread, you doofus. I told you to do a stock take,' he adds, before tutting at me. 'You're not looking for a change of career, are you? This one here is hopeless.'

I shrug. 'I am actually looking for a job, if you've got anything going.'

The man narrows his eyes at me. 'I thought you said you were a nurse.'

'I was, but I'm taking a break. I've been looking after my mum, but she's moving to a one-bedroom bungalow soon.'

'Couldn't cope with her, hey?'

His son – if that's who he is – shoots him a look of, '*You can't say that!*'

'It's her choice,' I reply, too diverted by Toby's comical expression to be annoyed. 'I think she wants her independence back,' I joke. 'She'd rather be around people her own age.'

The man looks amused. 'Have you worked in a bakery before?' he asks.

'No, but I had a summer job at a café when I was a teenager,' I tell him. 'And I'm a fast learner.'

'You're serious? You want a job?'

'Yes, seriously.'

Toby leans his elbows on the counter and regards me.

'Get your elbows off the work surfaces, for God's sake,' the man berates him. 'What's your name?' he asks me.

'Rose. Rose Thomson.'

'I'm Gavin, this is my son, Toby, and it just so happens our last girl was useless and got the nudge yesterday, so you can start tomorrow, if you like?'

'Really?' My eyes light up.

'Yep. Be here at seven a.m.'

That's early. 'Wow! Okay, I'll see you in the morning.'

'Oh, and you'd better clean that up.' He nods out of the window at Bicky, who's currently squatting on the pavement.

'Shit,' I curse, my face going bright red.

'You got that right,' Toby says drily.

Judy is at ours when I get home. She gets up to give me a hug. 'Hello, Rose,' she says. 'How are you?'

'Gutted that I didn't get another cupcake,' I reply with a smile, opening up the box to show them.

'Ooh,' Judy coos.

'We can share,' I say. 'They're enormous.'

'Where did you get them from?' Mum asks.

'That new bakery around the corner from the Town Hall and guess what!' I beam at them.

'What?' Judy and Mum ask in unison.

'I got a job there! I start tomorrow morning!'

There's a long pause where nobody says anything.

'That's wonderful,' Judy says eventually, although you'd hardly believe her from the lack of enthusiasm in her voice.

'But what about your nursing?' Mum asks, not even bothering to hide her disappointment.

'I told you, I need a break. A change will do me good.'

'But Rose—'

'I'm not talking about forever. It will be good to have a summer job while I decide what I want to do. All I need now is somewhere to live and I'll be sorted.'

Judy and Mum exchange a look.

'I might know someone who has a spare room,' Judy says carefully as Mum shifts in her seat.

'Who?'

'Angus.'

I slowly sit down on the sofa. 'How is he?' I ask.

'Not the best,' Judy replies downheartedly. 'His student lodger has finished his course, now. He could do with some company.'

'I don't think he'd want *my* company.'

'On the contrary, I think you could be the best thing for him at the moment. He's always been very fond of you, and I think he'd be better off with someone familiar, rather than another stranger.'

'Have you spoken to him about this?' I ask. I haven't seen Angus for months. I'm not sure we *are* that familiar any more.

'No, but if you're interested, I will.'

Despite everything, the thought of being closer to Angus again fills me with joy. I've missed him.

Chapter 15

Eliza

'I'm off!' I call to Michelle.

The bathroom door opens in a gust of steam.

'Are you going straight to *Roxy's* afterwards?' my flatmate asks, a faded blue towel wrapped around her bare body and her dark-red hair dripping wet from the shower.

'Depends on how it goes,' I reply. 'If it's quiet in town, I might come back here and drop off my guitar first, otherwise I'll see you at work.'

'Okay, see you later.'

Michelle and I waitress together at a burger joint in the Northern Quarter. It's quite new and it has a nice buzz about it, which makes for a very pleasant change from *Mario's*. I always thought I'd be leaving the Italian restaurant for a career in music, not more waitressing, but alas, life still hasn't panned out that way. I haven't given up, though. Not yet.

'Thank you,' I call after the small boy who has just dropped fifty pence into my guitar case. His mother smiles at me over her shoulder and I give her a nod and carry on singing.

I quite like this area of town. I rarely busk here, but Vikram the Juggler was in my usual spot earlier so I had to move on. He always draws a decent crowd, but this town ain't big enough for the two of us.

Two young children, a brother and a sister, pull on their mother's hand to get her to stop. The girl runs forward and starts to sway to the music. I smile at her and up my jaunty factor.

Dad once told me that my whole face lit up when I sang. He said I looked 'like an angel'.

My smile slips slightly at the memory of him, but I force it back into place as the woman passes her children some loose change to send in my direction before dragging them away.

I don't know what comes first, the hairs standing up on the back of my neck or me seeing him, but suddenly I'm locking eyes with Angus. He's standing stock still about twenty metres away. My song falters and he shakes his head slightly, willing me to continue, but I can't.

It's the first time I've seen him in months.

'Sorry,' I apologise to the group of teenagers who are listening. They don't care. They shrug and head into McDonald's as I pack away my things.

'You shouldn't have stopped,' Angus says, close to me now. Every nerve-ending in my body is on edge.

'I need to get home anyway,' I murmur. 'I've got to work tonight.'

'What time do you start?' he asks.

'Six,' I reply.

'Eliza, that's hours away,' he says sadly.

'I have to go,' I mutter, clicking my guitar case shut and slinging the strap over my shoulder.

'Wait,' he says strongly. 'Look at me.'

Reluctantly I do as he asks. It's a mistake. The expression in his eyes makes me want to cry.

'Hey,' he says as I crumble.

I turn and walk hurriedly away.

'Liza, wait!' he calls after me. A moment later he's by my side, keeping step.

'Angus, leave me alone. I don't want to see you.'

'Yeah, well, we don't always get what we want, do we?' he says bitterly, grabbing my hand and roughly dragging me to a halt on the pavement. 'I haven't spoken to you for so long. What are you doing now? Can we go for a coffee?'

I shake my hand free. 'Why?'

'Jesus, Eliza.' He glares at me. 'Don't I deserve half an hour of your precious time? After all these years?'

I shake my head miserably, but I can't disagree with him and he knows it.

'Okay,' I whisper.

His whole body visibly relaxes. 'There's a place around the corner,' he says with a sigh.

'What are you doing in town?' I ask, when we're sitting at a table opposite each other.

'I needed to pick up a few bits for the apartment.' He gives me an odd look. 'You do know Rose is moving into my spare room, right?'

I nearly knock myself out on the table. 'You are kidding me. How did *that* happen?'

'Don't you ever speak to your mum?' he asks with disbelief.

'Of course I do! I spoke to her a few days ago, but she didn't mention it.' Probably too scared I'd bite her head off.

He sighs. 'It was my mum's idea. She's got it into her head that I need a woman's company instead of another student, and with the spare room sitting there empty and Rose being homeless when your mum's house sale goes through, it seemed like a good solution.'

I don't know why the thought of this upsets me so much, the idea of Rose seeing Angus every day, especially since I've tried to avoid him completely.

The waitress brings over our order. I hope to swallow the lump in my throat along with my coffee.

'You've lost weight,' Angus says when she's gone. 'And you look pale. Are you okay?' he asks.

'I've been better,' I reply honestly. 'You?'

'Same.'

He has dark circles under his eyes and his face looks tired and drawn. His dark-blond hair is longer, shaggier. He looks like he hasn't taken care of himself, like he doesn't care *about* himself.

'Have you done any gigs lately?' he asks.

'A few. Just the usual venues.'

'You're still touring the working men's clubs?'

'Yeah.' Angus knows this was not supposed to be my plan. Perhaps he senses my discomfort because he drops the subject.

'It's good to see you.' His brown and green eyes are full of concern. 'Even though you look terrible,' he adds, deadpan.

Later, after we've passed the time chatting about small things, he offers to give me a lift home.

'It's okay, I can walk,' I reply.

'Let me drive you in my shitmobile.' He elbows me in my ribs.

'It's not a shitmobile,' I find myself saying. 'I've always liked your car.'

'Christ.' He glances at me with alarm. 'You've come over all sentimental. Are you feeling okay?' He tries to press the back of his hand to my forehead, but I bat him away.

'When is Rose moving in?' I ask unhappily as we walk. If he wants to drive me home, he can drive me home. I'm not going to argue.

'Saturday,' he replies. 'Why don't you come over, too? We could get a take—'

'No, thanks.'

He shakes his head, dismayed. 'Are you still not talking to each other? Why the hell not? It's so screwed up.'

'Our problems have been building for a long time,' I reply in a low voice. 'You know we've never really got on.'

He doesn't press the issue so we continue to walk to his car in silence.

I don't live far from the town centre, but it takes twenty minutes in traffic.

'Is this it?' Angus asks with apprehension when we arrive. He squints out of the front window at the sixteen-storey tower block that Michelle and I call home.

'Yep,' I reply with a wry grin, watching as he scopes out the group of youths standing on the corner.

'It looks dodgy as hell.'

'It's not as bad as it looks, I promise.' I get out of the car. 'Do you want to come up for a bit?'

Despite my attempts to avoid him, I'm in no rush to part company.

'Sure,' he says.

'You'll have to forgive the mess,' I say as I unlock the door.

'You should see my place,' he mutters, following me in.

'I bet Rose will have it sorted out in no time,' I say disdainfully, closing the door behind him. He ignores my jibe, looking around at the reasonably tidy living room. 'What mess?'

We have two pale-grey sofas with bright geometric-patterned pink and black cushions, a modern glass coffee table with a plant in the centre of it and, on the floor, a bobbly, dark-grey rug. There's a small balcony off the living room that is still overrun with plants from the last lady who lived here. I'm scared of heights so I never venture out there.

'Michelle must've tidied up,' I tell him. 'Avoid the kitchen, though, just in case.'

Too late, he's already on his way. The last couple of days' worth of plates are still piled high in the sink. 'That's nothing,' he says.

'Is it a competition?' I ask with amusement, throwing open the door to my bedroom. Clothes have been left where I took them off – I haven't done my washing in almost a week.

He purses his lips and cocks his head to one side. 'Nope. I still win.'

'How's your post stack?' I nod at the huge pile of envelopes, some of which I've opened, but haven't put away.

'About the same.'

He wanders over to the side table and I stiffen as he picks

141

up a card, lying facedown on the pile. He opens it up and reads it, his smile slowly edging away until it's gone. He puts the card back down again.

'Happy birthday for a couple of weeks ago,' he says quietly.

I nod quickly. 'Do you want another coffee?'

'Have you got any beer?' he asks.

'Er, yeah. I've got to be at work at six, though, remember?' It's getting close to five now.

'Don't worry,' he says ruefully. 'I'm not settling in for the night. I can give you a lift on my way home, if you like.'

'What are you, my taxi driver?'

'Take it or leave it.'

I smile at him. 'Okay, thanks.'

'Where do you work now?' he asks when I return from the kitchen with two beers – one for him and one for me.

'*Roxy's* in the Northern Quarter. The burger place.'

He nods. 'I know it. One of my colleagues went there last week for his leaving do. He said it was great.'

'How's your job at the paper?'

'It's cool. It keeps my mind occupied.' He takes a swig from his bottle. I do the same.

When I glance his way again, he's already looking at me.

'It is seriously good to see you,' he reiterates.

'It's good to see you, too,' I tell him honestly.

The key in the lock makes us both jolt. The door whooshes open and Michelle sweeps in, laden down with shopping bags.

'Hey!' she calls breezily, then stops suddenly in her tracks, staring at Angus. 'Oh,' she says, her eyes darting between us. 'Hi.'

'Hi,' he replies casually.

'Michelle, this is Angus. Angus, this is Michelle.'

Her eyes widen. 'Angus,' she says slowly, putting her bags down.

'Yes, *the* Angus,' I tell her wearily before she can ask.

She bounds over to shake his hand. 'Nice to meet you at last!' she exclaims, her grin almost cracking her face in half.

Angus returns the shake and glances at me, bemused. I shrug at him.

'Have you been shopping?' I ask her unnecessarily.

'Yeah. Quite busy in town today, wasn't it? How did you get on?' She nods at my guitar case.

'Alright.'

She reaches up and starts to unplait her hair. 'I'm just going to jump in the shower.'

'Angus said he'd give us a lift to work. Is that okay?' I check with him – I hadn't actually mentioned my flatmate.

'Of course.'

'Cool, thanks!' Michelle says, shutting the bathroom door with a bang.

'She seems like fun,' Angus says as we hear the shower turn on.

'She's certainly a bundle of energy.'

'It's good to have someone like that around.'

The look in his eyes hurts my heart. Maybe it's a good thing that he'll have Rose for company. But as soon as I think that thought, I feel miserable again.

Chapter 16

Phoebe

I am on such a high! I'm on Remy's home turf!

Yesterday, we drove for almost five hours straight back to Remy's old climbing playgrounds in the Cévennes National Park. Today we scaled a limestone peak and watched the Tour de France cyclists in their brightly coloured jerseys making their way up the mountain's hairpin bends, while helicopters roared over our heads.

Remy noticed that the river down below had carved out a sandy island in the shape of a heart. He pointed it out and kissed me before telling me that I'd changed his life. If I hadn't encouraged him to move from Turin, he wouldn't be doing his perfect job right now. I was so touched.

I'm so happy tonight. I may be getting ahead of myself, but I feel like I've turned a corner. I know I was right to stay here.

When I picture myself living out Angus's dream of settling in Sale, I can't help but shudder.

Sale made me. I wouldn't be the person I am without it.

That first climb at the leisure centre and all the trips I did with Dad – they're some of my happiest memories and I would never change growing up in that beautiful home with my beautiful family.

But I've moved on. And now I can say without a shadow of a doubt that I don't ever want to go back.

One of Dad's favourite quotes has just sprung to mind:

'Life can only be understood backwards, but it must be lived forwards.'

You may have been onto something there, Søren Kierkegaard.

I do want to live forwards, but I'd prefer not to contemplate what I've left behind. When I think about the future, I feel hopeful. Surely that's the way it should be.

Chapter 17

Rose

'Has your dad gone already?' I ask Toby. He's alone in the bakery, wiping down the worktops. Gavin is normally still here when I arrive, having baked for most of the night. Toby tends to come in when I do, and Gavin pops back in the afternoon to check up on things.

'He left a couple of hours ago,' he replies bluntly, barely glancing over at me.

'Is he okay?' I ask, hunting out my apron.

'He's fine,' he replies, but appears in no mood to elaborate so I shut up.

Toby doesn't say much. He's a far cry from his father, who seems to talk about anything and everything, as long as it's nothing of consequence.

'Did you bake these?' I ask, pointing to the baguettes in the cooling racks.

'Uh-huh,' he replies, coming over. 'They should be ready,' he says, so we load them onto a tray.

'I didn't know you could bake.'

He raises his eyebrows cynically. 'I've been Dad's slave since I was eight.'

'You don't enjoy it?' I ask, following him out of the bakery to the shop floor.

He shrugs. 'It's alright.'

Two by two we unload the baguettes from the tray into a tall wicker basket. They stand upright, straight and golden.

'Why do you do it if you don't like it?' I'm curious.

'Who else will?' he replies darkly.

It's not the first time I've wondered about his mother – where she is and what's happened to her.

'No, I mean, you're over eighteen, aren't you?' I follow him back into the bakery.

'Yeah, twenty-one,' he replies, checking to see if some of the other loaves are cool enough to move to the display baskets. I don't think they are, from the look on his face. We appear to be running late today.

'Didn't you think about staying in London? Going your own way?'

'Nah.' He pulls a face and pats his jeans pocket. 'I'm going to nip out the back for a fag.'

'Mind if I join you?'

He looks surprised. 'You smoke?'

'No, but if the loaves aren't ready, I may as well get some fresh air.'

'Well, it won't be fresh, but I'll stay as far away from you as possible.'

We go out into a small courtyard enclosed by a high brick wall. Weeds are sprouting through the cracks in the paving stones. Toby sits down on a low wall that used to form part of a planter box, judging by the greenery growing out of the soil. I sit beside him. He frowns at me.

'Do you really want to sit there?'

'It's fine. I'm used to passive smoking,' I say as Eliza's sneaky teenage cigarettes on her windowsill spring to mind. The smoke would often waft into my room, but I didn't hate it as much as I claimed.

I look up at the sky as he lights up. It's only a quarter past seven in the morning, but there's not a cloud to be seen. The forecast said it would be hot today. Perfect barbecue weather. I wonder if Angus owns a barbecue. I haven't seen one around. I could pick up a disposable this afternoon along with some grub.

'I moved into a new apartment at the weekend,' I reveal, bolstered by my plan for this evening.

'Yeah?' Toby doesn't seem that interested, but he's going to have to put up with my small talk because I've worked in silence alongside him for long enough, thank you very much.

'My mum's house sale is set to go through a week today. She's moved into her new place already, though. She's renting, so that makes it easier.'

'Yeah, you said.'

'Did I?'

'Yep.'

'Oh.'

We both fall silent again.

'You're not very talkative, are you, Toby?' I tease after a minute.

He glances at me, blowing smoke in the other direction. 'Not as talkative as you, Rose.'

He keeps a straight face, but he's teasing me in return and it makes me warm to him.

'Can I ask you a question?'

'I'm sure you will anyway,' he replies.

'Where's your mum?'

His dark eyes widen ever so slightly. 'She's at home,' he mutters, returning his gaze to the wall.

'Oh.' I'm taken aback. 'I figured, as neither of you talks about her—'

'She's not very well,' he explains, throwing his cigarette to the ground and stamping on it. 'That's why Dad stayed with her today.'

'Oh. I'm sorry,' I say quietly.

'We should open up. The loaves can't be far off.' He stands up before I can ask what's wrong with her. It's probably a good thing. I don't think my probing is going down too well.

It didn't feel as odd as I thought it would, moving into the apartment that should have belonged to Phoebe. Because she never lived in it herself, she didn't get the chance to put her mark on it. It makes it easier.

It's on the third storey of a new-build block near the train station. There's a decent-sized balcony off the living room with a view that reaches to the park and the doors fold right back, so it feels like you're outside, even when you're in.

Angus and Phoebe rented a furnished place in London so everything here was bought by Angus. A stylish marl-grey L-shaped sofa separates the open-plan living area from the dining space, and there's a cool yellow Perspex coffee table in front of it. I'm more of a Cath Kidston girl, personally, but I can't deny good taste when I see it. I love the giant orange Anglepoise floor lamp that kinks up and over the dining table, which in turn is surrounded by swivelling multi-coloured chairs.

'Guess what I've got for dinner!' I say to my new flatmate the moment he walks through the door. He looks momentarily startled to see me there. I wonder sometimes if he expects me to be Phoebe. 'A barbecue!' I pull out the disposable tray from the shopping bag and hold it up before going to the fridge. 'And I got burgers and salads and—' I glance up at the sound of his footsteps and see his face at the same time. 'What?'

'I'm so sorry,' he says regretfully as he rests his elbows on the island unit and gazes at me. 'I already have plans for tonight.'

On a Monday? 'Never mind,' I reply brightly, putting the food back in the fridge. 'It'll keep.'

'I'm so sorry, Rosie.'

I get a tiny dart of pleasure from hearing him call me Rosie. It's the first time I've heard it in way too long. 'Gus, forget about it,' I reply in return.

'Could we do it tomorrow?' he asks. 'The weather's going to hold out all week.'

'Of course we can.'

He smiles with relief. 'How about a drink before I jump in the shower?'

'Sounds good. What do you fancy?'

'I'll get them.' He spies the bottle on the counter on his

way to the fridge. 'You bought Pimm's and everything,' he notes with dismay.

'It'll keep, too,' I brush him off, feeling a bit embarrassed now at the effort I've gone to.

Even though it's only been a couple of days, I adore living here with Angus. I might've got a bit carried away in my enthusiasm for it.

'How about one now?' he suggests.

'Really?'

'Yeah! Let's do it!' He opens the fridge and pulls out the lemonade and ginger ale that I put in there earlier.

'I'll chop up some fruit,' I say, retrieving cucumber, strawberries and mint.

We stand side by side at the counter and a few minutes later, we're chinking each other's glass.

'Come on, let's go out onto the balcony.' He leads the way.

'This is such a great place,' I say when we're both gently reclining on steel designer deck chairs.

'Yeah, it's not bad,' he says. 'I'm glad you like it.' He flashes me a warm smile that heats up my insides.

'What are you up to tonight?' I ask.

'Er, just grabbing a bite to eat with a mate from the paper.' He glances at me and I wonder for a moment if he's going to invite me to join them, but he doesn't. 'How was work today?'

'It was good,' I reply. I tell him about Toby and his mum. 'I wonder what's wrong with her.'

'If he wants you to know, I'm sure he'll tell you.'

'It's just that, well, maybe there's something I could do to help, seeing as I'm a nurse.'

'I know you want to help, Rosie, but just be careful, okay?'

'I won't interfere, don't worry,' I assure him.

Mrs Dryden's hip has healed well enough for her to take care of Bicky herself now, but while I don't lament picking up after her dog, I have missed my daily walks. When Angus has gone, it occurs to me that I don't need a canine to go for a stroll, so I lock up the apartment and set off. Before I know it, I'm at the park around the corner from home.

Mum used to volunteer in the gardens here and I think about her as I wander along beside the flowerbeds, bursting with colour. She's settling into her new place better than even I'd hoped and it is an immense relief. Yesterday when I went over she had just come back from having coffee with one of her neighbours, and she's already been planting in the garden. I'm glad she's keeping busy. I hope she keeps it up.

A thought comes to me, then, about *Jennifer's*. The outside space is a mess, but with a few plants and a bit of a tidy up, we could put a table and chairs out there during the summer months for the staff to use. Access is through the kitchen so it's no good for customers, but we could open up the windows and provide a pretty view for them.

Mum might give me a hand, if not with the physical stuff, then at least with some suggestions about what to plant.

I walk on with a spring in my step, motivated by my plan. I'll ask Gavin about it in the morning. If he's back at work, that is. Toby was knackered this afternoon after being up half the night. I felt quite sorry for him. I really do wonder what the deal is with his mum. Is the bakery named after her? Why does she never come into the shop? What's wrong with her? Does Toby help to look after her? Is that why he hasn't left home? He and his dad don't seem to get on that well, so why do they work together if they don't have to? Has his dad forced him to stick around? But then, he's an adult. Surely he could leave whenever he wants.

Up ahead, a guy skateboards towards me along the pavement. I'm about to move to one side when I notice something familiar about his profile.

'Toby?' I call as he approaches.

'Hey.'

He skids to a stop and kicks up the back of his board, spinning it between his fingers as he catches it.

'Cool move,' I exclaim, impressed.

He shrugs and I feel a little silly, but then I'm distracted by his face.

'What happened to you?' I gasp, taking a step forward to look at the shiner on his right cheekbone. He flinches away.

'What happened?' I ask again, alarmed.

'I walked into a door,' he says, spinning his skateboard again.

I regard him with trepidation and concern, not about to be distracted by his tricks. The last time a patient told me they'd walked into a door, it turned out to be a domestic abuse case.

'It really fucking hurt,' he adds, dropping his board to the ground and hopping onto it, stepping down on the back and balancing the front in the air for a moment. 'What are you up to?'

'I felt like a walk.'

'Me too.' He pushes away and looks over his shoulder. 'Coming?'

'Er, sure.' I run to catch up with him. 'Did you put ice on it?'

'For a bit, yeah.'

'You should get some arnica cream on it, too.'

'It's fine. Honestly.'

'Hey, I've had an idea.' I'm feeling a little out of breath, now. I wish he'd slow down. 'How about we turn the back garden into a, well, a garden?'

He gives me a sideways look, his eyes narrowing.

I hastily continue. 'We could plant a few plants, take the frosting off the windows, put a table and chairs out there…'

He frowns. 'Sounds great, but who's got time to do any of that?'

'I was thinking that I could do it and maybe my mum could help. She loves gardening. She used to volunteer at the park.'

He doesn't comment and I've grown tired of hurrying.

'Sorry, but this is more like a jog than a walk and I'm really not that fit.'

'You look fit enough to me.'

I give him a funny look. Is he teasing me? Because it sounded like he was flirting. Neither is appropriate, frankly: I'm way too old for him.

'See you tomorrow, then,' he says, smirking at me over his shoulder as he skates away. I stand on the pavement and watch him for a moment before shaking my head and walking on.

He's a weird one.

Chapter 18

Eliza

'Hello!' My voice has gone up an octave. I'm at *Roxy's* and Angus has just walked through the door.

'Hey,' he replies with a wide smile. He's with another, slightly older man who looks vaguely familiar. 'This is my friend Stewart from work.'

'Hi.' My brow furrows. 'Have you been in before?'

'Yeah, last week with a few of the lads,' he tells me. 'The burgers were so good I thought I'd come back.'

'I hate to ask, but did you make a reservation?' I glance at Angus, but I already know his answer. He's not that organised.

'Sorry,' he says apologetically as I tut and grab two menus.

'Come with me.' I take them to a table for two in my section. 'I'll need you out by eight, though, is that okay?'

'We'll eat quickly,' Stewart promises.

I try to disguise how on edge I feel as I take their drinks

order. Angus and I went for months without laying eyes on each other and now I've seen him twice in one week. It's disconcerting.

It's also really lovely.

It's busier than usual for a Monday because we have a couple of big parties in so I don't have a whole lot of time to stay and chat, but sometimes I feel Angus's eyes on me and I can't help but glance over at him and smile.

'Eliza is a singer-songwriter,' he tells Stewart when I go to clear their plates after dinner.

'What sort of music do you play?' Stewart chips in with interest.

'It's kind of quirky, upbeat,' I reply.

'It's very cool,' Angus tells him earnestly. 'But she's too busy waitressing to line up new venues. Your dad would like her stuff,' he says casually.

'Yeah?' Stewart pays me a bit more attention, looking me up and down.

What's Angus up to?

'Stewart's dad is Joe of *Elvis & Joe's*,' Angus explains. Well, I don't imagine he's Elvis. 'Do you know the place?'

'Of course I do!' *Elvis & Joe's* is one of the city's hippest venues. Way out of my league, I'd say.

Stewart reaches into his pocket and pulls out his wallet, extracting a business card.

'Why don't you email me,' he says, handing it over. 'I can put you in touch with Dad.'

'That would be great,' I say, flashing a stunned look at Angus. I glance past him to the clock. It's nearly eight.

'Dessert?' I ask. Bugger the next customers; they can wait.

'Nah, I'm stuffed,' Stewart replies. 'Quick drink at the pub before I get back to the missus?' he suggests to Angus.

'Sure,' Angus replies with a nod.

'We'll just get the bill, please,' Stewart says to me.

I force a smile and hop to it.

After they've paid and left me a generous tip, Stewart goes downstairs to the toilet while Angus waits by the door. I need to get back to my customers, but I'm reluctant to leave him.

'What time will you finish tonight?' he asks me quietly as I smooth down the front of my red and white uniform.

'Around eleven, I think.'

'Can I come back for you?'

My heart flutters, but I speak before I can stop myself. 'Why? I mean, I usually catch the Metro. It's no trouble.'

'I'll come back for you,' he says decisively.

'What are you going to do to pass the next three hours?'

'Pub with Stew and then maybe I'll go and see a movie.'

'Okay.' I grin. 'Wish I could come.'

'Do you?' His face lights up.

A few people bustle in behind him. I glance over my shoulder to see that they – and I – have my boss's attention. 'Gotta go,' I tell him regretfully.

'I'll see you later.' He touches his fingers to mine.

I'm distracted for the rest of the night. Michelle corners me by the kitchen as I wait for the last of my customers' dessert order.

'I thought you didn't want to see him ever again,' she says.

'I didn't say that, did I?' I carry on before she continues. 'If

I did, it was in the heat of the moment. If Rose is living with him, why should I stay away?'

'Aah,' she says knowingly. 'It's the whole competitive sister thing going on.'

'I'm not competing with Rose.' Am I?

'You hate that she's living with Angus, don't you?'

I'm about to lie, but I can't be bothered. 'Yeah, it's pretty damn annoying. But it's typical of her. They were mates in London so it doesn't surprise me that she jumped right in there.'

'Well, I'm glad for you,' she says abruptly.

I flash her a mystified look. 'What did you say it like that for? He's just a mate. We're hanging out.'

'He's very good-looking, though, isn't he?' she says offhandedly.

'Oh, look, my ice creams are here,' I say sarcastically, picking them up from the counter and glaring at her as I go back upstairs to my last remaining table.

'Do you really have to live here?' Angus asks with distaste when we pull up outside my tower block half an hour later. He cuts the ignition, but the radio continues to play.

'Yes,' I reply firmly. 'It's fine. I'm fine. You don't have to worry.'

'I think I'll always worry about you, Liza.'

I remember him saying something similar to Rose once. He sounded like the big brother we never had. I try not to ponder that thought too much.

'How's it going with Rose?' I ask hesitantly.

'Good,' he replies, wriggling in his seat so he's facing me. 'She's easy to live with.'

I experience a spike of jealousy.

'She wanted to do a barbecue tonight, bless her,' he continues warmly, and my jealousy intensifies.

'Does she know you're here tonight?' I ask.

He shakes his head. 'I didn't mention it.'

'Why not?'

'I didn't think you'd want me to.'

I nod. 'Yeah, it's probably best to keep it quiet. I know Mum was warned not to tell me she was living with you.'

'Where was Michelle off to tonight?' he asks. He offered to give her a lift, too, but she declined.

'She's staying at her boyfriend's.'

'Are you seeing anyone at the moment?'

I'm taken aback by his direct question. 'No. Are you?'

He recoils. 'No.'

We sit in silence for a long moment. I still haven't made any move to get out of the car. Alt-J's 'Left Hand Free' is playing on his stereo. I like this song.

An impulsive thought comes to me. 'Have you got an early start? Shall we go for a drive?'

We don't talk much – in fact, I turn the music up and sing instead, and Angus bashes the steering wheel like a drum kit on the more upbeat songs, making me laugh.

It reminds me of how we used to be.

'Do you remember that picnic we had?' he asks after about half an hour. We're already out in the country, winding around the hills of the Peak District on a long, single-lane road.

'Of course I do,' I reply.

'I think we parked just around this corner.'

He slows right down and a moment later pulls onto a grassy verge. I sit up in my seat, looking out at the hills, which are overexposed and silvery white in the car's headlights.

He yanks on the handbrake and cuts off the engine, then opens his car door and hops out. 'Come on,' he says, slamming the door.

'Where are you going?' I call after him.

He doesn't answer, but I hear the rear door open and when I join him, he's sitting in the boot space of the Land Rover with his legs dangling out of the back. I perch beside him.

'Can you hear the stream?' he asks.

I listen for a moment. 'Yes.' It's tumbling over rocks nearby.

'Look up,' he whispers.

'Wow.' I gaze at the dark sky twinkling with stars.

'Are you cold?' He glances at my bare arms.

'Not really,' I reply. The heat from the July day has carried through to the evening, but I take the lightweight jacket he passes me, slipping my arms into the cool material. It smells of him.

'So, *Elvis & Joe's*, hey?' I say with a wry grin. 'You did that on purpose, didn't you?'

'Sorry I didn't give you any warning. Stewart hasn't stopped bleating on about your burgers, and then it occurred to me that we could drop in tonight.'

'Do you think he'll tell his dad about me?' I ask nervously.

'He will when he's heard you sing. I gave him a copy of your demo.'

'You still had one?' I ask with surprise.

160

'Of course,' he replies. 'I've still got a couple, actually, just in case I ever get a chance to give them to anyone important. I'm not lying when I say I like your music, you know.'

I'm touched, but I don't know what to say.

'It's been a while since I've heard any of your new stuff, though,' he adds.

'It's been a while since I've written anything new,' I confess. 'I only ever play covers at gigs these days.'

He glances at me with a frown. 'Why is that?'

'That's all they want at social clubs.' I sigh. 'It was kind of nice, the first time they asked me to do a few covers. The punters really got into it with everyone singing and clapping along. But the next time I went back, the manager wanted more of the same. That happened in venue after venue. I was only supposed to tour the working men's clubs for a couple of years, but two turned into five and… I don't know what's happened. I think I've lost confidence. That bloody demo didn't help.'

'What do you mean?' His eyebrows knit together.

'It was such a headache. I remember finding it so hard to choose between all of the songs I'd ever written and narrow them down to five. I used to think my earlier material was my best, but I worried that it sounded dated – plus I'd played it so much busking. In the end I went for variety and sent CDs off to a whole bunch of record companies. I didn't hear back from any of them. I probably should have stuck to a more cohesive sound.'

'I wish you'd asked for my opinion,' he says sadly.

I sigh again. 'Yeah.' My confusion over choosing which songs to use eventually led to me feeling unsure about myself.

Busking is the only time I ever really sing my own stuff any more, and I do enjoy it, but I'm not exactly raking it in.

'I hope Joe says yes,' I whisper. 'At least, I think I do.'

'I haven't rushed you into this, have I?' he asks tentatively.

'Yes.' I flash him a smile. 'But it's good. It's… just… Thank you,' I finish.

'You're welcome.' He reaches across and gives my shoulder a tender squeeze.

Chapter 19

Phoebe

Today we went on the Montenvers train from Chamonix up to Mer de Glace, France's largest glacier.

The mountains are lush at this time of year, the ground thick and leafy with ferns. There's no snow on the pine trees, but the branches still droop downwards as if laden with weight. They remind me of melted wax dripping down a candle.

The glacier is dirty grey and dusted with shingle, very different to the Bossons glacier, which is icy blue like Remy's eyes. But you can just make out the ice underneath, rolling like a huge frozen river down the mountain.

We caught a gondola to the bottom of the glacier and then walked down hundreds of steps to the grotto, which is sculpted fresh out of the ice every summer. The tunnels are lit with colourful light displays and along the way there are whole rooms carved out of the ice, with chairs, tables and frozen-solid beds in them. It made me think of Rose – she loves that sort of thing. But Eliza would probably like it too.

On the way back up the steps, I was laughing, telling Remy about that time when the school bully, Danny Riley, grabbed me and asked me if he pinched me, would my sisters feel it? Eliza kicked his shin so hard that he screamed like a little girl and let me go. She was the smallest of the three of us, for anyone looking closely enough to notice, but she was the bravest. Dad used to call her the runt of the litter – fondly – although I don't think he ever said it to her face.

I don't know why Rose has always given her such a hard time. Rose can be the kindest, sweetest, most giving person in the world – that's how most of us see her. But she's not like that with Eliza. With Eliza, she has no patience. With Eliza, she can be mean.

I remember one time at school during a P.E. lesson. When our classmates were picking teams for games, Eliza would usually get chosen towards the end because she's so uncoordinated – unless I was captain, and then I'd always call her name early on. But this time, Rose was captain, and she let Eliza stand there while she called out name after name. The numbers kept dwindling and Eliza was motionless, staring at her. Eventually the other captain took pity and picked her for his team, but I'll never forget the look in Eliza's eyes as she walked towards him. I could've hit Rose. I'd always tried to stay out of my sisters' arguments, but that time, I let rip.

Later I felt guilty because it was around that time that Mum and Dad decided to separate us into different classes at school. Rose was happy, but she didn't bank on me being the one to go with Eliza. I know she struggled that year. Eliza thought it served her right, but I felt so sorry for her.

Rose is naturally a jealous person and it's not something she can control, but I have wondered if there's a reason for why she's like that. She used to be very clingy with Mum when we were young. If Mum ever tried to leave the house for whatever reason and Rose wouldn't let her go, Mum would sometimes speak quite sharply to her. Rose would scream and cry and kick up such a fuss.

With only two parents and three of us going through the same stages of childhood, there just wasn't enough attention to go around.

Rose eventually got what she wanted when we moved to the new house and she and Mum bonded out in the garden. Eliza gave up trying to get Mum and Dad's attention and lost herself in her music instead, but I've always felt guilty about her being left out in the cold.

God, I do miss her. And I miss Rose, too. Despite how she is with Eliza, Rose has always been there for me, and if it really came down to it, I know she'd put aside her differences and be there for Eliza, too. I hope so, anyway.

Chapter 20

Rose

Gavin wasn't back yesterday and Toby was in a foul mood, but when we had a break, I got out the tube of arnica cream I'd brought in and offered to put some on him. He seemed quite touched.

'Didn't you like being a nurse?' he asked as I was applying it to his cheek, being careful not to press too hard and hurt him.

'Yes and no. I liked looking after people, but I found it hard to let go when nothing could be done to help them.'

'Yeah,' was all he said, but I could tell he understood.

He's pretty cute, you know. He's got that indie-rock, skater boy look. He's tall and skinny and his eyes are a warmer brown than I first thought.

'Is it okay if I take a set of keys to come back here this evening with my mum?' I ask Toby at the end of the week. 'I need to go and collect her and you won't want to wait around.'

'Er, sure, but they're the only ones we have.'

'You only have one set of keys?'

'We haven't got around to getting any more cut yet,' he explains.

'Well, I can nip out and do that tomorrow if you remind me. There's a key cutter down the road. But tonight I could just drop your keys back to you?'

He doesn't say anything.

I frown at him.

'Okay,' he agrees eventually. 'I'll write down our address.'

He doesn't seem very pleased about it.

That evening, Mum stands and surveys the interior of *Jennifer's*. She looks reasonably impressed, even more so when her eyes land on the cupcakes.

'Won't those go stale overnight?' she asks.

'Whoops, I forgot to put them away,' I say, going behind the counter to retrieve an airtight container.

She looks thwarted as I pop them, one by one, into the container.

'You can have some if you like, though?' I'll make sure the money finds its way into the till. I've already given her a loaf of bread today. That's one of the advantages of working here – free bread if there's any left over.

'Well, it's just that my new Bridge club is meeting tomorrow morning and I thought perhaps...'

'Of course,' I say quickly. 'How many are you?'

'Four,' she replies, looking pleased as I fill up a cardboard box for her.

'I'll leave them on the top. Let's not forget them,' I say.

'Thank you, darling.' She casts her eyes around the interior again. 'It's quite smart, isn't it?'

'It's a lovely place to work,' I say.

'Doesn't it get hot up here by the front window?' she asks.

'We leave the door open on warm days, but there's no through breeze, so it'd be nice to be able to open the windows at the back. Have a look.'

I take her through the bakery to the back door and we step outside.

'Okay.' Mum nods, surveying the scene as I surreptitiously kick Toby's cigarette butts around the corner of the planter box. 'It depends how easy you want this to be.'

'Very easy,' I say. 'I'll probably be doing most of it after hours.'

'I hope they're paying you,' she says indignantly.

'Highly unlikely,' I reply, adding, 'I want to do it, Mum.'

'Oh, Rose,' she says with frustration. 'I do wish—'

The sigh I let out is very loud and very dramatic. It does a good job of cutting her sentence short.

She takes the hint and cuts to the chase about what I could do to tidy the place up.

I look up Toby's address after I've dropped Mum off. It's not in a very nice part of Sale, but considering how lovely *Jennifer's* is, I'm expecting great things. Ten minutes later, I'm disappointed.

The front garden is overrun with brambles and the house beyond it is in a state of disrepair with white paint flaking off the red brickwork and the wooden windowsills rotting away.

Of course, they only moved here recently so maybe they got the house for a steal and plan to do it up. Yes, that must be it.

I unclick my seatbelt and get out of the car. Almost instantly I hear a man shouting, and I freeze when I realise that the sound is coming from inside Toby's house.

Suddenly the door flies open and Toby storms out, skate-board in hand.

'You get back here, right now!' Gavin shouts after him.

'Toby!' I hear a woman cry.

'Piss off!' Toby shouts back, kicking the door shut with a loud bang.

I watch with alarm as this scene unfolds and then a thought slams into me: *is Gavin responsible for the bruise on Toby's face?*

Toby spies me on the pavement and stops in his tracks. The rage on his face makes me want to return to my car and drive away at great speed.

'Give me the keys,' he snaps, striding purposefully towards me. Fumbling, I get his set out of my bag and offer them up. He swipes them from my extended fingers and shoves them into his pocket, glaring at me. Then he drops his board to the ground and skates off.

I don't know what comes over me, but I run after him.

'What are you doing?' he asks over his shoulder. I sense that some of his anger has already dissipated.

'Checking you're alright,' I say, struggling to catch up.

He skids to a stop around the corner from his house and digs into his pocket for his fags.

'I'm fine. You can go home now.' He nods back in the direction we came.

I shake my head and he sighs. He's completely unruffled as he stares down at me.

'You don't have anything to worry about,' he says calmly. 'He loses his temper sometimes, but he always keeps his cool at work.'

'I'm not worried about him hurting *me*,' I say with incredulity. 'I'm worried about him hurting *you*!' I reach up to touch the bruise on his face, but he catches my hand and laughs with disbelief.

'You think Dad did this?'

'Didn't he?' I ask with a meaningful look as he lets go of my hand.

He shakes his head as he's lighting his cigarette. 'Unbelievable.'

I stare at him with confusion.

'Haven't you ever shoved the door open a little too hard when you come out of the bakery?' he asks, continuing before I can pause to think. 'Well, that's what I did, and then I remembered I hadn't brought the rolls out so I turned around and smacked straight into it as it started to close. My dad may be a bit of an arsehole sometimes, but he's not violent.'

I realise he's telling the truth.

'You're hilarious,' he adds.

'I'm glad I entertain you.'

'Hey,' he calls, as I start to walk off. 'Sorry.' He sounds contrite. 'I know you mean well.'

'You make me sound like an interfering busybody,' I mutter with annoyance, coming to a standstill. 'And it's barms, not rolls. That's what we call them here in Manchester.'

He purses his lips and I can tell he's trying to keep a straight face.

'So what were you arguing about, then?' I dare to ask.

He sighs, wearily. 'He wanted to go to the pub, I wanted to go out. I'm his slave all day long so I'm buggered if I'm going to sit at home every night, too.'

'Why can't you both go out?' I ask.

'Mum wanted one of us at home.'

'What's wrong with her?' I ask gently, imploring him to open up to me.

His eyes dart down to meet mine and after a long moment, he says: 'She won't leave the fucking house.'

It turns out that his mother has anxiety issues which keep her housebound and, more often than not, bedridden. As a result, she's very overweight. Toby and Gavin are her sole carers.

'Dad inherited that shithole we live in from my great-aunt.' He shakes his head. 'That sounded really ungrateful, sorry, Aunt Bessie.' He glances up at the sky, but I don't know if he's being ironic. We're sitting on a bench in the park. 'Dad was her only living relative. Anyway, we sold our house in London and poured all of our money into buying the bakery. Dad thought it would be good to have a fresh start, but she's no better here than she was there.'

'I'm sorry,' I say quietly. 'And I'm also sorry for sticking my nose in. I bet that's the last thing you wanted.'

He shrugs. 'It's okay, Rose. You're alright, you know.'

I'm glad to hear he thinks so.

Angus is watching telly when I get home, a beer in one hand and a handful of crisps in the other.

'There you are!' he exclaims. 'Where have you been?'

'At the bakery with Mum and then I got caught talking to Toby.'

'I thought you must've gone out,' he says.

'Nope. I told you I didn't have any plans.'

'Yeah, Friday night.' He rolls his eyes. 'What are we like?' he says good-naturedly. He's been in remarkably good spirits all week.

I swear I heard him coming home in the middle of the night on Monday. I thought at the time it was an odd night to go boozing, but he didn't smell of alcohol the next morning. I hope he hasn't started seeing someone. I know he'll move on eventually, but I won't be very good at coping with it when he does.

'Do you want a beer?' he asks me, getting up from the sofa. 'Or a glass of wine?'

'Wine would be lovely, thanks.' I follow him into the kitchen where he retrieves a bottle from the fridge. His dinner plates are where he left them on the countertop.

'Have you eaten?' he asks.

'Nope, but I'm not that hungry. I might make a cheese toastie with this bread from *Jennifer's*.' I brought a ciabatta home with me.

His eyes light up. 'Would you do one for me, too?'

'Greedy sod,' I say with a grin, getting out the cheese and butter. 'Of course I can.'

He hasn't eaten well over the last year, judging by the weight he's lost, but he seems to have got his appetite back.

'Thanks, Rosie,' he says warmly, wrapping his arm around my shoulders and planting a kiss on my temple. 'I'm glad you're here.'

My insides fill with warmth. 'I'm glad I'm here, too,' I reply sincerely.

He smiles at me, his eyes twinkling. 'You don't miss your mum?'

'I still see her,' I reply a touch defensively. 'But it's nice to have the company of someone my own age again.'

I haven't exactly built up a social life since I returned to Manchester in October, nine months ago. My closest school friends moved away when I did, mostly settling in their university cities of choice. I have a couple of friends in Portsmouth where I studied and a few friends in London where I worked – some have visited over the last year, but I haven't much felt like going out.

'How's this week been at the bakery?'

'Good. I like the hustle and bustle of it. Being with Mum all day and night could be a bit depressing, if I'm honest.'

He nods, the light diminishing slightly from his eyes.

'But I'm not exactly going to meet Mr Handsome there and strike up a flirty conversation over a loaf of bread,' I add merrily.

'Well, you're not going to meet him here, either,' Angus points out, his jovial mood reinstalled.

I sigh. 'Yeah, I don't know what I'm going to do about that. You can't set me up with anyone from work, can you?'

'Christ no, none of them are good enough for you.'

'Are any of them attractive, though?' I ask playfully. 'To be honest, Gus, I could really just do with a shag.'

He gives me a look of horror. 'Too much information!' he cries.

I chuckle and carry on preparing the toasties.

*

The next day is Saturday, and to my surprise, Angus is up and out of the house before I even wake up. He leaves a note for me saying he's out for the day, which is particularly cryptic.

I wonder again if he is seeing someone and my chest tightens unpleasantly.

Last night was fun. Too much fun, in fact. I have quite a headache when I wake up at ten a.m. I take a couple of paracetamol and make myself a coffee, and then go and sit on the sofa.

If Angus brought another woman home, I can categorically say that I wouldn't like it. No, that's an understatement. I'd hate it. I like that we have this place to ourselves. And I kind of like having him to myself, too.

As soon as I think that thought, I'm filled with horror. I stand up and pace the room, flapping my hand in front of my face.

I'd better get out of here.

The completion date for the house sale is set for Monday, but this weekend it still belongs to our family, and I have a plan.

I've heard that the new owners intend to dig up part of the garden so they can build a conservatory. I hate the thought of Mum's cherished plants ending up in a skip, and if they won't be missed, why shouldn't I take some with me? Things are obviously tight for Gavin and his family, so it would save me asking for money for a garden renovation project.

I have to steel myself as I open the door of the house I grew up in. Cool air wafts out and engulfs me with an old familiar smell. A lump springs up in my throat, but I try to focus on the job at hand, heading straight for the back door and avoiding any glances up the stairs to our old bedrooms.

I walk across the recently cut lawn to the garden shed at the bottom. Earlier I realised with irritation that we forgot to ask the moving men to empty it out, but I'm sure the new owners will be able to use whatever we've left behind, and I can take some of the tools with me today.

I inhale deeply, listening to the sound of bees buzzing amongst the flowers and birds tweeting in the trees as I come to a stop in front of the old apple tree. My climbing rose is flaming brilliant orange amongst the green apple leaves. I bend forward and sniff at one of the blooms, and then my eyes fill with tears.

Dammit. I don't want to have any regrets about selling this house. It was the right thing to do, but God, it hurts. I steal a glance up at her bedroom window and swallow the lump in my throat. And then I get to work.

The garden shed smells musty, of damp, dank earth. I grab a fork, a spade and a stack of empty plastic plant pots. There are some old crates here that I can transport everything in, and there's even a big bag of compost that Mum never got round to using. My eye catches sight of the paint cans in the corner and I'm struck with another idea. I wonder if there's enough paint left to do the back wall.

A couple of hours later, I'm almost done. My hands are filthy, my dress is streaked with soil and my back is aching, but I feel content. I slump into a chair and put my feet up on the wrought-iron coffee table – yes, the removal men forgot to take the outdoor furniture, too. It was destined for a charity shop, but I'm thinking we'll keep it for the bakery. There are two single chairs, one two-seater bench and a matching coffee table, all painted duck-egg blue.

My eyes are drawn once more to my flaming rose. It's such a shame. It's too big and too entangled with the apple tree to even consider digging it up. I can't take it with me.

Or can I?

I grab Mum's old pocketknife from the pile of tools and stalk with purpose to the garden shed. I swear I saw some rooting hormone in here... Yes, there it is. I fill another empty plant pot with soil and walk back outside to the rose. I've seen Mum take cuttings, so I think I know what I'm doing. I cut off a stem at a 45-degree angle, dip the end into the rooting powder and shake off the excess before sticking it into the container of good soil. And then I repeat the process a couple more times. I'll take the cuttings back to Angus's with me and water them every day and, you never know, maybe one day they'll grow to be as beautiful as the rose flourishing in front of me now.

I head straight to *Jennifer's* after leaving home, bringing with me as much as I can fit in my car. I'll have to make another trip and I'll need Angus or Toby's help in bringing back the furniture, but we have tomorrow to do that.

It's Saturday today, and I'm not supposed to be at work, but as I don't have anything better to do, I decide to make a start on the garden.

I walk in to see a gorgeous young woman behind the counter. Who's she?

'Can I help you?' she asks, her eyes hovering on my cheek. I'm going to assume I'm smeared in dirt.

'Is Toby here?'

She turns to open the door to the bakery while I rub my cheek against my shoulder. 'Toby? There's someone here to see you,' she calls.

Toby appears a moment later. 'Hey,' he says.

'Who's that?' I mouth, glancing at the girl.

'Vanessa,' he replies, loud enough for her to hear.

'I'm Rose,' I tell her with a smile. 'I work here during the week.'

'Oh, right.' She looks away again, uninterested.

'What's up?' Toby asks.

As I fill him in, it occurs to me to wonder what he must think of me. A twenty-eight-year-old would-be-nurse turned shop-worker who has nothing better to do with her Friday nights or Saturday daytimes than come back to work. I must seem like a right bore.

I *am* a right bore. No wonder nobody wants me.

'Okay,' he says with a shrug, clearly not bothered one way or the other what I choose to do with my free time.

'Can you give me a hand carrying some stuff in from the car?'

After a while he comes out the back to have a smoke. 'How's it going?' he asks, perching on the planter box and lighting up.

'I feel like I'm getting RSI in my right hand from using this weed-killer,' I reply grumpily.

'Want me to do some squirting for you?'

I give him a wry smile, but hand over the bottle. 'Thanks. Just do the moss and the crap growing out of the cracks in the pavement.'

'Yes, Miss.' He squirts with his right and smokes with his left.

'So how long has Vanessa worked here?' I ask as I turn my attention to the planter box and start pulling out weeds.

'She started today,' he replies.

'She's very pretty.'

'She's alright.' He sounds nonplussed.

I glance over my shoulder at him. 'Not your type?'

'I don't have a type.'

'Do you have a girlfriend?' I ask with curiosity, struggling to pull up a particularly tenacious weed.

'Not at the moment.'

'You didn't leave anyone behind in London?'

'Nope. Did you?'

I humph. 'My boyfriend got his not-quite-ex-wife pregnant, so no.'

He pauses what he's doing. 'I didn't think you'd be the type to hook up with a cheater.'

'Well, I didn't know he was cheating on her at the time. He told me they were finished.'

He carries on squirting as I tug really hard at the weed. The leaves come off, but the roots stay intact.

'Bollocks,' I say.

'Want some Weedo?' He offers up the bottle.

'It's called Weedol. And no, what I really need is a fork.' I look around for Mum's bag of gardening tools. 'Damn, I left the tools in the car.' I stare with annoyance at my filthy hands.

'I'll go get them for you.'

'Er, okay. Thanks. My keys are in my bag. Side pocket,' I

direct as he reaches in and pulls them out. He throws his fag butt to the floor.

'Can you stop doing that? We're trying to tidy this place up.'

'Sorry, Miss,' he calls, unfazed.

I hope that nickname doesn't stick. I *do* feel like his bloody teacher, sometimes.

When he returns I barely glance up, too busy with the next round of weeds, but what I do see of his face is enough to make me do a double take.

He dumps the bag by my side. 'Are you an identical triplet?' he asks with astonishment.

He's holding an old photo of Phoebe, Eliza and me that I keep on the dashboard of my car. We're arm in arm on a beach in Somerset at the age of ten, wearing identical smiles and beaming straight at the camera.

'Give me that,' I snap, but a millisecond before snatching it I remember my dirty hands. 'Put it down. Put it in my bag.'

'What's the problem?' he asks, perplexed.

'I don't want the edges bent.'

'I'm not going to bend the edges, Rose.' He's really quite patronising for someone who's seven years my junior. 'If you care about it so much, why have you got it on your dash in full sun? The colour's fading.'

'I know,' I say, and to my mortification I'm suddenly fighting back tears. 'Just put it down.'

'Okay,' he says, startled at the look on my face. 'I'll put it in your bag.'

I swallow. 'Thank you. You should get back to work.'

He does as he's told, leaving me in peace.

Chapter 21

Eliza

'Well?' Angus asks, his face expectant as I walk out of *Elvis & Joe's*. I give him a sneaky thumbs-up along with a chuffed smile and he throws his arms around me.

'I was trying to be cool,' I say with a muffled voice against his shoulder.

'Bugger that,' he says, drawing away but keeping his hands on my upper arms. 'That's amazing. When?'

'Wednesday night, the week after next.'

'Wow! Lunch to celebrate?'

'Yes, I can actually eat, now.'

Stewart lined up the meeting with his dad after listening to my demo. I was so nervous earlier, I couldn't even stomach the croissants Angus brought over to my apartment. He came first thing this morning, armed with breakfast and a playlist of what he thought I should sing. It was very sweet of him.

'What are you up to for the rest of the day?' I ask as we walk.

He shrugs. 'I don't have any plans. I don't have much of a life these days, I'm afraid.'

'You're not alone,' I reply.

Soon afterwards we're seated on the pavement outside a pub in the Northern Quarter, not far from *Roxy's*. It's been baking hot all week and it's sheer bliss being able to have a drink with a friend in the sunshine.

'You look better,' I declare. He's had a haircut, but that's not it. He seems happier, healthier, a far cry from the ghost of a man who found me busking not even two weeks ago.

'I feel better,' he replies, leaning back in his chair and grinning.

'I can't believe you let Rose cut your hair last night.' I noticed he'd had a haircut when he arrived on my doorstep, but I got a sharp shock when he casually admitted that Rose did it when they'd both had a few drinks. 'I guess she's responsible for fattening you up, as well.'

He laughs. 'She's a good cook,' he agrees. 'She was out for most of yesterday evening, though, so I had to make do with a ready-meal.'

'Oh, poor you,' I say sarcastically. 'Where was she?'

'Hanging out with Toby, the boy she works with at the bakery.'

'Boy? How old is he?'

'Barely out of his teens. Rose is worried that he's having trouble at home.'

'Is she doing her lame duck routine again?' Angus doesn't respond to my snidey comment, but seriously, why *did* she give up nursing if she cares about looking after people so much?

'Which bakery does she work at again?' I ask, trying to sound more pleasant as he tells me.

'It's called *Jennifer's*. It's in Sale, around the corner from the Town Hall.'

'Does she like working there?'

'You know, you could just ask her these questions yourself.' He leans forward and rests his elbows on the table, regarding me pointedly.

'Forget it,' I grumble.

He smiles at me. The sun is bouncing off his pint and onto his face, making his mottled green and brown eyes dance in the light.

I aim for nonchalance with my tone. 'Well, I'm glad it's working out for you. If she's why you've perked up—'

'It's not just her,' he interrupts, pausing before adding, 'I'm glad to have you *both* in my life again. I wasn't sure I ever would.'

I can't hold his gaze for long. I take a sip of my cider and crunch on a chunk of ice.

He smiles a small smile. 'You seem a bit better, as well.'

If I do, it's because of him.

'But you're still too thin,' he adds.

'Maybe I should move in with you and Rose,' I say acerbically.

His smile widens.

'Never again,' I warn, before he gets any ideas.

We sit and chat for a couple of hours, eventually heading back to my apartment so I can get ready for work. Michelle is hanging out on the sofa, watching TV, but she goes to her room when we appear. I frown after her – she didn't need to make herself scarce.

'Coffee?' I ask.

'Sure.' Angus comes and stands in the doorframe, watching me.

'Do you work every night at *Roxy's*?' he asks.

'Pretty much. I need the money.'

He nods thoughtfully. 'Doesn't leave you much room for a social life, though.'

'I don't need one.'

'When was the last time you went on a date?' he asks.

'Oh God, here we go again.' I stare at the ceiling. 'I've got other things to worry about right now than men.'

'Rose wants me to set her up with one of the guys from my work,' he continues, not put off by my tone.

'Are you going to?' I ask casually, hoping the answer is yes.

'I told her I wouldn't,' he replies with a grin, and I can picture him hamming it up in his overprotective big brother role. *I bet Rose loved it*, I think meanly. 'But there is one guy that I think she might like,' he surprises me by saying.

'Really?'

'I don't know if she's serious about meeting someone, though.'

'Is she alright?' I find myself asking.

'I think she's been lonely,' he replies honestly. 'She says it's nice being around someone her own age again. I think it must've been hard at times, being with your mum all the time.'

I nod and change the subject.

The following week drags by. I keep hoping Angus will call, but he doesn't, so on Thursday I call him myself and ask what he's up to on Saturday. Saturday is a big busking day for me, but I don't want to go any longer without seeing him, so I'm willing to jack it in.

I'm crushed when he tells me that he's going away with his mum at the weekend – they're visiting old friends in Brighton.

'But I'm coming to your gig next week,' he tells me. 'Obviously.'

'Okay, that's good,' I reply half-heartedly.

On Wednesday night, six days later, I'm the most nervous I've ever been before a gig. It's been months since I last played to an audience at a social club and *Elvis & Joe's* is a far cry from that sort of venue – it's easily the nicest place I've ever performed. But that's not why I'm on edge. Nor is it because I'm worried about who will be watching or whether I'll remember my words. I know my songs inside out and back to front, and it doesn't matter how many people turn up because I'll be as comfortable with fifty as I would be with five.

No, what I'm nervous about is seeing Angus again.

I wish I felt as at ease with him as Rose does. She's always been so relaxed in his company, and no doubt she's feeling even more so now that they live together.

It still grates on me that she gets to see him every day, not that this is anything new. When they lived in London, Rose hung out with Phoebe and Angus all the time. I used to feel so left out, but I just couldn't imagine being part of that group, not with how I felt about Angus.

I don't really understand how Rose can be comfortable with Angus if she has feelings for him. *Does* she still have feelings for him? Has she *ever* been in love with him? Knowing

Rose, it was just an infatuation, another silly crush. She always was a hopeless romantic.

But what if she does love him? And what if her feelings are one day reciprocated?

The thought makes me want to throw up.

'You look nervous,' Michelle says, entering the small back-stage area where I'm waiting. I'm due to go on shortly.

'I'm fine,' I insist as she passes me a glass of water. 'Thanks.' I take a large gulp.

'There's a good crowd out there,' she tells me, impressed. 'All of the tables are full.'

'I'm sure they only came in for the food,' I say. Not that it matters. It's nicer to play to numbers, despite what I said earlier. 'Have you seen Angus?' I ask casually.

'Yep, he's here,' she replies. 'He's got a few mates with him.'

'Aw, really?' My heart swells and she smiles at me.

Once I'm sitting on a stool on the darkened stage with my guitar plugged into an amp, I scan the room. My eyes find Angus almost immediately. He's moved forward from the bar and is standing a few metres away with a beer in his hand. He raises it up to me, and as he smiles, my stomach somersaults.

Then the lights above the stage go on. I lean closer to the mic as the crowd noise dies down. Joe doesn't do announce-ments, he said, so I have to introduce myself. I'll say a few more words later, but right now I just want to get down to business with one of my quirkiest songs.

'Hi everyone. I'm Eliza Thomson and this song is called, "Don't Forget Your Toothbrush".'

I strum my guitar and start to sing.

*

'You were amazing!' Michelle enthuses as I step down from the stage. She's come around to the side to meet me and I'm so grateful for her support. My responding thank you is heartfelt.

Joe appears and opens the backstage door, jerking his head towards it.

'I'll just go and lock up my guitar,' I tell Michelle, glancing over my shoulder. I can't see Angus.

'That was a very nice set,' Joe says as the door closes behind us. 'I can't believe we haven't had you in before.'

'I'd love to come back,' I reply with a cheeky grin.

He chuckles. 'I'm sure we can arrange something. Give me a call in a couple of days or pop in if you're in town. We'll set something up.'

'Thank you!' I try to resist hugging him.

I put away my things and freshen up, swapping my T-shirt for one that isn't sweaty from being under the stage-lights. My hair is quite long at the moment and I'm wearing it in a single plait that drapes over my left shoulder. I need to get around to cutting it. My thoughts make the easy jump towards Rose, who recently cut Angus's hair for him.

I wonder if she knew about this gig. Did she in any small way want to come? As soon as I think the thought, I push it out of my head. I'm not about to go getting sentimental.

Michelle is waiting near the door when I return to the bar area.

'Do you know where Angus is?' I ask, cutting to the chase.

'He's at the bar, getting you a drink,' she replies with a smile.

'Come on, then,' I urge.

'Hey!' he says when we find him a moment later. He sweeps me up in a hug and crushes me to his hot, slightly damp body. He feels incredible. 'That was great,' he enthuses, pulling away. 'Best gig I've ever seen you do. Are you happy?'

'Yeah. I think so. Yes.'

'Here, I got you a beer.'

'Thanks.' We chink glasses.

'Which is the guy you think Rose might like?' I ask him a little later, furtively studying his friends.

'Evan, there.' He nods at a dark-haired, medium-height bloke wearing a white shirt and navy blazer.

'You reckon?' I wrinkle up my nose.

'You don't think she'd go for him?'

I shrug. 'I don't know. Maybe. Yeah, actually, she probably would.' He looks a bit too safe and middle-of-the-road for me. 'What was she doing tonight?' I ask.

'Just watching telly,' he replies casually.

'You didn't think about asking her to come?'

He looks confused. 'I thought you didn't want her to know we're seeing each other?'

I shift on my feet, suddenly uncomfortable. 'Don't you think it's a bit odd keeping it from her? I mean, why is it a secret?'

He looks nonplussed. 'Okay, no worries, I'll come clean tomorrow.'

'She's going to wonder why you didn't mention it. It's not like we're doing anything wrong.'

I blush as soon as the words come out of my mouth. Unfortunately, he notices. He stares down at me for a long moment, his mouth drawn out into a straight line. Then one of his mates interrupts and that's the last we say on the matter.

Angus drives Michelle and me home. My nerves are back in force as we walk into the apartment.

'I'm knackered, guys, I'm calling it a night,' Michelle says, raising a cheeky eyebrow at me as she goes in for a hug.

'Thanks for the lift, Angus,' she adds nonchalantly.

'You're welcome,' he replies. He sounds nervous too.

'Do you want a beer?' I ask him.

'No, I've had my limit,' he replies, slumping onto the sofa.

'Coffee? Tea?'

'A soft drink would be good. I'll be up all night if I have another caffeine hit.' He yawns and stretches, making his T-shirt ride up.

'I didn't realise you were driving tonight,' I call, heading into the kitchen.

'I wanted to give you a lift home.'

'Really?' I glance out the door at him. 'That was sweet of you.'

He doesn't say anything else as I get our drinks, joining him on the sofa. I sit at the other end, my knees up, facing him.

'So, I wanted to run something by you,' he says, looking awkward.

'Go on.' I'm immediately apprehensive.

'Don't look so worried,' he says with a small smile. He can talk. 'It's just that I've been asked to write a feature about themed hotels and I need to check out one that I think you'd like. It's called Hotel Gotham. Have you heard of it?'

I sit up straighter. 'The one in the old Bank building that's inspired by Batman?'

'That's it.'

'The rooftop bar there is supposed to be great!'

'And the restaurant is great, too. I know you probably can't get out of work on Saturday night, but do you want to come for dinner with me on Sunday?'

'Definitely!'

He grins. 'I don't know why I was worried about asking you.'

I pull a face at him. 'Neither do I, you moron. You should have known I'd jump at the chance to do anything Batman-related.'

We used to get so excited about comics when we were younger.

We chat for a little while, but soon I'm stifling yawns.

'You're knackered,' he notes. 'I should probably head off.'

'Sorry, no, you don't have to go,' I say.

'I'd better. I've got a deadline in the morning, but I'll see you on Sunday? I'm going to check in at around three p.m. and chill out so come whenever.'

I follow him to the door and lean against the wall, waiting for him to open it. I wish he wasn't leaving. He turns to face me.

'You were incredible tonight,' he says sincerely. 'Well done.'

He really means it, too. The words could sound glib coming from anyone else.

'Thank you again,' I reply seriously, looking up at him.

He doesn't make any attempt to leave, and as we continue to stand there facing each other, my heart begins to beat faster.

He sighs quietly, a pensive look in his beautiful eyes.

And then he speaks. 'I still care about you.'

I swallow, unable to look away, until his small step forward jolts me to my senses.

'Angus,' I say, startled. 'No.'

He touches his forehead to mine and takes my hand, silencing me. That's all he does. But my heart feels like it's about to catapult itself out of my ribcage.

'I'll see you Sunday. Any time after three,' he reminds me, and then he steps away, letting go of my hand to open the door.

'Wait...' I say, as he walks over the threshold.

He stops in his tracks, but doesn't turn around.

'Maybe don't say anything to Rose, after all,' I say.

He nods and I close the door behind him.

As soon as he's gone, my mind goes into overdrive.

What am I doing? Nothing has changed, not really. Phoebe might not be here, but Mum and Rose are, and what the hell would Judy think? Angus and I can't be together, not like that.

But the thought of going back to never seeing him makes me want to sob my heart out.

Michelle finds me on the sofa in exactly that state a few minutes later.

'Hey!' she exclaims, hurrying over to me. 'What's wrong?'

I shake my head. I'm crying, so talking isn't ideal right now.

She runs her hand across my hair, soothingly.

'What happened?' she asks. 'Are you thinking about Phoebe?'

'I'm always thinking about Phoebe!'

'Aw, Lize,' she says gently, still stroking my hair. 'I know I've said this before, but have you tried talking to her?'

'No.' I shake my head. 'I can't. I wouldn't even know where to start.' My bottom lip is trembling like crazy.

'Can it hurt to try?' she asks.

'Yes,' I bite back. 'It can hurt a lot.'

'I'm sorry,' she murmurs.

'It's okay. Maybe I just need to get some sleep. I'm sure I'll feel better in the morning.'

'It's been a pretty full-on night,' she agrees. 'You've had a lot on your plate.'

I nod and get up from the sofa, drying the tears from my eyes.

'Eliza?' She calls after me on my way to the bathroom.

'Yes?'

'Isn't it about time you put yourself first? If Angus is the one for you... I don't think Phoebe would want you to be unhappy.'

'Phoebe would *hate* me to be with Angus!' I hiss, my voice sounding choked.

'Are you sure about that? Because I'm not convinced,' she says.

I suddenly feel very weary. 'I'm so tired of doing the right thing,' I mumble.

'Try talking to her,' Michelle urges. 'Please. For me.'

I don't say anything as I head into the bathroom.

Chapter 22

Phoebe

It's the middle of the night and I've just had another bad dream. I keep having them. Remy has walked out of our bedroom because he said I called out Angus's name in my sleep. He's upset, but I can't even bring myself to go and comfort him – I feel too raw.

In my dream, Angus was with Eliza. They were passionately kissing and tearing each other's clothes off. I screamed at them both and they looked at me with annoyance, then went back to what they were doing. I kept trying to pull them apart, but they shoved me away and laughed, like my distress was one big joke to them. It was awful. I can't imagine getting back to sleep.

It's late morning now and I've been thinking about why I'm having so many nightmares. I've got too much on my mind at the moment, too many choices to make, and I keep shutting out my thoughts during the day. I think my subconscious is getting back at me during the night.

The thing is, every time Remy does something amazing, like climbs a mountain with me, takes me paragliding or even just kisses me here on the balcony with the mountains in the background, I fall deeper in love with him. I'm so deep, it's like I've tumbled into a crevasse and I can't get out. He holds my heart in his hands and if he crushes it, he'll crush me. I don't like feeling so dependent on him. Angus never made me feel like this. I could be myself with Angus, confident and happy. I'm not sure I appreciated that as much as I should have. Not once did I feel clingy or insecure. Have I made a mistake, letting him go?

Chapter 23

Rose

If I had a pound for every time I've heard someone say that they hate the smell of hospitals, I could probably buy myself a flight to Australia to visit my Uncle Simon. But you never hear that when you work in a bakery. Quite the opposite, in fact. There is something so heart-warming and life-affirming about the smell of freshly baked bread. I begin my days in the best possible mood.

Today, though, when I unlock the bakery door at seven a.m. using the spare key I had made, something is not quite right.

An indie rock song is blaring at high volume out of the bakery stereo, and when I open the door, Toby is sliding some rolls – he still can't get used to calling them barms – off a large metal tray and onto a wire rack. He's wearing a white T-shirt and has a white rag tied around his forehead, keeping his dark hair off his face. He looks a bit like he should be doing karate, not baking.

I go and turn the music down and he looks over at me.

'Did your dad have to leave early again?' I ask.

He gives me a dark look and then places his hands heavily on the worktop in front of him.

'He's at the hospital,' he says. 'Mum had a heart attack yesterday evening.'

'Oh no,' I hurry over to him, touching one hand to his flour-dusted forearm and the other to his back. His T-shirt is damp under my palm, a sign of how hot it is in here with all the ovens blaring.

'They think she'll recover. It was only minor. A *warning sign*,' he says bitterly.

'I'm so sorry. Are you okay?'

He straightens up, and our contact loosens. 'Yeah, but I'm running behind.'

'Have you been here on your own all night?' I ask with alarm, looking at the dozens of loaves of bread cooling on the wire racks.

He nods.

'You must be exhausted!'

No wonder he had his music on so loud. It's probably been keeping him awake.

'I'm fine,' he says wearily. 'This was the last batch.'

'Tell me what I can do to help.'

'Can you set up the shop? I could really use a cigarette break.'

'Of course.' I give him a sympathetic smile and go and get the cash register money from the safe. I've worked enough shifts now to know what to do to get started. The turnover from this place has been pretty incredible since its opening. Let's hope it keeps up like this.

*

Later, after our regular customers have been and gone, Toby fires up the coffee machine. He looks shattered, his actions slow and sluggish.

'Instead of drinking that, why don't you head home to bed?' I suggest in a no-nonsense tone. 'I can manage here.'

He shakes his head. 'I'd rather keep going.'

'What if your dad can't come in tonight?' I say. 'What then? You need to rest now, while you can.'

'I don't want to be at home.' He looks suddenly anguished.

'Hey,' I say gently, going over to give him a hug.

'I hate that place,' he mutters, looping his arms around my waist and resting his chin on the top of my head. He sighs loudly.

'Go for a lie down out the back, then,' I suggest, pulling away slightly to look up at him.

'Okay.' We let each other go and I watch him push through the bakery door with a sinking heart. Poor guy. 'Wake me up before the lunchtime rush,' he calls over his shoulder.

But when I nip into the bakery just before midday, I find him out cold on the floor, his lean body curled around a sack of flour. I can't bring myself to rouse him so I carry on alone.

It's two o'clock before he emerges, and by then the shop has quietened down. I've been run off my feet.

'Christ,' he mutters, rubbing his eyes. 'Why didn't you wake me?'

'You needed to rest more than I needed help,' I reply.

'Thanks.' He smiles at me sleepily and then yawns. I notice he's holding his mobile phone. 'Dad called from the hospital. They're keeping Mum in for a couple of days so he's going to need me to bake again tonight. You were right.'

'Toby, you have to go home,' I insist. 'Get some sleep in a proper bed.'

'Yeah, I will, after this shift,' he agrees.

'It's not going to be busy now,' I say, checking the time. 'I can manage. When do you need to come back?'

'Ten o'clock.'

'Bloody hell.'

'Dad does it every day,' he says with another yawn. 'I'll refresh the starter before I leave.'

The 'starter'? But a customer comes in so I let Toby go back into the bakery without asking.

I'm so knackered that evening that I crash out at nine, but only a few short hours later, a bad dream stirs me from sleep. I lie there for a while, wide awake and unable to doze off, and soon my thoughts drift to Toby. I know what it's like to lose a parent to a heart attack and no doubt he's terrified that his mum won't pull through. He has so much to deal with. Right now, he's at work all on his own. I check the time on my alarm clock. It's just after two o'clock in the morning. Am I really going to get back to sleep tonight? Or should I bite the bullet and go and help him?

A moment later, I'm out of bed and throwing on the first thing I lay my hands on in my wardrobe – black jeans and a navy top. Then I bundle my hair up into a bun and go to the kitchen to write Angus a note, letting him know where I've gone.

There's a chill in the air and the sky is sparkling with starlight beyond the orange street lamps as I get out of the car and walk along the pavement to *Jennifer's*. Sale is deadly quiet.

It's Friday night, well, Saturday morning, but everyone is at home tucked up in bed. Everyone except us.

I recognise the song that's playing when I enter the premises, but I'm so out of touch when it comes to cool music that I wouldn't have a clue who it's by.

I push open the bakery door and see Toby carrying a large, clear plastic container over to the wooden island unit.

'Hey!' I shout, knowing he's going to be freaked out when he sees me. 'Toby!'

But he's still completely oblivious. He tips an enormous blob of dough out onto the work surface and begins to fold the dough edges up and over, from the outside in, turning it to face him each time. I'm fascinated as I watch, and a moment later he's left with a smooth, round, elastic ball. He looks up and nearly jumps out of his skin.

'Holy shit!' he exclaims. 'What are you doing here?' He goes to turn the music down, but the loud chugging of machinery still fills the air.

'I couldn't sleep. Thought you might be able to use some help.'

'I think I might love you.' He exhales with relief as he strides around the worktop and engulfs me in a hug. My chest expands as I hug him back.

'Tell me what to do,' I prompt as he goes to check the contents of the Hobart – the large dough mixer standing on the floor.

'Pass me the caraway seeds,' he says, turning the machine off.

I do as he asks and he tips them into the dough, setting the machine going again.

'Can you grab me the *bannetons*, too?' He returns to the mound of dough waiting on the wooden countertop. 'You can help me shape the sourdough.'

'What are *bannetons*?' I ask.

He gives me a look of disbelief.

The *bannetons* turn out to be proving baskets, and some of ours are oval-shaped and made out of wood pulp while others are constructed out of round cane baskets. Sourdough, apparently, is a wetter dough, so if it's not contained in something, it will lose its shape and flop.

I flour the baskets while Toby uses a dough cutter to separate the dough into chunks, then I help him roll each one into shape and place them into the different-sized *bannetons*. He moves at a speed that makes my head spin, but I keep getting the dough stuck to my fingers.

'Use flour to get it off, not water,' he says, reading my mind as I glance at the sink. I dust my hands with flour and rub off the dough easily. 'You have to work quickly or the dough will stick again,' he warns.

He talks to me as he works, and I learn that being an artisan baker is all about the time it takes to do things. While working quickly at this stage is important, even more vital to the process is slowing things right down, because the longer something takes, the better it tastes.

Artisan bread is made using a combination of flour, water, salt, plus some kind of 'leaven' – the thing that makes the dough ferment and rise. French bread is made with fresh yeast, which comes in a packet like butter and smells pretty bad, but sourdough is naturally leavened using 'starter' or 'mother', as it's also called.

Toby jokes that his dad's 'mother' has been sitting in the fridge since time began, and every day it has to be fed with fresh flour and water to top it up. He tells me that some bakeries in France and Italy claim to have had their 'mother' on the go for centuries, being passed down generation to generation. It's pretty grim when you think about it, but he reiterates to me that the longer something takes, the better it tastes.

'You want to have a turn at baguettes?' he asks with a smile.

'Go on, then.'

'No flour on the work surface, only on your hands,' he directs me. 'A floury surface makes shaping the baguettes impossible. As long as the worktop is clean, they won't stick.'

I watch him do the first one, a blur of folding from the outside in, pointing the ends and rolling until the length is right. The whole thing takes him about ten seconds and then he's laying it lengthwise on a flour-dusted cloth that has been folded into a series of pleats for the baguettes to lie between.

'Chop chop,' he prompts.

I shake my head. 'I wouldn't have a clue where to start. I'll watch you do another one.'

At the end of the next ten seconds, I'm still none the wiser.

He smiles at my blank look and walks away from the counter, returning with a small piece of paper. 'Watch where I fold it,' he says.

He folds it from the outsides in. Then he folds it again. 'Imagine an invisible line in the middle. You're creating a spine,' he says, and I'm reminded of making paper aeroplanes with my sisters and Dad. He folds in the end edges to create a rounded-off shape, then folds the lengthwise edges again, until he's left with a long, thin piece of paper that looks a bit like a longboat. 'Now you roll the dough out until it's the right length. Okay?'

'Okay.' I nod and get to work, finding it easier to remember the folds when I think of it as a piece of paper. He still manages to make about ten baguettes in the time it takes for me to do one, and of course my hands are sticky with dough by the end of it.

'It takes practice,' he says as I rub flour on my fingers.

'You're very good at it. Have you really been baking since you were eight?'

'In the bakery, yeah, but I've been baking with Mum and Dad at home for as long as I can remember. Come on, we've got time to have a break while everything's proving. You want a coffee?' he asks.

'Sure.'

We go out into the shop and he switches on the machine. It's still dark outside, but dawn can't be far away.

'I think you enjoy baking more than you let on,' I say.

'It's a bit of a rush,' he confesses as he tips freshly ground coffee into the machine. 'I like working fast and under pressure. And the finished product is pretty beautiful.'

'Do you ever mess up?'

'Christ, yeah, on many occasions. Lesson number one: don't forget the salt. You need salt for flavour and it helps develop the gluten. Sometimes I'll be mixing the dough for ages, wondering why the hell it isn't doing what I want it to do. Dad will come in, pinch a piece of dough to taste it and tell me immediately where I've gone wrong. Lesson number two: don't pop out for a fag and forget to turn the mixer off.'

'What happens?' I ask.

'If you overwork the dough, the gluten bonds will over-stretch and be ruined. You know when you came in and I was folding it over?'

I nod.

'It looked smooth and elastic, right? Well, you can't get it to look like that. If you overwork it, it's wrecked. It has to go in the bin.'

'Why don't you use a timer?'

'I probably should because I get a bit distracted, but Dad never does. He knows the process by heart.'

From the reverence in his voice, he has way more respect for his dad than he lets on.

'Have you done many all-nighters with your dad?' I ask as the coffee machine spits and gurgles out coffee into the waiting cups.

'Not any more. We used to, back when Mum…' His voice trails off.

'When your mum what?' I prompt.

'When she was well, before she got so…' He shrugs, his back to me.

'Do you think this heart attack will spur her on to try to get better, maybe?' I ask tentatively.

'Who knows?' He passes me a cup.

'Thanks.'

He looks over at the cupcakes dwindling on the counter-top. 'We're going to run out today.'

'Who supplies them?' I ask. I've wondered before.

'Mum makes them,' he says to my surprise. 'This bakery was hers once. I mean, not this one, the first *Jennifer's* in East London. It's where she and Dad met.'

'Did she bake?'

'She did bake bread, but she was more into cakes and things.' He blows on his drink. 'She's been baking from home for years, though.'

'Does it still make her happy?'

'I'd like to think so,' he says, taking a sip of coffee. 'I might get ahead with prep for Sunday night.' Luckily the bakery is closed tomorrow, so no one has to work a night shift tonight, but it will be full steam again on Monday.

'What do you want me to do?' I ask, following him back into the bakery.

'Roast garlic, caramelise red onions, soak raisins or toast some seeds and nuts – take your pick.'

The baguettes go into the oven last, because they take the least time to cool, but when they're done, I stand for a moment and stare at the multitude of loaves cooling on the racks.

Bread has never looked so good. From fig and fennel and rye and caraway to garlic and rosemary and cumin and Gruyère, I feel like I could devour one of everything. Even the simple rustic white, or *pain au levain* as they call it in France, looks like a work of art.

I check the time on my watch. It's almost seven o'clock.

'Vanessa's going to be late,' he says with a raised eyebrow, reading a text on his phone. 'She says she'll be in at ten. You should go home and get some rest.' He lifts up the hem of his T-shirt and mops the sweat from his brow. His chest is pretty ripped, I note with surprise. 'I'll open up.'

'I can stay for a bit,' I reply, giving myself a little shake. 'I imagine we'll both be working at half-speed today. Unless you want me to leave because I stink?' He looks amused as I sniff my armpits. They're alright, thankfully. At least I had a shower when I came home last night.

'Thanks, Rose,' he says suddenly, coming over to give me a hug. I hug him back, and then jump in surprise as his hand lands on my backside. He pats it once, firmly. 'You're a star.'

'Thank you.' I blush as I pull away. 'It was a fun learning curve.'

'I'll get the float, you go and open up.' He smirks as he turns away.

It's only later, when a couple of our regular customers laugh as I'm getting their order that I realise what he's done. I glance over my shoulder to see a white, floury handprint on my right bum cheek.

'Toby!' I yell at him as our customers continue to laugh. 'You little git!'

He comes over and loops one arm around my neck, then whispers in my ear. 'Lesson number three: never wear black in a bakery.'

Chapter 24

Eliza

'I'm on the second floor,' Angus says when I call him to let him know that I've arrived at Hotel Gotham. 'I'll meet you by the lift.'

The 'Batman' building looks just like something that you'd find in one of the comics, an imposing stone and steel neoclassical design with arched art deco windows and even gargoyles on the roof.

Angus appears a moment after I step out of the lift. 'Hey,' he says warmly, his eyes widening. 'You look amazing.' He comes over to give me a peck on my cheek.

When Michelle and I checked out the hotel's website earlier, we saw that a lot of people make an effort to dress up. She convinced me to wear a 30s-inspired black dress from her wardrobe with my own high heels, but I stopped short of doing my hair in an up-do, instead blow-drying it to within an inch of its life so it falls glossily down my back.

'So do you,' I say with surprise. I was expecting him to be wearing his usual jeans and T-shirt, but he's donned smart black trousers and a white shirt, rolled up to his elbows with the top button open. His dark-blond hair is still a shaggy mess, though.

'Thought I'd make a bit of an effort to look less like the layabout that I actually am,' he whispers conspiratorially. 'Believe it or not, I've got a tie and suit jacket for later.' He glances towards the corridor where his room is and then checks his watch. It's almost five. 'Do you want to go straight up to the bar?' he asks.

'Er, sure.' I'm curious to see his room, but maybe I'll get to have a look later.

That thought leads to another and a blush creeps up my throat as we step back into the lift.

The hotel used to be the Midland Bank building and there are nods to its financial history throughout, with bags of fake money holding back the doors and, Angus tells me, toiletries resting on blocks of fake gold in the bathrooms. The restaurant has beautiful arched windows with views out over the city, but the rooftop bar is what really takes my breath away. Manchester's skyline is spectacular, and you can also sit right behind one of the gargoyles.

'What time did you check in?' I ask when we've ordered our drinks and sat down on a black bench seat, our backs resting against the outer walls of the grey-stone building. The sun is still high in the sky.

'About an hour ago. I've just been on the bed, reading.'

'What's your room like?' I ask.

'Very opulent. And there are Batman-shaped biscuits in a cookie jar.'

'Cool!'

'You can come and have one along with a cup of posh tea later if you like.' He says it casually and doesn't blush like I do at the thought of us being alone together in his room.

'So what have you been up to?' he asks.

'Joe called!' I exclaim. 'He wants me to do another gig the week after next – on a Friday night!'

'Wow, that's fantastic!'

I fill him in and we make our way through several cocktails as we sit and chat, the sun beginning to sink behind the rooftops. Suddenly we remember our dinner reservation and hightail it downstairs to the restaurant. We sit by one of the arched windows, looking out onto another art deco building. It's still light outside, but the table's candle has been lit regardless.

'Where did you tell Rose you were coming tonight?' I ask.

'I told her I was coming here.' He clears his throat. 'She thinks I'm seeing someone.'

'Oh. Did you put her straight?' I ask.

'Yeah. I mean, I'm not, am I?' He raises his eyebrows at me. 'But she seemed upset.'

'She probably thinks it's too soon,' I say flatly.

'It's been over a year,' he points out reasonably, before frowning. 'Anyway...'

The waiter comes over then, pouring ruby red wine into both our glasses. 'Are you ready to order?' he asks.

I'm glad of the interruption as I pick up my menu.

*

'Do you ever drive yourself mad thinking about the future?' Angus asks when we're well into our main courses.

'I try not to,' I reply.

He shakes his head. 'I'm not talking about ten years' time; I'm talking about two, three, ten thousand years away.'

'You don't think we will have blown each other up with nuclear bombs by then?' I ask.

'Who knows? But what if we haven't? What if the human race is still going strong and we haven't all been killed off by deadly viruses and world wars? I wonder who the superpowers will be. I'm not talking about comic book characters.'

'I know,' I say with a smile, wondering where he's going with this. It sounds like one of the bonkers conversations we used to have.

'The United States, the Soviet Union, the British Empire before World War II – they were all superpowers,' he says. 'But look back at history to Ancient Egypt, the Persian Empire, the Greeks and the Romans... Who will be the superpowers of the future?'

'China?' I suggest.

'Maybe. But what will the world be like? What will technology be like? Will any of these buildings still be standing? And if not, why not? What will make them fall? Will they be torn down and rebuilt bigger?'

'You'd drive yourself nuts thinking about it,' I say.

'Yeah, imagine being so overpowered by curiosity that you could literally drive yourself mad.'

'There's probably a medical term for that sort of thing,' I say with a giggle.

'Yeah, a term for the fatally curious. You wouldn't be able to switch off or fall asleep at night.'

I flash him a smile. 'I like it when you start to ponder the universe.'

He smiles back at me, his face and hair golden in the candlelight, and his eyes glinting beautifully. He's painfully gorgeous.

Out of the blue, I wonder if he used to have crazy conversations like this when he was with Phoebe.

But of course he did.

'What are you thinking?' he asks, sensing the change in atmosphere.

'Feebs,' I reply quietly.

I glance up in time to see him swallow, but then he looks down and places his knife and fork together on his plate.

'I'm stuffed,' he says.

'No room for dessert?' I double check.

'No, but you can.'

'I might just get a cup of tea, actually. I've had a bit too much wine.'

'Well, there's the posh tea and coffee in my room, and don't forget the biscuits.'

I smile. 'As if I could.'

Old-fashioned, pink-tinted newspapers titled *The Gotham News* hang over gold railings fixed to the walls as we walk down the corridor. Angus reaches his room and unlocks the door with a key card and I follow him inside.

The room is dark and sumptuous, a double bed in its centre with a fur throw draped casually over the end. I sit down on the only armchair and he offers up a glass jar. I smile and take a Batman-shaped biscuit, then he gets on with filling and boiling the kettle.

'What time have you got to be at work tomorrow?' I ask, trying to make small talk.

'Ten or so,' he replies, perching on the end of the bed, facing me. He rests his elbows on his knees and clasps his hands together and I catch a glimpse of his chest beneath his shirt.

'I'll be out of your way soon,' I say, nodding at the kettle as I hear it click off.

He gets to his feet to make our drinks and I relax back in the armchair and cross my legs. The bed dominates the small space and it's feeling a little warm in here.

When he turns around, he seems to jolt ever so slightly. His eyes graze my legs as he walks over and passes me a cup.

'When you look at me, do you ever see Phoebe?' I ask as he sits down.

He blanches. 'What? No!'

'Does it ever hurt to look at me?' I ask, as my mood takes a nosedive – a sure sign of too much alcohol. I'm on a destructive course now and I won't be able to stop it.

'Eliza,' he says with distress, placing his cup on a nearby table and coming to kneel on the carpet in front of me. He stares up at me. 'No. Obviously sometimes you remind me of her because you're her sister, but that's rare. Mostly you're just Liza.'

My eyes mist over. He sighs and takes my drink from me, before pulling me to my feet and into his arms. He's warm and strong and I let him hold me, my throat swelling uncomfortably.

He holds me tighter. 'I'm so thankful to still have you and Rose.'

Does he mean as friends? God, I don't know what I want.

I place my hands on his shoulders and break our contact, turning my face away. He tucks my hair behind my ears, prompting me to meet his gaze again. He cups my face with his hands.

'What are you—' I start to say, but he reaches up and touches his thumb to my mouth, silencing me. Then he replaces his thumb with his lips.

It is the sweetest kiss. It lasts no more than a couple of seconds and is incredibly gentle and tentative, but my knees feel weak as he breaks away.

'You shouldn't have done that,' I whisper, clutching his arms to keep steady. My heart is racing.

'Why not?'

I am intensely aware of the double bed directly behind him. It would be so easy to push him backwards and get totally and deliriously caught up in this moment.

But I can't do that.

Oh, but then he kisses me again.

The shivers rocketing up and down my spine are making my legs continue on their course towards jellification.

'Angus,' I whisper as he presses his lips to my jaw. 'We can't.'

'Yes, we can,' he murmurs gently.

Using great willpower, I put my hands on his chest and slowly push him away.

I'm startled to see his eyes flash with anger.

'You once told me that if I didn't want Phoebe, I couldn't have any of you,' he says in a low, dangerous voice.

I nod nervously. 'Maybe that still stands.'

'Bullshit!' he erupts, making me jump. I begin to pace the small area to the side of the bed as he rants. 'That is bullshit and you know it! She's not coming back. You and I are here. And we should be together. It would be about fucking time.'

The look in his eyes takes my breath away. He's so hot when he's riled up.

My willpower gives way and I take a step towards him. He sees me coming and closes the gap.

Where earlier it was tentative, now it is so fiery with passion that we could set light to the furniture.

He holds my face and kisses me with a frenzied urgency. I feel dizzy, but I attack him with just as much fervour. I don't want to stop. I can't stop. Stopping is futile and pointless. I need him. I want him, and damn it, I'm going to have him.

We pull each other down to the bed.

The morning comes and with it the guilt. The sense of déjà vu is extraordinary, but when I turn to see Angus sleeping peacefully beside me, I feel a sudden swell of determination. Last night was incredible. And I am hopelessly in love.

I press a gentle kiss to his shoulder and he stirs.

His beautiful eyes open and he looks momentarily confused. My heart skips a beat. Was he very drunk last night? Does he remember what happened? Does he know who I am? But then he smiles sleepily.

'Hello, trouble,' he whispers, putting all of my worries at

bay. He reaches over and places his hand on my cheek. 'Are you okay?'

'I think so,' I reply. 'Are you?'

He nods and slides his arm around me, pulling me against his bare chest. I sigh peacefully and snuggle into him, my palm flat against his stomach.

'Liza?' he asks after a moment.

'Yes?'

'Don't freak out later when you're alone. That killed me when we were eighteen.'

'I won't,' I promise, adjusting my position so I can look up at him. His eyes are full of trepidation.

'I love you,' I whisper, stroking my fingertips along his jaw.

His stressed expression melts away as he draws me up his body to kiss him. 'I love you, too,' he says against my lips.

But right then and there, I know that Michelle is right. I have to talk to Phoebe.

The air is damp with recent rainfall as I walk along the winding paths in the cemetery. A gust of wind blows the leaves on the trees, causing a cascade of raindrops to fall down on my head. I barely flinch.

I reach the gravestone and look down at the engraving.

Richard Thomson, beloved husband and father,
and Phoebe Thomson, beloved daughter and sister.
She was taken too soon from this earth.

I fall to my knees, the mud seeping up through the grass and soaking my skin.

'I'm sorry, Feebs, but I have to tell you something. I'm in love with Angus. I've loved him since the beginning.'

Tears spill out of my eyes as I speak and I can barely hold back my sobs.

'I'm so sorry. If you were here, this never would have happened. I've tried for so long to stay away from him, but I can't do it any more. I'm in such agony, missing you, and I feel like he's healing me. I hope you can accept it. I wouldn't expect you to be happy for me. I would give anything to have you back, and I know that would mean giving up Angus, but I feel incomplete without you. I love you so much. And I'm sorry. But I love him, too. And *he's* here. I hope you understand.'

I can't speak any more for the lump in my throat, but I stay there for a long time afterwards, with my hand on the gravestone and tears trekking down my cheeks.

Chapter 25

Phoebe

Guess what I did yesterday! I STOOD ON TOP OF MONT BLANC WITH DAD! We made it! We summited!

The scale of things up there was incredible. We weren't dwarfed by the mountains, we were midgetised by them. Microscopisized, even.

Mum used to accuse Dad of being selfish because she said he couldn't justify risking his life climbing when he had a wife and three young children at home.

But now I understand. When you're walking along a ridge, teetering on the brink between life and death, you've never felt so alive.

I can't believe this is my last page. Nor can I believe what I'm about to write. Deep breath: Dad has convinced me to go home with him. He's worried I'll lose perspective if I stay, and he's right. But I know it's going to kill me to say goodbye to Remy.

It's goodbye from me to you, too. What adventures I've had this year! It's been a blast.

So, au revoir.

Or, until we meet again…

Chapter 26

Rose

I'm in floods of tears as I close Phoebe's purple journal, my fingers trembling as I reattach the tiny padlock. That was her final entry, the last of her lovely, loping handwriting, and she's gone now, for good.

I've had her teenage diary in my possession for over a year since finding it in the loft on the same day that I uncovered Eliza's. But I never had any intention of reading Phoebe's – I had too much respect for her for that. I'm afraid the same couldn't be said for Eliza. My curiosity overruled any sense of right and wrong when it came to reading hers and no doubt she's still cross with me about it.

Back in May, when the anniversary of Phoebe's death was almost upon us, I went to bed feeling desperately sad. I wanted so much to feel close to her, to hear her voice again, so I dug out her old diary and I've been reading it on and off ever since.

I've tried to keep her alive by making it last for as long as possible, which goes against all of my instincts to devour it in one go, but now I've reached the end and it's like I've lost her all over again. It's so painful. I can't bear it.

I loved the way she wrote. I felt like I was right there with her as she had her 'proper pinch me moment', sitting on the balcony of her apartment in Argentière as she watched the sun set over the mountains. I lived through all of the climbs she did with Remy and their various adventures, like paragliding and daytrips to the ice grotto. Just a moment ago, I stood on top of Mont Blanc with her and Dad, after she'd finally persuaded him to visit her that summer. It was the last big climb they ever did together. And, of course, I also suffered her nightmares with her when she dreamed about Eliza kissing Angus, and Dad dying on a mountain. It all seems oddly prophetic.

I curl up into a ball on my bed and surrender to my emotions. Angus isn't around to hear me cry. He stayed at a hotel last night – he's writing a feature, apparently. I asked him outright if he was seeing someone, but he denied it.

I know he'll get another girlfriend eventually, but I will never get another sister. Despite what people think when they look at us, Phoebe was one of a kind. And she can't be replaced.

Sometimes I go back to the day Mum received the phone call, the one that told us we'd lost her. Eliza and I had been having a blazing row on the doorstep when the phone rang and Mum shouted out, 'IT'S PHOEBE!'

We automatically assumed that Phoebe was actually *on* the other end of the line and Eliza threatened to tell her everything about Angus, but then Mum let out the most agonising, inhuman sound, like her heart was being ripped from her chest. Eliza and I stared at each other in shock for only a split-second before racing inside. Mum was slumped on the floor in the kitchen, the phone clutched to her ear. I took the phone from her and the moment I discovered it was Josie, I knew.

'*Phoebe was caught in an avalanche*,' Josie managed to get out between sobs.

My triplet, one third of me, was gone forever.

'What's wrong?' Toby asks when I go into work. I did the best job I could with my concealer, but my eyes must still be red from crying.

'Nothing,' I mumble as his expression radiates concern. A moment later, my vision is obscured by tears.

'Hey,' he says gently, striding over to the front door. I hear him lock it.

'Don't, Toby, it's fine,' I protest. 'We can't open up late.' But he comes over and takes my arm, guiding me into the bakery.

'Tell me what's wrong,' he demands.

I crumble and a moment later his arms are around me, holding me as I cry.

'When you asked me if I was an identical triplet, I couldn't answer,' I say to him a little while later when I've calmed down enough to talk. We're sitting outside on the garden furniture from home. I painted the wall the weekend before last, but I haven't finished prepping the soil for the plants so we're still surrounded by plastic pots.

'It was the first time anyone had used the words "identical triplet" to me since Phoebe died,' I explain. 'And it shocked me when it occurred to me that I'm not sure if I technically am any more. Am I still a triplet, when one of the three of us is gone?' My voice sounds choked and I'm struggling to keep my tears under control.

'I don't know,' he replies quietly. 'Do you still feel like one?'

'Yes.' I nod.

'Then there's your answer.'

A sob escapes my mouth. He puts his arm around me and pulls me closer.

'Shhh,' he says soothingly, his warm breath tickling the top of my head. It feels as though our roles have been reversed. Now he's the adult, comforting the child. He's quite good at it, actually.

'You should go and open up,' I say eventually. 'The customers will be pounding down the door.'

'They can wait.'

'No, Toby, really, it's fine. Your dad wouldn't like it. Please go. I'll come back in shortly.'

'Okay.' He seems reluctant to leave, but leave he does.

I stay outside for another fifteen minutes, digging over the soil in the planter box to keep me busy and hoping the redness in my face will die down. There was a thunderstorm in the middle of the night and the ground is wet, so I make good progress.

When I'm feeling a bit more like myself, I head inside and wash my hands at the bakery sink before returning to the shop floor. Toby flashes me an encouraging smile as he finishes up with a customer. 'You okay?' he asks when they've gone.

There are still a couple of mums with babies drinking coffee in the small café area so we speak quietly.

'Yes. Thanks.'

'Mind if I pop outside for a fag?' he asks with a raised eyebrow.

'Go for it.'

He returns five minutes later.

'When are you going to put the plants in?' he asks.

'I planned to do it last weekend, but I was too zonked after our all-night baking session. Where are you going to go for your fag breaks when it's finished?' I ask pertinently.

'I don't know.' He shrugs. 'Maybe I'll quit. Smoking costs a packet. It's wiping me out.'

'Is that your only reason for stopping? Not the fact that it's incredibly bad for your health and makes your breath smell like sick?'

He looks a little put out.

'Sorry, that sounded worse than I meant it to.'

'Forget it,' he replies, staring at the blank space on the counter where the cupcakes used to be. His mum is due to come out of hospital tomorrow, but she won't be baking for a while.

'What are you doing tonight?' he asks suddenly, looking at me.

'Nothing, why?'

'Want to come to a gig in the city with me?'

'Er…'

'Have you already got plans?' he asks.

'No, but—'

'What? Something better to do on a Monday night? Come on, Rose, live a little. It'll do you good.'

'Wouldn't you rather go with someone your own age? One of your friends?' I ask.

'I don't have any friends my own age around here.'

'Neither do I,' I admit. 'Well, not any more. They've all moved away.'

He gives me a meaningful look.

'What about Vanessa?' I ask. 'She's young and beautiful.'

'Vanessa is dull,' he states.

'Fine,' I reply on a whim. 'I'll drive you there.'

'Jeez, Rose, you're not my mother.' He comes over and grasps my upper arms, giving me a little shake. 'Let's catch the Metro, have a few drinks. Let your hair down.' He glances at my bun and then back at my face.

'I think you'd get on better with my other sister,' I say sardonically.

I should have known the comment would come back to bite me. As soon as Toby and I are at the bar that night with drinks in our hands, he asks me about Eliza.

'We're not really talking to each other right now,' I explain, but of course, that utterance demands another explanation.

'We've got an hour before the band comes on,' he says. 'Spill.'

I take a deep breath and sigh loudly.

'I'm your only friend,' he reminds me, pretend seriously. 'Talk to me.'

I smirk at him. 'I do have one other friend in this city, you know. Angus, my flatmate. We've known each other since we were seventeen,' I explain.

'And he's *just* your flatmate?' He raises one eyebrow.

'Yeah.' I take a sip of my drink. 'I thought I was in love with him once, but he was with Phoebe. They were engaged to be married.'

'Whoa,' he says, his eyes widening.

'Before you start thinking I'm a horrible person, I should also tell you that Eliza fell for him, too, so it wasn't just me.'

'Christ, that's messed up.'

It's not the direction I was hoping this conversation would take, but I only belatedly realise my mistake.

I purse my lips. 'Yeah. You won't get any argument from us on that front,' I mutter.

'Did Phoebe know you both had the hots for him?'

I shake my head. 'I don't think so.'

He gives me a long, weighty stare.

'Eliza!' the big, burly man behind the bar suddenly exclaims. It doesn't take a genius to work out he's talking to me.

'I'm her sister,' I reply, used to this sort of thing happening, though it hasn't for a long while.

His jaw drops. 'You look just like each other.'

I shrug. 'We're identical...'

'Twins!' he finishes my sentence. 'I'm Joe,' he introduces himself.

'Rose,' I reply, bracing myself. Even Toby stiffened at the twins comment.

'You don't sing, do you? You two would look great up there.'

My expression is one of horror. 'No, I have no musical talent whatsoever.'

He shrugs, nonplussed. 'Well, maybe you could give your

sis one of these when you next see her. I've just had them mocked up.' He pulls out a photocopy of a flier from under the bar and hands it over. There's a picture of Eliza sitting on a stool, holding her guitar, mid-performance. She looks pensive. I feel a pinch as I stare at her image and then Toby distracts me by peering over my shoulder.

'Of course,' I tell Joe. He nods and goes off to serve another customer.

'Is she any good?' Toby asks me.

'You'd probably like her music.' I fold up the piece of paper, putting it into my bag. 'Can we go and find a table somewhere?' I want somewhere dark, somewhere private, where no one else is likely to mistake me for Eliza.

'Sure.' He picks up his drink and follows me because I'm already on my way.

My edginess melts away after my third vodka and cranberry, and when the band comes on – an indie-rock four-piece – I'm in a top mood. Toby went up to join the throng a few minutes ago, surprised that I wanted to stay seated. In fact, he looked at me like I had horns growing out of my head. I'm just worried about people mistaking me for Eliza, or Eliza herself lurking around somewhere. She's obviously a regular.

I catch a glimpse of Toby. He's wearing a dark T-shirt and jeans. I'm so used to seeing him in light-coloured clothing at the bakery, but black suits him. I feel a twinge of regret that I'm sitting here by myself, being boring. I'm out on the town at last – why aren't I making the most of it? What's the big deal if another person mistakes me?

I gulp down the last of my vodka and stand up. I'll start by going to the bar.

'Can I buy you a drink?' a man asks me within moments of me trying to flag down the bargirl. He's not bad looking. Kind of ordinary, but then so was Gerard and he managed to have two women on the go at the same time.

'Oh, it's fine, I'm getting two,' I reply.

'Have we met before?' he asks. 'You look kind of familiar.'

'I don't think so,' I say innocently.

'What's your name?' he asks.

'Rose.'

'That's a beautiful name,' he says. 'And you are a beautiful girl.'

I stifle a snort, but he doesn't seem to notice as he introduces himself. 'I'm Alan.'

A pair of hands land on my shoulders and I glance behind me to see Toby staring down at me with a slight frown. 'I couldn't see you at the table,' he says. 'I thought you'd gone.'

'Nah, just came to the bar. This is Adam,' I explain.

'Alan,' he corrects me, then: 'Sorry, mate, I didn't know she was with you.'

Alan makes himself scarce and I crack up laughing. 'Do I look younger than I am or do you look older?'

'Maybe a bit of both,' Toby says with wry amusement. 'You don't look twenty-eight.'

'Brilliant,' I reply with delight. 'You look older than twenty-one. You're *older than your years*,' I add wisely, trying to keep a straight face.

'You're pissed,' he points out the obvious, a smile tipping the corner of his lips.

He lifts his hand to get the bargirl's attention. She comes straight over.

'Can I get a glass of tap water?' he asks her. 'Large.'

'And I'll have a vodka and cranberry!' I chip in.

'And a beer,' he adds drily, passing me the water when it appears. 'Just drink it,' he says when I begin to protest.

'I'm supposed to be letting my hair down,' I say self-righteously. In fact, dammit, that's exactly what I'm going to do. I reach up and pull out the bobby pins, one by one, from my hair. It swings down into a ponytail. Nope. Don't want that. I tug out my hair tie and shake out my blonde locks.

Toby watches with a raised eyebrow, then gets his money out to pay the bargirl. 'Thanks.' He takes a sip of his beer and nods at the water. 'I don't want you to throw up on me later. I've got enough on my plate.'

I humph, but do as he asks, gulping it down in one go. I slam the empty glass back on the bar top.

'Come on, let's go and watch the band,' I say, hopping to my feet and heading towards the crowd with my vodka in hand.

Any cares I had about being recognised – or more likely, mistaken – have flown out of the window. I'm pissed as a newt and ready to enjoy myself!

'Urgh,' I say half an hour later when I'm hunched over a plant pot on the pavement.

'This would be easier if you hadn't let your hair down,' Toby muses acerbically, as he scoops back my hair into a makeshift ponytail.

'I don't think I'm going to be sick,' I tell him bravely, and he lets go of my hair as I straighten back up. I regard him with confusion. 'Did we eat?'

'No.' He half laughs.

'That was pretty stupid,' I state.

'Yeah. I guess. You want something?'

'Maybe we should.'

We set off down the street. 'How are you so sober?' I grumble.

'I'm not. I'm actually pretty drunk, just not in comparison to you.'

This gives me the giggles again.

'You don't get out much, do you?' he asks.

'No.' I fall silent. 'You're hanging out with a loser. Congratulations.'

'You're not a loser,' he says warmly, wrapping his arm around my shoulders and pressing a kiss to the top of my head. He's so tall. And really very good-looking. *Imagine what he's going to be like in a few years' time!*

Hot. As. Hell.

'Hey, how about a burger?' he asks, distracting me from my wayward thoughts.

We come to a stop outside a restaurant called *Roxy's*. The name sounds familiar, but I don't know why.

And then I see her. But of course. Mum told me that Eliza works here.

'No,' I say, backing away.

'Is that your sister?' Toby asks with amazement, following the line of my sight.

I come to a standstill on the pavement. I'm still staring at her. She's wearing a uniform: a red dress with a white apron, and her hair has been pulled up into a high ponytail. But despite the hairstyle she doesn't look like Phoebe. She looks too thin to be Phoebe. But she's still beautiful.

Even if I do say so myself.

I come to my senses, sobering up momentarily. Toby is still standing on the pavement, staring.

'You know, if you were a bit older, you'd be completely her type.'

I don't know why I just told him that.

'Really?' He raises one eyebrow, but doesn't stop looking at her. He seems fascinated.

I turn and walk away.

'Oi!' he calls, running after me. 'Where are you going?'

'Home. I think I need my bed more than food at this moment.'

'The Metro's this way.' He snatches my hand and tugs me to a stop.

In the same movement, I spin around to face him.

'I like you, Toby,' I find myself solemnly declaring. 'You're going to be a really good catch for someone one day.'

His dark eyes stare down at me. My stomach churns, but not from nausea. I suddenly feel very strange as I watch his eyebrows pull together. Then he breaks eye contact and stares over my head.

'Come on, Rose,' he says quietly. 'Let's get you home.'

Chapter 27

Eliza

'What are you doing here?' I ask with surprise when I finish my shift and come out of *Roxy's* to see Angus's Land Rover parked on double yellow lines. It's eleven thirty, which is later than usual for a Monday night.

'Can I give you a ride home?' he asks through the open window. He sounds on edge.

'Sure,' I reply hesitantly, wondering if something is wrong.

He looks stressed as he reaches across the passenger seat and opens the door for me. I go around to the other side of the car and climb in, glancing at him. 'Are you okay?'

'Yeah.' He nods and starts up the ignition, pulling away from the kerb. Nerves pulse through me when I realise that we haven't even kissed each other hello. Does he regret what happened between us? Is he going to be the one to end it this time?

When I left him this morning, I told him I was going to go to the graveyard. He didn't take the news well. His lips formed a dead-straight line and he could barely look at me.

'Is that really necessary?' he asked.

'I feel like I want to say something to her,' I told him.

'Like what?'

'I don't know, Angus, but it's nothing for you to be concerned about.'

He didn't seem convinced, but he had to get into work so we bade each other farewell and that was the last I've heard or seen of him all day.

I wasn't sure when we'd be able to hook up again. With my late-night shifts and his daytime ones, we're not going to cross over a whole lot. Unless he comes out late like this and risks Rose getting suspicious… We're going to have to tell her sooner or later. If we're still together.

'What are you thinking?' Angus asks.

'Nothing,' I reply.

'You just sighed. What were you sighing about?'

'Rose,' I reply quietly. 'And us.'

I swivel in my seat to face him, studying his side profile in the street lamps as we pass. From light to shade, orange to black.

'Do you have any regrets?' I ask in a small voice.

He glances at me and then flicks his indicator on, pulling up on the kerb.

'No,' he says firmly. He kisses me gently, but my lips part and I breathe in sharply, wanting more. 'Do you?' he whispers, hovering just millimetres from my mouth. He doesn't deepen the kiss like I'd like him to.

'No.'

We drive the rest of the way in silence and the atmosphere is charged. Last night, when we had sex, we'd been drinking. Tonight we are both stone-cold sober.

'Come up?' I ask uncertainly when we arrive at my apartment.

We walk side by side into the building. I press the button for the lift, and he conducts his usual examination of the graffiti in the lobby, the incongruous stains on the lino and the flickering fluorescent light over our heads.

A few minutes later, we're inside my apartment and I'm closing the door behind him.

'Michelle's staying at her boyfriend's tonight,' I say hesitantly.

He nods, taking my hands. We stand, staring at each other for a long moment. I still feel guilty. I can't help it. I just hope it doesn't eat me up.

I make the tiniest jerk of my head in the direction of my bedroom. He gives me the smallest nod in return.

We're both uneasy as we stand at the foot of my bed. I slide my arms around his waist, my hands skimming over the taut body underneath his T-shirt. He used to swim to keep fit. I'm guessing he still does.

He's so manly, so different to the boy I kissed almost a decade ago. And the way he was with me last night... That was very different from our heated fumblings as teenagers, too. But then I remember that the experience he has garnered over the years is down to Phoebe, and an unpleasant cold flush comes over me.

'Wait,' I whisper as his lips touch my jaw.

'What's wrong?'

'I can't— I'm thinking.'

The look on his face as he steps away from me is one of weary resignation. He knew this was going to happen.

'Come on,' he says quietly, taking my hand and walking towards the door.

'Where are we going?' I ask, confused.

'To the living room. We're just going to talk.'

'Really?' I pull a face as I hurry after him.

He tugs me down to one of the sofas, bringing me close so I'm nestled against his body with his arms around my waist. I can't see his face, but I can feel his chest vibrating as he speaks.

'Maybe we should slow this down,' he says gently. 'I don't want to screw it up.'

'But we've already had sex,' I say a touch indignantly, tensing under his fingers.

'I know. We were drunk.'

I blush, and now I'm glad he's not looking at me.

'But the next time we go to bed together,' he continues, 'I think we should be sober, and we both need to be totally okay about it.'

Now the urge to look at him is too great. 'Are *you* not okay with it?' I'm suddenly fearful as I twist round to look at him.

He pushes a strand of hair back from my face, staring at my forehead instead of my eyes.

'No, I can tell that you're not.' My voice wavers.

'Not completely,' he whispers, pulling me back against his chest. 'But I will be. I promise I will be.'

By now there's a lump in my throat. 'It *was* too soon.'

'Maybe. But it felt right. I don't want you to have any regrets.'

'I don't,' I reply. 'Do you?'

'Not at all,' he replies firmly, drawing me tighter. 'I've loved you for a long time.'

We both fall silent, but my mind is ticking over ten to the dozen.

Eventually I ask the question that's on my lips. 'How could you love Phoebe and me at the same time? I don't understand.'

'See, this is why we need to do this,' he says as I turn to face him again. I edge away slightly from him on the sofa. He meets my gaze apprehensively. 'There's so much we haven't talked about.'

I know he's right. This is going to eat away at me if we don't get it out in the open. Jealousy is an even more powerful emotion than guilt.

'Phoebe and I got serious so quickly,' he says, reaching over to take one of my hands. 'It's surprising, when I think about it in hindsight. Living next door to each other escalated things, but I was always curious about you.'

'Not Rose?'

'No.' He shakes his head. 'It was different with Rose. I liked her a lot, but I didn't feel drawn to her in the same way that I did with you.'

'You and I barely even spoke,' I say with a frown. 'Not until the evening that you threw that ball of paper into my room.'

He smiles.

'I kept the piece of paper,' I tell him.

'Did you?' he asks with surprise.

'I put it in my diary, the one that Rose stole,' I reveal bitterly. 'Did you know that she read about what we did in the tree house?'

His eyebrows jump up. 'No.'

'We had a massive row about it.'

'But surely you've forgiven her now, right?' he asks, perplexed. 'That can't be why you've fallen out for so long?'

'No,' I reply with a sigh. 'Rose and I have always rubbed each other up the wrong way. That argument was a long time coming. But now she just reminds me of Phoebe. It's easier for us both if we stay away from each other.'

Angus gives me a dejected smile and squeezes my hand. I slide closer and rest my face against his chest as his arm comes around me. We stay like that for a long time.

Chapter 28

Rose

Holy Mother of God, my *head*!

Urgh, and my stomach...

I make it to the toilet in time to heave into it. Why do people *do* this to themselves? How the hell am I supposed to go to work today?

I'm an hour late by the time I make it in, donning dark sunglasses.

'Afternoon,' Toby says wryly, handing over a loaf of bread to a customer as the door swings shut behind me. I open it back up for the customer.

'Don't you be smart with me, young man,' I berate him when we're alone. I walk around behind the counter.

'I'm back to being a young man, am I?' He hooks his thumbs through his belt loops and regards me with amusement. 'Last night I was *older than my years*,' he teases.

'Did I say that?'

'Don't you remember?' His brow furrows.

'I don't remember much,' I admit.

'Shame,' he says flippantly as he turns around to empty the coffee machine. 'It was a good night.'

I pop my sunglasses on top of my head. 'It *was* a good night, wasn't it?' I nod my head agreeably. The action makes it throb so I decide not to do that again.

'Coffee?' he asks.

'Yes, please.'

'How much water have you had to drink today?' He glances over his shoulder at me.

'Not much.'

'Go and down a glass.' He nods towards the bakery.

'Aah, I remember now,' I say good-naturedly. 'You *are* older than your years!'

He shrugs. 'My dad used to have a drinking problem.'

'Oh.' The humour leaves my face.

'It's not so bad any more,' he explains. 'But it still gets the better of him sometimes.'

'Sorry. That sucks.' I'm now lost for words.

'Water,' he says, nodding at the bakery door again.

I decide to just go ahead and follow his instructions.

Over the course of the morning, fragments of the night before start to slot into place. The first comes when I catch sight of the flier in my handbag. I remember the man behind the bar mistaking me for Eliza and me hiding away. Then I got chatted up by some random bloke, getting the giggles when he thought Toby and I were a couple. And I remember standing outside Eliza's restaurant and telling Toby that she'd have the hots for him if he were a bit older. And then, oh

God… What was it that I said? *That I liked him and thought he'd be a really good catch for someone one day!*

Argh!

A hot flush comes over me as I surreptitiously study him. I'm clearing a table in the café area and he's standing behind the counter staring straight ahead. He looks like he's in a bit of a daze, but then he glances over at me and I jolt to my senses, hastily getting on with clearing the table.

I acted very immaturely last night. For the rest of the day, I decide I'd better do my darndest to make up for it.

At four forty-five, our last customers have left. We close at five, but it's unlikely anyone else will come in this late in the day.

'You should go home and see your mother,' I say, adopting a tone of authority. She came out of the hospital today. 'I can lock up.'

'No, I want to get the starter ready and prep tonight's ingredients. Dad'll be knackered.'

'In that case, I'll help,' I say.

'It's alright. You look like you need your bed.'

I ignore him, heading into the bakery. A moment later, he joins me, looking confused at the sight of me putting on my apron instead of gathering my belongings.

'What are you doing?' he asks.

'I'll toast the nuts and seeds. You do the starter.'

He stares at me for a long moment. 'I said I can manage.'

'It's fine.' I flounce over to the cupboard and get out the stack of Tupperware containers containing the seeds, putting them on the counter and returning to retrieve the nuts.

I hear him sigh, but by the time I turn back around, he's already getting the jar of 'mother' out of the fridge.

'I don't know how your dad bakes on his own every night,' I say, as I sprinkle pumpkin seeds into one frying pan and poppy seeds into another. 'I think I'm still recovering from last Friday night.'

'Yeah, these next few weeks are going to be tough,' he agrees heavily.

'Maybe we should get someone else in,' I suggest. 'What are we going to do about the cakes?'

'I don't know, Rose,' he snaps, sounding frustrated.

I stare at him with surprise. 'Are you alright?' I ask with concern.

'Just… Quit mothering me. I don't need it.'

I feel a little sick as I stare back at him. 'I—'

'You're burning the seeds!' He storms over to the hob and I flinch and jump out of his way as he switches off the gas. I roughly drag my apron over my head and dump it on the worktop, grabbing my bag on my way out the door.

'ROSE!' I hear him call after me, but I'm already gone.

'Am I a mug?' I ask Angus later. I'm sitting half in, half out of the balcony door, staring at the rain. He's just walked in from work.

'What are you talking about?' he asks, coming over. He looks weary.

'Do you think I am?' I ask outright. 'Dad always used to say I was a giver, not a taker. But did he just mean that I'm a mug?'

'Of course not,' he scoffs. 'Being a good person doesn't make you an idiot.'

'Hmm,' I say, looking back out at the rain.

'What's this about?' he asks with a sigh, pulling up a chair and slumping into it. 'What's brought this on?'

'Just something Toby said,' I mumble. 'I've been trying to help him, but I don't know, maybe I'm overstepping the mark. I'm not sure he wants my help.'

'Well, that makes *him* the mug,' Angus says irately. 'You going into work like that in the middle of the night. I still can't believe you did that. He's bloody lucky and if he doesn't know it, then maybe I'll go in there and tell him myself.'

This makes me smile.

'You're not a mug, Rosie,' he says definitively. 'Now, what have you cooked for my dinner?'

I whack him on his chest and he laughs.

'Seriously, though,' he says, getting to his feet and going to the fridge. 'I don't think we have much in. Shall we get a takeaway?'

'Sure. I've got my appetite back now.'

'Where did it go?' he asks curiously as he opens the drawer for the takeaway menus and passes over a stack.

'I was pretty hungover earlier.'

'Were you? On a Tuesday?' He looks interested. 'What did you get up to last night?'

'Oh!' I remember what I was going to tell him. 'Toby and I went to see a band at this place called *Elvis & Joe's* in the Northern Quarter. Do you know it?'

'Er, yeah,' he calls after me as I march back into the hall to retrieve my bag.

I return with the flier. 'Look who has a gig there in a couple of weeks.'

238

I watch his face as I pass it over. Sure enough, his right eyebrow twitches.

Despite what I said on the doorstep that day we found out about Phoebe, I no longer believe that Angus and Eliza were having an affair. Eliza is nowhere near a good enough actress to pull off her reaction to my accusation, so whatever history they had I'm certain is behind them. I'll put Angus's eyebrow Tourette's down to that. 'The man there asked me to give this to her,' I continue. 'I'm seeing Mum in the next couple of days – she can pass it on.'

'Wow,' he says quietly, studying Eliza's image.

I swallow and fold my arms in front of my chest. 'I was wondering if maybe, I don't know, maybe we should go.'

He glances up at me quickly.

'Don't you miss her?' I ask.

'Do you?' he replies carefully.

I nod slightly.

The truth is, I've been missing Eliza for a while, now, ever since I read Phoebe's comments about us in her diary. I've always thought that Eliza considered me dull and boring. I thought that our personalities clashed and there was nothing we could do about it. I didn't really consider that I had been incredibly mean to her, growing up, and it had come from a place of jealousy and insecurity. It's hardly surprising that her resentment towards me built in return, and no doubt intensified in the years that I grew so close to Phoebe and Angus. If I put myself in her shoes, I know I would have found that unbearable.

I don't go into all of this with Angus, though. I'm still trying to come to terms with it myself.

'I do, a little,' I tell him. 'After the gig, Toby and I were going to get something to eat and we saw a restaurant called *Roxy's*. She was inside waitressing.'

'Oh, right,' he says.

'I'd forgotten that she'd left *Mario's*.'

Angus puts down the flier suddenly and gives me a beseeching look. 'Why don't you call her? Don't just turn up at her gig. You've got a lot to talk about.'

'I don't know,' I say. 'I just thought maybe it would be a small step in the right direction.' I've never been very supportive of Eliza and her music. I want to make up for it. 'Don't worry if you don't want to go.'

'It's not that,' he says. 'But God, Rose, this must be killing your mother. To lose one daughter and then have the others—'

'You don't have to spell it out, Angus, I know,' I say coldly. 'It's not like I want to be estranged from Eliza. Losing Phoebe was hard enough…' Tears spring up in my eyes and he pulls me towards him with a heavy sigh.

I bury my face against his collarbone, breathing in his familiar aftershave and trying to stave off my tears. Angus has always given the best hugs.

'It'll be okay,' he murmurs, rocking me comfortingly.

I pull away from him to dry my eyes and he lets me go. 'You're tired,' he says gently. 'You're probably experiencing an alcohol low. Pizza will help.'

I smile through my tears. 'Is that what you feel like?'

'You choose. Honestly. I'll eat anything.'

'Thai?' I ask timidly.

'Done.'

He takes the menu from me and goes over to the phone.

I forgot that the Thai restaurant doesn't deliver, so a short while later he heads down the street to pick it up. After ten minutes, there's a knock at the door. I'm assuming Angus has forgotten his keys so I don't think twice about opening it up. I start at the sight of Toby standing on the landing outside the apartment, his skateboard in one hand.

'What are you doing here?' I ask with surprise, glancing down the stairs. 'How did you get into the main lobby?'

'Some girl was coming out. She let me in.'

'They're not supposed to do that,' I say primly.

He gives me a long, poignant stare. 'Can I come in?' he prompts.

'Um, sure.' I step back to let him pass.

'I came to say sorry.' He looks shamefaced. 'I was out of order.'

'Forget about it,' I reply, leaning my back against the hall wall.

'I woke up this morning and decided to quit smoking,' he explains. 'I've been like a bear with a sore head all day.'

This news perks me up. 'Have you really quit?'

'Yeah.'

'Well done!' I enthuse.

He offers me a small smile, then reaches down and circles my wrist with his hand.

'I really am sorry,' he says quietly, stroking his middle finger across the top edge of my palm. My heart jumps as I stare back at him. And then the door opens and Angus bustles in.

'That place was chockers,' he starts, stopping in his tracks when he spies Toby, who drops my wrist like a hot potato.

'This is Toby,' I quickly pull myself together and make the introductions.

'Er, hi,' Angus says, giving him the once over.

Toby grabs the door before it closes. 'I've gotta go, but I'll see you tomorrow?'

I nod and he glances at Angus.

'See you later,' he says, then he turns and jogs down the steps.

Angus raises his eyebrows at me as he closes the door. 'So that was Toby, hey?'

'Yeah.' I wander back into the living room, feeling bizarrely jittery.

'He's not how I imagined him to look,' he comments, heading into the kitchen to unpack the takeaway.

'No?' I ask casually. I make it to the window in time to see Toby skating away along the pavement.

'I thought he'd be more of a skinny teenager,' Angus says.

I snort as a memory comes back to me. 'Last night I told him he was Eliza's type. She's too old for him, obviously, but she would have gone for him if she were a few years younger.'

Angus wrinkles up his nose. 'Really?' He sounds dubious.

'Yeah, you know how she was always into skater/indie boys.'

'I was one of them once,' he muses nostalgically. 'Until I had to get a proper job and tidy myself up.' He glances down at his attire – dark-grey cords and a light-blue designer T-shirt.

'You're still an indie boy, Gus,' I say fondly.

And you're still Eliza's type. But I don't say that part out loud.

Chapter 29

Eliza

'I want to tell her about us,' Angus says at the other end of the line.

It's Wednesday lunchtime and we're talking about Rose. He's just told me that she went into *Elvis & Joe's* on Monday night to watch a flipping gig! Since when does she go to gigs? What's more, Joe thought she was me and gave her a flier to pass on. Angus says he struggled to leave it sitting on the countertop instead of pocketing it to give to me himself.

'No,' I reply firmly, cradling the phone to my ear.

'Yes,' he insists. 'She's going to be really hurt when she finds out and she doesn't deserve that.'

'She'll just interfere! She'll think it's too soon. She won't understand.'

'Then we need to make her understand. I don't want to lie to her any more. It'll be worse in the long run. The longer this goes on behind her back, the harder it will be for her to forgive us.' He pauses. 'She misses you,' he says. 'She wants to see you.'

My heart clenches. 'Let's talk about it later,' I murmur.

After we end our conversation, I sit there for a moment, deep in thought, and a memory hits me out of the blue of Rose and me pretending to be each other's mirror images. We were at school and all of our classmates were laughing their heads off. I don't recall where Phoebe was – for once it was just Rose and me.

This recollection leads me straight into another one of us as teenagers shopping for dresses for an end-of-year disco. Phoebe and I had found outfits quickly and she'd gone off to meet up with Josie, but Rose was struggling. She was recovering from a bout of the flu and was feeling a bit weak, so I started to try on dresses for her, even twirling my hair up into a bun so I looked more like her. She laughed so much. But we found her a dress.

It's strange. When we were younger and Phoebe wasn't around, the gap between Rose and me would often close. But now that she's gone for good, it's wider than it's ever been.

Jolting out of my reverie, I check the time. I was supposed to go and see Mum this afternoon.

I grab my staff uniform. I'll have to head straight to work afterwards.

'You look well,' Mum says, once we're seated at her small kitchen table.

'So do you.' And she does. She's wearing smart trousers and a cream blouse and her dark blonde hair has been blow-dried into a tidy bob. She's even wearing a little make-up – something she hasn't bothered with for ages.

'New man on the scene?' she asks shrewdly.

'Nah.' I brush her off. 'You?' I raise one eyebrow.

'Well, Bert is pretty something when he's got his teeth in,' she jokes of her new next-door neighbour.

I smirk at her.

The cul de sac where Mum lives is only a short walk from the centre of Sale. Many of its current residents moved there to downsize and it has a retirement village feel about it with a strong, inclusive community. When I arrived, Mum was standing on the pavement, chatting away merrily to two of her new friends. As soon as they saw me, they wanted to know 'which one I was'.

I have to concede that maybe Rose was right all along. Mum's the perkiest I've seen her in a long time.

'Have you spoken to Rose recently?' she asks.

Gosh, that's even earlier than last time when she waited a good ten minutes before broaching the subject.

'No, Mum,' I reply wearily.

'I almost asked you both to come together. Make "sorting things out" part of the conditions.'

'Part of the conditions of what?' I ask with confusion.

She leans forward, her eyes bright. 'I plan to gift you and Rose some money from the house sale.'

I'm pretty taken aback.

'You shouldn't have to wait until I'm gone before you see your inheritance.' I flinch at this, but she continues, unabashed. 'I'd rather help while I'm still around to see you enjoy it. I haven't finished.' She holds up her palm to stave off my questions and then reaches across the table to take my hand, her expression one of motherly concern. I feel instinctively twitchy at the lecture I feel is coming.

'Darling, I'm worried about you. I've always been worried about you, what you're doing, where you're going, where you live,' she says with a barbed look. She was horrified the first time she saw the tower block and hasn't been back since. 'And who you're seeing,' she adds.

'I told you, I'm not seeing anyone.'

'Perhaps that's a good thing. I haven't exactly been enamoured with your choice of suitor over the years.'

I frown at her. 'Mum, you sound like something out of the Dark Ages.'

'I'm just being honest. You're twenty-eight, love.'

'You don't have to point any of this out.' I can feel myself getting worked up. 'I know I've been wandering through life a bit aimlessly, but things seem to finally be looking up.'

I tell her about my second gig at *Elvis & Joe's*.

'Does singing still make you happy?' she asks gently.

'Yes,' I reply with a small smile. 'I know I haven't hit the big time or anything, but I'm not ready to chuck in the towel, yet.'

Mum nods sympathetically, but doesn't let up. 'What about that horrid place you live?'

'It's handy for getting into work,' I say defensively. 'And anyway, it's all I can afford.'

'Not any more,' she says meaningfully. 'I don't like to think of you arriving home so late at night after your shifts. The thought of anything happening to you…' Her eyes well up with tears.

'Please don't cry,' I beg.

'You used to love catching the Metro into town from here,' she reminds me. 'If you moved nearby, I'd be able to see you more. I miss you, love. I like living here, but I miss you. We used to have such fun together. You made me feel younger.' She reaches for a tissue.

I reach for one, too. 'Rose used to think that I wore you out,' I state as we both sniff.

'Oh, you did. And you still do.' She casts her eyes to the ceiling. 'You always will, I suspect.'

I smile at her through my tears.

'You and Rose need to sort out your differences,' she implores. 'This can't go on any longer. You need to sort it out for all our sakes.' She pauses and takes a deep breath, and I sense that she's got something else to say – something she doesn't think I'm going to like. 'Perhaps I should have told you sooner, but Rose lives here in Sale.'

I nod.

'With Angus,' she adds on a release of breath.

My shoulders sag with relief. Is that all?

'I know,' I reply.

'Did she tell you?' she asks with astonishment.

'No, I heard about it on the grapevine.'

'And you don't mind?'

'No, Mum, it's fine.'

'I was worried you'd think she's stepping into Phoebe's shoes,' she says quietly.

As if I could accuse Rose of that, I think uncomfortably.

'But it was Judy's suggestion,' she continues. 'I was surprised, to be honest. I thought Angus might find it too hard…'

Her eyes well up again, but this time the tissue can't stop them from spilling over. I take her trembling hand and avert my gaze. It's the one thing I really, really struggle with, seeing Mum cry. I watched her go through hell after Dad's death. It almost did me in witnessing the worst of her grief after Phoebe died. I was more relieved than I let on when Rose left London and moved back home to Sale permanently. Finally I had someone else to share the burden. I'm not proud of it, but our blazing rows actually gave me an excuse to make a break for it.

'I don't think Angus looks at us and sees Feebs,' I find myself saying. 'He's always treated us as three very different people, just like you and Dad.'

I wish I could say the same for myself.

When I look at Rose, I *do* see Phoebe. When I look into the mirror, I see her, too. And it hurts, like shards of glass being stabbed through my heart.

So I try not to look in the mirror much.

And I also try not to look at Rose.

Chapter 30

Rose

'Are you still going to see your mum?' Toby asks towards the end of the day as he surveys the loaves of bread we have left. There are only three: a walnut and cranberry, a rye and caraway and a plain rustic white.

'That's the plan,' I reply, rubbing the back of my neck with my fingers.

Things were a bit weird between us when I came in this morning. After his visit to my home last night, I found it a little hard to look him in the eye. But over the course of the day we've settled into our usual banter.

'I'm knackered, though,' I add. 'I still haven't caught up on my sleep.'

'Come and sit down,' he urges, going over to the seated area and pulling out a chair.

I mosey over to him.

'Why are you so tired?' he asks, nodding pointedly at the

chair he's holding. I sit down, facing away from him. 'Were you up late last night with *Angus*?'

'What did you say his name like that for?' I jolt as his hands start to massage my shoulders. Wow, that feels amazing.

'He's the guy you and your sisters fell for, right?'

I freeze. 'Wait, how—?' I whip my head around to look up at him before remembering that I told him this on Monday night. 'Oh, that's right,' I say sardonically as I turn back around. 'Yeah, but we were just love-struck teenagers.' He doesn't comment and I begin to relax under his touch. 'Mmm. You are *really* good at this,' I say dreamily.

'So I've been told.'

'Who by?' My question comes out too quickly and I can hear the amusement in his voice as he replies.

'Just my mum.'

About half a minute passes while I try very hard to contain my curiosity, but I can't help myself. 'Have you had many girlfriends?'

'A few,' he says, working his thumbs in deeper.

'I could fall asleep here,' I murmur.

'I'll carry you to your mum's,' he jokes. 'You can take what's left of the bread, by the way. Your mum can share it with her friends.'

'Are you sure? Won't your parents want some?'

'No, Mum's supposed to cut down on carbs. We're in the wrong business,' he says drily.

'How is she?' I ask.

'She's okay. A health visitor is supposed to be dropping in this week. She won't leave the house to go to the weight loss clinic.'

'Is she agoraphobic? I mean, has she been diagnosed?'

'I'm not sure.'

'Did her symptoms start with panic attacks?' I ask.

'Maybe. I think she used to have them sometimes.'

'Do you know why? Was there something that happened, some reason that they started?'

'She was pretty cut up when my nan died. That was when I really started to notice her withdrawing from other people. But I think her first panic attack came after some wankers threw a brick through the bakery window.'

'That's awful!' I turn around to look at him. 'But there are things she can do that can help. I'll get some leaflets for her. There are self-help treatments she can do at home, and medication if nothing else helps, but the first step is just understanding what the condition is. Of course, the health visitors might already be advising her,' I say as I turn around again.

We fall silent. When he speaks, his tone is gentle.

'You were a good nurse, weren't you?'

People often said so, but his tone of voice implies that he doesn't require an answer from me. 'Maybe I'll go back to it one day, when I'm ready,' I say.

'Did you quit because of what happened to your sister?'

'Yeah,' I reply softly. He's hit the nail right on the head. 'Dealing with death and loss was too hard after that. I couldn't bear it.'

'I'm sorry,' he says, his hands resting on my shoulders.

'It's okay. Anyway, Mum needed me, too. It was a good time to come home.'

'She doesn't need you now, though.'

I glance over my shoulder at him. 'Are you trying to get rid of me?'

'Christ no, I'd be lost without you.'

He said I, not we.

I pat one of his hands and reach over to pull another chair out from the table. 'Well, you know I'm not going to be here for much longer.' I confessed quite early on that this was only a summer job.

He sighs and sits down beside me. 'I wish I could quit,' he says dejectedly, resting his elbows on the table and dropping his jaw into his palms.

'You can. You're an adult. You can do what you want.'

'How could I leave my dad with all of this to deal with?'

'He could employ someone else to help.'

'He wouldn't.'

'He employed me,' I point out. 'And the girl before me who couldn't cut the early mornings, and Vanessa. He might not like it, but he could get other people in, and who knows? Maybe your mum will be well enough one day to return to work herself.'

He's not cheered by this sentiment. 'I've been waiting for a long time for things to go back to the way they were when I was younger. They never will.'

'You don't know that.' I reach across and touch his forearm, pained by the emotion in his voice. 'Let me organise those leaflets. She could get better. Try to have faith. Around a third of people with agoraphobia eventually achieve a complete cure. Half see an improvement. Believe in her. Maybe she'll start to believe in herself.'

He takes a deep breath and exhales shakily. 'So where will you go?' he asks. 'When you leave here?'

'I'd like to go travelling,' I tell him wistfully. Reading about Phoebe's adventures has inspired me. I just need to save up enough money.

'Yeah? Where?'

'Europe, and Chamonix where Phoebe died.' I stare past him to the wall.

'What happened to her?' he asks softly.

'She went to Chamonix for her hen week, just before her wedding. She was caught in an avalanche.'

'Jesus.' He falls silent. 'Won't it be sad going to the place where she died?'

'I sort of hoped it might help. I thought I might feel closer to her somehow, following in her footsteps, seeing the things she wrote about in her diary.'

'Her diary?'

Damn. Walked right into that one.

'I found the one she kept when she was a teenager,' I confess. But he doesn't judge me, and I find myself telling him all about her visit to the grotto, the views from the top of Mont Blanc and her day to day life on the Aiguille du Midi. I sigh. 'Then again, I could just go and visit my uncle in Byron Bay.'

His eyes light up. 'I've always wanted go there. I wish flights to Australia weren't so expensive. Perhaps we should rob a bank and go together.'

The thought of this is oddly appealing.

'I'll walk with you for a bit,' Toby says a little later when we've locked up for the night. He drops his skateboard to the ground and pushes away from the pavement.

'I wish I had one of those,' I say. 'I always have to hurry to keep up with you.'

He raises one eyebrow at me. 'Can you skate?'

I crack up laughing. 'Are you joking? Look at me!'

I'm wearing ballet pumps and a white cardigan over a green and white summer dress with a hemline that floats around my knees.

'So?'

'Do I look like a skater girl to you? You honestly would get on so much better with Eliza,' I mutter.

'I can't imagine getting on better with anyone than I do with you.'

He says it so easily, but I realise with warm surprise that he's deadly serious.

'Have a go on my board if you like,' he says flippantly.

'Really?' My face breaks into a grin. The idea of me being able to ride a skateboard – hilarious! But also *really bloody cool*!

'Come through here.' He changes direction and heads off towards an alleyway.

'What, *now*?' I ask with alarm as I hurry after him.

'Just for a minute.' We arrive at a deserted space at the back of some shops and he kicks up the rear of his board, doing that spin thing between his fingers as he catches it.

'Now you're just showing off,' I say.

'You reckon?' There's a touch of sarcasm in his tone and I'm guessing that's the least of what he can do.

'Hop on,' he says, nodding at the board. It's plain and bashed at the edges with faded lime-green wheels.

I step on the end and emit a squeal as the front flies up.

He laughs under his breath and I jolt slightly as he places his hands on my hips to steady me. His touch is warm through the fabric of my dress. 'Take it easy. Put your foot here, and here.'

He kicks the board gently to demonstrate where he means and this time when I step on, I'm better balanced. I'd quite like his hands to stay where they were, though.

'Go on,' he prompts, so I push away from the ground and skate forward a few metres. 'Put your foot down on the tail to stop yourself,' he calls after me. I do what he says and almost fall off.

He chuckles as he lopes over.

'Do you ever skate on a ramp?' I ask, stepping back onto the board. I don't want to give up just yet. He stands facing me, and he's still taller than I am, even with the height of the apparatus I'm standing on.

'Sometimes.'

I edge my foot to the rear so the front tips up slightly, trying to get a bit of balance. 'Can you do that thing where they fly up at one end and spin around then zoom back down again?' I've seen that on TV and thought it was pretty cool.

He grins and shrugs. 'Yeah.'

'Really?' I am so impressed.

I could stay here for hours, but I remember I have somewhere to be.

'My mum's expecting me,' I say reluctantly.

He nods, skating ahead to the exit to the street. There's a small flight of stairs there and I watch in astonishment as he jumps up with his board and slides down on top of the handrail.

'Oi!' I hear someone shout at the bottom. 'No skateboarding!'

I run to catch up and see a policeman glaring at Toby as he kicks his board up and catches it. 'Sorry,' he apologises casually, then spins on his heels and walks backwards a couple of paces, his eyes steady on mine. 'See you tomorrow.'

'Okay. Bye.'

I don't know why I'm blushing as I turn and walk in the other direction.

'I wondered about making it part of the condition,' Mum says, eyeing me over the top of her teacup.

My jaw is on the floor. She's just broken the news about giving Eliza and me some money from the house sale. Now she wants us to kiss and make up.

I shake my head, coming to my senses. 'I agree with you that our fall-out has gone on for too long. I've already been thinking about calling her.'

Mum's whole face lights up with her smile. 'Really, love?'

'Yes.' I nod. 'Yes, and it has nothing to do with the money,' I add.

She takes a sip of her tea. 'I told her that you're living with Angus,' she says.

My face falls.

'But she already knew,' she adds.

'Really?' In that case, I'm surprised she hasn't come out of the woodwork to have a dig at me. 'Was she okay about it?'

'She seemed to be,' she replies. 'I don't know why we kept it from her in the first place, to be honest.'

'I didn't want her to think I was jumping the gun.'

She nods, understanding. My eyes are drawn to the photo frames on the bookshelves. There are pictures of Mum and Dad, and of Eliza, Phoebe and me. There are no photos of us on our own apart from individual school photographs at the age of five, but even these are side-by-side in a three-part hinged frame.

If Phoebe had married Gus, there would be a picture of them on their wedding day. The thought makes me want to cry. Will Eliza and I ever feature in a photo, just the two of us? I really shouldn't be thinking like this in front of Mum. I need to change the subject before I get upset so I say the first thing that comes to mind.

'I think Angus might be seeing someone.' I glance at Mum to see the pain cross her features and instantly regret opening my big mouth.

'I suppose it was bound to happen sooner or later,' she says quietly, placing her cup on the table. 'How do you feel about it?'

'Not that great,' I admit.

She nods perceptively. 'You've always had a soft spot for him.'

My face heats up and I'm about to splutter a denial, but she continues calmly.

'A mother knows these things. Do you still care about him in that way?'

I shake my head.

'Maybe just a little?' she pries.

'I don't know, Mum. That was a long time ago. I still care about him, of course. What about Eliza?' I ask, keen to move the conversation away from myself.

'What about her?'

'Do you think she has feelings for Angus?'

Her brow furrows. 'I'm not sure. Eliza is more difficult to read.'

So much for a mother knowing these things. I try not to take offence that I'm the predictable, transparent one.

'Well, it may not matter either way,' I say. 'Because like I said, I think he might have a new girlfriend.'

I leave Mum after a while so she can break bread – literally – with her friends. I want to spend the evening with Angus. I'm desperate to have a heart-to-heart with him and talk everything through. I hope he'll open up to me, but I also want to tell him that I intend to go to Chamonix. Maybe he'd like to come too.

I'll be going sooner rather than later, thanks to Mum. She approved of me using some of my inheritance to travel as long as I promise to do some serious soul-searching while I'm away. She'd like me to come back to England with a clear head and ideally get back to nursing. I'm still not sure, but maybe I'll feel better after some more time away from it.

Unfortunately, though, my plans for tonight amount to nothing because I return to the apartment to a message on the answerphone from Angus, saying he's going to be late.

I feel deflated as I slump onto the sofa and stare into space.

After a while, my thoughts drift to Toby. His dark-eyed stare. His lovely smile. He doesn't choose to show it very often, unless he's alone with me. There's certainly something about him. And he is very good on that skateboard. The memory of his move on the stair railings makes me feel a little flustered.

Fine, I'll admit it. I might have a bit of a crush on him. But he's only twenty-one! If Mum knew what I was thinking, she'd have a fit. Talk about unsuitable.

Too fidgety to sit there with my mind ticking over, I get up suddenly. I don't know where I'm going until I'm standing in the doorway of Angus's bedroom.

There's a window on the left that looks out onto a large cherry tree and a double bed backs up against the right-hand wall. Ahead of me is a bank of built-in wardrobes. In terms of furniture, it's minimal. In terms of mess, it's atrocious. *Why can't he put his clothes away?* I mutter inwardly, scooping up his T-shirts from the floor.

I bring one up to my nose to see if it needs a wash, thinking I'll put a load in, but all I can smell is his deodorant. My head spins as I breathe him in. I've always loved the way he smells.

I start to fold up the clean T-shirts and throw the dirty ones into a pile, then I go over to the wardrobes and open the double doors on the left, looking for somewhere to place his shirts.

But there is no space in this wardrobe for Angus's clothes. Instead the cavity is filled with boxes. I'm mystified. What's inside the boxes? And then I realise.

These are Phoebe's things.

It may surprise some people to hear it, but when we were children, I was the most accident prone of the three of us. Eliza was gawky and often clumsy, but when it came to heeding warnings, I was the one who would be most likely to disobey.

I was the one who'd touch the gas ring when I'd been told it was still hot.

I was the one who'd climb a ladder to see the view from the top of the apple tree.

I was the one who would come back downstairs at bedtime to eavesdrop on an argument between my parents.

I was the one who got burnt, who fractured bones, who tortured myself with fears of my parents getting a divorce.

I was the one who was ruled by my curiosity.

And now, *I* am sitting here surrounded by boxes containing the belongings of my lost sister. Clothes, make-up, jewellery, sunglasses, photo albums, an iPhone with the earphones still plugged in, pink and purple climbing rope with a knot still tied in it.

I can picture Phoebe practising her knots. Some of them were quite beautiful, her hands graceful as she threaded brightly coloured rope, crossing it this way and that.

'This is a clove hitch...'

'This is a figure of eight...'

'This is a bowline...'

'Watch me, Rose, I'll show you how to do it...'

She would leave bits of rope around the house. Mum was forever scooping them up and dropping them into her bedroom with a sigh, but Dad would watch her master one knot and then move on to teaching her another. I remember him saying that there were only three knots she really needed, but Phoebe was determined to learn them all. She loved impressing him.

We all wanted to stand out and be different, but Phoebe was the first of us to achieve that. She became the star of the show the moment she first scaled the climbing wall, with Dad proudly watching on. From that moment on, she shone the brightest, and she continued to do so right up until the day she died.

I pick up her perfume and spray some onto my wrist, bringing it up to my nose to inhale. She's all around me and it's almost too difficult to bear.

I miss her so much. I'd give anything to hear her voice again. I pull out the grey cashmere hoodie that's lying on the top of one box full of clothes and begin to cry as I shrug off my cardigan and pull it over my head, sliding my arms into the cosy-soft armholes. I hug the material to my chest, wanting to be engulfed by her. I search through the boxes for her favourite jeans and my heart jumps when I spy them. I'm still wearing my dress so I tuck the flimsy fabric into the waistband and go to the mirror, taking out my bobby pins as I go. My hair swings down into a high ponytail.

I stand for a long moment, staring at my sister. We look the same, except for our eyes. Where hers were bright and sparkling, mine are red and puffy. I slide down to the floor and sob my heart out, raising my wrist to my nose to inhale her perfume again. The lump in my throat is aching painfully, and it shows no signs of diminishing.

I reach into a box for one of the photo albums, but as I lift it out, I spy the navy and yellow notepad underneath.

My heart skips a beat.

I pick it up and skim through the pages and it's as I could hardly dare to hope: the dates tell me that this is Phoebe's most recent journal, the one she was writing when she died.

She's not gone. I can still hear her voice, if only I dare to read it.

I know full well that my curiosity will get the better of me.

Chapter 31

Eliza

'Sorry about that,' I say to Angus as I deliver his third cup of coffee of the evening.

My boss has been getting increasingly impatient with the amount of time I've been spending at this side of the room.

'Is your boyfriend going to sit there all night?' was his last grumble. We're not even busy. It's not like they need the table.

I asked Angus to come here so I could tell him about my meeting with Mum earlier. I had hoped my boss might let me leave early tonight – we had no reservations or big groups – but he's being a bit of an arse about it.

'Don't wait any longer for me,' I tell Angus downheartedly. 'I'll be here until ten thirty, eleven, I reckon.'

He shakes his head and offers me a small smile. 'I'm happy.'

'Eliza!' That's my boss again. I barely conceal my irritation as I turn away and head back over to him.

'Take Table 9's coffee order and then you can go.'

'Really?' I ask with delight.

'Quick before I change my mind.'

After the awkwardness of Monday night, Angus and I don't go back to my apartment and neither, of course, do we go back to his.

'I can't believe I haven't even seen where you live, yet,' I complain as we slide into a booth seat in a nearby pub.

He doesn't reply and the message is clear. Until Rose and I sort out our differences, I'm not going to.

It's an added incentive, I have to admit, but I'm still in no rush to come clean to my sister about Angus and face her wrath.

He wraps his arm around me and pulls me close so the whole right-hand side of my body is flush to his left. I drape my arm across his stomach and rest my face against his chest. It feels intimate, being here like this with him, never mind that we're in public. I tilt my face up and press a kiss to his neck. He holds me tighter in turn.

I wonder if he will ever feel like he's mine. Completely mine. How long will it take? Years, certainly. He was Phoebe's for almost a decade. How long before I can wipe clean the memory of the two of them together?

As soon as the thought occurs to me, I feel poisonous. And then I realise that I'm kidding myself, anyway. I'll never be able to forget that he should be with her.

Will it ever stop hurting, though?

'What are you thinking?' Angus asks quietly, with that uncanny knack of his.

'Do you still cry about her?' I don't know why, but this is the question that spills from my lips and I feel his flat stomach contract under my palm as a result.

'Sometimes,' he admits.

'Do you feel guilty being with me?'

'A little.' Again with honesty.

I break our contact, edging away from him.

'Don't go,' he says sadly.

The side of my body feels cold, where before it was warm.

'She would hate this,' I say, my voice wavering.

He shakes his head. 'I disagree. I think she'd want us to be happy.'

'Come on! She would *hate* us being together,' I say fervently.

'Liza, please don't,' he begs, reaching for my hand.

I let him take it, but it's limp.

My head is spinning with questions. I know the answers will drive me crazy and will only drum up more questions, but I need to ask them nonetheless.

'How many children did you want to have?'

Angus stares at me with dismay and, after a moment, his beautiful eyes fill with tears.

'She always wanted two when we were younger,' I tell him, not waiting any longer for his reply. 'A boy first and then a girl, three years later. Is that what she told you?'

He averts his gaze and nods.

I continue. 'She didn't want three. She wanted the boy to get her full attention and then she'd have a baby girl around the time her son went to nursery, so the new baby would have her at least some of the time. She had it all mapped out.'

To my surprise, he smiles slightly. 'She did,' he agrees, brushing away a tear. 'But you can't plan that sort of stuff.'

'No.' I nod, returning his shaky smile. 'You could have ended up with triplets, for all she knew.'

'Or two sets of twins.'

I laugh. 'When were you going to start trying for a baby?'

His smile drops from his face.

'Straight away,' I answer for him, sensing the truth.

He nods once and I feel a wave of nausea.

'Was that why she agreed to move back here? She was going to leave her job soon anyway?' I knew she wanted to write a book, so getting pregnant would have fallen in nicely with those plans.

He nods again. I let go of his hand.

'Why are you doing this to us?' he asks gravely.

'I can't help it,' I whisper. 'I need to know.'

'It's going to consume you.'

'But I need to know,' I reiterate. 'I need to know what your plans were, where you'd be. If we hadn't lost her, she could be expecting your son right now.'

'Stop it,' he begs.

I fall silent, but it's a momentary respite, because 'They' by Jem starts to play over the pub's sound system.

'Phoebe loved this song. She played this album relentlessly the year she met you.' My tone takes on a flippant edge.

'I remember,' he says, staring ahead in a daze.

'She used to be into dreamy, girlie stuff. Who did she like towards the end?'

'Mumford and Sons,' he replies dully. 'She played their second album on repeat.'

'I didn't even know she liked their first album,' I say. Phoebe and I had different taste in music. 'I really didn't know her that well, did I?'

'She still liked dreamy, girlie stuff, too,' he says.

But I'm not even listening. 'We'd grown apart over the years.'

He looks absolutely miserable as he hunches over the table and wraps his hands around his pint. 'I'm sorry,' he says.

'Yes, it *was* because of you,' I reply. 'And I was going to leave Manchester because of you, too.'

He doesn't even ask me to stop. He knows that I won't.

'If I could choose between having Phoebe here or being with you, I would choose Phoebe.'

'I know that!' Now he sounds angry as he stares at me, his eyes flashing. 'But for fuck's sake,' he hisses, 'she's not here. So why are you ruining this for us? You think that I wouldn't have found someone else eventually?'

I gawp at him, but he's not done.

'My life isn't over because Phoebe's gone. And neither is yours. I don't for a minute think that you wouldn't have gone off with some other guy sooner or later. And yeah, maybe you wouldn't have had this guilt with him, but if you think you could be happier with someone else, then what the hell are you doing here with me?'

It's a moment before I can speak. 'But isn't your guilt worse because you're with me rather than someone who never knew Phoebe?'

'No,' he snaps. 'Not really.' He shoves his hair back, still angry and frustrated. 'Most people want to know about their partner's past. And any girl I went out with might have been upset to hear I'd be married right now if my fiancée hadn't been killed doing Christ knows what up a mountain with some other guy!'

A cold flush comes over me. 'What are you talking about?' I ask.

'Phoebe!' he exclaims, not even bothering to lower his voice any more. 'What was she doing going rock climbing with someone who she used to be in love with?'

'Who?' I don't understand.

'Remy!'

'Phoebe was up the mountain with Remy? The same Remy from when she was eighteen?'

'Yes.' He looks anguished.

'I had no idea she was still in touch with him.'

'She wasn't.' He looks downcast. 'She bumped into him the night before she died and decided to go up the mountain on a whim. She hadn't climbed in years! Why would she do that?' He shakes his head, bewildered. 'She obviously still had feelings for him.'

'God,' I murmur.

'Was she having doubts?' I can see how confused he is. 'I'm sorry. I shouldn't be talking to you about this.' He shakes his head again, but it doesn't hurt as much as it should, witnessing his anguish over my sister. It's just as well, because he hasn't finished. 'I wanted to tell Rose about us tonight. I was going to convince you it was the right thing to do. But now I don't know. If you and I can't...'

My blood runs cold and his eyes well up again as he continues.

'Well, what would be the point of upsetting everyone for nothing?'

Chapter 32

Rose

'ROSE.'

Angus's voice rouses me from sleep and I'm disoriented as I come to.

'What the hell have you been doing?' His face is white with rage.

I realise with horror that I've fallen asleep on my bed, in amongst some of Phoebe's clothes. In fact, I'm still wearing one of her favourite going-out outfits: a navy shift dress and black high heels.

'I wanted to feel closer to her,' I whimper, getting down from the bed. His eyes rake over me from head to toe and his mouth drops open.

'Have you been playing dress up?' he asks with disbelief, backing out of the room.

'Gus, I'm sorry!' I call after him, stumbling in the heels.

I chase after him as he storms into his bedroom where everything is exactly as I left it. Jesus.

'I'm really sorry,' I say as he swoops down and scoops up a bundle of clothes.

'Get her things!' He points out of the door in the direction of my bedroom. I've never seen him so angry.

'I'll do it,' I start to say. 'I'll tidy up. Just go into the living room and wait.'

'Get them now!' he bellows at me.

I run out of his room and grab Phoebe's clothes from my bed, hurrying back in time to see him roughly shoving her possessions into the boxes.

'Gus, please,' I beg. 'I'll fold them up again.'

He storms over to me and I flinch as he snatches the items from my arms, turning to stuff them into the nearest box. He yelps suddenly, and I freeze. I tentatively step forward and place my hand on his back, and then he loses it completely.

'I'm so sorry,' I murmur. We're both sitting on the sofa in the living room, nursing cups of tea, but the last hour has been hell.

I've never seen Angus like that before. He'd already moved to this apartment in Manchester when Phoebe died and I was still in London, so I wasn't on-hand to witness his immediate grief. Now he is utterly distraught and he hasn't wanted me to touch him so I haven't known what to do with myself. I've had to watch while he's sobbed his heart out like a baby, all the while keeping me at bay.

He's no longer crying and he accepted my offer of tea, but asked me to get changed back into my own clothes first.

'I shouldn't have gone into your room,' I say.

'No, you shouldn't have,' he agrees in a low voice, blowing on the hot liquid in his cup.

'I'm so sorry,' I say again, totally ashamed. 'I'll never go in there again,' I find myself vowing. 'I just wanted to tidy it.'

'You don't have to do that, Rose,' he says, a little exasperated now.

'I was just trying to help.'

'I know, but please don't.'

My face heats up. There I go again, dishing out help where it's not wanted.

'What time is it?' I ask, stifling a yawn.

He checks his watch. 'One o'clock.'

'We're going to be knackered in the morning. Where were you tonight?' I ask.

He looks uncomfortable and doesn't reply instantly. Is this the time for our heart-to-heart? No. I'm not sure either of us can stomach it.

'Come on, then, we'd better get to sleep,' I say.

He nods, standing up.

'Hug?' I ask cautiously.

He opens up his arms in response. I step forward and they close around me, washing my worries away. My heart constricts as I rest my cheek against his chest. I feel so bad for hurting him. I breathe in deeply, trying to feel better again, but the scent I pick up is not from his usual deodorant. I go rigid and then step backwards, breaking our contact.

'What is it?' He cocks his head at the look on my face.

'Nothing,' I say. 'I'll see you in the morning. Goodnight.'

'Night,' he calls after me as I walk into my room, shutting the door and pressing my back against it.

I know who he's been with tonight. And I feel like I'm going to throw up.

I wait until Angus has left for work the following morning before venturing out of my room. I'm going to be late, but I'm handing in my notice anyway. The sooner I get out of this town, the better.

I can't believe that Angus has been seeing Eliza. How could they betray me like this? How could they betray Phoebe? Her grave has barely even settled and they're hopping into bed with one another.

Of everything Eliza has ever done, this is the worst.

A little voice inside my head reasons that whatever is going on between Angus and Eliza has nothing to do with me. But I shut it back down. It feels like a betrayal. So it is a betrayal.

I'm not even upset about it. I'm angry.

'Where have you been?' Toby demands to know when I flounce into work forty-five minutes late.

'I overslept,' I reply, barely cracking a smile at the customer who walked in the door behind me.

He looks put out at the lack of remorse in my voice, but doesn't pull me up on it while there are people around.

He corners me later when the lunchtime rush is over.

'Spill,' he says.

'Angus and Eliza are having an affair,' I hiss furiously, wiping down a table.

He looks stumped. 'Are they with other people?'

'No! They're just together! Together!'

'Is that technically an affair?'

I straighten up and glare at him. 'Phoebe only died a year ago.'

He shakes his head, perplexed, and I feel a wave of nausea because he doesn't understand.

'I'm handing in my notice,' I say flatly, reaching down to pick up a stack of plates.

His face falls as I turn towards the bakery.

'My mum is giving me some money,' I say over my shoulder. 'I want to go travelling and I want to go as soon as possible.'

The door swings shut behind him. He's followed me in here, but he's speechless.

'I'm sorry,' I say. 'I don't want to let you down. I'll work up until the end of the month so you'll have time to find someone else.'

His stare hardens. 'Whatever you want,' he mutters, backing out of the bakery.

He barely looks at me for the rest of the day.

I don't want to go home to Angus. I don't want to see his face. So I tell Toby I'll lock up and then head out the back.

I'm wrist-deep in dirt, planting orangey-red crocosmias when Gavin appears. I'm so lost in my thoughts that I nearly jump out of my skin when the back door bursts open.

'Jesus Christ!' he erupts. 'It's you! I thought it was a burglar scratching around out here.'

'Sorry, I wanted to finish the garden.'

'This going to be your legacy, eh?' he says drily. 'Toby told me you're leaving us.'

'Yeah, I'm afraid so.' I turn away from him and reach for another plant.

'We'll be sorry to see you go,' he says. 'Him especially.'

'He'll be alright.'

I'm alarmed when Gavin comes outside and perches on the edge of the planter box. I don't want company.

'I think you underestimate yourself,' he says. 'He needs you more than you realise.'

'Look, I can't be his mother! He already has one!'

Gavin's face turns puce and adrenalin makes my pulse race with the knowledge that I've overstepped the mark. But his colour fades back to normal almost instantly and he speaks before I can.

'If that's how you see it, there's nothing I can say to change your mind.' He gets to his feet. 'I'll stick a notice up in the window this evening, advertising for a replacement. You can leave as soon as we have one.'

'I'm sorry,' I blurt as he turns to go back inside.

'You've got nothing to be sorry for, Rose. I'm glad we had you for as long as we did.'

Then why do I feel so goddamn awful?

I go home soon afterwards, and I find myself hoping that Angus is out, even if that means he's with Eliza. Unfortunately, I hear the telly on as I come through the door.

'Hey,' he calls over his shoulder from his position on the living-room sofa. 'Where have you been? There's some pasta on the hob if you want to warm it up.'

'I'm not hungry,' I reply, opening the door to my bedroom.

'Rose?' he calls after me, confused. 'Are you okay?'

'I'm just tired. I'm going to go straight to bed.' I close my bedroom door behind me and lock it, without waiting for his response. Then I sit on the bed, reaching under the covers and pulling out the navy and yellow journal belonging to my sister.

Of course I still have it.

I may have let Angus take back Phoebe's clothes last night, but he wasn't getting this.

There's no padlock. Phoebe trusted Angus and there was no need to try to keep him out. The same can't be said for me.

I kick off my shoes and lie back on my pillows, opening it up to the first page.

Another year, another diary! she writes, and I can almost hear her bubbly voice speaking aloud to me.

It's going to be a crazy twelve months! Marriage, moving back to Manchester and who knows what else?

My eyes mist over and I smile through my tears. She's not gone after all. She's still here with me.

Chapter 33

Eliza

'Which one is it, Eliza or Rose?' Joe asks when I turn up at the bar on Friday at lunchtime.

'Eliza,' I reply with a smile.

'Did your sis give you the mock-up?' he asks.

'I haven't seen her yet,' I tell him.

'Never mind. I went ahead and got them printed.' He reaches under the bar and hands over a small stack of fliers. 'You can circulate them to your friends.'

'Great, thank you! Hopefully my boss will let me stick some up at *Roxy's* again.'

'Perfect. Now, what can I do for you? Drink?'

'Sure. Just water, please. I've got to get to work soon.'

I feel nervous as I watch him get a bottle of sparkling water out of the fridge. By the time he's turned around again, I've psyched myself up enough to ask my question.

'Joe?'

'Hmm?' He raises one eyebrow.

'Do you think there's any chance you might invite some of your record industry acquaintances to my next gig?'

'Aah.' He gives me a knowing look.

I wasn't planning on asking him for help until we'd got to know each other better, but then I thought, sod it. I can't keep putting things off. I just have to bite the bullet and go for it. Plus I need something to take my mind off Angus. We haven't spoken since Wednesday night.

'Well, I can't promise anything, but sure, I can ask a couple of old friends to come along. Don't get your hopes up, though, love. It's not easy to break in these days.'

'I know, and I won't,' I reply eagerly. 'Thank you!'

I walk out of there with a spring in my step. Next stop: Rose. I haven't given up on Angus and me, but there are things I need to sort out first.

The bakery where my sister works is in Sale town centre. Angus told me about it, but I wasn't expecting it to look *this* nice. I push open the door and get my second pleasant surprise at the sight of the hottie behind the counter.

'Hello,' I say, my eyes widening.

He frowns at me. Not the reaction I was expecting.

'You're not Rose,' he says.

'I'm Eliza. Is she here?' I ask.

'She's just nipped out. Does she know you're coming?'

'Nope.' I smile at him. 'Can I grab a cappuccino? I'll wait for her.'

'Take a seat.'

He's not very friendly, is he?

It's quite late in the day so there's no one sitting at the tables

276

in the rear. It's a good set-up, I muse as I wander back there, but I don't imagine there's much scope for tips. I wonder how Rose gets by. But then I doubt Angus charges her much in rent.

After a few moments, the guy comes over. It dawns on me who he might be.

'Are you Toby?' I ask.

'Yep,' he confirms, placing my coffee cup on the table.

Aha! Now I understand why Rose wanted to hang out with him after hours. But hold on, didn't Angus say he was practically a teenager?

The door opens and we're both distracted by the sight of Rose bustling in, struggling to carry what looks like a heavy bag of soil. This is getting curiouser and curiouser.

She halts in her tracks, her eyes darting between Toby and me.

'What are you doing here?' she splutters, her grip on the bag slipping. Toby rushes forward and takes it from her.

'She came in looking for you,' I hear him say and they seem to exchange a meaningful glance.

I have a feeling he knows more about me than I'm comfortable with.

'I'll put this out the back.' He heaves the enormous bag over his shoulder, much like I imagine he would a sack of flour. He doesn't look at me again as he goes through the door behind the counter.

Rose dusts her hands off and hesitantly approaches, but after a couple of steps, her chin juts out and she holds her head higher.

I think Angus might've read this wrong. She doesn't look to me like someone who wants bygones to be bygones.

'What do you want?' she asks.

'I wanted to see you,' I reply.

'Why?'

'Bloody hell, Rose, don't you think we need to sort this out, for Mum's sake if not our own?'

'I thought I wanted to see you, too, but your timing sucks.'

I'm baffled. 'What do you mean?'

'I know about you and Angus.'

My stomach is instantly overcome with nausea.

'Did he tell you?' I ask.

'Did he fuck,' she snaps and I balk because Rose rarely swears.

'Hey.'

We both start at the sound of Toby's voice. He pushes the door behind the counter open again and jerks his head towards it. Okay, so I agree that we shouldn't be having this conversation in a public place, even if it is currently deserted.

'Come with me,' Rose mutters, leading me past Toby and out through the bakery to a back door. A moment later we're standing in a small courtyard, enclosed by a high brick wall, the back face of which has been painted a vibrant mauve. It's the exact same shade as the colour of our rear garden wall at home, but this thought distracts me for only a second.

'How did you find out?' I ask as Rose closes the door behind us.

She gives me a look of disgust. 'I could smell your perfume on him when he hugged me the night before last.'

My head spins. 'Does he know you know?'

'No.' She shakes her head. 'What you get up to is your own

dirty business. I'll be gone soon and the two of you can shack up and shag each other to death, for all I care.'

'Not likely at this rate,' I say unhappily. 'Listen, we were going to tell you. He wanted to tell you on Wednesday night—'

'How long has it been going on?' she interrupts.

'God, only a few days.'

Now it's her turn to balk. 'Days?'

'Since Sunday.' I feel suddenly very deflated. 'You thought we'd been together longer.'

She nods.

'I bumped into him around the same time as you moved in with him.'

She looks mildly shifty. 'You knew about that.'

'Yeah.' I nod ruefully.

She sighs. 'I thought you'd be angry.'

'I was,' I admit before waving her away. That's not the most important issue at hand here. 'Listen, I didn't tell you about Angus because I knew you'd say it was too soon. And it *was* too soon.' My voice trembles. 'I haven't been able to stop thinking about Phoebe and how upset she'd be. It will probably always be too soon, for you and for us. I don't know what's going to happen, but Angus and I didn't leave each other on good terms on Wednesday night. We might be over before we've even started.'

Rose takes a deep breath and lets out a long sigh. I'm not sure if it's with relief.

'I don't even want to be in the same room with him at the moment,' she murmurs.

I close my eyes briefly in resignation. 'I'm sorry we hurt you.'

She doesn't speak. This is not an easy conversation to have, but I need to be honest with her.

'What you read about in my diary,' I start. 'That night with Angus in the tree house was the beginning and also the end. It was the first time we'd ever kissed. Sunday night just gone was the second. He was never unfaithful to Phoebe. They were on a break ten years ago and he wanted it to be permanent. I pretty much pushed them back together.' I swallow. 'Angus loved Phoebe, and he would have married her and they would have been very happy together. But I knew he had feelings for me, too, and it hurt too much to watch him move forward with Feebs. I missed you both badly when you were living in London together. Yes, you too,' I say when I see the look on her face. 'But I couldn't be around Phoebe and Angus. I still loved him and no other guy ever stood a chance while he was in the picture. I know you cared for him, too,' I say carefully. 'I know you still do. But you never loved him, Rose.'

'How would you know how I felt?' she snaps.

But I continue, and I'm not trying to hurt her, it just needs to be said. 'And he has never loved you, either. Not the way he loved – *loves* – me.'

Her eyes well up with tears. 'Well, I hope it all works out for you both, then,' she says.

I'm not at all convinced she means it.

Chapter 34

Rose

'Are you okay?'

I'm still standing in the courtyard, staring at the space recently vacated by Eliza.

I turn to look at Toby. 'Yeah. I'll be back in shortly,' I reply.

'I've locked up,' he tells me. 'You want to talk about it?'

'No. I'm still trying to get my head around it myself.'

He nods.

'She and Angus really seem to love each other,' I find myself blurting, despite what I've just said about not wanting to talk. 'I used to believe I loved him too, but Eliza thinks what I felt wasn't even on the same page, let alone the same book.'

'She doesn't know how you felt.'

'No, she's right. I don't think I've ever really loved anyone. I'm twenty-eight and I've never been in love. How sad is that?'

He sits down on the wrought-iron bench seat and stares up at me with those dark eyes of his. He pats the space beside him.

I go and sit down.

'Why does it bother you so much?' he asks. 'You've still got the rest of your life ahead of you.'

'Phoebe didn't,' I point out sadly. 'But by the time she'd died, she'd already been in love twice.' With Angus and Remy. 'I always used to think that Eliza went after men who were bad for her, but her heart was with Angus all along, so she had a reason for doing that. The more I think about it, the more I think that maybe I'm the one with the problem.'

He doesn't say anything for ages and I sit there, my mind ticking over.

'If you sort things out with Eliza, will you still leave?' he asks eventually.

'Yes. I want to go to Chamonix and around Europe generally, maybe even Australia. I never took a year out between school and university so I think it would do me good. And Mum likes the idea of me seeing the world. She's healthy and relatively happy right now. If I leave it too long, I might not feel able to go.'

He leans forwards, resting his elbows on his knees.

'Can I meet your mum before I go?' I ask tentatively.

He swallows, his Adam's apple bobbing up and down. 'What's the point?'

'I will come back eventually, you know,' I say gently. 'And we can keep in touch, right? We can still be friends?'

He turns and stares at me directly. As the seconds

tick by and he doesn't speak, butterflies take over my stomach.

He shouldn't be looking at me like this. I'm too old for him.

'Toby?' I ask warily. 'Friends?'

He abruptly averts his gaze and gets to his feet. 'Yeah, of course,' he says.

I'm still avoiding Angus so I stay on at *Jennifer's* again that night and Gavin and I cross paths once more.

'Working late?' he asks with surprise as I wash my hands at the bakery sink.

'I wanted to finish off the outdoor space before the weekend. It's done now,' I add.

'Let's have a look, then.'

I lead the way outside and he stands and stares at the sight before him. As well as the wall, I've painted some of the old crates that I used to carry the pot plants. They're now a dark blue and lined with heavy-duty black polythene, acting as higgledy-piggledy plant boxes. I've taken out a few of the paving stones along the back wall to create a small garden bed and filled the space with sizzling orangey-red crocosmias, burnt-orange helianthemums and flaming red dahlias. The exotic colours seem to smoulder in the late afternoon sun and are set off beautifully against the painted wall. I've filled the planter box with aromatic herbs like sage, rosemary, thyme and mint. The duck-egg blue outdoor furniture from home complements the colour scheme.

'Just gorgeous, Rose,' Gavin says, shaking his head with amazement. 'Jenny would love it.'

This is the first time he's mentioned his wife, so I'm honoured to hear it.

'Make sure you give me your receipts so I can reimburse you,' he adds.

'No,' I tell him. 'Most of the plants were free, and anyway, I wanted to do this. Plus, it's not like I ever asked for your permission.' I meant to check with him, but in the end I cracked on with Toby's approval.

'I might not be the most generous of bosses, but I don't want you being out of pocket. I insist,' he says.

'Okay, thank you.' I sense this is not an argument I'm going to win. 'I've also planted some bulbs,' I reveal. I dug them up from home, too. 'You'll see them in the spring. This space will be bursting with orange and red tulips and yellow daffodils. The flowers I've planted are perennials, so provided they don't get taken out by a harsh winter frost, they should come back year after year.'

I found I remembered a lot from my gardening sessions with Mum all those years ago.

'Jenny loves fairy lights,' Gavin reveals with a fond smile. 'She'd have them all around the walls. I can imagine her sitting out here, decorating her cupcakes.'

'Do you think she'll come to see it?' I ask hopefully.

He shrugs, his smile fading slightly. 'Who knows? We're working on it. Thank you for the leaflets, by the way.'

I rang and asked a former colleague to post some.

We wander back into the bakery and I grab my things.

'I meant to say,' Gavin says as he ties up his apron. 'Someone phoned me earlier, asking about the position. Are you sure you want to leave us?'

My stomach squeezes, but I nod. 'I'm going to take some time out to go travelling,' I tell him. I've already been on the internet researching my route.

'Is that right? Never understood the lure, personally. I like what I know.'

I smile at him. 'Toby doesn't take after you, then.'

'Toby?' He scoffs as he pours water into the Hobart's large silver mixing bowl. 'You've got to be joking, right? He likes what he knows, too.'

This is probably one of those moments where I should keep my nose out of other people's business and not interfere, but a leopard can't change its spots overnight.

'Toby told me he'd love to go to Australia,' I reveal.

'Did he?' Gavin looks surprised as he grabs the flour.

'But he doesn't feel like he can leave you with so much on your plate.'

He pauses mid motion, then puts the flour back on the counter with a thump and gives me a hard stare. 'Is that what he said?'

I stand my ground. 'Yes.'

'Hmm. Well, he'd bloody well better start saving, then,' he mutters, getting on with his task. 'Flights to Oz cost a bomb.'

Angus's Land Rover is parked on the road outside the apartment when I get home, but he's not in the living room and his bedroom door is closed. I'm concerned, so, despite his recent insistence on privacy, I knock on his door. He can have his apartment back to himself when I'm gone.

He doesn't answer so I cautiously open the door. He's

curled up in a foetal position on the bed, dressed in black jeans and a blue T-shirt.

'Angus?' I ask softly, but he doesn't answer, and while I wait and watch, his chest rises and falls, slowly and evenly.

He's facing away from me so I tiptoe around to the other side of his bed. He's out cold and looks peaceful, but even sleep can't disguise the dark circles under his eyes. I have to fight the urge to reach down and brush his hair away from his face.

I care about him so much, I think to myself. I always have and I always will.

The end wardrobes are slightly ajar and I can't resist pushing them shut as I pass, but they spring back open again and reveal Phoebe's possessions spilling haphazardly out of the boxes. Her grey hoodie is on the top, and I feel a wave of guilt as I reach in and take it, leaving Angus's room and quietly closing the door behind me.

I'm confused as I get on with preparing vegetables for a stir-fry. I'll make enough dinner for Angus, too, just in case he wakes up and feels like joining me. I wasn't sure if he'd be here tonight. I thought he might be with Eliza, but from what she said, they're keeping their distance from each other. It must be so confusing for them both.

I feel a sudden swell of jealousy at the thought of them together. Why does it bother me so much?

Fragments of Eliza's diary scribblings come back to me, and when I think about the way she wrote about him, with such longing and such passion, I pause. Did I ever write with that emotion?

I never read my own diary around the time that I rediscovered it in the loft, but I did bring it here with me.

I leave the cooking preparations on the kitchen worktop and go into my bedroom, closing the door behind me. Five minutes later, I'm sitting on my bed with the third and final purple journal in my hands.

Half an hour later, I'm still sitting there, squirming with discomfort.

I sound like a lovesick teenager. I *was* a lovesick teenager. The first half of the diary sees me go through four different crushes that I had on various boys at school, and when Angus finally comes on the scene, my ridiculousness jumps up a level.

'I've just seen Angus and Phoebe kissing. My heart hurts so much, I know I'm going to cry myself to sleep.

I love him. I love him! Why did he have to fall for her? If only he loved me instead.'

My face is hot with embarrassment as I read. I sound twelve, not eighteen. I thought I was the mature one, heading off to university before my sisters, but I can see now that I was anything but.

Angus doesn't appear for dinner and, after surfing the net for flights and hotel deals, eventually I retire to my bedroom to read some more of Phoebe's diary. In this entry, it's May Bank Holiday and we'd all gone to Primrose Hill for a picnic together – Josie and Craig, included. I remember that day – Gerard got called into work at the last minute, but I still had a lovely time with my sister and friends. I can almost feel the warm sun on my face as I read about it…

I wake up, sweating and anxious.

I stumble to the bathroom, catching sight of my reflection

in the mirror. No wonder I feel so hot; I put on Phoebe's cashmere hoodie before I went to bed in lieu of PJs, and I'm boiling inside it.

I press a cold, damp flannel to my face before leaving the bathroom, flicking off the light as I go.

I come to a sudden stop. Angus is standing in the doorway of his bedroom, naked except for his boxer shorts. He seems unsteady on his feet, as though he's still half asleep.

Horror engulfs me as I remember what I'm wearing, and I can't take it off because I have nothing on underneath. I'm about to ask if he's alright, but he speaks first.

'Phoebe?' he whispers.

My insides turn to ice.

'Rose.' I shake my head quickly. 'Angus, it's me, it's Rose.' My voice doesn't sound like my own.

'Why are you doing this to me?' he asks, anguished. He looks so lost that I can't bear it. I run over to him and throw my arms around his neck.

'I'm sorry,' I cry.

He stands, frozen under my touch, and then his hands slowly slide around my waist.

'You feel like her,' he whispers, his grip on me tightening. I tense as he nestles his face against my neck and hair and breathes in deeply. 'And you smell like her.'

I push him away, stumbling backwards. His eyes are shining in the dark light.

'Are you trying to make me mistake you for her?' he asks quietly, almost sinisterly.

'No.' I shake my head fervently, unable to believe that we're having this conversation.

'Because it wouldn't be the first time I'd fucked up like that, would it?'

'Angus, stop it!' I say with distress, detesting his tone. It's not like him to be cruel, but I know he's trying to hurt himself as much as he's hurting me.

'Go back to bed,' he says dully, turning away from me.

'I know about you and Eliza!' I call after him. His footsteps falter. 'I saw her today.'

I hear his fast intake of breath, but he keeps his back to me.

'She came to see me at the bakery. She and I are going to be okay,' I tell him weakly. 'We'll work out our differences.'

'I'm happy for you,' he replies in a monotone before going into the bathroom and shutting the door behind him.

I toss and turn for the rest of the night, eventually giving up in the early hours of the morning. I shower and get dressed in a distinctly 'Rose' outfit: a red and white floral-patterned dress which is fitted at the waist and kicks out into a full skirt around the knee, then I go into the kitchen and make a pot of tea.

Angus emerges sooner rather than later, and from the weary look on his face, he's been awake half the night, too.

'I'm sorry about—'

We both speak at the same time.

'I'm sorry,' I mumble, hurrying over to give him a hug. I stiffen only briefly when he hugs me back, but there are no signs of him going weird on me again.

'Me too,' he says, releasing me. 'I never should have said those things to you.'

'It's okay.' My eyes fill with tears. 'It was my fault for taking her hoodie again. I'll get it for you now.'

He grabs my arm to stop me from leaving. 'You don't have to,' he says firmly, pulling me back. 'She was your sister. I should never have made you give me her things back. That was wrong of me. You can take what you like of hers. The other night, I'd just come back from seeing Eliza and I was in a bit of a state. Seeing you in Phoebe's clothes sort of tipped me over the edge. I'm sorry.'

I bite my lip, staring at the floor.

'So, you know about us?' he asks gently, bending down in an attempt to make eye contact. I meet his gaze.

'Yes.'

'I should have told you I was seeing her.' He sounds contrite.

'I understand why you didn't,' I reply. 'I'll admit I have mixed feelings about it.'

He rakes his hair back from his face and goes to sit on the sofa with a heavy sigh. I join him. Time for our heart-to-heart, it seems.

'To be honest, I'm not sure if it'll go further than this.' He looks drawn. 'We're both pretty messed up.'

I raise my hand.

'Yes, you too,' he says with a wry smile. 'I guess it was to be expected.'

'Maybe I should never have moved in with you.' I sound depressed.

'Don't say that,' he mutters. 'I'm glad you did.'

'I won't be here for much longer.'

I belatedly fill him in about my plans.

'You want to go back to where Phoebe died?' He looks shocked.

'Yes. I know it's going to be hard, but I hope it'll also be sort of beautiful. Phoebe wanted me to see the things that she saw on her year out. I want to go to the top of the Aiguille du Midi, I want to hike across a mountain and see the view down through the valley. I was actually wondering if you might consider coming?'

His mouth falls open. He shuts it again. 'No, I couldn't. I couldn't bear it. I can't believe you can.'

'I was going to ask Eliza, too,' I say.

This time his lips tilt up at the corners. 'Are you mad? She'd never agree to do that.'

I laugh under my breath. 'You're probably right.' For one she's scared of heights, for another she hates prolonged good-byes. 'But I thought I'd ask her anyway. I'm sure I'll end up going on my own.'

He actually looks quite impressed.

'Have you spoken to Josie recently?' I ask him, and I don't know why, but his whole expression becomes strained. 'What's wrong?' I ask.

He shakes his head. 'Josie and I haven't been in touch for months, but I've been meaning to call her. I need to talk to her about something.'

'What?' I ask.

'I'm hoping she'll tell me everything she knows about Phoebe and Remy.'

Now it's my turn to look shocked as he fills me in.

Chapter 35

Eliza

I'm working the Saturday lunchtime shift at *Roxy's*, but on my way out the door, Rose rings me.

'Eliza, it's Rose.'

'Hi,' I reply with surprise.

What follows is a head-fuck of a conversation about Remy, Josie and Phoebe's purple diary from her gap year because, it turns out, my dear sister recently read that, too.

'You are opening a whole can of worms,' I warn, deadly serious. Maybe Phoebe's secrets are meant to go with her to the grave.

'Angus needs to know,' she tells me.

This makes me feel even more uneasy. 'Does Angus think that Phoebe wanted to be with Remy?' And if she did, does he believe it will absolve him of his guilt about me? Talk about a dangerous game to play.

'I don't think so, but something was going on,' Rose

replies. 'I'm heading to London tomorrow to catch up with Josie. Do you want to come with me?'

I somehow find myself agreeing.

Josie lives in a mezzanine apartment in Dartmouth Park, north London. We went to school together for a few years, but she was primarily Phoebe's friend. I've never been to her house, and I feel like an outsider as she and Rose give each other an emotional hug hello in the poky hallway.

'How are you?' Josie asks with concern, stroking Rose's hair and staring poignantly into her eyes.

'I'm okay,' Rose replies with a nod, patting Josie's hand. Rose glances my way and steps aside so Josie can greet me, too.

'Hey, Eliza,' she says.

Our embrace is brief, and afterwards she leads us down a flight of stairs to the lower-ground floor. It's open plan with the kitchen at the front and the living room at the back over-looking the garden. A small brown-haired boy is playing with a train set on a grey rug.

'He's grown,' Rose gushes, falling to her knees beside him. 'Harry, you're such a big boy now,' she says in a saccharine voice.

'Where's Craig?' Rose asks of Josie's husband.

'He's playing tennis with Ned,' Josie replies, making small talk as she fills up the kettle. 'I've just had Amber and Katy over, actually.'

'How are they?' Rose asks warmly.

'Really good. Katy is walking now.'

I switch off because I don't know who these people are. I

wasn't part of this life here in London, and it stings to remember that Phoebe and Angus were.

'How's Angus?' Josie asks, snatching my attention again.

'He's okay,' Rose replies, flashing an uncomfortable glance my way. Who should be answering that question? The one who he comes home to every night or the one who he recently had sex with?

But Rose continues to take the lead in the conversation, and when Josie joins us, carrying a tray of teacups and a matching teapot, my sister relays Angus's concerns.

'He doesn't understand why Phoebe went climbing with Remy. Do you know if they'd kept in touch?'

'If they did, then she lied to me,' Josie replies. 'But I think she was telling the truth. Remy just appeared at our table one night. He seemed stunned to see her, but Phoebe was really calm, almost like she knew he was going to be there. It didn't make sense.'

'Do you think they'd pre-arranged it?' I ask, getting involved.

She shakes her head. 'I don't think so, not from his expression. Phoebe said later that she had a feeling she'd see him again. I nearly fell off my chair when she asked him if she could go on his climb the next day.'

Apparently, Remy had sat down with them for a while. From what Josie could tell, it was the first time he and Phoebe had seen each other in years.

'The way they were with each other...' Her brow furrows as she tries to explain it. 'They were quite tentative, you know? A little unsure of one another.'

Rose and I nod in unison.

'Anyway,' Josie continues. 'Remy mentioned that he was taking some Americans on a day climb from the Aiguille du Midi and Phoebe came right out with it and asked if she could go. I smiled at her because I thought she was joking. She'd been teasing me about climbing a mountain since we'd got there. I soon realised she was deadly serious.' She winces at the unfortunate turn of phrase.

'Please tell us everything,' Rose implores, gathering herself together. 'Even if it's just something you suspect.' She glances at me and I nod, encouraging her to go on. I want to get to the bottom of this, too.

Josie takes a sip of her tea and places the cup back on the saucer. It clatters slightly, like she's nervous. 'I feel like I'm betraying her by conjecturing,' she says quietly. 'I honestly don't know what was going through her mind, but there definitely seemed to be something between them. I didn't know Remy that well and I never saw him when he was going out with Phoebe, but the way they were looking at each other... It was quite... intimate. I felt like I was intruding. Phoebe actually spoke in French when she asked him if she could go on the climb, but I understood her. He shrugged and laughed, but said she could if she wanted to, and I understood that, too. I jokily accused them of speaking in code, so they reverted to English, and when she got down to the nitty-gritty details about meeting points and what time they were setting off, I couldn't believe what I was hearing. He left us to it after that.'

'Did they kiss each other goodbye?' Rose pries curiously.

Josie nods miserably. 'Two kisses, but he lingered on his second kiss, and when he left she was blushing. She said to me, "Don't look at me like that". I tried to talk her out of it, but she was adamant that she wasn't doing anything wrong. She said I could have a day shopping and she'd be back before dinner.'

Her nose turns bright red and a split-second later, her eyes well up with tears.

I get to my feet and go to the back door, relieved to find it unlocked. I walk out into the small garden, desperate for fresh air. In the house, I can hear noses being blown. I try to focus on the sound of an aeroplane roaring high above.

Luckily Harry starts to kick up a fuss about something, so Josie has to pull herself together. I reluctantly return indoors, nodding at Rose as she flashes me a look of sympathy. She knows I'm not good with other people's tears.

'Anyway, that's all I can tell you,' Josie says, Harry now attached to her hip. 'The next morning when I knocked on her bedroom door, she was already gone.'

'She didn't leave a note?' Rose asks.

Josie nods. 'It just said—' her voice breaks. 'It just said that I had nothing to worry about, and that she'd see me later for drinks on the balcony.'

She clutches her hand to her throat, trying to keep the tears at bay, and then she turns her face and smiles brightly at her child. 'Oh dear me,' she says with forced cheer. 'Silly old Mummy.' She glances over at us as tears roll down her cheeks. 'I guess we'll never know what was going through her mind in those last few hours.'

Rose reaches for her handbag and pulls out a yellow and navy notepad.

'Maybe this holds the answers,' she says quietly.

'Oh Christ,' I mutter, looking away.

'What's that?' Josie asks warily, placing her wriggling son back on the rug and joining us on the sofa. 'Is that Phoebe's journal?'

'Yes,' Rose admits.

I lift my head and bite my lip, watching their exchange.

'Rose, what are you doing?' Josie shakes her head, worriedly. 'You shouldn't read that. It's private.'

'Hallelujah,' I say.

Rose flashes me an annoyed look. 'I disagree,' she replies firmly. 'If she were still alive, yes.'

I scoff at this and she has the grace to look embarrassed. She read *my* diary without any such qualms.

'But she's not here to care either way, and it makes me feel closer to her. I feel like I can hear her talking to me,' she explains.

Josie's eyes well up again. I pour some more tea and take a large gulp, wincing as the hot liquid scalds my throat.

'Anyway, I haven't finished it yet,' Rose continues seriously. 'I'm trying to make it last.'

'Have you checked out her last entry?' Josie asks cautiously, curiously.

Rose shakes her head.

I don't know whether Josie is more relieved or disappointed.

'Well, that was fun,' I mumble on the train home, staring out of the window. Rose ignores me. When I look back at her, I'm shocked to see that she has Phoebe's diary open in her hands.

'Are you kidding me?' I gasp, my throat closing up at the

sight of Phoebe's familiar handwriting. 'Rose!' I have an intense urge to get out and pace the aisle, but I'm in a window seat.

'You know, you should read this,' she says flippantly.

'There is *no way* I could!' I hiss.

'It's a fantastic insight into her character,' she continues.

'What I didn't know, I didn't deserve to know,' I tell her bitterly, remembering how I'd allowed us to grow apart.

'Fine,' she snaps. 'I won't read it now if it bothers you.' She closes the book up, but leaves it on her lap. 'Thank you for coming with me,' she says after a moment. 'I know it was awkward for you, being there.'

'Do you miss London?' I ask, changing tack and twisting in my seat to look at her. 'You seemed so happy there.'

She pauses for thought. 'I was. I miss Josie and my other friends. Sometimes I miss the hospital.'

'Why don't you go back? I mean, I like the bakery and everything. It seems like a nice place to work. But it's not really you. You've always had a proper job, a proper career. You seemed like you were going places, unlike me. I've never had any direction.'

'What?!' she exclaims. 'You had the most direction of all of us! All you ever wanted to do was play your guitar and write songs.'

'And where has it got me? Nowhere.'

'What about that gig you've got coming up?' she asks. 'That place seems like a great venue.'

'Speaking of which,' I say, setting off on a tangent, 'what were *you* doing going to a gig? You never go to gigs!'

She shrugs. 'Toby asked me,' she replies casually. 'We hang out a little.'

'Mmm, I can see why.'

She frowns. 'It's not like that.'

I whack her on the arm. 'I'm messing with you.'

She blushes and looks down at her lap. I stare at her for a moment, feeling an unusual warmth towards her. Another memory strikes me from out of nowhere. We must've been about fourteen and Phoebe had gone for a sleepover at Josie's house. Josie had recently moved to Manchester from York, and all three of us had taken a liking to her. Rose actually got in there first, volunteering at school to take Josie under her wing, but as usual, the object of our platonic affection had eventually migrated towards Phoebe. Phoebe always had the most friends, the most Facebook likes – you get the picture. Anyway, on this one evening, Mum and Dad had gone out to dinner, and I'd started to feel feverish. Rose dosed me up with medicine and cooled me down with a damp flannel, staying by my bedside until Mum and Dad got home. I felt very close to her that night.

'Why did you leave nursing?' I ask. 'You were good at it.'

So she confides in me about Roger and his sixteen-year-old daughter Bianca, who died two hours apart after being involved in a hit-and-run car accident – and she tells me about the mother and young brother they left behind. She opens up about Tara, the one-year-old baby who died of meningitis, and her grief-stricken parents Lana and Michael. And she cries, and I want to cry, too. And I find myself hugging my sister on that train, trying to comfort her in a way that she only allowed Phoebe to do in the past. And I wish that Phoebe were here now, because she'd do a far better job than I ever could.

Chapter 36

Rose

I feel shattered but also strangely light-hearted as I climb the stairs on Sunday evening, opening the door and expecting to see Angus sitting in his usual place on the sofa. But the lights are off, and he comes out of his bedroom as I pull the door shut behind me.

'Hey,' I say. He looks exhausted and a little tense.

'How did it go?' he asks.

'Good,' I reply, indicating the living room. He follows me through, collapsing on the sofa and putting his bare feet up on the coffee table. His arms are folded over his chest protectively.

He barely meets my eyes, staring at his feet as I fill him in.

I'm too scared to tell him that I have Phoebe's diary. I can't risk him taking it away from me.

He sighs heavily when I've finished. 'I really didn't want to have to talk to him.'

'Who?'

'Remy,' he says.

Gosh. No, that wouldn't be fun. 'Do you have contact details for him?' I ask hesitantly.

'I know which tour company he works for. I thought that one day I might want to hear about Phoebe's final moments.' He looks pained, but he holds it together. It's more than can be said for me. He passes me a tissue and flashes me a sad smile, then he re-crosses his arms over his chest.

'And you haven't wanted to speak to him until now?'

'I don't want to speak to him now, either,' he replies in a low voice. 'Even less so, after hearing what Josie said. But I really want to move on from this.'

I have a sudden moment of clarity. He wants to put it to rest because of Eliza.

I experience a pang, but not of jealousy. I feel for him. And I feel for her.

'Don't you think you should call Eliza?' I ask carefully.

'I don't know,' he replies quietly and I notice the muscles on his arms flexing as he increases his grip on his elbows. 'I thought she might need some space. I thought I might need some, too, to be honest. It's been a rough few days.'

I shift uneasily. Some of that is down to me going through Phoebe's things. 'Isn't it her gig on Friday night?' I ask.

His eyes widen and he sits forward tiredly, placing his feet on the floor. 'That had completely slipped my mind,' he says, dragging his hand over his mouth.

'We have to go,' I tell him.

He glances at me. 'You too?'

I shrug. 'Why not? I go to gigs now.'

He shakes his head good-naturedly and I smirk.

'Come on, Gus, it's going to be okay, you know. You and Eliza have only just got started. Properly, I mean. I know you had a thing ten years ago.'

He doesn't deny it or try to explain.

'I'm just not sure she'll ever be able to get over her guilt about Phoebe.' He sounds so jaded. I get up and go to sit next to him.

'She will. It'll just take time,' I say, running my hand up and down his back soothingly.

'She doesn't believe Phoebe would have ever been okay with her and me. Eliza has always been utterly black and white about it. I was with Phoebe first, so she always said I was Phoebe's and could never be hers.'

He's never spoken to me so openly before about my sisters. We've never had that sort of relationship. I'm not sure I like it, but I continue rubbing his back, encouraging him to go on.

'Phoebe and I had just broken up when Eliza and I kissed, but that didn't stop Eliza from freaking out. She wouldn't see me or speak to me. She was *really* upset when I told her what happened between you and me.'

My hand on his back freezes. A moment later I let it drop to my lap, too uncomfortable to touch him now. He stays hunched forward, talking to me over his shoulder, but not expecting me to make eye contact. It's a small relief.

'The awful thing was, *literally* the night before, I'd told her I thought you were all so different.' He laughs unhappily. 'Then I fucked up at that party by kissing you.'

'You were drunk.' I try to sound reasonable, but I feel

mortified that we're having this conversation at all. 'And I didn't exactly stop you,' I add, squirming in my seat.

To my dismay, he turns to look at me properly, a curious expression on his face. 'No, you didn't, did you?' he says. 'Not at first. You did eventually.'

'I came to my senses,' I say. 'Oh God, Angus.' I bury my burning face in my hands. 'I might've had a bit of a crush on you too.'

'*Did you?*' He reels backwards with astonishment.

I peek at him through my fingers. 'This is so embarrassing.'

He looks bemused. 'What the hell? *Why?*'

'I don't know,' I say, shrugging helplessly. 'Let's just say that there were many times when I wished you were a triplet, too.'

I giggle and with my amusement as permission, he cracks up laughing and falls back onto the sofa.

The next morning, I'm still feeling reasonably cheerful when I go into work, but the look on Toby's face when I walk through the door takes some of the edge off.

'Morning,' he says grumpily.

'What's up with you?' I ask him outright.

'Nothing,' he replies.

The cupcakes on the counter divert my attention. They're beautifully decorated with icing all of the colours of the rainbow.

'Wait, did your—'

'Mum baked them,' he completes my sentence.

'Wow! She's feeling a bit better, then?' I ask with delight.

'I guess so,' he mutters, pushing through the door to the bakery.

I stare after him, but a customer arrives so I have to focus on attending to them.

As soon as there's a break in our customer traffic, I peek into the bakery, but Toby is nowhere to be seen. I don't want to leave the shop floor unattended so I go to the windows at the back and wrench one of them open.

'Oi!' I exclaim with annoyance at the sight of him perched on the bench seat, an almost burnt-out fag in his right hand.

He puts the butt to his lips and inhales deeply, glaring at me through a wisp of smoke.

'I thought you'd quit?'

He throws the butt down and grinds his heel onto it as he exhales.

'Why should you care?' he mutters, sounding like a teenager.

'Oh, grow up, Toby,' I snap, closing the window again.

I'm expecting him to be in a mood for ages, so I'm surprised when he apologises on his return.

'Sorry,' he says in my ear, touching his hand on my arm. He lets go and leans up against the counter.

'It's okay,' I reply, still a little put out.

'Dad's found a replacement for you,' he tells me quietly.

I glance at him with surprise. 'Has he? That was quick.'

'She's a single mum and she asked if she can start as soon as possible. He told her she could come in a week from today.' He stares at me despondently.

'Oh.' I'm shocked. 'That's so soon. So he wants me to finish on Friday?'

He nods slowly, meaningfully.

'Wow. Guess I'd better get on with sorting out my train ticket, then. No time like the present, hey?'

He leans forward and I start in surprise as his hand finds mine.

'I'm going to miss you.'

'I'm going to miss you, too,' I reply, meeting his dark-eyed stare. The door whooshes open and he sighs, dropping my hand as he straightens up. 'What can I get for you?' he asks the customer.

An idea occurs to me during the day, but it's not until I'm standing on the pavement and Toby is locking up that I pluck up the courage to ask him.

'Will you come to Eliza's gig with me on Friday night?' I shift on my feet. 'I was thinking it could be sort of like my leaving do.'

'Sure,' he replies casually, making me wonder why I didn't ask earlier. He shoves his keys into his jeans pocket. 'Have you sorted things out with her, then?' he asks.

'We're moving in the right direction,' I reply, telling him about our trip to London. Before I know it, we're halfway to Angus's and have passed the turning to his house.

'Erm, has your dad mentioned anything to you about a conversation we had?' I ask edgily, remembering what I said to Gavin.

Toby raises an inquisitive eyebrow. 'No? What about?'

'I sort of told him that you'd like to go travelling, but you didn't want to leave him with so much to deal with.'

His shoulders slump. 'Rose!'

'Sorry!' I exclaim. 'It just sort of came out! He wasn't angry, though. He just said you'd better get saving.'

He shakes his head at me, but he's not annoyed. 'I've been saving for a car for ages,' he reveals.

'Can you drive?' I ask with surprise.

'Of course I can bloody drive,' he exclaims.

'Sorry, it's just that I only usually see you on a skateboard.'

'Dad would let me borrow his car, but I never damn well go anywhere, do I? Christ.' He shakes his head. 'I really need to get a life.'

And I really need to sort out my travel plans.

Chapter 37

Eliza

'Hey.'

'Hey.'

I'm on the phone to Angus. I rang him, but from the tone of his voice, the call is unwelcome.

'You sound down,' I say, my stomach awash with nerves.

'I'm trying to find some answers,' he replies. 'But I'm not getting very far. I wanted to do something that might help us move forward.'

I feel a rush of relief, but also disappointment. 'Without the guilt?' I ask, continuing before he can answer. 'You're fooling yourself. I don't think there is any closure in this for you. I don't think Phoebe had any intention of cheating on you with Remy. She was coming back home to marry you. And you've got to be okay with that. *I've* got to be okay with that.' Hot tears well up in my eyes. 'I *want* to be okay with that,' I add desolately.

'I wish we were having this conversation in person,' he

says quietly. 'Because I'd really like to hold you right now.'

'I'd really like that too,' I reply, dragging a finger under my eye to protect my mascara from tears. 'But I've got to get to work.'

'Rose and I are coming to your gig on Friday night,' he tells me.

'Are you?' This makes me smile.

'Yeah. So I'll see you then, okay?'

'Okay.'

The next couple of days drag by. I resist calling Angus again and he doesn't call me. It hurts a little, but I figure we'll be seeing each other in person on Friday night, and hopefully we'll both feel better after the time apart.

But that philosophy goes out of the window when his home number flashes up on my Caller ID on Friday morning.

My heart jumps as I answer the phone. 'Angus?'

'It's Rose,' my sister replies, and a wave of disappointment crashes through me, followed swiftly by an after flow of self-reproach. 'Mum says you're coming this way today?'

'That's right,' I reply. I'm starting a fresh apartment search. I haven't yet told Angus that I'm planning to look for somewhere in Sale. With Rose leaving, I'd like to be closer to Mum. And obviously I want to be closer to him, too.

'Is everything okay?' I ask, detecting an edge to Rose's tone.

'Yes, but I'd like to see you before tonight if there's any way you can swing by. It's my last day today, but Toby says I can pop home for an hour.'

'You want to meet me at Angus's?' I check, feeling odd about the idea.

'Yes. Is that okay?' She sounds hesitant.

'It's fine.' I try to shrug off my unease. 'How's eleven o'clock for you?'

'Perfect,' she says with what sounds like relief.

I wonder what this is about.

It doesn't feel right walking into Angus's apartment for the first time and being welcomed by Rose. Angus has impeccable taste and I can't help but feel proud as I stand in the airy open-plan living space and take in the surroundings. I just wish he were here himself to show me around.

'Where are the bedrooms?' I ask Rose, pointing questioningly back towards the hall.

She nods. 'I'm on the right.'

I poke my head around her door and smile at the neatly made up double bed with its floral bedcover. It couldn't be further from what Angus would choose if he were decorating the room.

'What's so funny?' Rose asks, put out at the look on my face.

'Nothing,' I reply with a smirk. 'It's a lovely room. Is that Angus's there?'

'Yes.' She nods, but appears perturbed when I walk over to have a sneaky peek. It would be a serious case of double standards if she asked me to respect his privacy. But I'm sure he wouldn't mind.

I push open the door and walk into his room. At the sight of his unmade bed, my mind is swamped with flashbacks of our night together. He has a white and grey spotted duvet cover and it's been thrown back from the bed as though he's just hopped out. The pillow still has an indentation from his head on it, I notice, and I'm suddenly overwhelmed with an intense longing to hold him tightly and have him hold me in return.

'So,' Rose says, dragging my attention back to her. 'I don't have a lot of time before I need to get back to work, but there's something I want to show you.'

My brow furrows. 'What?' I ask as I follow her back into her bedroom.

'This.'

I can barely believe it when she pulls out that flipping diary again.

I'm about to give her an earful, when she thrusts it, open, in front of my face.

'"I know that Eliza keeps her distance because she's in love with Angus",' she says, and my jaw hits the floor. Does she remember it, word for word?

She continues. '"And I know that he has feelings for her, too."'

The blood drains from my face and I sit, shakily on her bed, taking the diary from her as I do so.

'She wrote this the night before she died. She'd known how you felt for years,' Rose says gently. 'And she was okay about it. Better than okay,' she adds as my heart leaps with hope. 'Look,' she says, pointing to another paragraph. 'She felt guilty about getting to Angus first, because she knew you two would have made a great couple. But she also knew you would never take him from her, even if they weren't together any more.'

My eyes skip over Phoebe's words, my head spinning as I try to make sense of everything.

Rose paraphrases for me. 'She says that she would have had to fall spectacularly out of love with Angus for you two to have ever stood a chance. And she said that while you knew that she still had feelings for him, you wouldn't have touched him with a bargepole.'

But it's the sentence between these two that gets my attention, and my blood runs cold as I read it aloud:

'"If Angus and Eliza are meant to be together, the stars and planets will have to align to make it happen."' My face crumples. 'Oh God.'

'No, no, no,' Rose says, horrified. 'Don't think like that! That's not why I showed you this! This is what you have to remember. Eliza!' She shakes me slightly, trying to pull me together. 'You saw him first! It was you! I read it in your diary. Your biggest mistake was not fighting for him. Neither of us ever fought Phoebe for anything! Luck just fell her way. She was like that and we all loved her for it, but she did enjoy being the centre of attention. You were always so fiercely protective of her, but her light blinded us at times and we have to remember that this is *our* life now. And we can't waste it. You've got to let it go. Move on. Angus loves you and you love him and I won't let you be unhappy any longer. I won't accept it.'

'Does he know about this?' I choke out.

'Hell, no,' she replies. 'You should have seen how mad he got when I found her things. He would have seriously flipped out if he knew I'd been reading her diary, too.'

'What things?' I ask, confused.

'In the wardrobe in his bedroom.' She looks uncomfortable as she tells me how Angus lost his rag.

'That must've been upsetting,' I say.

'It was,' she replies, and her discomfort seems to increase. 'You were right, you know. I never loved him. I've been through crush after crush and have never really loved any man, not even Gerard, even though on paper he should've been a perfect catch. Apart from his not-ex-wife,' she adds hastily. 'I don't know what my problem is. I do want to settle down, but maybe I need to *find myself* first,' she says in a silly voice. 'I think it will do me good to get away for a while, sort out what I really want from my life. But I'm going to miss you. I really am.'

'I'm going to miss you, too.' And I mean it so much it hurts.

The last time I played at *Elvis & Joe's*, I was nervous. This time, my nerves are out of this world. Joe has told me that a couple of people from a local indie label have accepted his invitation to drop in tonight. He's going to introduce them to me afterwards. I'm trying not to get my hopes up – I need to keep my cool – but it's hard. And of course, I'm also incredibly on edge about seeing Angus again.

There's a knock on the door, likely to be Michelle returning with my drink. I could do with some Dutch courage, but I never drink alcohol before a show. 'Come in,' I call, smiling as she pokes her head around the door.

'Look who I found on their way in.' She opens the door wider to reveal Rose – and Angus.

My heart flips. He looks so gorgeous in his old denim jeans and one of his faded band T-shirts.

'Hi!' I put my guitar down and hop to my feet, going to greet Rose first before turning to Angus.

'Hey,' he says, and he gives me a slightly awkward hug before retreating. My heart sinks, but I try not to let it show, taking the glass Michelle hands me.

'Cheers.' I raise my soft drink.

'Empty-handed,' Angus replies with a smile, holding his palms up. 'We were just on our way to the bar.'

'Toby's there,' Rose reminds him. The three of them came together. 'I'll help him. See you after?' she asks me.

'Definitely. Hopefully I'll be able to relax more then.'

Michelle makes herself scarce along with Rose, so Angus and I find ourselves alone.

'How are you feeling?' he asks, pulling up a chair and sitting down. He rests his elbows on his knees.

'Nervous,' I admit, picking up my guitar again. I've already tuned it and it doesn't need doing again, but I feel like I want something to hide behind.

'Would you rather I left you to get your head together?' he asks with concern.

'No!' I exclaim. 'No, I'm glad you're here,' I state firmly.

He smiles a small smile, and I have an urge to put my guitar down, climb onto his lap, push his hair back from his face and kiss him.

'You look beautiful,' he says earnestly.

I glance down at my appearance, self-consciously. 'Really? I wasn't sure if I should go with something more colourful.' I'm wearing a long-sleeve, sheer-black, floaty top that is fitted under my chest and bares my midriff, along with skinny dark blue jeans and silver sandals. I've styled my hair in a single fishtail plait.

'Black suits you. And I like your hair like that, too.'

The look in his eyes melts my heart. I prop my guitar up against the wall and lean forward, running my right hand up his tanned forearm. He catches my fingers with his other hand and pulls me towards him, and then I'm where I wanted to be a moment earlier, straddling his lap and staring straight into his beautiful mottled eyes. He places his hands on my hips and edges me closer.

'I missed you,' he whispers.

'I missed you, too,' I whisper back, stroking my thumbs down the side of his warm face and raking my fingers through his sexy dark-blond hair. He stares back at me.

There's a knock on the door.

'Come in,' I call, stifling a sigh. I'm a little shocked when I see it's Joe, not Michelle. I clamber off Angus's lap and straighten up, but Joe just looks tickled.

'Angus, right?'

They shake hands and he turns back to me.

'I just wanted to say hi. Is there anything you need?'

'No, I'm fine, thank you,' I say with a tense smile.

Angus presses my shoulder. 'I'll leave you to it.'

I watch him go with regret, but it's time to psyche myself up, anyway.

Chapter 38

Rose

'Actually, can you make mine a vodka and cranberry?' I say to Toby, changing my order from wine at the last moment.

'Is this going to be messy like last time?' he asks me when the bargirl has gone off to get our drinks.

'I hope not,' I scoff.

'Shame,' he says, glancing north of my forehead to my admittedly looser-than-normal up-do. 'I liked it when you let your hair down.'

I cringe. 'I thought you thought I was out of control.'

'You were. You were fun,' he says with amusement.

'Oh God, am I one of those people who are only fun when they're drunk?' I moan. 'I'm a right bore most of the time.'

He grins at me. 'No, you're not.'

His expression is full of warmth and the seconds tick by as he meets my gaze. I raise my eyebrows at him as the bargirl returns with our drinks.

Angus chooses that moment to join us, and it's just as well, because the look in Toby's eyes is unsettling me.

'Aah, cheers for that,' Angus says, picking up his pint and downing a third of it.

'How's Eliza?' I ask, trying to make casual conversation, even though I feel anything but.

'She's alright.' He spies some people he knows. 'Hey, Stewart!' he calls. 'Evan!'

'Shall we move closer to the stage?' I ask Toby, feeling a little skittish.

'Sure,' he replies, but then Angus comes back over with his colleagues from work: Stewart, whose dad owns the bar, and Evan, who looks like he's just got back from holiday, judging by his impressive tan. I discover he works on the newspaper's travel desk.

After chatting for a while, we all move towards the stage together. When Eliza appears, the noise around the bar area dies down, but not completely. She sounds cool, calm and collected as she introduces herself over the sound system, and I feel a swell of pride as she starts to strum her guitar. She leans in close to the microphone to sing. She has a beautiful voice, soulful and expressive, and her lyrics are clever and quirky. There are a few chuckles from around us as she sings a punch-line, rewarding her audience with a charming grin.

I cast a glance at Angus. He's staring up at Eliza, his face alight with some emotion. I'm taken back to a time in our early twenties when Phoebe and Angus were together again after their year-and-a-half hiatus. I'd gone to visit Phoebe at university and Angus was there. She took part in a rock climbing competition and he stood at the bottom of the rock wall and watched her scale the heights. He was so proud when she won. He was so full of love. And those are the emotions I'm witnessing on his face right now.

He loved Phoebe. And he loves Eliza. It must be possible to love two people at once, because the proof is right here in front of me.

Toby nudges me, and I welcome the distraction because I'm on the verge of tears. 'She's good,' he says, impressed.

'Yes.' I nod, still trying to control my emotions. 'She is.'

It's not too late for us. At times, Eliza and I have felt like the worst of enemies, but we could be the best of friends. If only we can stop taking each other for granted.

I'm pretty tipsy by the time Eliza joins us later, and she seems entertained as I throw my arm around her neck.

'I'm not saying this because I'm drunk,' I say, hanging off her. 'But I am really, really proud of you.'

'Aw, thanks Rose,' she replies. She is totally sober.

'I mean it!' I exclaim. 'And Angus is proud, too. You should have seen his face when he was looking up at you. He really loves you.'

She stares back at me, suddenly serious.

'Look at you two,' Joe interrupts. 'Are you sure you can't sing, love?' he asks me.

I shake my head and giggle.

'Ready to be introduced?' he asks Eliza.

She looks nervous as they move away together. Angus comes to stand by my side.

'What do you think of Evan?' he asks.

'Oh.' I furrow my brow as I stare past Angus to his colleague in question. 'Yeah, he's alright.'

'Don't sound too enthusiastic,' he jokes with a grin.

'I'm leaving in a couple of days. There's no point.'

'What happened to,' and he affects my voice: '"To be honest, Gus, I could really just do with a shag".'

I whack him on his stomach and he doubles over, laughing.

'What was that about?' Toby asks as I turn away, mock disgusted.

'Angus is trying to set me up.'

'With who?' he asks.

'Evan.' Pause. 'I'm not interested.' I glance up to see Toby studying me. He's certainly very confident with his eye contact, I muse. It makes him seem older.

Eliza joins us again after a while and plays catch-up by doing a couple of shots at the bar. She and Angus seem so relaxed in each other's company. It's bizarre for me, witnessing the reality of their relationship when they've both let down their defences. I feel like I have to realign my perspective. They laugh a lot and they're very tactile with each other – I'm not entirely comfortable with it, but I'm sure I'll get used to it with time. I have to.

No, I want to.

'I'd like to go dancing,' I find myself announcing towards closing time.

'Do you want to hit a club?' Toby asks. 'Jase and I went to a place last Saturday that was pretty cool.'

His friend from London came to stay with him last weekend.

'Yeah! Let's see if the others are up for it.'

'Really?' Eliza asks with astonishment when I make the suggestion.

'Why not?' I reply.

She turns to Toby and prods his chest. 'What have you done to my sister?'

He rolls his eyes, but he's smiling.

'So are you coming or not?' I demand to know.

Eliza glances at Angus. He gives her a meaningful look and she turns back to me.

'No,' she says.

'Are you sure?' And then it dawns on me. 'Aah. You're going to have an early night, aren't you?'

She shifts on her feet. 'Maybe.'

In that case, I might see her in the morning. I'm not sure how I'll feel about that, but right now I'm too drunk to care.

The club is full of youngsters and I have second thoughts as I wait for Toby to come back from the bar. I spied a vacant booth and made a beeline for it, to his amusement, but I can see him from here. He looks so comfortable, so chilled. He fits right in with this crowd. His ripped denim jeans sit low on his narrow hips, held up with a chunky black belt. He's wearing a black T-shirt that must've shrunk in the wash with the way it's riding up at his side. The skin of his waist is exposed as his body twists to lean against the bar top.

He really is sexy.

The girls to his right seem to think so, too. I watch as one of them, a beautiful girl with long dark hair turns to say something to him. He smiles and answers, and then he's being served.

The bargirl is young and sexy, too, and she stares at him with a smile as she listens to his order.

What am I doing here? I think suddenly. I don't belong. I should be tucked up in bed.

And then I remember that Eliza is probably back at the apartment with Angus and I'm not sure I can cope with that, yet, either.

The next thing I know, Toby is returning to our table.

'I feel like I'm cramping your style,' I say as he slides in next to me. I must've sobered up because I can't imagine joining the sweaty throng on the dance floor now.

'What are you talking about?' he asks, baffled.

'Those girls up at the bar. You could've been in there. But instead you're keeping the old age pensioner company.'

'Jesus,' he mutters, his eyes wide with disbelief. 'Rose,' he says loudly, swivelling on the booth seat to face me. 'Cut it out.'

'Sorry, but I'm almost a decade older than you!'

'No, you're not,' he scoffs. 'You're six years older – that's closer to half a decade.'

'I'm twenty-eight and you're twenty-one. That's seven years.'

'I'm twenty-two soon. I round it down.'

'It doesn't matter anyway. You're right, I shouldn't be so bothered about it.'

'Why *are* you so bothered?' he asks me outright.

'I don't know.' I shrug, wanting to change the subject. 'So dish the dirt, then. Did you pull when you came here last weekend?' I try to sound more nonchalant than I feel, but the truth is I've been dying to ask all week.

He shakes his head. 'No.'

I pick up my drink and take a large gulp, trying to regain my earlier buzz. I'm thinking too much, and his close proximity tonight is making me inexplicably nervous.

'Have you always gone out with guys the same age as you?' he asks.

I sense that we're crossing into dangerous territory, given the undercurrent prevailing between us, but I find myself answering.

'No,' I reply. 'My last boyfriend was eight years older than me. And that was a mistake.'

'Because he was older?'

'No, because he was a tosser.' I take another sip of my drink. 'What about you?'

'All but one of my girlfriends have been older than me.'

'Really?' My voice sounds squeaky. 'How much older?'

He shrugs. 'When I was eleven, my first girlfriend was twelve. When I was fifteen, I went out with a girl two years older, and at seventeen, my girlfriend was three years older than me.'

'Wow.'

'And then when I was twenty-one, she was six-and-a-bit years older,' he says with a smirk, taking a sip of his beer and regarding me out of the corner of his eyes.

Wait. 'What?' I splutter, then I roll my eyes, realising he's teasing me.

'Drink up, let's go and dance.' He nods at my vodka and cranberry.

Bugger it. I down it in one and plonk my glass back on the table. He slides out of the booth and leads the way.

The drink has gone straight to my head, but I am still all too aware of the female attention Toby is receiving as he makes his way through the crowds. If he notices, he doesn't show it.

Luckily a song I recognise comes on as we approach the dance floor, and it's not too long before my self-consciousness fades away and I start to enjoy myself. It helps that Toby is a great dancer. After about half an hour or so, he puts his hand on my waist, his touch scorching the skin under my top.

'Drink?' he asks in my ear, pulling away to look into my eyes.

I nod, feeling suddenly feverish, as well as hot and sweaty. 'Back in a sec.'

He goes off to the bar, leaving me on the dance floor alone. Bizarrely, I don't mind. It's only taken me twenty-eight years, but I seem to have finally lost my inhibitions.

Scrap that, I think, less than a minute later when I rouse the attention of a couple of wasted lads. One of them starts to gyrate his way towards me, but I dance in the opposite direction before he can make contact. It doesn't put him off, unfortunately, and I begin to feel uncomfortable as they move closer. This goes on for a while – them circling me and me trying to move away – and then, to my immense relief, I see Toby approaching. He doesn't have any drinks on him and he looks annoyed, and then suddenly a pair of hot sweaty hands land on my hips and one of the guys gyrates right up against my arse. I'm disgusted.

'Oi!' Toby shouts, wrenching me away from his sweaty grasp. He shoves the drunken offender hard on his chest. 'Leave her alone!' he yells, turning back to me. 'You alright? I saw them from the bar.'

God, he's gorgeous. My vision is right in line with his lips. I inadvertently step closer to him and I notice his eyes widen fractionally. I place my hand on his lovely slim hips, my thumb brushing over the bare skin under his T-shirt. I feel his stomach retract as he breathes in and then his hands are cupping my face and his mouth is on mine.

I feel giddy as his tongue edges my lips apart, but I'm powerless to stop our kiss from deepening. Desire rockets through me as he pulls me closer, my chest pressing against his ribcage. Shivers are ricocheting up and down my spine in waves and my legs feel shaky. He breaks away.

No, no, what's he doing? That was the best kiss of my life and I don't want it to end, but he takes my hand and pulls me off the dance floor. A moment later, we're in the dark against a wall, kissing again.

My head is spinning as I slip my hands around his waist. He kisses my jaw, and I gasp as he nibbles at my earlobe. I feel breathless and jittery and a little beside myself, if I'm being honest. I've had too much to drink and I'm confused about what's happening. I'm making out with a twenty-one-year-old and my head tells me that's wrong, despite what the rest of my body says.

It takes immense – *immense* – willpower to place my hand on his stomach and firmly push him away.

'We can't do this,' I murmur, my heart constricting. 'I'm too old for you.'

His expression softens slightly. 'No, you're not.' He tries to pull me back against him, but my hand is still raised.

'Please,' I beg, trying so hard to be strong and adult about it. 'I'm leaving on Sunday.'

His hands are back on my hips. 'You're making excuses.'

'If I am, then I am. There has to be a reason for that.'

'I don't want you to go,' he says dully, his fingers slipping underneath my top. 'Don't go.' I jolt as they trace the line of my waistband.

'I have to.' I force myself to take a step backward. 'I need to do this for myself. I've spent my life looking after other people. This is for me.'

He leans against the wall and folds his arms, broodingly. We're now standing a foot apart, still too close, but I don't want to move away any further.

'I get it,' he says. 'I understand. But you must know that there's something here.' He motions to the two of us. 'I care about you. A lot.'

'Trust me,' I say, trying to keep it together. 'In ten years' time, you'll look back and know that I was right. You'll get so much life experience over the next few years. We're in different places right now. You're barely in your twenties and I'm heading towards my thirties. I should be settling down, not acting like a teenager.'

'My parents got together when they were eighteen, and they're still together,' he says adamantly. 'Despite everything, they love each other. My dad works his fingers to the bone, and it's all for us. He would do anything for Mum and me.'

The passion in his eyes takes my breath away, but I steel myself to keep my distance.

'I can't do it, Toby,' I say flatly, shaking my head. 'It doesn't feel right.'

He stares at me despondently. 'If this doesn't feel right, then I can't imagine what ever will.'

Chapter 39

Eliza

'Are you sure about this?' Angus hesitates with his key in the lock.

'It's a bit bloody late now,' I snap jokily. 'We've come all the way to Sale. Do you think I'm going to go and crash on Mum's floor?'

He smiles as he opens the door, flicking on lights as he leads me inside.

Neither of us is wasted, but neither of us is sober, either, which is how we agreed it should be the next time we went to bed together. That idea seems to have flown out of the window. I really hope Rose doesn't come home anytime soon.

'Did Rose tell you I came here earlier today?' I ask.

'Did you?' He looks taken aback.

I remember what she said about him being angry if he discovers she's reading Phoebe's diary. I don't want to land her in it. 'I was in the area, flat hunting.' I look around. 'This is a great apartment.'

'Thanks. Do you want something to drink?' he asks, his eyebrows pulling together.

'Just take me to your bedroom, Angus.'

He looks amused as he nods, his fingers running slowly down the length of my arm as he comes to stand close beside me. He gazes into my eyes, and my heart is in my throat as I stare up at him. Then his fingers close around my hand and he leads me into his room. He closes the door behind me and locks it, and then his hands are on my bum and he's lifting me from the floor. I wrap my legs around his waist and he presses my back against the door, his mouth finding mine.

I'm glad he's supporting me because my entire body turns to jelly with his kisses. When he carries me to the bed, I notice it's still unmade, but then I'm not thinking about anything other than his lips on my bare stomach and his tongue tracing the sensitive skin around my bellybutton ring.

'I like this top,' he murmurs. 'I've wanted to kiss you here all night.'

I shudder with longing and claw at his T-shirt. He straightens up and tugs it over his head, revealing his leanly muscled, honey-coloured chest.

He lifts my top over my head and unclasps my bra, skimming his fingers over the curves of my body. I frantically reach for the buttons on his jeans, but I'm too clumsy and he takes over instead.

I want him on top of me. I want to feel the weight of his body pressing into mine. I want to feel consumed by him, so I pull him down, gasping as our skin collides. We kiss

passionately, and a minute later we shed the last of our clothing and he takes me completely.

Afterwards we lie in the dark, side by side, staring into each
other's eyes.

'We were supposed to be sober,' I remind him.

'What are you doing tomorrow night?' is his response,
accompanied by a cheeky grin.

'Working,' I reply with a smile.

'Bunk off,' he urges.

'I can't. It's our busiest night of the week.'

'Sunday, then?' he suggests. 'We'll go on a proper date.'

'Really?'

'Yeah.' He kisses me gently. 'How do you think tonight
went?'

The corners of my lips tilt downwards. 'Okay, I think.'

He props himself up on one elbow and stares at me gravely.
'What is it?'

'Joe introduced me to two men from Red Vox Records,'
I reply weakly.

'And?' he prompts.

'The head guy left straight after meeting me so that was
a bit gutting, but his second-in-command stayed and talked
to me for a bit.'

I'm still trying to come to terms with what he said. The
man, Sean Nottingham, reminded me of Dad, quite fatherly
and nurturing, and his advice was kind, but truthful.

Angus looks concerned as he reaches over and runs his
fingers along my arm, from my shoulder to my wrist.

'It's okay,' I tell him. 'I'm okay.'

Deep in my heart, I knew it already. The record industry is a tough place and labels are only taking on bright young things. No one else is getting a look in. But Sean asked me if I had considered other roles within the music industry. He said that his boss, the head of the label who had already left, needed a new PA. They hadn't advertised for the position yet, and he said that they could do without the stress. It would be a junior role and I'd be an all-round dogsbody, starting at the bottom and hopefully working my way up.

'What do you think?' Angus asks tentatively after I fill him in.

'I think that I love you for always believing in me.'

He leans forward and plants a tender kiss on my lips. When he pulls away, I have tears in my eyes. 'But I also think that it might be time to try something else.'

'You don't have to give up on your music,' he says seriously.

'I know. I'd like to still do gigs, but God...' I shake my head as the reality of what Sean is offering starts to sink in. 'It would be pretty amazing to be able to leave waitressing for a job in the record industry.'

He nods, impressed. 'I'll say.'

'Sean said there'd be perks. I'd be able to go to gigs, and sometimes I'd get to go on album shoots and that sort of thing.'

'It sounds right up your street.'

'Yeah.' I smile at him, feeling a belated bubble of excitement.

Dad always used to say that we needed to discover our passion in life and then find a way to do it. He said that we'd meet like-minded people, doing what we love. This is my chance to meet people in the music industry, and who knows what the future might hold? Maybe one day I'll get to write songs for the next big thing, or even sing backing vocals for another artist. I'm not set on being the front person – I just want to get by, doing what I love.

The more I think about it, the more at peace I feel.

Angus kisses me again. 'I'm so proud of you,' he murmurs. 'Your dad would be proud, too.'

'Thank you,' I murmur, my nose prickling.

The sound of a key in the lock makes me start.

'It's just Rose,' he whispers.

'I hope she'll be okay about me being here in the morning,' I whisper back, fretting as I listen to her go into her room and close the door behind her.

'She'll have to be.' He kisses the tip of my nose. 'Everyone will have to be. I don't want to be apart from you again. From now on, we're in this together.'

Chapter 40

Rose

The next morning, my headache feels like the least of my problems. I lie there for a while in bed, contemplating the events of the night before. I can't believe I kissed Toby. What was I thinking?

Eventually I get out of bed and go into the kitchen to fill up the kettle. I'm just downing a glass of water and a couple of headache tablets when Angus walks in.

'Are you making filtered coffee?' he asks, sleepily planting himself on a stool at the island unit. He's wearing low-slung PJ bottoms and nothing else, but I'm unaffected by the eye-candy moment.

'Yeah, you want one?' I ask.

'Please,' he says, and suddenly he looks awkward.

'Am I making two or three?' I ask pointedly.

'Three, please,' he replies sheepishly.

'*Okaaay* then.' The words come out sounding a bit arsey, and as I turn around to get out the cups, I hear him sigh.

'Rosie, please don't—'

'It's fine,' I interrupt, glancing at him over my shoulder. 'I won't give her a hard time, I promise.'

His shoulders sag with relief. 'Good. Thank you.'

'Is it safe to enter?' my sister calls from the doorway, seemingly naked except for the T-shirt of Angus's she's wearing.

'Yes, there was no need for his big brother pep talk,' I reply wryly.

She grins as she ambles over, hopping onto a stool beside Angus. They exchange intimate smiles.

It's eerie seeing them together like this. I guess in some ways it's good that they hooked up before I went away. It would be harder to come home to them already being a full-blown couple.

'So,' Eliza says, leaving a significant pause before continuing. 'How was it with Toby last night?' She raises a knowing eyebrow at me and my face heats up in response. 'Rose!' she admonishes, a grin splitting her face.

'What? No!' I want to tell her that she's got the wrong idea. In fact, how did she know to ask her meaningful question about Toby in the first place? 'We're just friends!' I insist.

'There is nothing platonic about the way you two look at each other,' she says. 'Tell me what happened!' she urges, and it's obvious that whatever denials I issue will be ignored. 'Did you kiss him?'

I groan, hiding my face.

'You did!' Eliza exclaims. I don't deny it.

'Wait, you kissed Toby?' Angus interjects with confusion.

'Yep,' Eliza gleefully confirms.

Angus gawps at me. '*Noooo!*'

'What's the big deal?' Eliza brushes off his horrified reaction.

'He's practically a teenager!' Angus exclaims.

'He's twenty-one, almost twenty-two,' I find myself correcting him. He still looks taken aback. 'I know, I know.' I press my fingers to my flaming cheeks. 'You don't have to tell me. I made a mistake.'

Eliza shoves Angus's arm. 'Back in your box, big brother. This is sister territory.'

Angus looks put out as he sits back on his haunches.

'Why was it a mistake?' Eliza asks me. 'He's an adult. You're an adult. Plus he's sexy as hell.'

'Oi!' Angus butts in, outraged.

'And he really, really likes you,' Eliza continues, ignoring Angus. 'Plus, the feeling is mutual. I can tell,' she adds as I stare at her. 'You're stupid if you're going to pass up a hottie like that. He won't stay single for long.'

I gather myself together. 'No, he won't. And I need to be okay with that.' I try to project the tone of a mature adult, something I'm supposed to be. 'I want to settle down, get married and have kids. I want what my friends have, what you two will no doubt have in the not too distant future.'

They both shift on their seats like two peas in a pod, but neither of them denies it.

'You're still looking for Prince Charming,' Eliza states, matter-of-factly.

'Yes,' I confirm with a decisive nod.

'Well,' she says, 'just remember that he might not come in the package you're expecting.'

*

Last night, the taxi journey home was unbearably tense. I didn't want to talk about what had happened, so Toby just sat there on the other side of the car, staring humourlessly out of the window. It was only when we arrived at my place that he met my eyes.

'Come and say goodbye tomorrow,' he said.

I nodded and climbed out of the car.

'Rose,' he called after me, so I turned around and looked back in at him. 'I mean it,' he said. 'Don't go without saying goodbye.'

'I won't,' I vowed. He seemed to relax marginally.

Now I can't believe I made such a promise.

Surely it would be better for both of us if we had a clean break? But no, I do want to stay friends, and anyway, there's something I've been meaning to give him.

Toby is behind the counter with Vanessa when I walk into *Jennifer's*. He takes one look at me and jerks his head towards the bakery, holding the door back to let me go through. Out in the garden, I notice the windows to the café area are closed and the frosting is still in place.

'I hope you're going to take off the frosting or open up the windows when I'm gone,' I say. 'I didn't do all of this for nothing, you know.'

He smiles, despite himself. 'Sorry, I didn't quite get around to doing it earlier, but I will. I promise. Dad's talking about turning one of the windows into an outside door so people can come out here to drink their coffees. He really loves what you've done.'

'That's a great idea,' I say, thrilled. 'How's your head?' I ask, pulling up a single chair.

'Head's fine. Heart's the problem,' he replies, sitting down opposite me.

My face does its usual trick of heating up like a radiator, but he seems remarkably cool as he stares back at me.

'I brought you this.' I try to compose myself as I place the plant pot on the low table.

I re-potted one of the rose cuttings I took from home and covered it with a plastic bag to create a greenhouse environment. The other two I'm giving to Mum and Eliza. They're just starting to shoot. I take off the bag now to show Toby, patting the soil down around the cutting as I explain where it came from.

'When I'm back, I'll plant it in the garden for you. The orange colour will work well with the crocosmias and helianthemums.'

He's staring at me sadly. I tuck a loose piece of hair behind my ear.

'You'll have to spritz it with water every—'

My sentence is cut short by him reaching across and brushing my cheek with his thumb.

'Dirt,' he explains, rubbing it from his hands and meeting my eyes again. 'It's funny, I've got this overriding memory of Mum baking in the kitchen at home. She always had flour on her face. With you it's soil.'

I shake my head, smiling sadly. 'I wouldn't make a good baker, would I?'

'You'd make a better gardener,' he replies.

It's a lightbulb moment. I gawp at him, open-mouthed.

'What is it?' he asks.

'I think I've just worked out what I want to do with my life,' I tell him.

He looks bemused.

'I don't want to go back to nursing. And it's not just because I'd find it too hard. When I think about it, I didn't really choose a nursing career in the first place. It's not what I love, what I'm passionate about.' I look around and laugh a little. '*This* is what I'm passionate about.' Tears sting my eyes and I feel bizarrely emotional. 'I love gardening.'

I don't think I was destined to be a nurse, I think I was meant to work outside in the garden, wind, rain or shine. Gardening was Mum's hobby – it was her passion. Nursing was her job. She missed her vocation, just as I missed mine. But it's not too late.

I find myself laughing giddily.

'Does this mean you won't go away?' Toby asks, still a little bemused, but mostly hopeful.

My face falls. 'No. I'm going. I have to.'

I do want to follow in Phoebe's footsteps, but this is not just about doing what Phoebe did and seeing what Phoebe saw. This is about closure. Then I'm going to go my own way and see the world.

'How long will you be away?' Toby asks downheartedly.

'I don't know. Maybe a year, maybe less.' I'm taking the train to Paris tomorrow and after a few days I'll head to Chamonix. I thought about travelling around Europe first, like Phoebe did, but I think I'll have too much on my mind, knowing that the Alps are waiting for me. I'll go to Europe afterwards before flying down to Brisbane in December.

'My uncle and his partner are having me to stay at their house in Byron Bay for Christmas,' I tell Toby. 'After that, I'll backpack around Australia and come back via Asia.'

'I'm envious,' he admits.

'Start saving,' I respond with a smile.

He stares at the cutting on the table.

'My mum said she'll pop in to check on the garden for me,' I tell him. 'Maybe you should make watering the plants one of the new girl's jobs.'

He shakes his head. 'Nah. I'll do it.'

'Well, while you're out here, don't start up smoking again,' I warn.

My heart flutters as he stares at me levelly.

'Will you keep in touch?' he asks eventually. 'Text me?'

'Do you want me to?'

'Of course.' He gives me a reproachful look. 'Despite you throwing yourself at me last night, you're still my friend.'

'I did not throw myself!'

He laughs at my outraged expression and gets to his feet. 'Give us a hug.'

I pull a face at him, but stand up and prepare myself for goodbye. His arms fold around me and he holds me tight.

'I'll miss you,' he whispers into my ear. 'Thank you for everything.'

'I'll miss you, too,' I whisper back. I let him go before I start to cry.

Chapter 41

Eliza

Rose left today. I feel pretty down about it. We had dinner with Mum last night. She kept getting all misty-eyed at the sight of us together. It made me feel bad that our silence had gone on for so long.

I thought Mum would be upset about Rose's Chamonix plan, but she seems to understand. I'm still not sure I do. But I do feel torn about my decision not to go with her. For me, it's too difficult, and it's definitely too soon. But it gives me comfort to know that Chamonix isn't going anywhere, not that I imagine I'll ever want to do what Rose is doing.

I feel oddly disloyal being in Angus's apartment without Rose. She didn't live here for long, but her aura is stamped all over it. I'm miserable as I wander into her bedroom and see the duvet cover stripped and her possessions packed away in boxes in the wardrobe.

'Will you get another tenant?' I ask Angus, wondering

what he'll do with Rose's belongings if he does. He already has one wardrobe stuffed full of Phoebe's things.

'I was going to talk to you about that,' he says. 'You're looking for somewhere to live—'

'No, Angus,' I interrupt. 'It's too soon.'

'Just hear me out.' He takes my hands and stares into my eyes. 'We've known each other for years. We know what we're getting into. If you're moving here to Sale, you're going to be at my apartment loads anyway. At least, I hope you are,' he says with a hopeful smile. 'I want to wake up with you. I want to have breakfast with you and kiss you goodbye before I go to work. If the PA thing doesn't pan out and you decide to carry on waitressing, I want you to come home to me.'

I've got to hand it to him: it's a good argument.

'What will people think?' I ask.

'What people?' he replies with a frown. 'I don't care what anyone thinks. If they have a problem with us being together, they'll get over it when they see how happy we are.'

'Happy? You and I fight like cats and dogs,' I point out with a wry smile.

He grins. 'You keep me on my toes, that's true. But I love that about you. And you know I'm always going to give it to you straight.'

I stand up on my tiptoes and give him a kiss. 'I know. I trust you.'

'So move in with me,' he says simply. The look in his eyes is making my heart melt. I have a strange reality-check moment where I can't believe we're together like this. The only man I've ever really wanted wants *me*.

'What about Rose?' I ask, trying to stay focused.

'She'll be okay with it. She'll have to accept it like our mums will have to accept it.'

'No, I don't mean… I mean, I know she'll be okay with us eventually.' She's been amazing so far. 'But what about when she comes back? What if she still wants to live with you?'

'Well, I presume you won't be sleeping in *her* bed,' he says with meaning.

I smirk at him and step away, wandering into his bedroom. I stand and stare at the wardrobes. The double wardrobe to the left is the only one that doesn't open up onto the space directly in front of the bed. And it's full of Phoebe's things.

'Why did you put Feebs's things in the left-hand wardrobe?' I ask. 'And not the one over there?' I point to the right, the furthest up against the far wall and the most difficult to access.

'When I started to unpack, she was on her hen week,' he says quietly. *And still alive*, he doesn't have to add. 'I was trying to get the apartment sorted before she came back.'

I remember Rose was on her way out of the door to help him when we received the phone call about Phoebe.

'You gave her the best wardrobe,' I state. It doesn't need acknowledging, because it's obvious.

'I'll empty it out,' he says, in that same low voice.

I walk over to the wardrobe. It's open a crack, and when I pull at the doors, I can see why. Phoebe's clothes are in a right state, spilling out of the boxes inside.

'It doesn't normally look like that,' Angus says, sounding on edge.

'I know,' I reply. 'Rose told me what she did.' I cast a look at him over his shoulder. 'Do you mind?' I ask, indicating the contents in front of me.

He shakes his head, but he looks uncertain. He's worried that today is going to go horribly wrong.

'It's okay,' I try to reassure him. 'It's okay.'

He nods again and comes forward as I lift Phoebe's clothes from the top of the first box and lay them carefully on the bed.

'Rose wanted to keep some of her things,' he tells me in a husky voice. I have a lump in my throat, too. 'I said that she could.'

'She would have liked that,' I reply, tracing my fingers over a red chiffon blouse. 'Did Phoebe wear this to work?' I ask.

He nods and I spy a multi-coloured knitted jumper peeking out from underneath a couple of other garments. I pull it out. 'She had this when we were teenagers,' I murmur.

'She liked slobbing around in it in front of the telly,' he tells me with a sad smile.

I bring it up to my nose. 'It still smells of her. Everything does.'

A tear rolls down my cheek and he reaches out and touches my arm.

'I'm okay,' I say gently, going to sit on the bed. I look up at him. 'Did you know that Phoebe knew I was in love with you?'

His expression changes only a little. He nods and kneels down at my feet so now he's the one staring up at me. He places his hands on my thighs. 'And she knew that I had feelings for you, too,' he says.

I cover his hands with mine. Neither of us breaks eye contact.

'I read her diary.' He's admitting what I had just in this

moment realised. 'I had to know what was going through her mind,' he says.

'That's how you found out about Remy?' I ask.

He nods. 'She'd told me about him on her year out, so I was shocked to see his name on the accident report. And then Phoebe's things came back from Chamonix, including the notepad that she used to sometimes write in. I resisted reading it for a very long time, but it was always there, taunting me. Finally I couldn't stand it any longer. Have you read it?' he asks.

'No.' I shake my head. 'Rose told me what it said.' Whoops, I've just blown her cover. 'She has it now,' I confess.

'I know,' he replies with a wry smile. 'I knew she'd taken it.'

'You should have told her you knew. She was worried you were going to flip out.'

He tuts with mock despair before his expression grows serious again. 'Are you alright?' he asks me.

'Yes.' I nod, surprised at how alright I am.

'Are you still okay to go on our date?'

'Definitely.' I smile at him and then turn to look at the mess on the bed. 'Let's get these things packed away neatly first, though.'

'Okay,' he agrees, standing up.

I shed a few more tears as we unpack and fold up Phoebe's clothes, but Angus lets me be, and I feel a welcome sense of relief once it's done. We leave the boxes in the left-hand wardrobe. If I do move in with him, we'll cross that bridge when we come to it, but for now, I'm at peace.

*

As soon as I see the picnic hamper, I know where we're going. It's late afternoon by the time we arrive, and the sun is casting long shadows across the hills of the Peak District. We park up in our usual secluded spot on a grassy verge, and Angus swings open the back door of the Land Rover. His music wafts out of the car as we set up our picnic on the rug, but the volume is low enough to not drown out the sound of the nearby stream or the birds chirping as they fly overhead.

'Did you and Phoebe ever come here?' I ask, and immediately wish that question hadn't come to mind.

'No.' He shakes his head, and I feel a swell of relief. There's something so lovely about this being our place. Just ours.

'Show us your bits, then,' I prompt, remembering what he said to me the first time we came here.

He grins and pulls out grapes, millionaire shortbread and salt and vinegar crisps.

'You've even got the same food!' I exclaim, sitting up straighter.

He laughs and pulls out a bottle of sparkling wine. 'And this is for you. I'm driving so I won't drink.'

'Aw.' I lean across and give him a chaste kiss before taking the bottle and putting it back in the bag. 'I don't want to drink alone, and anyway, remember what we said about being sober tonight.' I say it flippantly, but my face betrays me.

He raises one eyebrow and then crawls over in my direction. He kisses me on my lips softly, but deepens it after a moment, so I fall back against the rug, pulling him with me.

We're secluded from view here, and I don't think the sheep in a nearby field count. As he unbuttons my jeans, I hazard a guess that we're not waiting until tonight...

I cry out as he takes me, but then he stills, and it's so intense, being this close to him, this connected. It's almost unbearable.

'I love you,' he says against my lips.

I clasp his face in my hands and stare into his eyes, which are brimming with emotion, just like mine. 'I love you, too, Angus Templeton. I'll love you for the rest of my life.'

Chapter 42

Rose

I'm standing on a balcony of a chalet in Argentière, staring up at the nearby mountains soaring into the crystalline blue sky. I take a deep breath and slowly exhale.

This is the exact same chalet where Phoebe and Josie stayed on their hen trip and tonight I will be sleeping in Phoebe's bed. Josie was worried when I asked for every minute detail, but I tried to reassure her that I'm not losing my mind. I just want to feel close to my sister.

Right now, though, I feel cold.

I shiver and go back inside, sliding the door shut behind me before crawling onto the sofa and pulling a thick, woolly blanket up to my neck.

But I know that nothing I do will make me warm.

It's been a week since I left England. I stayed in Paris for a few days, trying to soak up the atmosphere and prepare myself for what lay ahead. Then I took a train down to Saint Gervais and caught the Mont Blanc Express up through the valley to Chamonix, staring out of the window at the imposing mountains growing gradually bigger with each mile, heightening the tension that I would soon arrive at the town where Phoebe felt so at home.

From my position on the sofa I stare up at the mountains again, scarcely able to believe that my dad and sister used to climb them. The melting ice cascading down the rocks looks like a white waterfall, as though God has upended a carton of milk on them. It is absolutely breathtaking. I feel a pang of homesickness and wish Mum, Eliza or Angus were here with me to share this experience. Or Toby…

Reaching over to the coffee table, I pick up Phoebe's purple diary and her iPhone with the headphones still attached. I plug in the earpieces and press play, listening as the dreamy strains of a song by an artist called Greta Svabo Bech waft out. Then I open the diary and begin to read. I want Phoebe's experiences to be fresh in my mind when I go to the top of the Aiguille du Midi tomorrow.

It's early September, and around 20 degrees in Chamonix town centre and partly sunny. I'm wearing Phoebe's grey hoodie and I feel snug as I stand on a bridge, looking down at the milky green river rushing noisily below, before striding uphill to the main part of the town. Chamonix is pretty and it has a nice vibe, with people sitting on the pavement outside restaurants and cafés. I walk down a shopping street and through a square, gazing up at the surrounding mountains. They start off green near the bottom and grow increasingly white as they project into the sky. In places the slopes are banded with dark green pine trees, in others they're striped with cables that carry the ski lifts, not that anyone will be skiing for a while. Far over my head, brilliantly coloured parachutes float this way and that, attached to the nutcases who deem it a good idea to jump off a mountain.

My sister was one of those nutcases, I muse with admiration tinged with sadness. Remy took her paragliding on their first proper date.

I'm intrigued to meet this man, after everything I've read about him, but I'll have to wait a few days. He's currently with a group of mountaineers on Mont Blanc, but he has promised to text me on his return. I hope he wasn't too shocked to receive my email. He didn't let on if he was.

I've already bought my extortionately priced Aiguille du Midi ticket – thank goodness for Mum because I never would have been able to afford to do everything I'm doing with my meagre bakery earnings – so after a while I head back down the hill to the cable car entrance and join the queue winding inside.

When I'm standing inside a cabin packed with people, the door whooshes shut and we begin our flight away from Chamonix. I emit a squeal along with most of the other passengers as we sail up and over the pylons, and I remember Phoebe saying that she'd never tire of the sound.

I turn to look at the girl who's manning the car: she's young and pretty with chocolate-brown eyes, and her straight, dark hair is partly tied back from her oval-shaped face. For a moment I picture Phoebe in her place, with blonde hair instead of brown and wearing the same dark uniform and I have to fight back tears. I look down to see us clear the tree line, and then we're passing over rocks and grass and disembarking to switch cable cars at the middle station.

On the next car, I manage to secure a spot near the front and grip the handrail for support as crisp mountain air streams in through a crack in the window. Very soon the rocks below us are covered with snow, and in the distance I can make out tiny red and orange tents on an enormous white expanse. What did Phoebe write when Dad came over and climbed Mont Blanc with her? They weren't *dwarfed* by the mountain, they were *microscopisized* by it. I don't think it's even a word in the English language, but it should be. I can see what she meant.

The cable car breaks through the clouds to cheers of delight and I look in dazed awe at the mountain peaks protruding through the fluffy whiteness. It's almost otherworldly – the sun is bright and the sky is as blue as blue can be.

Our ascent becomes almost vertical and only a metre or so in front of me is a sheer rock face, too steep for even snow to cling on to, although a multitude of icicles manage it. I suddenly feel quite dizzy with vertigo. A small group of climbers to my left are walking along a steep, narrow ridge and I can barely believe my eyes. It looks so dangerous – and Phoebe and Dad used to do that sort of thing often!

The dizziness I'm feeling worsens as I step out of the car and follow the crowd down the stairs. I feel distinctly unsteady as I walk onto a wide metal footbridge, astonished at the low height of the handrails on either side. Cloud hovers only ten metres below, so I have no idea how far the drop would be if I were to topple over the railings. Around me, majestic brown and grey snow-splatted mountaintops pierce the sky, but I feel too giddy and short of breath to appreciate the view. Is this what altitude does to you? I honestly had no idea. I've never been this high before in my life.

Feeling rigid with fear, I force myself to turn and study the building wrapped around one jagged peak. I find it astonishing that people managed to build up here. Who clung to the mountaintop and hammered in that nail? Are they absolutely mental?

It occurs to me that somewhere inside that mass of manmade material is the staff apartment, and then I realise that I'm standing on the footbridge where Remy and Phoebe shared their first kiss. I'm amazed that she felt relaxed enough to smile, let alone kiss anyone up here or stay overnight with only one colleague for company. I'd be far too scared to do that, yet she was only eighteen and stayed up here on a fairly regular basis.

The panoramic viewing platform is at the top of the building, past the café and shop, I recall from Phoebe's diary, but I feel too shaky to climb any higher right now. I decide to go and take a look at the ice cave instead.

Once over the footbridge and into the tunnel, I feel slightly safer. I pause for a moment to try to compose myself, standing clear of the melting ice dripping from the ceiling. Most of the people passing by are climbers, wearing backpacks adorned with ice axes and ropes, and harnesses around their waists, jangling with carabiners, slings, camming devices and other essential climbing gear. Harnesses have always reminded me of oversized charm bracelets and I have a flashback to Phoebe and Dad, fully geared-up as they set off early from a campsite in Wales. Mum, Eliza and I were huddling miserably around the campfire in the drizzle, trying to keep warm, but Dad and Phoebe were buzzing with excitement about their imminent climb. Nothing seemed to scare Phoebe. Nothing except for falling hopelessly and uncontrollably in love with Remy.

When I read about her fears in her diary, I couldn't believe she chose to leave him behind, that she chose home and safety instead of the rollercoaster of emotions she experienced with him. But maybe she regretted it. Maybe that was why she was willing to risk her life to spend one more day with him.

Again, I'm curious to meet this man.

I move on from where I'm standing, and it's not long before I reach the ice cave and beyond it the ridge where Remy and his cousin Amelie came in off the mountain.

Carved out scallop shapes give the walls around me the appearance of whipped egg white, and ahead the light is blinding as it reflects off the snowy slopes. This is the same ridge that I saw earlier from the cable car and it looks just as steep. I feel nervous at the sight of some approaching climbers. They're tethered together by rope, but *still*... It seems like it would be so easy to lose their footing and slip, pulling down others with them.

The horror of Phoebe's death hits me with the impact of a punch to the stomach and my heart starts to beat faster. The feeling intensifies, and suddenly it seems like a very real possibility that I'm going to faint.

'Are you okay?' I'm vaguely aware of a young climber asking this question. I try to be brave and nod my head, but he isn't buying it. 'It's the altitude,' he says in an American accent. 'You should think about going back down.'

I nod again and stumble away from him, slipping on the slushy ice and snow under my feet.

'Do you need some help?' he calls after me.

I shake my head and feel my way out of the ice cave.

I'm still in a state of vertiginous terror as I climb back onto the cable car. I feel like I'm at the top of a very, very tall ladder and have to turn around and climb down the first rung without losing my footing.

The cable car sets off slowly, and as we come back through the cloud, the grey rocks emerge and the air is dark and gloomy. But I feel a wave of relief that I'm on my way back down again. I was thinking about getting off at the intermediate stop, but right now I just want to put my feet down on flat ground.

Chamonix is not particularly pretty from this height – a grey, dull stretch of buildings running all the way down the valley – but it's a welcome sight to me.

That evening, I sit out on the balcony and try to make sense of the day I've had. I feel very low, like I've let Phoebe down by not appreciating what she loved. Her diary descriptions are completely alien compared to my experience. The top of the Aiguille was stunning, yes, but how could I admire its beauty when my heart was in my throat and I found it difficult to breathe?

I can see how Phoebe felt inspired here, and I understand how she wanted to be up there on top of the world, but I can't imagine actually going through with what she did. She was adventurous, brave and self-assured.

We couldn't be more different.

I don't feel as close to her tonight. And it makes me feel sad.

The valley before me is shrouded in darkness and the pine trees look black, not green. But beyond the trees, the mountains are still light in colour, the sky above blue as it fades into night.

The reality of Phoebe dying up there suddenly hits me again, and I have to hurry back inside before I lose it.

I sob my heart out that night. At one point, Eliza's name pops up on my Caller ID and I feel unbearably alone as I let the phone ring. She wouldn't know how to handle me like this. I cry myself to sleep soon afterwards.

The next morning, when I wake up, I lie there for a long time wondering if I've been very stupid by thinking that I could – *should* – do this. I feel like I dreamt my trip up the mountain yesterday. I don't want my stay to be plagued by grief and despair, so eventually I get up and resolve to pull myself together.

When I made the decision to go travelling by myself, I felt liberated. Not exactly free – the thought of what awaited me here gave me a knot in my stomach that feels a long way from unravelling – but I knew it would do me good to go out on my own. The last time I felt like that was when I went to university, but between then and now I've lost some of my confidence and independence. I'd like to get it back.

The purpose of this trip is to honour Phoebe, to try to keep her memory alive. I don't want to crumble every time I visit one of her old haunts. I want to appreciate the things she saw and respect the things that she did.

I reach for her diary and have a flick through before making a decision. Today I'm going to go on the Montenvers train to visit the grotto.

*

The little red train departs from Chamonix and I smile at the young family sitting opposite before turning to stare out of the window at the ferns nestled in amongst the rocks as we chug steeply up the mountain.

Mer du Glace, France's largest glacier, is 7km long and 200m deep, and its name translates to Sea of Ice. The grotto is dug out every summer because the glacier moves about 70m a year, and there are hundreds of steps to walk down before you reach it. Eventually I make it into the huge, cold tunnel of ice. It's lit by colourful lights and I take photos of the various 'rooms' that I pass along the way. Phoebe was right: this is totally up my street. I try not to think about how she wanted to bring both Eliza and me back here with her.

Later I head to the restaurant in the Grand Hotel for lunch. It's an imposing rectangular granite-stone building several storeys high, but is cosy inside, with wooden-panelled interiors. I order the *tartiflette* – a traditional Savoyard dish made with potatoes, reblochon cheese, lardons and onions. The calories are sky high, but I need comfort food right now. I'm battling loneliness – and grief.

I wish I could have persuaded Eliza to come. I remember that she called me last night and I send her a quick, breezy text to tell her what I'm up to. I'd love to talk to her, but politeness gets the better of me – I'd feel too rude having a conversation on my phone in the middle of a restaurant.

We do talk to each other that night, while I'm sitting outside on the balcony with a glass of wine in my hand.

'It's stunning here,' I tell her. 'I can see why Phoebe was so drawn to the mountains.'

'You're not planning on moving, are you?' she asks with alarm.

I laugh. 'No. This is her place, not mine, but it is beautiful.'

'Is it hard?' she asks quietly.

'A little,' I admit.

We both fall silent. She doesn't want me to elaborate, and I don't want to burden her with my tales of woe.

'I wish you were here,' I say.

'I'm glad I'm not,' she replies indignantly, making me smile again. 'Where are you at the moment?' she asks.

'On the balcony, looking up at the mountains. They're only a few hundred metres away, across a valley dotted with chalets and a hell of a lot of pine trees. It's getting dark now, but you can see the top of the Aiguille du Midi from here.'

'What's that?' Eliza asks.

'The mountain Phoebe worked on during her gap year,' I reply.

'Oh,' she says, leaving a long pause before adding sadly: 'I wish I'd spoken to her more that year. I hardly know anything about what she got up to.'

'Neither did I,' I'm quick to correct her. 'I learnt almost everything I know from pilfering her diary. I was having too much fun at university to think twice about you two.' I say this teasingly, but the comment has a lot of truth to it. I also avoided Phoebe after my mortifying faux pas with Angus. Yes, shame on me.

'What have you done since you got there?' she asks, so I fill her in, steering clear of my freak-out yesterday.

'When are you seeing Remy?' she eventually asks.

'He's back from his climbing trip tomorrow. I'll give him a call in a couple of days if he hasn't got in contact by then.'

I imagine he's less enthusiastic to meet me than I am to meet him.

To my surprise, Remy lives only a five-minute walk from where I'm staying. He's invited me to his place for a coffee and I'm nervous as I follow his directions through the streets of Argentière two days after my conversation with Eliza. His apartment is located within a five-storey traditional chalet, not dissimilar to mine, and when he answers the intercom, it's in English.

'Hello?'

He's expecting me.

'Hi, Remy, it's Rose,' I confirm, my stomach a tangle of anxiety.

'I'm on the second floor.' This time I hear his French accent clearly.

'Okay, thanks,' I reply as the door buzzes open.

The air inside the chalet is cool, and the sound of my booted footsteps reverberates around the walls and stone floor as I make my way up the stairs. Nearing the top of the second flight, I hear a door click open, and by the time I reach the top, Remy is standing on the landing.

He has short, dark-brown hair and a neatly trimmed beard. His eyes are startlingly blue and they widen as I smile at him. A moment later, the blood drains from his face.

'Hello,' I say, feeling a pang of sympathy as the triplet effect takes hold.

He starts and comes to his senses, stepping back from the door and holding it open.

'Come in, come in,' he says.

He's wearing dark blue jeans and a yellow T-shirt and his face, legs and forearms are tanned and lean. The edgy feeling in my stomach intensifies as I walk into his apartment.

'Can I get you a coffee or something cold to drink?' he asks. He sounds uneasy, so it's not just me.

'I'd love a coffee,' I reply.

'Take a seat,' he says, heading off into the kitchen.

His apartment is even closer to the mountains than mine is, with the same sliding doors opening up onto a large balcony. I sink onto the pale-blue sofa, the cushions having given up the ghost some time ago. The coffee table is wooden and solid and the rug under my feet is bordering on threadbare. The walls are painted ochre and there's graphic art hanging on them.

'I like your apartment,' I say when Remy returns with our drinks.

'The furniture belonged to my grandmother,' he tells me with a smile, handing me a mug and sitting in a faded brown leather armchair. He crosses one leg over the other, resting his ankle on the opposite knee. It's a relaxed gesture, but I'm pretty sure he's anything but.

'Thank you for agreeing to meet me.' I decide to get straight to the point.

'It's okay,' he says, placing his chin on his upended palm. His eyes keep darting away from me, like it hurts to look at me for too long, but they keep finding their way back to my face. A morbid fascination.

I didn't hesitate to get in contact with Remy because I already felt like I knew him, but now I don't know what to say.

'Sorry,' I blurt. 'I know this is weird. It's weird for me, too. I've read so much about you that I feel like we're already friends, but this is harder than I thought it would be.'

'Phoebe told you about me?' He looks confused. He probably thinks he misunderstood me.

'No.' I shake my head. 'Not really. When she came back from France ten years ago, she went straight to university. I read about you in her journal.'

He looks taken aback. 'I remember her writing in that.' He swallows. 'What did she say?'

'She wrote about everything you did together. Well, not *everything*.' I blush. 'But she wrote about how you met, your first date, visiting the grotto, the trails you hiked and the mountains you climbed.'

He looks shaken, but I continue.

'I'm trying to understand. What happened on the day she died? What happened on the night before? I know that you met her in a bar in Chamonix, but had you pre-arranged it? Did you know she was going to be there?'

'No,' he says firmly. 'I was stunned to see her.'

'She claimed that she wasn't very surprised to see you.'

'She wasn't,' he acknowledges, leaning forward in his seat. He rests his elbows on his knees, clasping his hands together.

'She said it felt like fate,' I add.

He stares ahead in a daze. 'It did.'

'You know she was getting married, right?' I didn't mean that to sound as sharp as it came out.

'Of course. She told me,' he frowns. 'I wasn't trying to win her back. I was just pleased to be able to catch up with her. We hadn't seen each other in years, but I'd thought about her often and I was glad to see her again. She seemed happy.'

'She was,' I say in a tiny voice.

He looks pained and a second later his blue eyes fill with tears.

I press on, but more gently. 'She asked to go climbing with you, right?'

He nods, his eyes spilling over. He brushes his tears away, but his bottom lip is trembling and I have an urge to go over and hug him.

'I should have said no.' He looks down at his hands for a long moment before lifting his eyes to meet mine again. 'I didn't know she hadn't climbed in years. Why did she stop? She used to love it so much.'

To my alarm, I realise that he actually expects me to answer this question.

'Er, I don't know.' I think for a moment. 'Angus didn't climb,' I tell him, feeling like I'm betraying Gus by admitting it.

He nods thoughtfully, but the gesture transforms into a headshake.

'What?' I prompt.

He looks full of despair. 'We used to work so well as a team, but that morning we lost a lot of time. She was holding the group up. There were three other experienced climbers, but she didn't have the speed or the ability to keep up with them, although she was trying. She was embarrassed, but she didn't want to give up.' He shakes his head again, fighting back tears. 'I didn't even think to ask if she was fit enough because I just assumed that she would be.'

'Could her death have been avoided?' I feel shell-shocked. 'Was it her fault?'

'No, Rose, it was *my* fault!' He raises his voice, anguished. 'She shouldn't have been up there in the first place! I'm a mountain guide. I should know who's fit to climb and who's not. That's my job!'

This time I do get up and go over to him because I can't bear to sit there watching him suffer alone. I kneel at his feet and put my arms around his neck, and a moment later he breaks down, his arms encircling my back. We hold each other as we sob – two strangers who are unfamiliar, yet so familiar to each other in the most unusual of ways. I *look* like his lost love, I *feel* like his lost love, and it's like *I* know *him* intimately, because I've been inside my sister's head reading about him.

'I should have said no to her,' he cries, his voice stifled by my shoulder.

I tighten my grip on him. 'No one ever said no to Phoebe.'

For some reason, my comment seems to calm us both down, and only a minute or so passes before we gather ourselves together. Remy excuses himself to go and get a box of tissues, and when he returns, we both blow our noses loudly and smile at each other shyly as I return to my spot on the sofa.

But the worst is not yet over.

'How did she die? I want to know everything,' I remind him with quiet but strong determination. If ever there were a time when my curiosity could burn me, this would be it, but there's no suppressing that part of my personality now.

'We were caught in an avalanche,' he says.

I already know this, but I want to understand what it was like and I say as much. 'Please tell me everything you can remember. Every detail.'

He swallows and stares ahead in a daze. 'It was like being hit with wet cement. Heavy. And we could hear it coming. It sounded like snakes hissing.'

My eyes widen. 'So she knew she was going to die?'

He shakes his head, glancing at me. 'Yes, she was frightened. The look in her eyes haunts me at night. But Phoebe was such a positive person, such a fighter. She hadn't changed *that* much. I don't believe she thought she would die. Your father taught her avalanche survival techniques – I remember her repeating his advice on one of our climbs years ago, things like try to swim through the snow and keep an air gap in front of your mouth...'

He's more animated now, like his mind is on what he knows and what he's comfortable with, rather than our difficult subject. I bring him back to the hellish reality of it soon enough.

'I keep having nightmares about her being stuck under the freezing snow, trying to get out,' I say, as a new stream of tears begins to cascade down my cheeks.

He shakes his head. 'It wasn't like that, at least, not for Phoebe. For Phoebe it was quick. It was instant.'

This time it's he who gets up and comes over to me. He sits beside me and closes his warm hands around mine, turning me to face him.

'She was killed by a large block of ice, Rose.' He swallows. 'I saw it happen.'

'Oh God.'

He increases the pressure on my hands. 'It was quick. I promise you, she didn't suffer.'

'But she was scared?' I ask.

'Momentarily, yes. But icefall struck us before the snow. The size of the block that hit her... She could never have survived it. We were roped together and both of us were torn clean off the mountain. We cartwheeled down with the snow. I'd sent the rest of our group on ahead, so they saw what happened and contacted mountain rescue. I was wearing an avalanche transceiver and we weren't buried very deep so they managed to locate us relatively quickly and dig us out. If they hadn't, I would have died, too.'

'But you say Phoebe never stood a chance?' I ask in a choked voice.

'No. She was still tethered to me, and I knew with the utmost certainty that she was already gone.'

I gulp back a sob and a moment later we both break down.

I was too anxious to eat lunch today, so when Remy asks if I'd like to go out for a bite to eat with him, I agree. We walk down the hill to Argentière's small town centre and into a bar.

'What can I get you?' Remy asks me.

'A white wine, please.'

'Go grab us a table. I'll bring the drinks over. Here, take a menu, too.'

After we've placed our food order, we settle in for a chat, and I feel more relaxed now that we've got the hard stuff out of the way. Remy asks where I've been since leaving the UK so I fill him in about Paris and I'm aware of him searching my face, studying every tiny detail as he tries to make sense of the fact that I look exactly like the girl he used to love.

'It's uncanny, isn't it?' I say softly. 'If Eliza were here, you'd be even more freaked out.'

He jolts, startled. 'Sorry, I didn't mean to stare. Yes, it is strange, and that top you're wearing… Is it…?'

'Hers,' I confirm. It's this damn grey hoodie again.

'I thought it looked familiar. I think she was wearing it the night I saw her again. The night before…'

'I'm so sorry,' I say with concern. All of Phoebe's possessions from her hen trip were returned to Angus – this top included. 'I didn't even think twice when I put it on this morning. Do you want me to take it off?'

He waves me away. 'No, it's fine. Really, it's fine,' he tries to reassure me. 'So how do you like Chamonix?'

'It's not quite how I expected,' I reply a little downheartedly.

He looks intrigued, and slightly perturbed, perhaps because I've been talking quite enthusiastically up until now. 'In what way?'

'It's beautiful,' I'm quick to acknowledge. 'I mean, it's absolutely stunning. But I sort of expected to come here and walk in Phoebe's shoes. I thought it would make me feel closer to her, but so far she's seemed all the more alien to me. She and I are *so* different. Practically the only thing we have in common is how we look.'

He reaches across the table and presses my hand. 'I'm sorry. I hate to think of you having a bad experience here. How much longer are you planning on staying?'

'Another week or so.'

'I have a few days off. Perhaps I could show you around a bit? Show you the Chamonix I know?'

'I'm not going rock climbing,' I state firmly, just to make it perfectly clear.

He shakes his head and looks away from me, very serious all of a sudden. 'No,' he says. 'No, there's no chance of that.'

The next morning, Remy is in a brighter mood when he turns up outside my chalet in a silver-grey Nissan X-Trail. There are two mountain bikes perched on the roof racks.

'What are they for?' I ask him warily.

'Can you ride a bike?' he asks in return, a twinkle in his bluer than blue eyes.

'Yes,' I reply hesitantly.

'Then hop in,' he says with a grin.

'I haven't ridden in a long time,' I warn as he pulls out of the car park.

'It's not something you forget,' he teases. 'And I promise you it's not a difficult ride.'

We're going to Le Tour, which Remy tells me is a ski area in the winter and a great place for hikes in the summer. It's only around a five-minute drive to the upper end of the valley. When we arrive, Remy unloads the bikes from the roof, while I fumble around with the helmet he's brought for me.

'Here, let me help you,' he says, coming over to adjust the chinstrap. I'm struggling.

'How is Amelie, by the way?' I find myself asking.

He looks at me with surprise.

'Sorry, I feel like I know her, too,' I explain. 'She visited you and Phoebe a few times during that summer.'

I also know from Phoebe's most recent diary that she lost touch with Cécile. She wrote that Cécile had moved to Germany, but she would have attempted to catch up with her if she'd still been here.

Remy smiles and nods. 'Yes, she did. She's very well, thank you for asking. She got married last year, but no babies yet. Here you go,' he says, wheeling one of the bikes towards me. 'Climb on and I'll just check the seat doesn't need adjusting.'

I do as he says.

'Perfect,' he comments. 'Feel okay?'

'Yes.' I nod.

'I'll lead, but tell me if I'm going too fast or too slow,' he says.

The latter is unlikely.

We bike up the mountain on a not too difficult trail and then stop off for lunch. There's no snow at this time of year, but the view from the café is stunning – we can see down the entire Chamonix valley with the Mont Blanc range in the distance.

The trip is so much fun, thrilling and a little scary at times, but mostly exhilarating.

'Thank you so much,' I say to Remy on the car journey home. 'I really enjoyed that.'

My cheeks are rosy red from the cool mountain air and my hair has come loose with the wind and the motion of bouncing over the rocky ground. I feel happy.

'I'm glad to hear it.' He returns my smile. 'What now? Have you dinner plans?'

'No, but you don't have to—'

'I want to,' he cuts me off. 'There's a restaurant in Chamonix that I think you'd like.'

'You do actually look a little different to each other,' Remy says from across the table.

'Oh?' I say, pleasantly surprised that he thinks so.

'I can't quite put my finger on it, but I'm sure I could tell you apart.' He sits forward in his seat. 'What do you do, Rose?'

'I'm not really sure, to be honest,' I reply with a smile.

He raises an inquisitive eyebrow so I tell him about how I quit nursing, and how I've rediscovered my passion for gardening.

'What about you?' I ask warmly. 'Do you like your job?'

His smile falters and he looks down at the table. 'I did and, yes, I still do. It took me a while to go back to work after the accident.'

'Were you hurt?' I ask gently. I don't want to lose it here, and neither does he, I'm sure, so we won't stay with this subject for long.

'I fractured my ribs, but it was mainly only surface cuts and bruises. I was very lucky.' His eyes are shining as he glances up at me. 'I'm sorry,' he whispers.

'Stop,' I say quickly, touching my hand to his. 'If you hadn't sent the rest of your group on ahead, it sounds like you all could have…'

He swallows and I take a deep breath and try to compose myself.

'I didn't mean to bring it up again, but I'm glad you're still working as a guide. Phoebe was happy to hear that you were doing a job that you loved, even though I think she was a little envious.'

'Oh, it also has its drawbacks,' he tells me wryly. 'The worst thing is turning people back when the conditions aren't right or you don't think they're ready for it. Getting so close to the summit of Mont Blanc and then telling clients who've paid a lot of money that it's not going to happen… I deal with some very disillusioned people.'

'When are you next going up?' I ask.

'In a few days' time. I have a group of Australians coming.'

'Tell me about the climb you did with Phoebe and Dad,' I prompt.

I'm glad to sit and listen to him, watching as he grows increasingly animated talking about his favourite hobby. It sounds like he got on well with Dad – they had a mutual respect for each other – although Remy did say it was sometimes a case of too many cooks.

'I joined them on their preparation climb, in the lead-up to their Mont Blanc ascent. The White Lady was something they planned to do just the two of them,' he explains. 'Anyway, your father wanted to lead, but I was used to doing that.' He smiles good-naturedly. 'Phoebe encouraged me to let him have his way.'

I laugh, remembering how pig-headed Dad could be at times. He wouldn't have let a young upstart get one over him. 'Well, he certainly had a lot of experience,' I say diplomatically.

'That wasn't why I bowed down to him,' Remy replies with a smirk. 'I just didn't want to piss off my girlfriend's father.'

We both laugh.

It is the loveliest evening, which is surreal considering the tragedy that brought us together.

'Your climbs do sound amazing,' I say when he's finished regaling me with stories.

'You've really never been tempted?' he asks.

'I couldn't think of anything worse.'

He smiles. 'Are you afraid of heights?'

'No, it's not that. Although I did feel incredibly unsteady at the top of the Aiguille du Midi. I was a bit freaked out,' I admit. 'I wanted to go across to Helbronner, but I needed to get back down again.'

'That's a shame,' he says, looking disappointed on my behalf. 'It is the most incredible journey, travelling over crevasses, surrounded by mountain peaks.'

'Now you're making me feel bad that I missed it,' I say with a little laugh.

'I'll go back with you tomorrow, if you like?'

I decide to take Remy up on his offer, so the next day, we return to the Aiguille du Midi. I still feel short of breath and a bit giddy, but I'm not nearly as anxious with him by my side.

We catch one of the tiny, four-person egg-like cable cars to Italy, which glides over the glacier and wild crevasses below. I'm by no means relaxed, but I feel somewhat better equipped to be able to enjoy the view without worrying too much that I'm going to faint.

In Helbronner, we visit the crystal museum before going to the café for lunch.

'I forgot you used to live in Turin with an Italian girl-friend,' I say after Remy orders in fluent Italian.

He shakes his head as we take our food to a table. 'I wish I had access to *your* diaries. You have an unfair advantage.'

I laugh and sit down. 'My diaries are horrendous. I was such a love-struck idiot as a teenager.'

He raises one eyebrow.

'I read them recently,' I explain, cracking open my can of Diet Coke. 'I went through *a lot* of crushes.'

On the return journey, Remy asks me about Angus. 'You say he didn't climb.'

'No.'

'But he and Phoebe got on well?'

'Very well,' I reply. 'They had a lot of fun together.'

I sound a bit defensive, but I'm uncomfortable talking about Angus to Remy.

'I don't think Angus had anything to do with Phoebe stopping climbing,' I say. 'He never would have tried to prevent her from doing something that made her so happy. Now I think about it, it's more likely that she stopped because Dad died. It probably upset her too much to go on her own.'

Remy nods thoughtfully, staring out of the window.

Sometimes I think it's a blessing that Dad died before Phoebe. I don't know how he would have coped, knowing that he set her on a track towards her death. But then, he understood the risks. They both did. To me, climbing is a selfish sport. To them, it was as fundamental as breathing.

'Where were you when you lost her?' I ask quietly, following Remy's gaze across the jagged peaks, the snow catching the afternoon sunshine and reflecting it back to us blindingly.

'I'll show you when we get back to the Aiguille,' he replies quietly.

I feel like I'm going to throw up as we take the elevator to the top terrace, and I'm shaking as Remy leads me to the railings and puts his hand on my back, but he doesn't make me wait before telling me what I need to know.

'There,' he says, pointing. 'We were on Mont Blanc du Tacul, just in front of Mont Blanc.'

My throat has swollen up painfully, so all I can do is stare.

'She joined our group on a preparation climb for Mont Blanc,' he tells me gently, 'like the one we did with your father. We were planning to turn around at the top of Mont Blanc du Tacul and come back here.'

I nod again. Tears are streaming down my cheeks and it's a wonder they're not freezing into tracks in the cold air.

When I thought about doing this trip, it occurred to me that I could bring some pages of Phoebe's diary to scatter on the wind. But now the idea seems too melodramatic, so I stand there in silence and remember her instead.

I remember her sitting on the grass in the park, making daisy chains to drape around my neck...

I remember her climbing up the rock wall in Sale, looking down at the rest of us with a deliriously proud grin on her face...

I remember her running into the bedroom that we shared in London and waggling her bottom at me, while wearing those damned unicorn knickers that we all fought over...

I remember her laughing...

I remember her crying...

I remember my sister, my beloved sister, one part of me, despite how different we were, and when I open my mouth to say goodbye, a sob comes out instead, and it's Remy I turn to for comfort.

'Thank you for being here for me,' I whisper. 'I honestly don't know how I would have coped doing this alone.'

'I'm happy I had a chance to meet you, Rose. I really do wish you and your sister all the best. You can come back and see me anytime.'

'Thank you,' I say, but I know in my heart that it's time to shut the book on this chapter.

I call Mum a couple of days later, before I leave Argentière.

'I can't believe it!' she squawks down the phone, making me flinch. 'Why didn't you tell me that Eliza and Angus were together?'

In the midst of my own dramas, I'd forgotten the ones that were going on at home.

'Has she told you, then?' I say wryly.

'She's moving in with him! Into his room, not yours, *his*!'

I laugh. 'I know, Mum.'

'And you're okay about it?' she asks.

'Yes, I'm okay about it,' I confirm. Not happy, just okay. But I hope that will change with time.

'Well, that's something, at least.'

'What did Judy say?' I ask.

'She's very apprehensive,' Mum replies, and I feel a pang of sympathy for Eliza because I know she was worried about Judy's reaction. 'I think she's concerned that Angus is trying to replace Phoebe, but—'

'He's not,' I interrupt. 'Who are we kidding? Phoebe can't be replaced and Eliza is her own, unique person.

Angus has always cared about her. And Phoebe knew it. She understood it. In fact, she even felt a little bit guilty about it because she got to Angus first and she knew Eliza was heartbroken.'

'You sound like you know an awful lot about it,' Mum says, disconcerted.

More than I should, that's for sure.

'I just want everyone to be happy,' I reply.

'That's good,' she says. 'Because I do, too. And,' she adds, 'so does Judy. She and Angus had a proper heart-to-heart and she's given them her blessing.'

I'm really pleased to hear it.

'So,' I say, changing the subject. 'Have you been into the bakery lately?'

'Oh, I meant to tell you!' she exclaims. 'I met Toby's mother!'

'You didn't?' I gasp.

'I did! She was outside in the garden when I went to check on the plants. She seemed nice, if a little shy. She said to pass on her regards to you.'

I'm astonished. Delighted. And as soon as we hang up, I find myself calling Toby's mobile.

'You took your time about it,' he says when I tell him it's me, and the sound of his deep, dry voice makes me feel instantly jittery.

'How are you?' I ask with a smile. 'I heard your mum has been into the bakery?'

'Yeah,' he says warmly. 'It's been pretty amazing, the turnaround.'

'What happened?' I ask.

'I sort of lost it with her a few days after you left. Ended up shouting my head off.'

'Oh.'

'Yeah, I felt really bad about it at the time,' he says heavily. 'But, I don't know, it seemed to spur her on. She seems determined to do what she can to get better.'

'I'm so pleased to hear it.'

'It's a lot down to you,' he says seriously.

'No, I didn't do anything.'

'You did. More than you know.'

We both fall silent and I hug my knees to my chest. I have to remind myself that nothing has changed – he's still too young for me – but I can't ignore how much I've missed talking to him.

'Where are you now?' he asks.

'I'm in Chamonix. Well, Argentière, the next village along. I've been here for a few days, but I'm going to Geneva tomorrow.'

'How's it been?'

'Surprisingly therapeutic,' I reply.

'You thought it would be, right?'

'I hoped, but I was worried I'd screwed up by coming here.' He listens as I fill him in.

'It's so picturesque,' I say. 'You should see the view from my chalet.'

'Send me a selfie of you on the balcony,' he prompts.

'Okay, I will do as soon as I get off the phone.'

In the background, I hear a couple of lads shouting.

'Where are you?' I ask, confused.

'At the park,' he replies.

'Send me a selfie, too,' I say before I can think better of it.

We end our call and I go out onto the balcony and hold my phone aloft, trying to catch the snowy, sunlit tops of the mountains in the background. I check the photo and press send, and a moment later receive his.

He's lying on the grass in the late afternoon sunshine. His face is bathed in a golden glow and his dark eyes have flecks of toffee-brown in them as he stares into the lens. I shiver. Another text comes in from him, a response to the photo I sent.

'Beautiful,' he says.

I shiver again and force myself to put my phone away.

'I don't know what your problem is,' Eliza says to me on the phone as I stand outside a shop in Geneva. I've been inside taking photos of shelves bursting with cuckoo clocks, cow-bells and penknives, and now I've just stupidly admitted that I can't stop thinking about Toby.

'He's twenty-two, now, anyway,' she comments. 'They had balloons up when I went into *Jennifer's* yesterday.'

'Shit! I can't believe I forgot his birthday!'

'Don't worry, the new girl was showering him with attention.'

'What's she like?' I ask nervily.

'Ha! Gotcha,' she says, instantly cottoning on to my jealousy. I squirm in my seat. 'Late thirties, very mumsy. Can't see it happening.'

'The point is,' I say, trying to regain control of the conversation, 'Mum struggled for years to get pregnant, and my biological clock is ticking, too.'

'You're not even thirty!' she exclaims.

'But Toby's nowhere near ready to settle down.'

'No, I don't imagine he is, but Jesus, Rose, what's the big rush? Why are you so desperate to shack up and have kids? People do that a lot later in life now.'

'That's easy for you to say. You have Angus.'

'Angus and I aren't in any hurry,' she states firmly. 'Your problem is that you think you can plan how your life is going to pan out. You're like Phoebe in that respect. But love doesn't have an order. It happens when it happens.'

'I'm not in love. I just have a stupid crush.' Another one.

'Whatever. You have to work this out on your own.'

In the next couple of months, I travel through Germany, Holland, Belgium, France, Portugal, Spain and Italy. I visit the Bauhaus museum in Berlin, ride a bicycle along the canals in Amsterdam and eat too much chocolate in Bruges. The Sistine Chapel is closed, but I tour the Vatican in Rome, window shop in the grand arcades of Milan and snigger at the size of the statues' willies in Florence, trying my best to look impressed at the mastery of Michelangelo's David. I eat too many tapas at the Mercado San Miguel in Madrid and tone my legs walking up most of the seven hills in hot and sticky Lisbon, and I sit on a beach in Biarritz, watching the surfers with the Pyrenees mountains in the background.

It's a small world when you're riding the train tracks of Europe, and I bump into the same people more than once. At first I feel out of place – like I don't belong with so many youngsters on their gap years – but soon I find I have things in common with people and make friends, regardless of age.

I speak to Eliza regularly, and she seems as keen as I am to strengthen our sisterly bond. She's now a personal assistant to the head of an indie record label and she loves the role, but they work her to the bone. She doesn't mind – she's much happier being surrounded by musos instead of demanding, unappreciative customers. She's also thrilled that Joe wants her to continue to play regular gigs – I've asked Angus to record a couple of songs next time and email them to me.

I spoke to Angus before I left the Alps and gently brought him up to date with everything Remy said. It was a heart-wrenching conversation and I'm not sure that it answered all of his questions, but I think he's coming to terms with it and is ready to lay Phoebe to rest. He's committed to Eliza, one hundred per cent.

I talk to Mum too, of course, and I also frequently text and call Toby. I've given up trying to control my attraction to him. Who knows where we'll be in a year when I return? For now, we're friends, and I'm not going to fight it.

Eventually I end up back in Paris, ready for my flight to Brisbane the next day.

Eliza calls me when I'm at the top of the Eiffel Tower.

'I can't believe you're so close and I can't see you,' she says.

'You should've come over here for the weekend,' I say, trying to swallow my mouthful of *pain au chocolat*. I'm eating on the run.

'Why didn't you suggest it!' she cries, sounding traumatised.

I laugh. 'Don't worry about it. It's only just occurred to me, to be honest.'

'It's going to be horrible without you here at Christmas,' she says miserably.

'It's going to be hard for me, too,' I agree.

I've tried not to think about it too much. The first Christmas without Phoebe was unbearable. The second will be almost as challenging, but with every year that passes, we just have to believe that it will get easier.

'Have you spoken to Toby recently?' she asks.

'Last night. We speak quite regularly. Why?'

'Still think it's a crush?'

'Oh, I don't know, Eliza.' I feel my face start to warm.

'Don't be so prickly, Rose,' she teases.

'Bugger off,' I reply, making her hoot with laughter. 'I do like talking to him,' I admit when she composes herself. 'And I miss him much more than I could ever have imagined I would.'

'But do you *fancy* him?' she asks in a cheeky voice.

'He can be quite flirty on the phone,' I confide. 'I don't discourage him, but I probably should.'

'You like it too much.'

'Mmm.' I feel like my face is about to catch alight.

'Good,' she says, and I can practically hear her smile cracking her features.

I end the call soon afterwards because the tower is swaying slightly and it's making me feel nauseous. The world seems keen to let me know that I'm not so great at heights, after all.

Toby rings me an hour later as I'm wandering alongside the river on my way to a museum.

'We only spoke last night,' I say, but I'm smiling as I locate a bench to perch on.

'Eliza said you're missing me.'

'Has she been into the bakery?' It's Saturday.

'She comes in all the damn time, giving me grief.'

I laugh. 'Do you ever think she's me when she walks through the door?'

'Never,' he replies quite seriously. 'But I wish she *was* you. I miss you.'

'I miss you too, but, Toby…' I sigh. 'You know I'm going to be away for a long time, right? Who knows what's going to happen. You shouldn't wait for me.' Even as I say it, I feel a wave of nausea about the idea of him being with someone else.

'*Do* you miss me?' he asks after a long pause.

'Of course.' I sit up straighter. 'You're not in Paris, are you?'

'Do you wish I was?'

'*Are* you here?' I scan the crowds urgently.

'No, I'm not,' he tells me, and I'm unprepared for the disappointment I feel. 'Sorry. It's my mum's birthday,' he explains. 'We're having a small family celebration at the bakery tonight. She's not ready to go out to a restaurant or anything yet.'

'Oh. That sounds really lovely.' I try to sound like I mean it because I do. I have no idea why I feel like crying.

'What time is your flight tomorrow?' he asks.

'Nine forty-five in the evening.'

'Will you text me when you get there?'

'Sure.' My mobile bill alone will wipe out my budget if I keep making phone calls once I'm Down Under.

'Are you okay?' he asks gently.

'I'm fine!' Honestly, though, my throat is swollen and if I try to say more than two words, he'll hear how choked I sound.

'Rose,' he says quietly.

I burst into tears.

'Hey!' He's mortified.

'I'm sorry!' I reply, gulping for air. 'I just thought for a moment that you were here.'

'I'm really sorry,' he says, but he sounds more amused than apologetic.

I brush away my tears and gather myself together.

'I'm glad you want me there so much.' He's a bit too pleased with himself, but I don't deny it. The phone is pressed up against my ear and it's leaving a painful impression, but I'm still sad when he makes a move to end our call.

'Listen, I'd better go,' he says reluctantly. 'Vanessa's out the front on her own and it sounds quite busy.'

'Are you in the garden?' I ask.

'Yes.'

'With the windows open?'

'Just a crack. I've taken the frosting off,' he answers my next question before I can ask it.

'Good.'

We both fall silent for a long moment, but I know he's smiling. He speaks first.

'I love you, Rose. Have a safe flight and remember to text me,' he reiterates.

'Okay, I will.'

After we end the call I stare down at the phone in my hand, stunned. Did Toby just tell me he loves me?

Despite their refutations, I go through the next few hours hoping that Toby and Eliza have indeed concocted an elaborate plan to sneak over to Paris and surprise me, but by the time I'm tucked up in bed that night, I have to concede that they were telling the truth. I fall asleep feeling disheartened and lonely, and the feeling doesn't leave me all the next day.

On Sunday night I board a long flight to Brisbane via Dubai, and on Tuesday I step off a plane into a cool Australian morning.

My Uncle Simon and his partner Katherine meet me at the airport, and I'm happy to be in the company of family again.

Simon is my favourite of Dad's three brothers. Uncle Jack lives in Scotland, but he's a cantankerous old git who doesn't like visitors – although Phoebe and Dad used to drop in on him when they went on climbs there. Our other uncle, Gerry, lives in America with his third wife and we barely see him at all, but Simon has come to visit often – he and Dad were very close.

I've only met Katherine on three separate occasions and one of those times was when she came to Dad's funeral, but I really like her. I'd actually forgotten that she's thirteen years older than Simon, because a stranger wouldn't be able to guess if they saw them standing side-by-side.

The first time I met her, she had long greying hair, but she's gradually cut it shorter and it's currently layered into a tawny brown mid-length style with dark-blonde highlights.

As for Simon, he's now the same age Dad was when he died and he's grown to look more like him over the years. I feel a pang as his face breaks out into his brother's grin, but the unfamiliar Aussie twang in his accent soon has me smiling again.

Simon and Katherine used to live in Sydney, but they moved to Byron Bay a few years ago and opened up an art gallery. It's only a week until Christmas so by the time I arrive the town centre is jam-packed with tourists here for the festive season and we sit in bumper-to-bumper traffic all the way down the hippie-tastic main street.

Katherine's nephews are coming over with their families for Christmas, but I have a couple of days to get over the worst of my jetlag before they arrive. I've never met them before, but my uncle assures me that I'll love them. At least, he hopes so, because apparently it's going to be a bit of a squash.

I don't know why he's worried. The house is huge with four double bedrooms and a large open-plan living area that opens up onto a wide balcony on the first floor. They have an infinity pool down below which has the most incredible view, broken only by two tall palm trees in the sloping garden. A white sandy beach stretches all the way along the coast, with a multitude of surfers riding the cool, blue waves. Katherine and Simon actually live on a hill overlooking Wategos Bay, which is just over a five-minute drive to much busier Byron. Simon tells me there's a beautiful walk from here up to the lighthouse and Australia's easternmost point.

Simon is right: I really like Katherine's nephews and their families, although he was also right about the house feeling crammed now there are eleven people staying in it.

Sam is warm and friendly and his wife Molly is a blast, making me laugh every time she pretends to be completely harassed by her three boisterous children.

Nathan is less outgoing than his brother, but just as warm, and his wife Lucy and I hit it off immediately. Although she's often distracted by the demands of their unbearably cute eighteen-month-old son, Finn, we find time to chat and bond over our shared love of Somerset while nursing cups of tea out on the balcony. Lucy spent quite a few years growing up in England and her mum has a place in Dunster, not far from where my Aunt Suzie lives. I think I might have actually been to her mum's teashop in the past.

After a few days, it occurs to me that my jetlag is kind of a blessing because I'm naturally waking up early – I wouldn't stand a chance of a sleep-in with all the noise created by the children each morning. I love that the house is full and lively because it's helping to take my mind off an approaching Christmas without Mum and Eliza, not to mention Phoebe. But two days before Christmas, Simon notices me taking a couple of headache tablets at breakfast and encourages me to head down to the beach for some peace and quiet. I sit on the cool white sand and stare out at the ocean, watching the surfers expertly navigating the waves.

'G'day,' I hear a voice say and look to my left to see Nathan walking towards me, carrying a surfboard. His black wetsuit has been rolled down to his waist and his dark hair is wet from the surf.

'I didn't know you were down here,' I say, trying not to gawp at his chest. Lucy's a lucky girl.

'Yeah, I'm just going back up. You staying here for a bit?' he asks. 'I think Lucy wants to bring Finn down for a play in the sand.'

There goes my peace and quiet. Not that I mind.

'I'll be here,' I say.

'Cool, see ya later,' he says, and my eyes follow him as he wanders off along the beach, his tanned feet making imprints in the sand.

'Is that my competition?' I hear a deep, familiar voice say.

My heart nearly jumps out of my chest as I shoot my head around to see Toby standing behind my right shoulder.

'Oh my God!' I murmur, scrambling to my feet.

He raises one eyebrow at me.

'Oh my God!' This time I squeal it, throwing myself at him.

He laughs as his arms close around me.

'Oh my God!' I say, pulling away to look at him.

'You're starting to worry me now, Rose,' he says drily. 'Have you lost the ability to speak?'

'Holy shit!' I exclaim.

He looks thoroughly entertained.

'What are you doing here?' I demand to know, gawping at the wide khaki green straps coming over his shoulder and then grabbing his arm and turning him to see the enormous backpack on his back. 'You're not!' I gasp.

'I am,' he replies with a grin. 'Turns out I won't be buying a car yet after all.'

'Oh my God!'

'Rose!' He shakes me slightly. 'Are you happy to see me?'

'Are you kidding? Oh my God, are you coming backpacking with me?'

'Oh my God, only if you want me to,' he replies, mimicking me and then smiling.

'Of course I want you to.' Tears fill my eyes.

'Aw,' he says, wrapping his arms around me and holding me close.

He feels so amazing, so real. I feel a bubble of something burst inside my chest, and it's not excitement, it's more than that.

381

'Who was the surfer?' he asks wryly, and now it's my turn to tease. I pull away and shrug.

'Oh, you know, just a guy I've got to know.'

He stiffens and I crack up laughing, unable to keep up the pretence.

'It's Nathan, Katherine's nephew! He's married.'

Toby doesn't look particularly amused by the joke. I continue to laugh myself silly.

'You're so immature,' he mutters, making me laugh more. He grins and unclicks his backpack, dropping it onto the sand with a thump before pulling me down beside him.

He loops his arms around his knees and stares straight ahead. 'Seriously, though,' he begins, looking a little on edge. 'I don't want to cramp your style. If you don't want me to travel with you—'

'Toby, I can't think of anyone else I'd rather go travelling with. I can't actually believe it, but I'm so happy you're here.'

'Thank Christ for that,' he says, exhaling with relief.

'How did it come about, though?' I ask. 'Were your parents okay about you leaving? How on earth did you even know where to find me?'

He reaches across and takes my hand. Butterflies start up in my stomach at the feeling of his warm, firm grasp. 'Yes, they were happy about it. In fact, they encouraged me to go.'

I beam at him, unable to contain my delight about the entire scenario.

'As for how I knew where to find you, well, I had a little help with that.'

'Eliza,' I hazard a guess. 'She knew when I spoke to her in Paris, didn't she?'

'Oh, she's known for weeks now,' he replies flippantly, flashing me a grin.

'Does my uncle know?' I ask with a frown, wondering if he'll offer to put Toby up, too.

'Yeah, he knows. Didn't you wonder why he sent you down to the beach?'

I shake my head with amazement. 'I can't believe you were all in on it.'

He turns his head to look at me, and my stomach flips over as his dark eyes lock me in a stare. Maybe Eliza is right: Prince Charming doesn't always come in the package you're expecting. When you meet someone you really, really like – possibly, *likely* love – then you'd be stupid not to see where it leads.

Toby reaches over and brushes my cheek. 'Sand,' he whispers.

'Not soil,' I reply, taking his hand and holding it to my face.

He leans forward and kisses me.

We stay on the beach for a far too brief time, with Toby claiming to want to go up to the house to introduce himself. I'd like longer with him alone, but I oblige, and when we walk up the hill, I notice an unfamiliar car parked on the steep driveway.

'Is that yours?' I ask him.

'Nope,' he replies, pulling my hand towards the property's steps. I'm out of breath by the time we reach the ground-floor level of the house, and what little breath I have left leaves me when I see who's sitting on the edge of the infinity pool with their feet dangling in the water.

'How bloody long does it take to walk up from the beach?' Eliza asks, trying to keep a straight face as Mum beams at me from beside her.

'OH MY GOD!' I scream.

'Here we go again,' Toby says drily.

'I can't believe you all came. I just can't believe it,' I say later when Eliza and I are sitting at the table on the balcony, a beer in her hand and a glass of wine in mine. They dropped Toby to the beach earlier. He carried his heavy backpack to keep up the pretence, bless him.

'We've had it planned for *ages*,' she says, looking like the cat that got the cream. 'I had to check you were serious about Toby first, though.'

I laugh and shake my head, glancing into the house at him. He's helping out in the kitchen, stirring something in a saucepan. Perhaps he senses me watching, because he looks over his shoulder at me and smirks. My pulse speeds up.

'Angus couldn't come?' I ask, returning my attention to Eliza.

'No.' She shakes her head, sadly. 'He couldn't get time off work, but you know what he's like about his mum. He wouldn't have wanted to leave her on her own at Christmas for too long anyway.'

'Do you miss him? No,' I answer my own question. 'It's only been a day or two.'

She shrugs and grins sheepishly. 'I still miss him, though. But I'm sure we'll survive without each other for a couple of weeks, and the sex is going to be *crazy* when I go back.'

'Too much information!' I exclaim, making her laugh.

Lucy and Molly come out onto the balcony to join us. I hear the cracking open of bottles and glance inside again to see Nathan passing Toby a beer. They chink bottles and then Sam comes into the room and they go through the process again.

Mum is sitting beside Simon on the sofa, bouncing a giggling baby Finn on her lap. Molly and Sam's three kids tear out onto the balcony and then run back inside again with Katherine in tow.

'This house is shrinking by the moment,' I muse, making everyone laugh.

Mum ends up sharing my bed and Eliza kips on the floor of our bedroom on a blow-up mattress. Toby chooses to sleep on the sofa upstairs, having been given the option of that or the second bunk bed in the kids' room. By the time we set off backpacking, we'll probably be desperate to have just each other for company. I'm looking forward to getting to know him better, but we'll have plenty of time for that.

Christmas Day is a raucous affair, and although Phoebe is never far from my mind, nor Mum's or Eliza's, I am sure, we have a good day and I'm just so very happy that we're all together like this. I feel sorry for Eliza that she doesn't have Gus around – even *I* miss him – but she'll be back with him soon enough. I imagine Christmas is hard for him without Phoebe, too, but his mum has a good shoulder for him to cry on.

On Boxing Day, Eliza and I find ourselves sitting alone on the beach. Mum has gone for a wander along the shore with Katherine, and Toby is surfing with Nathan. At the moment, they're sitting upright on their boards, waiting for a decent wave. They seem to be having a good chat.

'Nice view,' Eliza says with a smirk.

'Get off,' I reply.

'I'm talking about Nathan.'

'What would Angus say?' I admonish.

She laughs. 'He knows he's the only man for me.' She pauses, before saying quietly: 'It's only ever been him.'

'Check out the look on your face,' I tease. 'You've gone all puppy-dog-like.'

She grins at me. 'You have exactly the same expression when you're staring at Toby.'

I purse my lips at her. 'You once said I looked like that over Angus.'

She shakes her head. 'No, that was different. I've seen you go through crushes, but that's not what this is with Toby. I could tell from the way I saw you together at my gig. I'm really glad you're giving him a chance.'

I shrug. 'We'll see how it goes.'

'That's all you can do.'

We're going out in town tonight to see a live band – Toby, Eliza, Nathan, Lucy, Sam and Molly. Mum has convinced a slightly freaked out Katherine and Simon that the three of them will more than be able to handle four kids. Nathan and Sam are the closest things Katherine and Simon have to children – Katherine took them in when they lost their parents, but they were teenagers at the time. Mum, on the other hand, raised triplets, so she's more than capable, even at her age.

Triplets...

'I'm so glad you're here,' I say to Eliza, resting my cheek against her shoulder.

'Me too.' She wraps her arm around me and draws me close.

'I miss her so much,' I whisper.

She hugs me tighter, but I don't want to cry, and neither, as I well know, does she.

'Do you remember that time that Joanne Osborn tried to test our telepathic powers and you guessed that Phoebe wanted pizza for dinner?' I say, trying to sound light-hearted.

Eliza laughs. 'I do! You were so cross that I got it right.'

Eliza speaks next. 'What about the time we all went to Hannah Longstaff's birthday party and everyone freaked out when you and Phoebe said: "Oh *please* can we play musical chairs?" in exactly the same pitch at exactly the same time?'

I laugh loudly. 'That's right! I'd forgotten that one. What about when bully boy Danny Riley said to you: "How do you know which one you are?"' I affect his dumb voice. 'And you sarcastically replied: "Gosh, I don't know. I look in the mirror and even I get confused."'

She hoots with laughter and we fall back on the sand, staring up at the sky.

It's my turn next. 'Remember that time Phoebe went climbing with Dad and you tried to teach me to play the guitar?'

'You weren't having it,' she replies sardonically.

'I was just jealous that you were so good and I was so crap, but I appreciated your effort.' I reach across and pat her knee. She makes a swipe for my hand and holds it to her chest. 'You and I both got our periods that same weekend,' I recall.

'That's right!' Eliza exclaims. 'Phoebe was quite put out!'

We both laugh. 'She didn't get hers for another few months. She was gutted,' I say.

'We've been through a lot together, haven't we?' She squeezes my hand.

I squeeze hers back. 'We have. Every single awkward phase. We were meant to be together, right from the beginning.'

'That's kind of comforting,' she murmurs.

'It is,' I agree.

A shadow falls over us and we raise our heads to see Mum standing a few feet away on the sand.

'Look at you two,' she says warmly. 'Let me take a photo.'

As Eliza and I press our cheeks together and smile up at Mum, I think of the photo frames on Mum's bookshelves in her new house. Months ago I wondered if Eliza and I would ever feature in a photo of just the two of us. And now I know that we will.

It *is* just the two of us now. Eliza and Rose. Rose and Eliza.

But in our hearts, we will *always* be triplets.

Acknowledgements

It's been ten years since the publication of my debut novel, *Lucy in the Sky*, and I still want to pinch myself. Thank you to my readers for making me laugh and cry (usually in happiness – phew) with all of your social media interactions and outstanding online reviews. I feel very lucky to be doing what I love every day, but I wouldn't enjoy it nearly as much if you weren't all so sweet to me, so I'm truly grateful. Please continue to help spread the word about my free book club, *The Hidden Paige*, which I created as a way of showing my appreciation for your support. Visit paige-toon.com and sign up to receive exclusive extra content from me, including short stories, hidden chapters and competitions.

Thank you to my amazing editor, Suzanne Baboneau, who has helped to make the last ten years some of the best of my life. You're always there when I need you – and for this book I needed you quite a lot. You're my rock.

Thank you to Emma Capron for her brilliance with everything book-related, and indeed to the entire team at Simon & Schuster. I adore each and every one of you and I am indebted to you for your decade of enthusiasm and support of my books. Cue another Mexican wave!

Thanks also to my fabulous agent Lizzy Kremer and the team at David Higham for everything that they continue to do behind the scenes.

I have a few people to thank for their research help, but Melanie Fowler – wow – you went above and beyond! Mel works on the

Aiguille du Midi cable car in Chamonix and she really brought my characters' adventures to life by sharing her experiences with me.

Thanks also to Natalie Collingwood for her crazy, fun and insightful account of what it was like to work as a seasonnaire, and to Emma and Justin Guest, whose apartment in Argentiere formed the backdrop for part of this story (email jus@jguest.net for details).

Huge thanks to Helen Underwood for sharing her vast knowledge of baking and for allowing me to watch her at work. I have a new appreciation of artisan bread. Check out whitecottagebakery.com if you'd like to see some of her creations.

Thank you also to Keith Chadwick for his help with questions relating to Toby's mum's condition.

Huge thanks to Laura Betts for raising money for CLIC Sargent (for children with cancer: clicsargent.org.uk) by entering an auction to see her name appear in this book. She very sweetly donated the prize as a birthday gift to her sister, Becky, but I managed to include them both.

Heartfelt thanks to all of my lovely friends who have put up with my chatter about imaginary people for the last ten years – so many of you have offered valuable help and I truly appreciate it. I want to say an extra big thank you to Jane Hampton and Sarah Horsborough for reading the first draft of this book and giving me such valuable feedback.

And of course, thank you to my parents, Jen and Vern Schuppan and my parents-in-law Helga and Ian Toon for all their support.

Finally, thank you to my beautiful little children, Indy and Idha – mostly just for making me smile – and my husband and best friend, Greg. You've been pivotal to my career in so many ways, and frankly, I don't know what I'd do without you.

New to Paige Toon?

Turn the page to read the first

chapter of her last book...

THE
SUN IN
HER EYES

Available now in paperback and eBook

Prologue

Recently Doris had not been able to stop thinking about the little girl. Of course, she had thought about her ceaselessly after the accident, but that had been over twenty-six years ago and Doris was now in her nineties with decades of memories at her disposal.

'*Please… You have to tell her…*' the woman had said with her last few breaths. The memory made Doris wince, the pain almost as potent now as it had been back then.

Doris tried to shut out the images that filled her head, but it was no use. The woman would not be silenced, not then and not now. Even sleep brought Doris no peace, and she was so very tired these days.

Doris had taken the woman's hand, not knowing how to tell her that her daughter was unconscious in the back of the car she was driving. But a moment later, the woman was gone, her dying words ringing in Doris's ears.

The little girl had stirred, a stuffed toy clutched in her arms, and Doris's fractured heart had split at the sight of two cobalt-blue eyes opening and flinching at the same sunlight that had been the likely cause of her mother veering off the road.

If only she knew what had happened to the girl, perhaps she could let go, move on, sleep without the nightmares. She had told the policeman what the woman had said before she had died, but had not made certain that the message was passed on to the child. Should she have told the girl herself, as she had promised?

In that instant, Doris knew what she needed to do. She would write a letter, and she would ask her son to help her track down the child, who would of course be a grown woman by now. Her name was Amber, Doris hadn't forgotten. Amber Church. It was time to come good on her promise.

The Story of
Amber Church, the Girl
With the Sun in Her Eyes

Chapter 1

It has been a shit of a day.

It started off badly when I woke up for the second time that week to find myself in bed alone without my husband beside me. Ned had been socialising with his boss – again – and I found him out cold on the sofa, reeking of stale booze and cigarettes. *Her* cigarettes, to be precise. His boss is very much female and very much attracted to him. Or so I suspect.

My first thought was to pour a glass of water over his head, my second was that it might ruin our brown-suede sofa, so I resisted. Then I spied a little pile of vomit on his shoulder and soon realised that it was not so little and not entirely on his shoulder.

'Ned, you *idiot*!' I shouted at the top of my voice, making him jolt awake, his hazel-coloured eyes wide open with terror and his sandy hair sticking out every which way.

'What?' he gasped.

'You've thrown up on the sofa! Clean it up!'

'No! I'm sleeping,' he snapped. 'I've got a pounding head ache,' he added, throwing his arm over his face. 'I'll do it later.'

'Get up and do it NOW!' I yelled.

'NO!' he yelled back, just as vehemently.

It was safe to say that our honeymoon period was well and truly over.

I was seething as I got ready for work, banging about and ranting about how selfish and pathetic my husband was. I didn't give a second thought to the couple who have just moved in downstairs, so when I *slammed* the front door and *stomped* down the communal stairs, I was a bit surprised to come face-to-face with one of them.

'Thank you *very* much for waking up my baby,' the woman of about my age had said sarcastically, her face purple with rage as a child screamed blue murder in the background. 'He only got to sleep two hours ago after being up all night. *I* was lucky enough to get a whole hour before the banging in your flat started.'

'I'm so sorry,' I replied, shamefaced. 'I had an argum—'

'Just keep it down in future, yeah?' she interrupted.

I felt guilty and on edge for the entire walk to the Tube station.

That was when the fun *really* began.

Thanks to severe delays on the Northern Line, the station was backed up with commuters mimicking bumper-to-bumper traffic all the way down into the darkest depths of the tunnels.

By the time I arrived at work, I was hot, flustered and forty-five minutes late. Not only that, but the heat from the Underground had made my wavy auburn hair go lank and sweaty. It was a bad-hair day, to boot.

I hurried into the office, so full of apologies that I thought I might burst, and then came to a sudden stop. I work as a commodities broker in a start-up company in the City, and the flurry of activity that usually greeted me somehow seemed off. Spying me, my boss clicked his fingers and motioned for me to join him.

'You're late.'

'I'm sorry—'

'Never mind,' he interrupted. 'HR want to see you.'

He nodded to his office, and I headed warily towards it. Most of my colleagues were carrying on as normal, but I noticed a few empty seats. I caught my next-door neighbour Meredith's eye and registered pity, but by then I'd reached my boss's office.

The two people from HR asked me to close the door and take a seat.

I was being made redundant. Five of us were going, right then, right now. In fact, four had already gone.

I would be paid three months' salary, but would be missing out on my substantial bonus that was due in less than two months' time.

I felt sick to my stomach.

Brokering is not the most reliable employment, nor is it something I wanted to do. I chose to go into teaching when I left university, after getting a First in Mathematics. Some of my fellow students thought I was mad not to opt for a better-paid job when I had so many choices laid out in front of me. I bumped into one of them last summer and he told me that he'd got involved in a start-up company that was raking in millions. He gave me his card and said that he could put me in touch with someone if I was interested in quitting my teaching job.

He caught me at exactly the right time. I needed a change. Unfortunately, I was unwittingly destined for another one.

Bob, one of the building's security guards, kept me company while I packed up my stuff. His presence wasn't necessary – I wasn't going to stash my PC in my handbag. Although, saying that, I did swipe a couple of pens when he was looking the other way.

Then I had to do the hellish journey in reverse, this time my head spinning with questions about what I was going to do next.

Eventually I made it back to our flat on the second floor of a three-storey terraced house in Dartmouth Park, an area of London that's not far from Tufnell Park, Highgate and Archway, depending on who's asking.

The place still reeked of Ned's antics the night before; he'd barely attempted to clean up his vomit. So *I* did, seething as I rubbed and scrubbed at the stain.

Like I said, it has been a shit of a day. And it's only lunch time.

I sigh heavily as the credits on the television programme begin to roll. What now? I should phone Ned to let him know about my job, or lack thereof, but even the thought of speaking to him annoys me. He hasn't even called me to apologise.

A moment later, my mobile rings. I bet that's him, and about time, too.

I dig out my phone from my bag, but it's not a number I recognise. If it's those idiots calling about Payment Protection Insurance again, I'll give them an earful.

'Hello?' I say irritably.

'Amber, it's Liz,' my dad's partner replies in her usual clipped, restrained tone.

My dad and Liz have been together for seventeen years, but have never married. I keep wishing she'll leave him so he can find someone nicer, because he'll never be the one to walk away. Dad likes an easy life.

'Hi, Liz,' I reply coolly, wondering why she's ringing me on my mobile when it's so expensive. Oh, of course, she doesn't know that I'm now unemployed. That's going to be fun news to break.

'I'm calling about your dad,' she says. I instantly tense up. 'He's had a stroke.'

My heart leaps into my throat and my face prickles all over. 'Is he okay?'

'We don't know yet,' she admits, sounding like she might cry. Liz wouldn't normally be seen dead crying, so this is bad. 'I found him on the floor in the bathroom. He couldn't speak or, at least, I couldn't understand what he was saying. He sounded drunk, only worse, and I saw that his face looked strange – sort of droopy on one side. He couldn't move his arm and then I realised the whole right-hand side of his body had just stopped working.'

'Oh God,' I murmur.

'I called an ambulance straight away and they've brought us to the Acute Stroke Unit at the Royal Adelaide Hospital. They've taken him off to have a CT scan. I wanted to let you know as soon as I could.'

'Oh God,' I repeat, unable to find the vocabulary to utter anything else. 'Is he—'

'I don't know, Amber,' she cuts me off, sounding like the

Liz I'm all too familiar with. 'I don't know anything yet,' she adds with frustration. 'All they've told me is that it was very, very lucky that I was there. The faster he's treated, the more likely it is that the damage will be less. I don't know what would have happened if I'd gone to the movies with Gina. I had a bit of a sore throat so I stayed at home.'

'Will you call me—'

'I'll call when I know more,' she interrupts, completing my sentence for me.

'Should we come home?' I ask, fear tying knots in my stomach.

'We'll talk later,' she snaps. 'I've got to go! His consultant has just come in.'

'I'm at the flat,' I tell her quickly, but she's already hung up.

I feel so helpless. Dad and Liz live in Adelaide, South Australia, where I grew up, and I'm here in London on the other side of the world.

On autopilot, I take the home phone out of its cradle and dial Ned's number.

He doesn't even bother to say hello. 'What are you doing at home?' he asks instead, obviously seeing the caller ID.

'I've been made redundant.'

He gasps, but I cut him off before he can speak.

'But I'm calling because my dad has had a stroke.'

There's silence at the other end of the line, and then I hear him exhale.

'Oh baby,' he says in a low voice.

At the sound of his empathy, I break down.

'You poor thing,' he murmurs. 'Do you want me to come home?'

'You don't have to,' I cry. Please do, though.

'I'm on my way,' he says gently. 'I love you.'

I text Liz to ask her to call me at home when she can before taking my iPad and going to lie down in the bedroom. Ned arrives three quarters of an hour later and I hear him taking off his big winter coat in the hall before coming to find me. He pauses in the doorway, looking all dishevelled in his unironed grey shirt and jeans.

'Hey,' he says quietly, smiling sorrowfully at me.

I slide my hand towards him in a small peace offering. He sighs heavily and sits on the bed, taking my hand. 'What did Liz say exactly?'

I repeat our conversation.

'What about your job?' he asks next, so I fill him in about that, too.

'What an arsehole,' he mutters about my boss, shaking his head and squeezing my hand.

'Mmm.' My expression darkens as I stare at him. My ex-boss is not the only arsehole around here.

Finally he has the grace to apologise.

'I'm sorry about earlier.' He looks down at our hands, still entwined.

'I can't believe you shouted at me,' I reply. 'After throwing up on the sofa—'

'I know, I know,' he cuts me off. Ned *hates* having his nose rubbed in his mistakes.

This argument could go on for days – they certainly have in the past – but there are bigger things to worry about, so I bite my tongue.

'I've been looking at flights back to Australia,' I tell him miserably, reaching for my iPad. 'The prices are horrendous, but at least we're past Christmas.' It's the middle of February, which is still summer Down Under, but December and January are the peak times.

'Do you think you should go?' he asks.

'Definitely,' I reply. 'I can get on a flight the day after tomorrow.'

'Really? Okay. I guess in a way it's good timing. *Not* good timing,' he quickly corrects himself when he sees me gape at him. 'You know what I mean.' His leg starts jiggling up and down. 'At least you can stay out there for as long as you're needed.'

'Will you come?' I ask hopefully.

'Amber, I can't,' he replies regretfully. 'I wish I could, I really do, but I'm so busy at work.'

A dark feeling settles over me.

'Hey.' He pats my shoulder. 'You know I can't just drop every thing. I have to go to New York the week after next—'

'With Zara?' I interrupt. That's his boss.

'Yes.' His brow furrows. 'Don't be like that,' he scolds mildly. 'You know this job is important to me, to us.'

'I don't know why you won't just admit that she fancies you,' I say hotly.

'She doesn't!' he insists. 'She only split up with her husband a couple of months ago.'

'She's only just got married!' I exclaim, hating that he's defending her.

'She doesn't fancy me,' he repeats. 'I was looking forward to telling you some good news, but...' His voice trails off and he stares out of the window.

'What?' I ask, sitting up straighter.

'Max and Zara promoted me today. Zara told me last night that they were going to.'

'What sort of a promotion?' My voice sounds like it's coming from somewhere else, rather than from me.

'Creative Director.' He shrugs and his cutesy, bashful smile makes an appearance.

'You've only been working there for two years and she's making you Creative Director?' Doesn't fancy him, my arse!

All humour vanishes from his face. 'It's almost two and a *half* years, and maybe I'm better at my job than you give me credit for.' At that, he walks out of the room.

'Ned!' I call out in dismay, hurrying after him. He's already in the kitchen, loudly making himself a coffee. 'I'm sorry,' I say. 'I know you're brilliant. What did they say?' I prompt.

Ned's a creative at a rapidly expanding advertising firm in central London. Last year they were bought out by a New York agency, and his trip there in less than a fortnight will be the first time he's visited the office.

Max Whitman is the Executive Creative Director and one of the three founding partners of the firm, KDW. Zara is the Managing Director and oversees everyone in the company. She's only thirty-three. I don't like her very much, the handful of times I've met her.

She's thin and very tall – a lot taller than me because I'm only five foot four – and she has dead-straight, white-blonde hair that she usually wears scraped back from her face, which is all angles and cheekbones. She's striking, I'll give her that, but she couldn't look more different from me with my petite frame and long auburn locks. Sometimes she wears the same sort of trendy horn-rimmed glasses I used to, but I've since had laser-surgery on my eyes. We can both carry off red lipstick, but I'm not sure that constitutes much of a similarity.

Ned goes to get the milk out of the fridge, not looking at me. 'Tate's gone to work in the New York office now, so they need a replacement here,' he says, closing the fridge door with more force than it requires. Tate was Ned's line manager and one of the firm's so-called creative geniuses.

'Does that mean you'll be answering directly to Max?' I ask. That constitutes a big step up. Max is the top dog.

'Yes,' he replies. 'Him, and Zara, still, to an extent.'

A wave of pride goes through me as his good news belatedly sinks in. 'That really is amazing,' I say, stroking his arm.

'It's a lot more money,' he replies with a grin, leaning back against the counter. 'I'll have to do a few more late nights, probably need to buy some suits.' He glances down at his crumpled attire and shrugs with amusement.

'Aw, but I love your shabby appearance,' I say with down-turned lips, and though it might sound to an outsider like I'm teasing, he knows that it's true.

He chuckles and takes me into his arms.

'Well done,' I say, hugging him tightly.

'Thanks, baby,' he murmurs. His voice is muffled against the top of my head. He's about six foot tall and towers above me. 'I'm sorry about your news.'

I feel a wave of nausea at the reminder that Dad's had a stroke and I've been made redundant.

'Hey,' Ned says softly, as my eyes well up with tears and I sniff.

At least I've saved up enough money to be able to afford

the flight back to Australia, and I'll have three months' worth of wages to live on.

'I wish you could come with me,' I say.

'I do, too. But maybe it's for the best that I can't,' he adds carefully. 'You'll be able to focus on your dad.'

'Maybe.'

I know he's psyched about his promotion and would rather be celebrating than commiserating. But maybe that's unfair.

He smiles and holds me at arm's length, trying to jolly me up. 'And you can catch up with Tina and Nell.'

And Ethan, my mind whispers before I attempt to squash the thought.

But it won't go willingly, and suddenly my head is full of the beautiful dark-haired boy that I fell for all those years ago.

Ethan, Ethan, Ethan...

My first love. Who never loved me back.

Despite all the tears I've cried over him, despite all the heartache I've endured, I'd still give anything to see him again.

And now I'm going to.